Gods and Fighting Men

Lady I. A. Gregory

Contents

GODS AND FIGHTING MEN

BY

Lady I. A. Gregory

DEDICATION TO THE MEMBERS OF THE IRISH LITERARY SOCIETY OF NEW YORK

My Friends, those I know and those I do not know, I am glad in the year of the birth of your Society to have this book to offer you.

It has given great courage to many workers here--working to build up broken walls--to know you have such friendly thoughts of them in your minds. A few of you have already come to see us, and we begin to hope that one day the steamers across the Atlantic will not go out full, but come back full, until some of you find your real home is here, and say as some of us say, like Finn to the woman of enchantments--

"We would not give up our own country--Ireland--if we were to get the whole world as an estate, and the Country of the Young along with it."

AUGUSTA GREGORY.

PREFACE

I

A few months ago I was on the bare Hill of Allen, "wide Almhuin of Leinster," where Finn and the Fianna lived, according to the stories, although there are no earthen mounds there like those that mark the sites of old buildings on so many hills. A hot sun beat down upon flowering gorse and flowerless heather; and on every side except the east, where there were green trees and distant hills, one saw a level horizon and brown boglands with a few green places and here and there the glitter of water. One could imagine that had it been twilight and not early afternoon, and had there been vapours drifting and frothing where there were now but shadows of clouds, it would have set stirring in one, as few places even in Ireland can, a thought that is peculiar to Celtic romance, as I think, a thought of a mystery coming not as with Gothic nations out of the pressure of darkness, but out of great spaces and windy light. The hill of Teamhair, or Tara, as it is now called, with its green mounds and its partly wooded sides, and its more gradual slope set among fat grazing lands, with great trees in the hedgerows, had brought before one imaginations, not of heroes who were in their youth for hundreds of years, or of women who came to them in the likeness of hunted fawns, but of kings that lived brief and politic lives, and of the five white roads that carried their armies to the lesser kingdoms of Ireland, or brought to the great fair that had given Teamhair its sovereignty, all that sought justice or pleasure or had goods to barter.

II

It is certain that we must not confuse these kings, as did the mediaeval chroniclers, with those half-divine kings of Almhuin. The chroniclers, perhaps because
they loved tradition too well to cast out utterly much that they dreaded as Chris-
tians, and perhaps because popular imagination had begun the mixture, have mixed
one with another ingeniously, making Finn the head of a kind of Militia under Cormac MacArt, who is supposed to have reigned at Teamhair in the second century,
and making Grania, who travels to enchanted houses under the cloak of Angus,
god of Love, and keeps her troubling beauty longer than did Helen hers, Cormac's
daughter, and giving the stories of the Fianna, although the impossible has thrust
its proud finger into them all, a curious air of precise history. It is only when one
separates the stories from that mediaeval pedantry, as in this book, that one rec-
ognises one of the oldest worlds that man has imagined, an older world certainly
than one finds in the stories of Cuchulain, who lived, according to the chroniclers,
about the time of the birth of Christ. They are far better known, and one may be
certain of the antiquity of incidents that are known in one form or another to every
Gaelic-speaking countryman in Ireland or in the Highlands of Scotland. Sometimes
a labourer digging near to a cromlech, or Bed of Diarmuid and Crania as it is called,
will tell one a tradition that seems older and more barbaric than any description of
their adventures or of themselves in written text or story that has taken form in the
mouths of professed story-tellers. Finn and the Fianna found welcome among the
court poets later than did Cuchulain; and one finds memories of Danish invasions
and standing armies mixed with the imaginations of hunters and solitary fighters among great woods. One never hears of Cuchulain delighting in the hunt or
in woodland things; and one imagines that the story-teller would have thought it
unworthy in so great a man, who lived a well-ordered, elaborate life, and had his
chariot and his chariot-driver and his barley-fed horses to delight in. If he is in the
woods before dawn one is not told that he cannot know the leaves of the hazel from
the leaves of the oak; and when Emer laments him no wild creature comes into her
thoughts but the cuckoo that cries over cultivated fields. His story must have come

out of a time when the wild wood was giving way to pasture and tillage, and men had no longer a reason to consider every cry of the birds or change of the night. Finn, who was always in the woods, whose battles were but hours amid years of hunting, delighted in the "cackling of ducks from the Lake of the Three Narrows; the scolding talk of the blackbird of Doire an Cairn; the bellowing of the ox from the Valley of the Berries; the whistle of the eagle from the Valley of Victories or from the rough branches of the Ridge of the Stream; the grouse of the heather of Cruachan; the call of the otter of Druim re Coir." When sorrow comes upon the queens of the stories, they have sympathy for the wild birds and beasts that are like themselves: "Credhe wife of Cael came with the others and went looking through the bodies for her comely comrade, and crying as she went. And as she was searching she saw a crane of the meadows and her two nestlings, and the cunning beast the fox watching the nestlings; and when the crane covered one of the birds to save it, he would make a rush at the other bird, the way she had to stretch herself out over the birds; and she would sooner have got her own death by the fox than the nestlings to be killed by him. And Credhe was looking at that, and she said: 'It is no wonder I to have such love for my comely sweetheart, and the bird in that distress about her nestlings.'"

III

One often hears of a horse that shivers with terror, or of a dog that howls at something a man's eyes cannot see, and men who live primitive lives where instinct does the work of reason are fully conscious of many things that we cannot perceive at all. As life becomes more orderly, more deliberate, the supernatural world sinks farther away. Although the gods come to Cuchulain, and although he is the son of one of the greatest of them, their country and his are far apart, and they come to him as god to mortal; but Finn is their equal. He is continually in their houses; he meets with Bodb Dearg, and Angus, and Manannan, now as friend with friend, now as with an enemy he overcomes in battle; and when he has need of their help his messenger can say: "There is not a king's son or a prince, or a leader of the Fianna of Ireland, without having a wife or a mother or a foster-mother or a sweetheart of the

Tuatha de Danaan." When the Fianna are broken up at last, after hundreds of years of hunting, it is doubtful that he dies at all, and certain that he comes again in some other shape, and Oisin, his son, is made king over a divine country. The birds and beasts that cross his path in the woods have been fighting men or great enchanters or fair women, and in a moment can take some beautiful or terrible shape. One thinks of him and of his people as great-bodied men with large movements, that seem, as it were, flowing out of some deep below the narrow stream of personal impulse, men that have broad brows and quiet eyes full of confidence in a good luck that proves every day afresh that they are a portion of the strength of things. They are hardly so much individual men as portions of universal nature, like the clouds that shape themselves and re-shape themselves momentarily, or like a bird between two boughs, or like the gods that have given the apples and the nuts; and yet this but brings them the nearer to us, for we can remake them in our image when we will, and the woods are the more beautiful for the thought. Do we not always fancy hunters to be something like this, and is not that why we think them poetical when we meet them of a sudden, as in these lines in "Pauline":

"An old hunter
Talking with gods; or a nigh-crested chief
Sailing with troops of friends to Tenedos"

IV

One must not expect in these stories the epic lineaments, the many incidents, woven into one great event of, let us say, the story of the War for the Brown Bull of Cuailgne, or that of the last gathering at Muirthemne. Even Diarmuid and Grania, which is a long story, has nothing of the clear outlines of Deirdre, and is indeed but a succession of detached episodes. The men who imagined the Fianna had the imagination of children, and as soon as they had invented one wonder, heaped another on top of it. Children--or, at any rate, it is so I remember my own childhood--do not understand large design, and they delight in little shut-in places where they can play at houses more than in great expanses where a country-side takes, as it were, the impression of a thought. The wild creatures and the green things are more to them than to us, for they creep towards our light by little holes and crevices. When they imagine a country for themselves, it is always a country where one can wander without aim, and where one can never know from one place what another will be like, or know from the one day's adventure what may meet one with to-morrow's sun. I have wished to become a child again that I might find this book, that not only tells one of such a country, but is fuller than any other book that tells of heroic life, of the childhood that is in all folk-lore, dearer to me than all the books of the western world.

Children play at being great and wonderful people, at the ambitions they will put away for one reason or another before they grow into ordinary men and women. Mankind as a whole had a like dream once; everybody and nobody built up the dream bit by bit, and the ancient story-tellers are there to make us remember what mankind would have been like, had not fear and the failing will and the laws of nature tripped up its heels. The Fianna and their like are themselves so full of power, and they are set in a world so fluctuating and dream-like, that nothing can hold them from being all that the heart desires.

I have read in a fabulous book that Adam had but to imagine a bird, and it was born into life, and that he created all things out of himself by nothing more important than an unflagging fancy; and heroes who can make a ship out of a shaving have but little less of the divine prerogatives. They have no speculative thoughts to wander through eternity and waste heroic blood; but how could that be otherwise, for it is at all times the proud angels who sit thinking upon the hill-side and not the people of Eden. One morning we meet them hunting a stag that is "as joyful as the leaves of a tree in summer-time"; and whatever they do, whether they listen to the harp or follow an enchanter over-sea, they do for the sake of joy, their joy in one another, or their joy in pride and movement; and even their battles are fought more because of their delight in a good fighter than because of any gain that is in victory. They live always as if they were playing a game; and so far as they have any deliberate purpose at all, it is that they may become great gentlemen and be worthy of the songs of poets. It has been said, and I think the Japanese were the first to say it, that the four essential virtues are to be generous among the weak, and truthful among one's friends, and brave among one's enemies, and courteous at all times; and if we understand by courtesy not merely the gentleness the story-tellers have celebrated, but a delight in courtly things, in beautiful clothing and in beautiful verse, one understands that it was no formal succession of trials that bound the Fianna to one another. Only the Table Round, that is indeed, as it seems, a rivulet from the same river, is bound in a like fellowship, and there the four heroic virtues are troubled by the abstract virtues of the cloister. Every now and then some noble knight builds himself a cell upon the hill-side, or leaves kind women and joyful knights to seek the vision of the Grail in lonely adventures. But when Oisin or some kingly forerunner--Bran, son of Febal, or the like--rides or sails in an enchanted ship to some divine country, he but looks for a more delighted companionship, or to be in love with faces that will never fade. No thought of any life greater than that of love, and the companionship of those that have drawn their swords upon the darkness of the world, ever troubles their delight in one another as it troubles Iseult amid her love, or Arthur amid his battles. It is one of the ailments of our speculation that thought, when it is not the planning of something, or the doing of something or some memory of a plain circumstance separates us from one another because it makes us always more unlike, and because no thought passes through another's ear unchanged. Companionship can only be perfect when it is founded on things, for things are always the same under the hand, and at last one comes to hear with envy of the voices of boys lighting a lantern to ensnare moths, or of the maids chattering in the kitchen about the fox that carried off a turkey before breakfast. This book is full of fellowship untroubled like theirs, and made noble by a courtesy that has gone perhaps out of the world. I do not know in literature better friends and lovers. When one of the Fianna finds Osgar dying the proud death of a young man, and asks is it well with him, he is answered, "I am as you would have me be." The very heroism of the Fianna is indeed but their pride and joy in one another, their good fellowship. Goll, old and savage, and letting himself die of hunger in a cave because he is angry and sorry, can speak lovely words to the wife whose help he refuses. "'It is best as it is,' he said, 'and I never took the advice of a woman east or west, and I never will take it. And oh, sweet-voiced queen,' he said, 'what ails you to be fretting after me? and remember now your silver and your gold, and your silks ... and do not be crying tears after me, queen with the white hands,' he said, 'but remember your constant lover Aodh, son of the best woman of the world, that came from Spain asking for you, and that I fought on Corcar-an-Dearg; and go to him now,' he said, 'for it is bad when a woman is without a good man.'"

V

They have no asceticism, but they are more visionary than any ascetic, and their invisible life is but the life about them made more perfect and more lasting, and the invisible people are their own images in the water. Their gods may have been much besides this, for we know them from fragments of mythology picked out with trouble from a fantastic history running backward to Adam and Eve, and many things that may have seemed wicked to the monks who imagined that history, may have been altered or left out; but this they must have been essentially, for the old stories are confirmed by apparitions among the country-people to-day. The Men of Dea fought against the mis-shapen Fomor, as Finn fights against the Cat-Heads and the Dog-Heads; and when they are overcome at last by men, they make themselves houses in the hearts of hills that are like the houses of men. When they call men to their houses and to their country Under-Wave they promise them all that they have upon earth, only in greater abundance. The god Midhir sings to Queen Etain in one of the most beautiful of the stories: "The young never grow old; the fields and the flowers are as pleasant to be looking at as the blackbird's eggs; warm streams of mead and wine flow through that country; there is no care or no sorrow on any person; we see others, but we ourselves are not seen." These gods are indeed more wise and beautiful than men; but men, when they are great men, are stronger than they are, for men are, as it were, the foaming tide-line of their sea. One remembers the Druid who answered, when some one asked him who made the world, "The Druids made it." All was indeed but one life flowing everywhere, and taking one quality here, another there. It sometimes seems to one as if there is a kind of day and night of religion, and that a period when the influences are those that shape the world is followed by a period when the greater power is in influences that would lure the soul out of the world, out of the body. When Oisin is speaking with S. Patrick of the friends and the life he has outlived, he can but cry out constantly against a religion that has no meaning for him. He laments, and the country-people have remembered his words for centuries: "I will cry my fill, but not for God, but because Finn and the Fianna are not living."

VI

Old writers had an admirable symbolism that attributed certain energies to the influence of the sun, and certain others to the lunar influence. To lunar influence belong all thoughts and emotions that were created by the community, by the common people, by nobody knows who, and to the sun all that came from the high disciplined or individual kingly mind. I myself imagine a marriage of the sun and moon in the arts I take most pleasure in; and now bride and bridegroom but exchange, as it were, full cups of gold and silver, and now they are one in a mystical embrace. From the moon come the folk-songs imagined by reapers and spinners out of the common impulse of their labour, and made not by putting words together, but by mixing verses and phrases, and the folk-tales made by the capricious mixing of incidents known to everybody in new ways, as one deals out cards, never getting the same hand twice over. When one hears some fine story, one never knows whether it has not been hazard that put the last touch of adventure. Such poetry, as it seems to me, desires an infinity of wonder or emotion, for where there is no individual mind there is no measurer-out, no marker-in of limits. The poor fisher has no possession of the world and no responsibility for it; and if he dreams of a love-gift better than the brown shawl that seems too common for poetry, why should he not dream of a glove made from the skin of a bird, or shoes made from the skin of a fish, or a coat made from the glittering garment of the salmon? Was it not Aeschylus who said he but served up fragments from the banquet of Homer?--but Homer himself found the great banquet on an earthen floor and under a broken roof. We do not know who at the foundation of the world made the banquet for the first time, or who put the pack of cards into rough hands; but we do know that, unless those that have made many inventions are about to change the nature of poetry, we may have to go where Homer went if we are to sing a new song. Is it because all that is under the moon thirsts to escape out of bounds, to lose itself in some unbounded tidal stream, that the songs of the folk are mournful, and that the story of the Fianna, whenever the queens lament for their lovers, reminds us of songs that are still sung in country-places? Their grief, even when it is to be brief like Grania's, goes up into the waste places of the sky. But in supreme art or in supreme life there is the influence of the sun too, and the sun brings with it, as old writers tell us, not merely discipline but joy; for its discipline is not of the kind the multitudes impose upon us by their weight and pressure, but the expression of the individual soul turning itself into a pure fire and imposing its own pattern, its own music, upon the heaviness and the dumbness that is in others and in itself. When we have drunk the cold cup of the moon's intoxication, we thirst for something beyond ourselves, and the mind flows outward to a natural immensity; but if we have drunk from the hot cup of the sun, our own fullness awakens, we desire little, for wherever one goes one's heart goes too; and if any ask what music is the sweetest, we can but answer, as Finn answered, "what happens." And yet the songs and stories that have come from either influence are a part, neither less than the other, of the pleasure that is the bride-bed of poetry.

VII

Gaelic-speaking Ireland, because its art has been made, not by the artist choosing his material from wherever he has a mind to, but by adding a little to something which it has taken generations to invent, has always had a popular literature. One cannot say how much that literature has done for the vigour of the race, for one cannot count the hands its praise of kings and high-hearted queens made hot upon the sword-hilt, or the amorous eyes it made lustful for strength and beauty. One remembers indeed that when the farming people and the labourers of the towns made their last attempt to cast out England by force of arms they named themselves after the companions of Finn. Even when Gaelic has gone, and the poetry with it, something of the habit of mind remains in ways of speech and thought and "come-all-ye"s and poetical saying; nor is it only among the poor that the old thought has been for strength or weakness. Surely these old stories, whether of Finn or Cuchulain, helped to sing the old Irish and the old Norman-Irish aristocracy to their end.

They heard their hereditary poets and story-tellers, and they took to horse and died fighting against Elizabeth or against Cromwell; and when an English-speaking aristocracy had their place, it listened to no poetry indeed, but it felt about it in the popular mind an exacting and ancient tribunal, and began a play that had for spectators men and women that loved the high wasteful virtues. I do not think that their own mixed blood or the habit of their time need take all, or nearly all, credit or discredit for the impulse that made our modern gentlemen fight duels over pocket-handkerchiefs, and set out to play ball against the gates of Jerusalem for a wager, and scatter money before the public eye; and at last, after an epoch of such eloquence the world has hardly seen its like, lose their public spirit and their high heart and grow querulous and selfish as men do who have played life out not heartily but with noise and tumult. Had they understood the people and the game a little better, they might have created an aristocracy in an age that has lost the meaning of the word. When one reads of the Fianna, or of Cuchulain, or of some great hero, one remembers that the fine life is always a part played finely before fine spectators. There also one notices the hot cup and the cold cup of intoxication; and when the fine spectators have ended, surely the fine players grow weary, and aristocratic life is ended. When O'Connell covered with a dark glove the hand that had killed a man in the duelling field, he played his part; and when Alexander stayed his army marching to the conquest of the world that he might contemplate the beauty of a plane-tree, he played his part. When Osgar complained as he lay dying, of the keening of the women and the old fighting men, he too played his part; "No man ever knew any heart in me," he said, "but a heart of twisted horn, and it covered with iron; but the howling of the dogs beside me," he said, "and the keening of the old fighting men and the crying of the women one after another, those are the things that are vexing me." If we would create a great community--and what other game is so worth the labour?--we must recreate the old foundations of life, not as they existed in that splendid misunderstanding of the eighteenth century, but as they must always exist when the finest minds and Ned the beggar and Seaghan the fool think about the same thing, although they may not think the same thought about it.

VIII

When I asked the little boy who had shown me the pathway up the Hill of Allen if he knew stories of Finn and Oisin, he said he did not, but that he had often heard his grandfather telling them to his mother in Irish. He did not know Irish, but he was learning it at school, and all the little boys he knew were learning it. In a little while he will know enough stories of Finn and Oisin to tell them to his children some day. It is the owners of the land whose children might never have known what would give them so much happiness. But now they can read this book to their children, and it will make Slieve-na-man, Allen, and Benbulben, the great mountain that showed itself before me every day through all my childhood and was yet unpeopled, and half the country-sides of south and west, as populous with memories as are Dundealgan and Emain Macha and Muirthemne; and after a while somebody may even take them to some famous place and say, "This land where your fathers lived proudly and finely should be dear and dear and again dear"; and perhaps when many names have grown musical to their ears, a more imaginative love will have taught them a better service.

IX

I need say nothing about the translation and arrangement of this book except that it is worthy to be put beside "Cuchulain of Muirthemne." Such books should not be commended by written words but by spoken words, were that possible, for the written words commending a book, wherein something is done supremely well, remain, to sound in the ears of a later generation, like the foolish sound of church bells from the tower of a church when every pew is full.

W.B. YEATS.

PART ONE: THE GODS.

BOOK ONE: THE COMING OF THE TUATHA DE DANAAN.

CHAPTER I. THE FIGHT WITH THE FIRBOLGS

It was in a mist the Tuatha de Danaan, the people of the gods of Dana, or as some called them, the Men of Dea, came through the air and the high air to Ireland.

It was from the north they came; and in the place they came from they had four cities, where they fought their battle for learning: great Falias, and shining Gorias, and Finias, and rich Murias that lay to the south. And in those cities they had four wise men to teach their young men skill and knowledge and perfect wisdom: Senias in Murias; and Arias, the fair-haired poet, in Finias; and Urias of the noble nature in Gorias; and Morias in Falias itself. And they brought from those four cities their four treasures: a Stone of Virtue from Falias, that was called the Lia Fail, the Stone of Destiny; and from Gorias they brought a Sword; and from Finias a Spear of Victory; and from Murias the fourth treasure, the Cauldron that no company ever went away from unsatisfied.

It was Nuada was king of the Tuatha de Danaan at that time, but Manannan, son of Lir, was greater again. And of the others that were chief among them were Ogma, brother to the king, that taught them writing, and Diancecht, that understood healing, and Neit, a god of battle, and Credenus the Craftsman, and Goibniu the Smith. And the greatest among their women were Badb, a battle goddess; and

Macha, whose mast-feeding was the heads of men killed in battle; and the Morrigu, the Crow of Battle; and Eire and Fodla and Banba, daughters of the Dagda, that all three gave their names to Ireland afterwards; and Eadon, the nurse of poets; and Brigit, that was a woman of poetry, and poets worshipped her, for her sway was very great and very noble. And she was a woman of healing along with that, and a woman of smith's work, and it was she first made the whistle for calling one to another through the night. And the one side of her face was ugly, but the other side was very comely. And the meaning of her name was Breo-saighit, a fiery arrow. And among the other women there were many shadow-forms and great queens; but Dana, that was called the Mother of the Gods, was beyond them all.

And the three things they put above all others were the plough and the sun and the hazel-tree, so that it was said in the time to come that Ireland was divided between those three, Coll the hazel, and Cecht the plough, and Grian the sun.

And they had a well below the sea where the nine hazels of wisdom were growing; that is, the hazels of inspiration and of the knowledge of poetry. And their leaves and their blossoms would break out in the same hour, and would fall on the well in a shower that raised a purple wave. And then the five salmon that were waiting there would eat the nuts, and their colour would come out in the red spots of their skin, and any person that would eat one of those salmon would know all wisdom and all poetry. And there were seven streams of wisdom that sprang from that well and turned back to it again; and the people of many arts have all drank from that well.

It was on the first day of Beltaine, that is called now May Day, the Tuatha de Danaan came, and it was to the north-west of Connacht they landed. But the Firbolgs, the Men of the Bag, that were in Ireland before them, and that had come from the South, saw nothing but a mist, and it lying on the hills.

Eochaid, son of Erc, was king of the Firbolgs at that time, and messengers came to him at Teamhair, and told him there was a new race of people come into Ireland, but whether from the earth or the skies or on the wind was not known, and that they had settled themselves at Magh Rein.

They thought there would be wonder on Eochaid when he heard that news; but there was no wonder on him, for a dream had come to him in the night, and when he asked his Druids the meaning of the dream, it is what they said, that it would not be long till there would be a strong enemy coming against him.

Then King Eochaid took counsel with his chief advisers, and it is what they agreed, to send a good champion of their own to see the strangers and to speak with them. So they chose out Sreng, that was a great fighting man, and he rose up and took his strong red-brown shield, and his two thick-handled spears, and his sword, and his head-covering, and his thick iron club, and he set out from Teamhair, and went on towards the place the strangers were, at Magh Rein.

But before he reached it, the watchers of the Tuatha de Danaan got sight of him, and they sent out one of their own champions, Bres, with his shield and his sword and his two spears, to meet him and to talk with him.

So the two champions went one towards the other slowly, and keeping a good watch on one another, and wondering at one another's arms, till they came near enough for talking; and then they stopped, and each put his shield before his body and struck it hard into the ground, and they looked at one another over the rim. Bres was the first to speak, and when Sreng heard it was Irish he was talking, his own tongue, he was less uneasy, and they drew nearer, and asked questions as to one another's family and race.

And after a while they put their shields away, and it was what Sreng said, that he had raised his in dread of the thin, sharp spears Bres had in his hand. And Bres said he himself was in dread of the thick-handled spears he saw with Sreng, and he asked were all the arms of the Firbolgs of the same sort. And Sreng took off the ty-ings of his spears to show them better, and Bres wondered at them, being so strong and so heavy, and so sharp at the sides though they had no points. And Sreng told him the name of those spears was Craisech, and that they would break through shields and crush flesh and bones, so that their thrust was death or wounds that never healed. And then he looked at the sharp, thin, hard-pointed spears that were with Bres. And in the end they made an exchange of spears, the way the fighters on each side would see the weapons the others were used to. And it is the message Bres sent to the Firbolgs, that if they would give up one half of Ireland, his people would be content to take it in peace; but if they would not give up that much, there should be a battle. And he and Sreng said to one another that whatever might happen in the future, they themselves would be friends.

Sreng went back then to Teamhair and gave the message and showed the spear;

and it is what he advised his people, to share the country and not to go into battle with a people that had weapons so much better than their own. But Eochaid and his chief men consulted together, and they said in the end: "We will not give up the half of the country to these strangers; for if we do," they said, "they will soon take the whole."

Now as to the Men of Dea, when Bres went back to them, and showed them the heavy spear, and told them of the strong, fierce man he had got it from, and how sturdy he was and well armed, they thought it likely there would soon be a battle. And they went back from where they were to a better place, farther west in Connacht, and there they settled themselves, and made walls and ditches on the plain of Magh Nia, where they had the great mountain, Belgata, in their rear. And while they were moving there and putting up their walls, three queens of them, Badb and Macha and the Morrigu, went to Teamhair where the Firbolgs were making their plans. And by the power of their enchantments they brought mists and clouds of darkness over the whole place, and they sent showers of fire and of blood over the people, the way they could not see or speak with one another through the length of three days. But at the end of that time, the three Druids of the Firbolgs, Cesarn and Gnathach and Ingnathach, broke the enchantment.

The Firbolgs gathered their men together then, and they came with their eleven battalions and took their stand at the eastern end of the plain of Magh Nia.

And Nuada, king of the Men of Dea, sent his poets to make the same offer he made before, to be content with the half of the country if it was given up to him. King Eochaid bade the poets to ask an answer of his chief men that were gathered there; and when they heard the offer they would not consent. So the messengers asked them when would they begin the battle. "We must have a delay," they said; "for we want time to put our spears and our armour in order, and to brighten our helmets and to sharpen our swords, and to have spears made like the ones you have. And as to yourselves," they said, "you will be wanting to have spears like our Craisechs made for you." So they agreed then to make a delay of a quarter of a year for preparation.

It was on a Midsummer day they began the battle. Three times nine hurlers of the Tuatha de Danaan went out against three times nine hurlers of the Firbolgs, and they were beaten, and every one of them was killed. And the king, Eochaid, sent a messenger to ask would they have the battle every day or every second day. And it is what Nuada answered that they would have it every day, but there should be just the same number of men fighting on each side. Eochaid agreed to that, but he was not well pleased, for there were more men of the Firbolgs than of the Men of Dea.

So the battle went on for four days, and there were great feats done on each side, and a great many champions came to their death. But for those that were alive at evening, the physicians on each side used to make a bath of healing, with every sort of healing plant or herb in it, the way they would be strong and sound for the next day's fight.

And on the fourth day the Men of Dea got the upper hand, and the Firbolgs were driven back. And a great thirst came on Eochaid, their king, in the battle, and he went off the field looking for a drink, and three fifties of his men protecting him; but three fifties of the Tuatha de Danaan followed after them till they came to the strand that is called Traigh Eothaile, and they had a fierce fight there, and at the last King Eochaid fell, and they buried him there, and they raised a great heap of stones over his grave.

And when there were but three hundred men left of the eleven battalions of the Firbolgs, and Sreng at the head of them, Nuada offered them peace, and their choice among the five provinces of Ireland. And Sreng said they would take Connacht; and he and his people lived there and their children after them. It is of them Ferdiad came afterwards that made such a good fight against Cuchulain, and Erc, son of Cairbre, that gave him his death. And that battle, that was the first fought in Ireland by the Men of Dea, was called by some the first battle of Magh Tuireadh.

And the Tuatha de Danaan took possession of Teamhair, that was sometimes called Druim Cain, the Beautiful Ridge, and Liathdruim, the Grey Ridge, and Druim na Descan, the Ridge of the Outlook, all those names were given to Teamhair. And from that time it was above all other places, for its king was the High King over all Ireland. The king's rath lay to the north, and the Hill of the Hostages to the northeast of the High Seat, and the Green of Teamhair to the west of the Hill of the Hostages. And to the north-east, in the Hill of the Sidhe, was a well called Nemnach, and out of it there flowed a stream called Nith, and on that stream the first mill was built in Ireland.

And to the north of the Hill of the Hostages was the stone, the Lia Fail, and it used to roar under the feet of every king that would take possession of Ireland. And the Wall of the Three Whispers was near the House of the Women that had seven doors to the east, and seven doors to the west; and it is in that house the feasts of Teamhair used to be held. And there was the Great House of a Thousand Soldiers, and near it, to the south, the little Hill of the Woman Soldiers.

CHAPTER II. THE REIGN OF BRES

B ut if Nuada won the battle, he lost his own arm in it, that was struck off by Sreng; and by that loss there came troubles and vexation on his people. For it was a law with the Tuatha de Danaan that no man that was not perfect in shape should be king. And after Nuada had lost the battle he was put out of the kingship on that account.

And the king they chose in his place was Bres, that was the most beautiful of all their young men, so that if a person wanted to praise any beautiful thing, whether it was a plain, or a dun, or ale, or a flame, or a woman, or a man, or a horse, it is what he would say, "It is as beautiful as Bres." And he was the son of a woman of the Tuatha de Danaan, but who his father was no one knew but herself.

But in spite of Bres being so beautiful, his reign brought no great good luck to his people; for the Fomor, whose dwelling-place was beyond the sea, or as some say below the sea westward, began putting tribute on them, the way they would get them under their own rule.

It was a long time before that the Fomor came first to Ireland; dreadful they were to look at, and maimed, having but one foot or one hand, and they under the leadership of a giant and his mother. There never came to Ireland an army more horrible or more dreadful than that army of the Fomor. And they were friendly with the Firbolgs and content to leave Ireland to them, but there was jealousy between them and the Men of Dea.

And it was a hard tax they put on them, a third part of their corn they asked, and a third part of their milk, and a third part of their children, so that there was not smoke rising from a roof in Ireland but was under tribute to them. And Bres made no stand against them, but let them get their way.

And as to Bres himself, he put a tax on every house in Ireland of the milk of hornless dun cows, or of the milk of cows of some other single colour, enough for a hundred men. And one time, to deceive him, Nechtan singed all the cows of Ireland in a fire of fern, and then he smeared them with the ashes of flax seed, the way they were all dark brown. He did that by the advice of the Druid Findgoll, son of Findemas. And another time they made three hundred cows of wood with dark brown pails in place of udders, and the pails were filled with black bog stuff. Then Bres came to look at the cows, and to see them milked before him, and Cian, father of Lugh, was there. And when they were milked it was the bog stuff that was squeezed out; and Bres took a drink of it thinking it to be milk, and he was not the better of it for a long time.

And there was another thing against Bres; he was no way open-handed, and the chief men of the Tuatha de Danaan grumbled against him, for their knives were never greased in his house, and however often they might visit him there was no smell of ale on their breath. And there was no sort of pleasure or merriment in his house, and no call for their poets, or singers, or harpers, or pipers, or horn-blowers, or jugglers, or fools. And as to the trials of strength they were used to see between their champions, the only use their strength was put to now was to be doing work for the king. Ogma himself, the shining poet, was under orders to bring firing to the palace every day for the whole army from the Islands of Mod; and he so weak for want of food that the sea would sweep away two-thirds of his bundle every day. And as to the Dagda, he was put to build raths, for he was a good builder, and he made a trench round Rath Brese. And he used often to be tired at the work, and one time he nearly gave in altogether for want of food, and this is the way that happened. He used to meet in the house an idle blind man, Cridenbel his name was, that had a sharp tongue, and that coveted the Dagda's share of food, for he thought his own to be small beside it. So he said to him: "For the sake of your good name let the three best bits of your share be given to me." And the Dagda gave in to that every night; but he was the worse of it, for what the blind man called a bit would be the size of a good pig, and with his three bits he would take a full third of the whole.

But one day, as the Dagda was in the trench, he saw his son, Angus Og, coming to him. "That is a good meeting," said Angus; "but what is on you, for you have no good appearance to-day?" "There is a reason for that," said the Dagda, "for every evening, Cridenbel, the blind man, makes a demand for the three best bits of my share of food, and takes them from me." "I will give you an advice," said Angus. He put his hand in his bag then, and took out three pieces of gold and gave them to him.

"Put these pieces of gold into the three bits you will give this evening to Cridenbel," he said, "and they will be the best bits in the dish, and the gold will turn within him the way he will die."

So in the evening the Dagda did that; and no sooner had Cridenbel swallowed down the gold than he died. Some of the people said then to the king: "The Dagda has killed Cridenbel, giving him some deadly herb." The king believed that, and there was anger on him against the Dagda, and he gave orders he should be put to death. But the Dagda said: "You are not giving the right judgment of a prince." And he told all that had happened, and how Cridenbel used to say, "Give me the three best bits before you, for my own share is not good to-night." "And on this night," he said, "the three pieces of gold were the best things before me, and I gave them to him, and he died."

The king gave orders then to have the body cut open. And they found the gold inside it, and they knew it was the truth the Dagda had told.

And Angus came to him again the next day, and he said: "Your work will soon be done, and when you are given your wages, take nothing they may offer you till the cattle of Ireland are brought before you, and choose out a heifer then, black and black-maned, that I will tell you the signs of."

So when the Dagda had brought his work to an end, and they asked him what reward he wanted, he did as Angus had bidden him. And that seemed folly to Bres; he thought the Dagda would have asked more than a heifer of him.

There came a day at last when a poet came to look for hospitality at the king's house, Corpre, son of Etain, poet of the Tuatha de Danaan. And it is how he was treated, he was put in a little dark narrow house where there was no fire, or furniture, or bed; and for a feast three small cakes, and they dry, were brought to him on a little dish. When he rose up on the morrow he was no way thankful, and as he was going across the green, it is what he said: "Without food ready on a dish; without milk enough for a calf to grow on; without shelter; without light in the darkness of night; without enough to pay a story-teller; may that be the prosperity of Bres."

And from that day there was no good luck with Bres, but it is going down he was for ever after. And that was the first satire ever made in Ireland.

Now as to Nuada: after his arm being struck off, he was in his sickness for a while, and then Diancecht, the healer, made an arm of silver for him, with movement in every finger of it, and put it on him. And from that he was called Nuada Argat-lamh, of the Silver Hand, for ever after.

Now Miach, son of Diancecht, was a better hand at healing than his father, and had done many things. He met a young man, having but one eye, at Teamhair one time, and the young man said: "If you are a good physician you will put an eye in the place of the eye I lost." "I could put the eye of that cat in your lap in its place," said Miach. "I would like that well," said the young man. So Miach put the cat's eye in his head; but he would as soon have been without it after, for when he wanted to sleep and take his rest, it is then the eye would start at the squeaking of the mice, or the flight of the birds, or the movement of the rushes; and when he was wanting to watch an army or a gathering, it is then it was sure to be in a deep sleep.

And Miach was not satisfied with what his father had done to the king, and he took Nuada's own hand that had been struck off, and brought it to him and set it in its place, and he said: "Joint to joint, and sinew to sinew." Three days and three nights he was with the king; the first day he put the hand against his side, and the second day against his breast, till it was covered with skin, and the third day he put bulrushes that were blackened in the fire on it, and at the end of that time the king was healed.

But Diancecht was vexed when he saw his son doing a better cure than himself, and he threw his sword at his head, that it cut the flesh, but the lad healed the wound by means of his skill. Then Diancecht threw it a second time, that it reached the bone, but the lad was able to cure the wound. Then he struck him the third time and the fourth, till he cut out the brain, for he knew no physician could cure him after that blow; and Miach died, and he buried him.

And herbs grew up from his grave, to the number of his joints and sinews, three hundred and sixty-five. And Airmed, his sister, came and spread out her cloak and laid out the herbs in it, according to their virtue. But Diancecht saw her doing that, and he came and mixed up the herbs, so that no one knows all their right powers to this day.

Then when the Tuatha de Danaan saw Nuada as well as he was before, they gathered together to Teamhair, where Bres was, and they bade him give up the kingship, for he had held it long enough. So he had to give it up, though he was not very willing, and Nuada was put back in the kingship again.

There was great vexation on Bres then, and he searched his mind to know how could he be avenged on those that had put him out, and how he could gather an army against them; and he went to his mother, Eri, daughter of Delbaith, and bade her tell him what his race was.

"I know that well," she said; and she told him then that his father was a king of the Fomor, Elathan, son of Dalbaech, and that he came to her one time over a level sea in some great vessel that seemed to be of silver, but she could not see its shape, and he himself having the appearance of a young man with yellow hair, and his clothes sewed with gold, and five rings of gold about his neck. And she that had refused the love of all the young men of her own people, gave him her love, and she cried when he left her. And he gave her a ring from his hand, and bade her give it only to the man whose finger it would fit, and he went away then the same way as he had come.

And she brought out the ring then to Bres, and he put it round his middle finger, and it fitted him well. And they went then together to the hill where she was the time she saw the silver vessel coming, and down to the strand, and she and Bres and his people set out for the country of the Fomor.

And when they came to that country they found a great plain with many gatherings of people on it, and they went to the gathering that looked the best, and the people asked where did they come from, and they said they were come from Ireland. "Have you hounds with you?" they asked them then, for it was the custom at that time, when strangers came to a gathering, to give them some friendly challenge. "We have hounds," said Bres. So the hounds were matched against one another, and the hounds of the Tuatha de Danaan were better than the hounds of the Fomor. "Have you horses for a race?" they asked then. "We have," said Bres. And the horses of the Tuatha de Danaan beat the horses of the Fomor.

Then they asked was any one among them a good hand with the sword, and they said Bres was the best. But when he put his hand to his sword, Elathan, his father, that was among them, knew the ring, and he asked who was this young man. Then his mother answered him and told the whole story, and that Bres was his own son.

There was sorrow on his father then, and he said: "What was it drove you out of the country you were king over?" And Bres said: "Nothing drove me out but my own injustice and my own hardness; I took away their treasures from the people, and their jewels, and their food itself. And there were never taxes put on them before I was their king."

"That is bad," said his father; "it is of their prosperity you had a right to think more than of your own kingship. And their good-will would be better than their curses," he said; "and what is it you are come to look for here?" "I am come to look for fighting men," said Bres, "that I may take Ireland by force." "You have no right to get it by injustice when you could not keep it by justice," said his father. "What advice have you for me then?" said Bres.

And Elathan bade him go to the chief king of the Fomor, Balor of the Evil Eye, to see what advice and what help would he give him.

BOOK TWO: LUGH OF THE LONG HAND.

CHAPTER I. THE COMING OF LUGH

Now as to Nuada of the Silver Hand, he was holding a great feast at Teamhair one time, after he was back in the kingship. And there were two door-keepers at Teamhair, Gamal, son of Figal, and Camel, son of Riagall. And a young man came to the door where one of them was, and bade him bring him in to the king. "Who are you yourself?" said the door-keeper. "I am Lugh, son of Cian of the Tuatha de Danaan, and of Ethlinn, daughter of Balor, King of the Fomor," he said; "and I am foster-son of Taillte, daughter of the King of the Great Plain, and of Echaid the Rough, son of Duach." "What are you skilled in?" said the door-keeper; "for no one without an art comes into Teamhair." "Question me," said Lugh; "I am a carpenter." "We do not want you; we have a carpenter ourselves, Luchtar, son of Luachaid." "Then I am a smith." "We have a smith ourselves, Colum Cuaillemech of the Three New Ways." "Then I am a champion." "That is no use to us; we have a champion before, Ogma, brother to the king." "Question me again," he said; "I am a harper." "That is no use to us; we have a harper ourselves, Abhean, son of Bicelmos, that the Men of the Three Gods brought from the hills." "I am-a poet," he said then, "and a teller of tales." "That is no use to us; we have a teller of tales ourselves, Ere, son of Ethaman." "And I am a magician." "That is no use to us; we have plenty of magicians and people of power." "I am a physician," he said. "That is no use; we have Diancecht-for our physician." "Let me be a cup-bearer," he said. "We do not want you; we have nine cup-bearers ourselves." "I am a good worker in brass." "We have a worker in brass ourselves, that is Credne Cerd."

Then Lugh said: "Go and ask the king if he has any one man that can do all these things, and if he has, I will not ask to come into Teamhair." The door-keeper went into the king's house then and told him all that. "There is a young man at the door," he said, "and his name should be the Ildanach, the Master of all Arts, for all the things the people of your house can do, he himself is able to do every one of them." "Try him with the chess-boards," said Nuada. So the chess-boards were brought out, and every game that was played, Lugh won it. And when Nuada was told that, he said: "Let him in, for the like of him never came into Teamhair before."

Then the door-keeper let him pass, and he came into the king's house and sat down in the seat of knowledge. And there was a great flag-stone there that could hardly be moved by four times twenty yoke of oxen, and Ogma took it up and hurled it out through the house, so that it lay on the outside of Teamhair, as a challenge to Lugh. But Lugh hurled it back again that it lay in the middle of the king's house. He played the harp for them then, and he had them laughing and crying, till he put them asleep at the end with a sleepy tune. And when Nuada saw all the things Lugh could do, he began to think that by his help the country might get free of the taxes and the tyranny put on it by the Fomor. And it is what he did, he came down from his throne, and he put Lugh on it in his place, for the length of thirteen days, the way they might all listen to the advice he would give.

This now is the story of the birth of Lugh. The time the Fomor used to be coming to Ireland, Balor of the Strong Blows, or, as some called him, of the Evil Eye, was living on the Island of the Tower of Glass. There was danger for ships that went near that island, for the Fomor would come out and take them. And some say the sons of Nemed in the old time, before the Firbolgs were in Ireland, passed near it in their ships, and what they saw was a tower of glass in the middle of the sea, and on the tower something that had the appearance of men, and they went against it with Druid spells to attack it. And the Fomor worked against them with Druid spells of their own; and the sons of Nemed attacked the tower, and it vanished, and they thought it was destroyed. But a great wave rose over them then, and all their ships went down and all that were in them.

And the tower was there as it was before, and Balor living in it. And it is the reason he was called "of the Evil Eye," there was a power of death in one of his eyes, so that no person could look at it and live. It is the way it got that power, he was passing one time by a house where his father's Druids were making spells of death, and the window being open he looked in, and the smoke of the poisonous spells was rising up, and it went into his eye. And from that time he had to keep it closed unless he wanted to be the death of some enemy, and then the men that were with him would lift the eyelid with a ring of ivory.

Now a Druid foretold one time that it was by his own grandson he would get his death. And he had at that time but one child, a daughter whose name was Eth-linn; and when he heard what the Druid said, he shut her up in the tower on the island. And he put twelve women with her to take charge of her and to guard her, and he bade them never to let her see a man or hear the name of a man.

So Ethlinn was brought up in the tower, and she grew to be very beautiful; and sometimes she would see men passing in the currachs, and sometimes she would see a man in her dreams. But when she would speak of that to the women, they would give her no answer.

So there was no fear on Balor, and he went on with war and robbery as he was used, seizing every ship that passed by, and sometimes going over to Ireland to do destruction there.

Now it chanced at that time there were three brothers of the Tuatha de Danaan living together in a place that was called Druim na Teine, the Ridge of the Fire, Goibniu and Samthainn and Cian. Cian was a lord of land, and Goibniu was the smith that had such a great name. Now Cian had a wonderful cow, the Glas Gaibhnenn, and her milk never failed. And every one that heard of her coveted her, and many had tried to steal her away, so that she had to be watched night and day.

And one time Cian was wanting some swords made, and he went to Goibniu's forge, and he brought the Glas Gaibhnenn with him, holding her by a halter. When he came to the forge his two brothers were there together, for Samthainn had brought some steel to have weapons made for himself; and Cian bade Samthainn to hold the halter while he went into the forge to speak with Goibniu.

Now Balor had set his mind for a long time on the Glas Gaibhnenn, but he had never been able to get near her up to this time. And he was watching not far off, and when he saw Samthainn holding the cow, he put on the appearance of a little boy, having red hair, and came up to him and told him he heard his two brothers that were in the forge saying to one another that they would use all his steel for their own swords, and make his of iron. "By my word," said Samthainn, "they will not deceive me so easily. Let you hold the cow, little lad," he said, "and I will go in to them." With that he rushed into the forge, and great anger on him. And no sooner did Balor get the halter in his hand than he set out, dragging the Glas along with him, to the strand, and across the sea to his own island.

When Cian saw his brother coming in he rushed out, and there he saw Balor and the Glas out in the sea. And he had nothing to do then but to reproach his brother, and to wander about as if his wits had left him, not knowing what way to get his cow back from Balor. At last he went to a Druid to ask an advice from him; and it is what the Druid told him, that so long as Balor lived, the cow would never be brought back, for no one would go within reach of his Evil Eye.

Cian went then to a woman-Druid, Birog of the Mountain, for her help. And she dressed him in a woman's clothes, and brought him across the sea in a blast of wind, to the tower where Ethlinn was. Then she called to the women in the tower, and asked them for shelter for a high queen she was after saving from some hardship, and the women in the tower did not like to refuse a woman of the Tuatha de Danaan, and they let her and her comrade in. Then Birog by her enchantments put them all into a deep sleep, and Cian went to speak with Ethlinn. And when she saw him she said that was the face she had seen in her dreams. So she gave him her love; but after a while he was brought away again on a blast of wind.

And when her time came, Ethlinn gave birth to a son. And when Balor knew that, he bade his people put the child in a cloth and fasten it with a pin, and throw him into a current of the sea. And as they were carrying the child across an arm of the sea, the pin dropped out, and the child slipped from the cloth into the water, and they thought he was drowned. But he was brought away by Birog of the Mountain, and she brought him to his father Cian; and he gave him to be fostered by Taillte, daughter of the King of the Great Plain. It is thus Lugh was born and reared.

And some say Balor came and struck the head off Cian on a white stone, that has the blood marks on it to this day; but it is likely it was some other man he struck the head off, for it was by the sons of Tuireann that Cian came to his death.

And after Lugh had come to Teamhair, and made his mind up to join with his father's people against the Fomor, he put his mind to the work; and he went to a quiet place in Grellach Dollaid, with Nuada and the Dagda, and with Ogma; and Goibniu and Diancecht were called to them there. A full year they stopped there, making their plans together in secret, the way the Fomor would not know they were going to rise against them till such time as all would be ready, and till they would know what their strength was. And it is from that council the place got the name afterwards of "The Whisper of the Men of Dea."

And they broke up the council, and agreed to meet again that day three years, and every one of them went his own way, and Lugh went back to his own friends, the sons of Manannan.

And it was a good while after that, Nuada was holding a great assembly of the people on the Hill of Uisnech, on the west side of Teamhair. And they were not long there before they saw an armed troop coming towards them from the east, over the plain; and there was a young man in front of the troop, in command over the rest, and the brightness of his face was like the setting sun, so that they were not able to look at him because of its brightness.

And when he came nearer they knew it was Lugh Lamh-Fada, of the Long Hand, that had come back to them, and along with him were the Riders of the Sidhe from the Land of Promise, and his own foster-brothers, the sons of Manannan, Sgoith Gleigeil, the White Flower, and Goitne Gorm-Shuileach, the Blue-eyed Spear, and Sine Sindearg, of the Red Ring, and Donall Donn-Ruadh, of the Red-brown Hair. And it is the way Lugh was, he had Manannan's horse, the Aonbharr, of the One Mane, under him, that was as swift as the naked cold wind of spring, and the sea was the same as dry land to her, and the rider was never killed off her back. And he had Manannan's breast-plate on him, that kept whoever was wearing it from wounds, and a helmet on his head with two beautiful precious stones set in the front of it and one at the back, and when he took it off, his forehead was like the sun on a dry summer day. And he had Manannan's sword, the Freagarthach, the Answerer, at his side, and no one that was wounded by it would ever get away alive; and when that sword was bared in a battle, no man that saw it coming against him had any more strength than a woman in child-birth.

And the troop came to where the King of Ireland was with the Tuatha de Danaan, and they welcomed one another.

And they were not long there till they saw a surly, slovenly troop coming towards them, nine times nine of the messengers of the Fomor, that were coming to ask rent and taxes from the men of Ireland; and the names of the four that were the hardest and the most cruel were Eine and Eathfaigh and Coron and Compar; and there was such great dread of these four on the Tuatha de Danaan, that not one of them would so much as punish his own son or his foster-son without leave from them.

They came up then to where the King of Ireland was with the Riders of the Sidhe, and the king and all the Tuatha de Danaan stood up before them. And Lugh of the Long Hand said: "Why do you rise up before that surly, slovenly troop, when you did not rise up before us?"

"It is needful for us to do it," said the king; "for if there was but a child of us sitting before them, they would not think that too small a cause for killing him." "By my word," said Lugh, "there is a great desire coming on me to kill themselves." "That is a thing would bring harm on us," said the king, "for we would meet our own death and destruction through it." "It is too long a time you have been under this oppression," said Lugh. And with that he started up and made an attack on the Fomor, killing and wounding them, till he had made an end of eight nines of them, but he let the last nine go under the protection of Nuada the king. "And I would kill you along with the others," he said, "but I would sooner see you go with messages to your own country than my own people, for fear they might get any ill-treatment."

So the nine went back then till they came to Lochlann, where the men of the Fomor were, and they told them the story from beginning to end, and how a young well-featured lad had come into Ireland and had killed all the tax-gatherers but themselves, "and it is the reason he let us off," they said, "that we might tell you the story ourselves."

"Do you know who is the young man?" said Balor of the Evil Eye then.

"I know well," said Ceithlenn, his wife; "he is the son of your daughter and mine. And it was foretold," she said, "that from the time he would come into Ireland, we would never have power there again for ever."

Then the chief men of the Fomor went into a council, Eab, son of Neid, and Seanchab, grandson of Neid, and Sital Salmhor, and Liath, son of Lobais, and the nine poets of the Fomor that had learning and the gift of foreknowledge, and Lobais the Druid, and Balor himself and his twelve white-mouthed sons, and Ceithlenn of the Crooked Teeth, his queen.

And it was just at that time Bres and his father Elathan were come to ask help of the Fomor, and Bres said: "I myself will go to Ireland, and seven great battalions of the Riders of the Fomor along with me, and I will give battle to this Ildanach, this master of all arts, and I will strike his head off and bring it here to you, to the green of Berbhe." "It would be a fitting thing for you to do," said they all. "Let my ships be made ready for me," said Bres, "and let food and provisions be put in them."

So they made no delay, but went and got the ships ready, and they put plenty of food and drink in them, and the two swift Luaths were sent out to gather the army to Bres. And when they were all gathered, they made ready their armour and their weapons, and they set out for Ireland.

And Balor the king followed them to the harbour, and he said: "Give battle to that Ildanach, and strike off his head; and tie that island that is called Ireland to the back of your ships, and let the destroying water take its place, and put it on the north side of Lochlann, and not one of the Men of Dea will follow it there to the end of life and time."

Then they pushed out their ships and put up their painted sails, and went out from the harbour on the untilled country, on the ridges of the wide-lying sea, and they never turned from their course till they came to the harbour of Eas Dara. And from that they sent out an army through West Connacht and destroyed it altogether, through and through. And the King of Connacht at that time was Bodb Dearg, son of the Dagda.

CHAPTER II. THE SONS OF TUIREANN

And Lugh of the Long Hand was at that time at Teamhair with the King of Ireland, and it was showed to him that the Fomor were after landing at Eas Dara. And when he knew that, he made ready Manannan's horse, the Aonbharr, at the time of the battle of the day and night; and he went where Nuada the king was, and told him how the Fomor had landed at Eas Dara and had spoiled Bodb Dearg's country; "and it is what I want," he said, "to get help from you to give battle to them." But Nuada was not minded to avenge the destruction that was done on Bodb Dearg and not on himself, and Lugh was not well pleased with his answer, and he went riding out of Teamhair westward. And presently he saw three armed men coming towards him, his own father Cian, with his brothers Cu and Ceithen, that were the three sons of Cainte, and they saluted him. "What is the cause of your early rising?" they said. "It is good cause I have for it," said Lugh, "for the Fomor are come into Ireland and have robbed Bodb Dearg; and what help will you give me against them?" he said.

"Each one of us will keep off a hundred from you in the battle," said they. "That is a good help," said Lugh; "but there is a help I would sooner have from you than that: to gather the Riders of the Sidhe to me from every place where they are."

So Cu and Ceithen went towards the south, and Cian set out northward, and he did not stop till he reached the Plain of Muirthemne. And as he was going across the plain he saw three armed men before him, that were the three sons of Tuireann, son of Ogma. And it is the way it was between the three sons of Tuireann and the three sons of Cainte, they were in hatred and enmity towards one another, so that whenever they met there was sure to be fighting among them.

Then Cian said: "If my two brothers had been here it is a brave fight we would make; but since they are not, it is best for me to fall back." Then he saw a great herd of pigs near him, and he struck himself with a Druid rod that put on him the shape of a pig of the herd, and he began rooting up the ground like the rest.

Then Brian, one of the sons of Tuireann, said to his brothers: "Did you see that armed man that was walking the plain a while ago?" "We did see him," said they. "Do you know what was it took him away?" said Brian. "We do not know that," said they. "It is a pity you not to be keeping a better watch over the plains of the open country in time of war," said Brian; "and I know well what happened him, for he struck himself with his Druid rod into the shape of a pig of these pigs, and he is rooting up the ground now like any one of them; and whoever he is, he is no friend to us." "That is bad for us," said the other two, "for the pigs belong to some one of the Tuatha de Danaan, and even if we kill them all, the Druid pig might chance to escape us in the end."

"It is badly you got your learning in the city of learning," said Brian, "when you cannot tell an enchanted beast from a natural beast." And while he was saying that, he struck his two brothers with his Druid rod, and he turned them into two thin, fast hounds, and they began to yelp sharply on the track of the enchanted pig.

And it was not long before the pig fell out from among the others, and not one of the others made away but only itself, and it made for a wood, and at the edge of the wood Brian gave a cast of his spear that went through its body. And the pig cried out, and it said: "It is a bad thing you have done to have made a cast at me when you knew me." "It seems to me you have the talk of a man," said Brian. "I was a man indeed," said he; "I am Cian, son of Cainte, and give me your protection now." "I swear by the gods of the air," said Brian, "that if the life came back seven times to you, I would take it from you every time." "If that is so," said Cian, "give me one request: let me go into my own shape again." "We will do that," said Brian, "for it is easier to me to kill a man than a pig."

So Cian took his own shape then, and he said: "Give me mercy now." "We will not give it," said Brian. "Well, I have got the better of you for all that," said Cian; "for if it was in the shape of a pig you had killed me there would only be the blood money for a pig on me; but as it is in my own shape you will kill me, there never was and never will be any person killed for whose sake a heavier fine will be paid than for myself. And the arms I am killed with," he said, "it is they will tell the deed to my son."

"It is not with weapons you will be killed, but with the stones lying on the ground," said Brian. And with that they pelted him with stones, fiercely and roughly, till all that was left of him was a poor, miserable, broken heap; and they buried him the depth of a man's body in the earth, and the earth would not receive that murder from them, but cast it up again. Brian said it should go into the earth again, and they put it in the second time, and the second time the earth would not take it. And six times the sons of Tuireann buried the body, and six times it was cast up again; but the seventh time it was put underground the earth kept it. And then they went on to join Lugh of the Long Hand for the battle.

Now as to Lugh; upon parting with his father he went forward from Teamhair westward, to the hills that were called afterwards Gairech and Ilgairech, and to the ford of the Shannon that is now called Athluain, and to Bearna nah-Eadargana, the Gap of Separation, and over Magh Luirg, the Plain of Following, and to Corr Slieve na Seaghsa, the Round Mountain of the Poet's Spring, and to the head of Sean-Slieve, and through the place of the bright-faced Corann, and from that to Magh Mor an Aonaigh, the Great Plain of the Fair, where the Fomor were, and the spoils of Connacht with them.

It is then Bres, son of Elathan, rose up and said: "It is a wonder to me the sun to be rising in the west to-day, and it rising in the east every other day." "It would be better for us it to be the sun," said the Druids. "What else is it?" said he. "It is the shining of the face of Lugh, son of Ethlinn," said they.

Lugh came up to them then and saluted them. "Why do you come like a friend to us?" said they. "There is good cause for that," he said, "for there is but one half of me of the Tuatha de Danaan, and the other half of yourselves. And give me back now the milch cows of the men of Ireland," he said. "May early good luck not come to you till you get either a dry or a milch cow here," said a man of them, and anger on him.

But Lugh stopped near them for three days and three nights, and at the end of that time the Riders of the Sidhe came to him. And Bodb Dearg, son of the Dagda, came with twenty-nine hundred men, and he said:

"What is the cause of your delay in giving battle?"

"Waiting for you I was," said Lugh.

Then the kings and chief men of the men of Ireland took their armour on them, and they raised the points of their spears over their heads, and they made close fences of their shields. And they attacked their enemies on Magh Mor an Aonaigh, and their enemies answered them, and they threw their whining spears at one another, and when their spears were broken they drew their swords from their blue-bordered sheaths and began to strike at one another, and thickets of brown flames rose above them from the bitterness of their many-edged weapons.

And Lugh saw the battle pen where Bres, son of Elathan, was, and he made a fierce attack on him and on the men that were guarding him, till he had made an end of two hundred of them.

When Bres saw that, he gave himself up to Lugh's protection. "Give me my life this time," he said, "and I will bring the whole race of the Fomor to fight it out with you in a great battle; and I bind myself to that, by the sun and the moon, the sea and the land," he said.

On that Lugh gave him his life, and then the Druids that were with him asked his protection for themselves. "By my word," said Lugh, "if the whole race of the Fomor went under my protection they would not be destroyed by me." So then Bres and the Druids set out for their own country.

Now as to Lugh and the sons of Tuireann. After the battle of Magh Mor an Aonaigh, he met two of his kinsmen and asked them did they see his father in the fight. "We did not," said they. "I am sure he is not living," said Lugh; "and I give my word," he said, "there will no food or drink go into my mouth till I get knowledge by what death my father died."

Then he set out, and the Riders of the Sidhe after him, till they came to the place where he and his father parted from one another, and from that to the place where his father went into the shape of a pig when he saw the sons of Tuireann.

And when Lugh came to that place the earth spoke to him, and it said: "It is in great danger your father was here, Lugh, when he saw the sons of Tuireann before him, and it is into the shape of a pig he had to go, but it is in his own shape they killed him."

Then Lugh told that to his people, and he found the spot where his father was buried, and he bade them dig there, the way he would know by what death the sons of Tuireann had made an end of him.

Then they raised the body out of the grave and looked at it, and it was all one bed of wounds. And Lugh said: "It was the death of an enemy the sons of Tuireann gave my dear father." And he gave him three kisses, and it is what he said: "It is bad the way I am myself after this death, for I can hear nothing with my ears, and I can see nothing with my eyes, and there is not a living pulse in my heart, with grief after my father. And you gods I worship," he said, "it is a pity I not to have come here the time this thing was done. And it is a great thing that has been done here," he said, "the people of the gods of Dana to have done treachery on one another, and it is long they will be under loss by it and be weakened by it. And Ireland will never be free from trouble from this out, east and west," he said.

Then they put Cian under the earth again, and after that there was keening made over his grave, and a stone was raised on it, and his name was written in Ogham, And Lugh said: "This hill will take its name from Cian, although he himself is stripped and broken. And it was the sons of Tuireann did this thing," he said, "and there will grief and anguish fall on them from it, and on their children after them. And it is no lying story I am telling you," he said; "and it is a pity the way I am, and my heart is broken in my breast since Cian, the brave man, is not living."

Then he bade his people to go before him to Teamhair, "But do not tell the story till I tell it myself," he said.

And when Lugh came to Teamhair he sat in the high seat of the king, and he looked about him and he saw the three sons of Tuireann. And those were the three that were beyond all others at Teamhair at that time for quickness and skill, for a good hand in battle, for beauty and an honourable name.

Then Lugh bade his people to shake the chain of silence, and they did so, and they all listened. And Lugh said: "What are your minds fixed on at this time, Men of Dea?" "On yourself indeed," said they. "I have a question to ask of you," he said. "What is the vengeance each one of you would take on the man that would kill your father?"

There was great wonder on them when they heard that, and one of the chief men among them said: "Tell us was it your own father that was killed?" "It was indeed," said Lugh; "and I see now in this house," he said, "the men that killed him, and they know themselves what way they killed him better than I know it." Then the king said: "It is not a death of one day only I would give the man that had killed my father, if he was in my power, but to cut off one of his limbs from day to day till I would make an end of him." All the chief men said the same, and the sons of Tuireann like the rest.

"There are making that answer," said Lugh, "the three men that killed my father; and let them pay the fine for him now, since you are all together in the one place. And if they will not," he said, "I will not break the protection of the king's house, but they must make no attempt to quit this house till they have settled with me."

"If it was I myself had killed your father," said the king, "I would be well content you to take a fine from me for him."

"It is at us Lugh is saying all this," said the sons of Tuireann among themselves. "Let us acknowledge the killing of his father to him," said Iuchar and Iucharba. "I am in dread," said Brian, "that it is wanting an acknowledgment from us he is, in the presence of all the rest, and that he will not let us off with a fine afterwards." "It is best to acknowledge it," said the others; "and let you speak it out since you are the eldest."

Then Brian, son of Tuireann, said: "It is at us you are speaking, Lugh, for you are thinking we went against the sons of Cainte before now; and we did not kill your father," he said, "but we will pay the fine for him the same as if we did kill him." "I will take a fine from you that you do not think of," said Lugh, "and I will say here what it is, and if it is too much for you, I will let you off a share of it." "Let us hear it from you," said they. "Here it is," said Lugh; "three apples, and the skin of a pig, and a spear, and two horses, and a chariot, and seven pigs, and a dog's whelp, and a cooking-spit, and three shouts on a hill. That is the fine I am asking," he said; "and if it is too much for you, a part of it will be taken off you presently, and if you do not think it too much, then pay it"

"It is not too much," said Brian, "or a hundred times of it would not be too much. And we think it likely," he said, "because of its smallness that you have some treachery towards us behind it." "I do not think it too little of a fine," said Lugh; "and I give you the guarantee of the Tuatha de Danaan I will ask no other thing, and I will be faithful to you, and let you give the same pledge to me." "It is a pity you to ask that," said Brian, "for our own pledge is as good as any pledge in the world." "Your own pledge is not enough," said Lugh, "for it is often the like of you promised to pay a fine in this way, and would try to back out of it after."

So then the sons of Tuireann bound themselves by the King of Ireland, and by Bodb Dearg, son of the Dagda, and by the chief men of the Tuatha de Danaan, that they would pay that fine to Lugh.

"It would be well for me now," said Lugh, "to give you better knowledge of the fine." "It would be well indeed," said they.

"This is the way of it then," said Lugh. "The three apples I asked of you are the three apples from the Garden in the East of the World, and no other apples will do but these, for they are the most beautiful and have most virtue in them of the apples of the whole world. And it is what they are like, they are of the colour of burned gold, and they are the size of the head of a child a month old, and there is the taste of honey on them, and they do not leave the pain of wounds or the vexation of sickness on any one that eats them, and they do not lessen by being eaten for ever. And the skin I asked of you," he said, "is the pig skin of Tuis, King of Greece, and it heals all the wounds and all the sickness of the world, and whatever danger a man may be in, if it can but overtake the life in him, it will cure him; and it is the way it was with that pig, every stream of water it would go through would be turned into wine to the end of nine days after, and every wound it touched was healed; and it is what the Druids of Greece said, that it is not in itself this virtue was, but in the skin, and they skinned it, and the skin is there ever since. And I think, too, it will not be easy for you to get it, with or without leave."

"And do you know what is the spear I am asking of you?" he said. "We do not," said they. "It is a very deadly spear belonging to the King of Persia, the Luin it is called, and every choice thing is done by it, and its head is kept steeped in a vessel of water, the way it will not burn down the place where it is, and it will be hard to get it. And do you know what two horses and what chariot I am asking of you? They are the chariot and the two wonderful horses of Dobar, King of Siogair, and the sea is the same as land to them, and there are no faster horses than themselves, and there is no chariot equal to that one in shape and in strength.

"And do you know what are the seven pigs I asked of you? They are the pigs of Easal, King of the Golden Pillars; and though they are killed every night, they are found alive again the next day, and there will be no disease or no sickness on any person that will eat a share of them.

"And the whelp I asked of you is Fail-Inis, the whelp belonging to the King of

Ioruaidh, the Cold Country. And all the wild beasts of the world would fall down at the sight of her, and she is more beautiful than the sun in his fiery wheels, and it will be hard to get her.

"And the cooking-spit I asked of you is a spit of the spits of the women of Inis Cenn-fhinne, the Island of Caer of the Fair Hair. And the three shouts you are to give on a hill must be given on the Hill of Miochaoin in the north of Lochlann. And Miochaoin and his sons are under bonds not to allow any shouts to be given on that hill; and it was with them my father got his learning, and if I would forgive you his death, they would not forgive you. And if you get through all your other voyages before you reach to them, it is my opinion they themselves will avenge him on you. And that is the fine I have asked of you," said Lugh.

There was silence and darkness on the sons of Tuireann when they heard that. And they went to where their father was, and told him the fine that had been put on them. "It is bad news that is," said Tuireann; "and it is to your death and your destruction you will be going, looking for those things. But for all that, if Lugh himself had a mind to help you, you could work out the fine, and all the men of the world could not do it but by the power of Manannan or of Lugh. Go then and ask the loan of Manannan's horse, the Aonbharr, from Lugh, and if he has any wish to get the fine, he will give it to you; but if he does not wish it he will say the horse is not his, and that he would not give the loan of a loan. Ask him then for the loan of Manannan's curragh, the Scuabtuinne, the Sweeper of the Waves. And he will give that, for he is under bonds not to refuse a second request, and the curragh is better for you than the horse," he said.

So the sons of Tuireann went to where Lugh was, and they saluted him, and they said they could not bring him the fine without his own help, and for that reason it would be well for them to get a loan of the Aonbharr. "I have that horse only on loan myself," said Lugh, "and I will not give a loan of a loan."

"If that is so, give us the loan of Manannan's curragh," said Brian. "I will give that," said Lugh. "What place is it?" said they. "At Brugh na Boinn," said Lugh.

Then they went back again to where Tuireann was, and his daughter Ethne, their sister, with him, and they told him they had got the curragh. "It is not much the better you will be for it," said Tuireann, "although Lugh would like well to get every part of this fine he could make use of before the battle with the Fomor. But he would like yourselves to come to your death looking for it."

Then they went away, and they left Tuireann sorrowful and lamenting, and Ethne went with them to where the curragh was. And Brian got into it, and he said: "There is place but for one other person along with me here." And he began to find fault with its narrowness. "You ought not to be faulting the curragh," said Ethne; "and O my dear brother," she said, "it was a bad thing you did, to kill the father of Lugh of the Long Hand; and whatever harm may come to you from it, it is but just." "Do not say that, Ethne," they said, "for we are in good heart, and we will do brave deeds. And we would sooner be killed a hundred times over," they said, "than to meet with the death of cowards." "My grief," said Ethne, "there is nothing more sorrowful than this, to see you driven out from your own country."

Then the three pushed out their curragh from the beautiful clear-bayed shore of Ireland. "What course shall we take first?" said they. "We will go look for the apples," said Brian, "as they were the first thing we were bade bring. And so we ask of you, curragh of Manannan that is under us, to sail to the Garden in the East of the World."

And the curragh did not neglect that order, but it sailed forward over the green-sided waves and deep places till it came to its harbour in the east of the world.

And then Brian asked his brothers: "What way have you a mind to get into the garden? for I think," he said, "the king's champions and the fighting men of the country are always guarding it, and the king himself is chief over them." "What should we do," said his brothers, "but to make straight at them and attack them, and bring away the apples or fall ourselves, since we cannot escape from these dangers that are before us without meeting our death in some place." "It would be better," said Brian, "the story of our bravery and our craftiness to be told and to live after us, than folly and cowardice to be told of us. And what is best for us to do now," he said, "is to go in the shape of swift hawks into the garden, and the watchers have but their light spears to throw at us, and let you take good care to keep out of their reach; and after they have thrown them all, make a quick flight to the apples and let each of you bring away an apple of them in your claws, and I will bring away the third."

They said that was a good advice, and Brian struck himself and the others with his Druid rod, and changed them into beautiful hawks. And they flew towards the garden, and the watchers took notice of them and shouted on every side of them, and threw showers of spears and darts, but the hawks kept out of their reach as Brian had bade them, till all the spears were spent, and then they swept down bravely on the apples, and brought them away with them, without so much as a wound.

And the news went through the city and the whole district, and the king had three wise, crafty daughters, and they put themselves into the shape of three ospreys, and they followed the hawks to the sea, and sent flashes of lightning before them and after them, that scorched them greatly.

"It is a pity the way we are now," said the sons of Tuireann, "for we will be burned through and through with this lightning if we do not get some relief." "If I can give you relief I will do it," said Brian. With that he struck himself and his brothers with the Druid rod, and they were turned into three swans, and they went down quickly into the sea, and the ospreys went away from them then, and the sons of Tuireann went into their boat.

After that they consulted together, and it is what they agreed, to go to Greece and to bring away the skin of the pig, with or without leave. So they went forward till they came near to the court of the King of Greece.

"What appearance should we put on us going in here?" said Brian. "What appearance should we go in with but our own?" said the others. "That is not what I think best," said Brian; "but to go in with the appearance of poets from Ireland, the way the high people of Greece will hold us in respect and in honour." "It would be hard for us to do that," they said, "and we without a poem, and it is little we know how to make one."

However, they put the poet's tie on their hair, and they knocked at the door of the court, and the door-keeper asked who was in it. "We are poets of Ireland," said Brian, "and we are come with a poem to the king."

The door-keeper went in and told the king that there were poets from Ireland at the door. "Let them in," said the king, "for it is in search of a good man they came so far from their own country." And the king gave orders that everything should be well set out in the court, the way they would say they had seen no place so grand in all their travels.

The sons of Tuireann were let in then, having the appearance of poets, and they fell to drinking and pleasure without delay; and they thought they had never seen, and there was not in the world, a court so good as that or so large a household, or a place where they had met with better treatment.

Then the king's poets got up to give out their poems and songs. And then Brian, son of Tuireann, bade his brothers to say a poem for the king. "We have no poem," said they; "and do not ask any poem of us, but the one we know before, and that is to take what we want by the strength of our hand if we are the strongest, or to fall by those that are against us if they are the strongest." "That is not a good way to make a poem," said Brian. And with that he rose up himself and asked a hearing. And they all listened to him, and it is what he said:

"O Tuis, we do not hide your fame; we praise you as the oak among kings; the skin of a pig, bounty without hardness, this is the reward I ask for it.

"The war of a neighbour against an ear; the fair ear of his neighbour will be against him; he who gives us what he owns, his court will not be the scarcer for it.

"A raging army and a sudden sea are a danger to whoever goes against them. The skin of a pig, bounty without hardness, this is the reward I ask, O Tuis."

"That is a good poem," said the king; "but I do not know a word of its meaning." "I will tell you its meaning," said Brian. "'O Tuis, we do not hide your fame; we praise you as the oak above the kings.' That is, as the oak is beyond the kingly trees of the wood, so are you beyond the kings of the world for open-handedness and for grandeur.

"'The skin of a pig, bounty without hardness.' That is, the skin of a pig you own is what I would wish to get from you as a reward for my poem.

"'The war of a neighbour against an ear, the fair ear of his neighbour will be against him.' That is, you and I will be by the ears about the skin, unless I get it with your consent.

"And that is the meaning of the poem," said Brian.

"I would praise your poem," said the king, "if there was not so much about my pig-skin in it; and you have no good sense, man of poetry," he said, "to be asking that thing of me, and I would not give it to all the poets and the learned men and the great men of the world, since they could not take it away without my consent. But I will give you three times the full of the skin of gold as the price of your poem," he said.

"May good be with you, king," said Brian, "and I know well it was no easy thing

I was asking, but I knew I would get a good ransom for it. And I am that covetous," he said, "I will not be satisfied without seeing the gold measured myself into the skin."

The king sent his servants with them then to the treasure-house to measure the gold. "Measure out the full of it to my brothers first," said Brian, "and then give good measure to myself, since it was I made the poem."

But when the skin was brought out, Brian made a quick sudden snatch at it with his left hand, and drew his sword and made a stroke at the man nearest him, and made two halves of him. And then he kept a hold of the skin and put it about himself, and the three of them rushed out of the court, cutting down every armed man before them, so that not one escaped death or wounding. And then Brian went to where the king himself was, and the king made no delay in attacking him, and they made a hard fight of it, and at the end the King of Greece fell by the hand of Brian, son of Tuireann.

The three brothers rested for a while after that, and then they said they would go and look for some other part of the fine. "We will go to Pisear, King of Persia," said Brian, "and ask him for the spear."

So they went into their boat, and they left the blue streams of the coast of Greece, and they said: "We are well off when we have the apples and the skin." And they stopped nowhere till they came to the borders of Persia.

"Let us go to the court with the appearance of poets," said Brian, "the same as we went to the King of Greece." "We are content to do that," said the others, "as all turned out so well the last time we took to poetry; not that it is easy for us to take to a calling that does not belong to us."

So they put the poet's tie on their hair, and they were as well treated as they were at the other court; and when the time came for poems Brian rose up, and it is what he said:

"It is little any spear looks to Pisear; the battles of enemies are broken, it is not too much for Pisear to wound every one of them.

"A yew, the most beautiful of the wood, it is called a king, it is not bulky. May the spear drive on the whole crowd to their wounds of death."

"That is a good poem," said the king, "but I do not understand why my own spear is brought into it, O Man of Poetry from Ireland."

"It is because it is that spear of your own I would wish to get as the reward of my poem," said Brian. "It is little sense you have to be asking that of me," said the king; "and the people of my court never showed greater respect for poetry than now, when they did not put you to death on the spot."

When Brian heard that talk from the king, he thought of the apple that was in his hand, and he made a straight cast and hit him in the forehead, so that his brains were put out at the back of his head, and he bared the sword and made an attack on the people about him. And the other two did not fail to do the same, and they gave him their help bravely till they had made an end of all they met of the people of the court. And then they found the spear, and its head in a cauldron of water, the way it would not set fire to the place.

And after a while they said it was time for them to go and look for the rest of the great fine that was on them, and they asked one another what way should they go. "We will go to the King of the Island of Siogair," said Brian, "for it is with him are the two horses and the chariot the Ildanach asked of us."

They went forward then and brought the spear with them, and it is proud the three champions were after all they had done. And they went on till they were come to the court of the King of Siogair.

"It is what we will do this time," said Brian, "we will go in with the appearance of paid soldiers from Ireland, and we will make friends with the king, the way we will get to know in what place the horses and the chariot are kept." And when they had settled on that they went forward to the lawn before the king's house.

The king and the chief men that were with him rose up and came through the fair that was going on there, and they saluted the king, and he asked who were they. "We are trained fighting men from Ireland," they said, "and we are earning wages from the kings of the world." "Is it your wish to stop with me for a while?" said the king. "That is what we are wanting," said they. So then they made an agreement and took service with him.

They stopped in the court a fortnight and a month, and they never saw the horses through that time. Then Brian said: "This is a bad way we are in, to have no more news of the horses now than the first day we came to the place." "What is best for us to do now?" said his brothers. "Let us do this," said Brian, "let us take our arms and gather our things together, and go to the king and tell him we will leave the country and this part of the world unless he will show us those horses."

So they went to the king that very day, and he asked them what did they mean by getting themselves ready for a journey. "You will hear that, high king," said Brian; "it is because trained fighting men from Ireland, like ourselves, have always trust put in them by the kings they guard, and we are used to be told the secrets and the whispers of any person we are with, and that is not the way you have treated us since we came to you. For you have two horses and a chariot that are the best in the world, as we have been told, and we have not been given a sight of them yet." "It would be a pity you to go on that account," said the king, "when I would have showed them to you the first day, if I had known you had a wish to see them. And if you have a mind to see them now," he said, "you may see them; for I think there never came soldiers from Ireland to this place that were thought more of by myself and by my people than yourselves."

He sent for the horses then, and they were yoked to the chariot, and their going was as fast as the cold spring wind, and the sea was the same as the land to them.

And Brian was watching the horses closely, and on a sudden he took hold of the chariot and took the chariot driver out and dashed him against the nearest rock, and made a leap into his place himself, and made a cast of the Persian spear at the king, that went through his heart. And then he and his brothers scattered the people before them, and brought away the chariot.

"We will go now to Easal, the King of the Golden Pillars," said Brian, "to look for the seven pigs the Ildanach bade us bring him."

They sailed on then without delay or drawback to that high country. And it is the way the people of that country were, watching their harbours for fear of the sons of Tuireann, for the story of them had been told in all parts, how they had been sent out of Ireland by force, and how they were bringing away with them all the gifted treasures of the whole world.

Easal came to the edge of the harbour to meet them, and he asked was it true what he heard, that the king of every country they had gone to had fallen by them. Brian said it was true, whatever he might wish to do to them for it. "What was it made you do that?" said Easal. Brian told him then it was the oppression and the hard sentence of another had put them to it; and he told him all that had happened, and how they had put down all that offered to stand against them until that time.

"What did you come to this country now for?" said the king. "For the pigs belonging to yourself," said Brian; "for to bring them away with us is a part of the fine." "What way do you think to get them?" said the king. "If we get them with good-will," said Brian, "we are ready to take them thankfully; and if we do not, we are ready to do battle with yourself and your people on the head of them, that you may fall by us, and we may bring away the pigs in spite of you." "If that is to be the end of it," said the king, "it would be a pity to bring my people into a battle." "It would be a pity indeed," said Brian.

Then the king whispered and took advice with his people about the matter, and it is what they agreed, to give up the pigs of their own free will to the sons of Tuireann, since they could not see that any one had been able to stand against them up to that time.

Then the sons of Tuireann gave their thanks to Easal, and there was wonder on them to have got the pigs like that, when they had to fight for every other part of the fine. And more than that, they had left a share of their blood in every other place till then.

Easal brought them to his own house that night, and they were served with food, and drink, and good beds, and all they could wish for. And they rose up on the morrow and came into the king's presence, and the pigs were given to them. "It is well you have done by us, giving us these pigs," said Brian, "for we did not get any share of the fine without fighting but these alone." And he made a poem for the king then, praising him, and putting a great name on him for what he had done.

"What journey are you going to make now, sons of Tuireann?" said Easal. "We are going," they said, "to the country of Ioruaidh, on account of a whelp that is there." "Give me one request," said Easal, "and that is to bring me with you to the King of Ioruaidh, for a daughter of mine is his wife, and I would wish to persuade him to give you the whelp without a battle." "That will please us well," they said.

So the king's ship was made ready, and we have no knowledge of what happened till they came to the delightful, wonderful coast of Ioruaidh. The people and the armies were watching the harbours and landing-places before them, and they knew them at once and shouted at them.

Then Easal went on shore peaceably, and he went to where his son-in-law, the king, was, and told him the story of the sons of Tuireann from beginning to end.

"What has brought them to this country?" said the King of Ioruaidh. "To ask for the hound you have," said Easal. "It was a bad thought you had coming with them to ask it," said the king, "for the gods have not given that much luck to any three champions in the world, that they would get my hound by force or by good-will." "It would be better for you to let them have the hound," said Easal, "since they have put down so many of the kings of the world."

But all he could say was only idleness to the king. So he went then to where the sons of Tuireann were, and gave them the whole account. And when they heard the king's answer, they made no delay, but put quick hands on their arms, and offered to give battle to the army of Ioruaidh. And when they met, there was a brave battle fought on both sides. And as for the sons of Tuireann, they began to kill and to strike at the men of Ioruaidh till they parted from one another in the fight, so that Iuchar and Iucharba chanced to be on one side, and Brian by himself on the other side. It was a gap of danger and a breaking of ranks was before Brian in every path he took, till he came to the King of Ioruaidh in the battle pen where he was. And then the two brave champions began a fierce fight together, and they did not spare one another in it. And at the last Brian overcame the king, and bound him, and brought him through the middle of the army, till he came to the place where Easal was, and it is what he said: "There is your son-in-law for you, and I swear by my hand of valour, I would think it easier to kill him three times than to bring him to you once like this."

So then the whelp was given to the sons of Tuireann, and the king was unbound, and peace was made between them. And when they had brought all this to an end, they bade farewell to Easal and to all the rest.

Now as to Lugh of the Long Hand, it was showed to him that the sons of Tuireann had got all the things that were wanting to him against the battle with the Fomor; and on that he sent a Druid spell after them to put forgetfulness on them of the rest of the fine that they had not got. And he put a great desire and longing on them to go back to Ireland; so they forgot that a part of the fine was wanting to them, and they turned back again toward home.

And it is the place where Lugh was at the time, at a gathering of the people for a fair on the green outside Teamhair, and the King of Ireland along with him. And it was made known to Lugh that the sons of Tuireann were landed at Brugh na Boinn.

And he went into the city of Teamhair, and shut the gate after him, and he put on Manannan's smooth armour, and the cloak, of the daughters of Flidais, and he took his own arms in his hand.

And the sons of Tuireann came where the king was, and they were made welcome by him and by the Tuatha de Danaan. And the king asked them did they get the fine. "We did get it," said they; "and where is Lugh till we give it to him?" "He was here a while ago," said the king. And the whole fair was searched for him, but he was not found.

"I know the place where he is," said Brian; "for it has been made known to him that we are come to Ireland, and these deadly arms with us, and he is gone into Teamhair to avoid us."

Messengers were sent to him then, and it is the answer he gave them that he would not come, but that the fine should be given to the king.

So the sons of Tuireann did that, and when the king had taken the fine they all went to the palace in Teamhair; and Lugh came out on the lawn and the fine was given to him, and it is what he said: "There is a good payment here for any one that ever was killed or that ever will be killed. But there is something wanting to it yet that it is not lawful to leave out. And where is the cooking-spit?" he said; "and where are the three shouts on the hill that you did not give yet?"

And when the sons of Tuireann heard that there came clouds of weakness on them. And they left the place and went to their father's house that night, and they told him all they had done, and the way Lugh had treated them.

There was grief and darkness on Tuireann then, and they spent the night together. And on the morrow they went to their ship, and Ethne, their sister, with them, and she was crying and lamenting, and it is what she said:

"It is a pity, Brian of my life, it is not to Teamhair your going is, after all the troubles you have had before this, even if I could not follow you.

"O Salmon of the dumb Boinn, O Salmon of the Life River, since I cannot keep you here I am loath to part from you.

"O Rider of the Wave of Tuaidh, the man that stands best in the fight, if you come back again, I think it will not be pleasing to your enemy.

"Is there pity with you for the sons of Tuireann leaning now on their green shields? Their going is a cause for pity, my mind is filled up with it.

"You to be to-night at Beinn Edair till the heavy coming of the morning, you who have taken forfeits from brave men, it is you have increased our grief.

"It is a pity your journey is from Teamhair, and from the pleasant plains, and from great Uisnech of Midhe; there is nothing so pitiful as this."

After that complaint they went out on the rough waves of the green sea; and they were a quarter of a year on the sea without getting any news of the island.

Then Brian put on his water dress and he made a leap, and he was a long time walking in the sea looking for the Island of the Fair-Haired Women, and he found it in the end. And he went looking for the court, and when he came to it, all he found was a troop of women doing needlework and embroidering borders. And among all the other things they had with them, there was the cooking-spit.

And when Brian saw it, he took it up in his hand and he was going to bring it with him to the door. And all the women began laughing when they saw him doing that, and it is what they said: "It is a brave deed you put your hand to; for even if your brothers were along with you, the least of the three times fifty women of us would not let the spit go with you or with them. But for all that," they said, "take a spit of the spits with you, since you had the daring to try and take it in spite of us."

Brian bade them farewell then, and went to look for the boat. And his brothers thought it was too long he was away from them, and just as they were going to leave the place they were, they saw him coming towards them, and that raised their courage greatly.

And he went into the boat, and they went on to look for the Hill of Miochaoin. And when they came there, Miochaoin, that was the guardian of the hill, came towards them; and when Brian saw him he attacked him, and the fight of those two champions was like the fight of two lions, till Miochaoin fell at the last.

And after Miochaoin had fallen, his three sons came out to fight with the three sons of Tuireann. And if any one ever came from the east of the world to look at any fight, it is to see the fight of these champions he had a right to come, for the greatness of their blows and the courage of their minds. The names of the sons of Miochaoin were Core and Conn and Aedh, and they drove their three spears through the bodies of the sons of Tuireann, and that did not discourage them at all and they put their own three spears through the bodies of the sons of Miochaoin, so that they fell into the clouds and the faintness of death.

And then Brian said: "What way are you now, my dear brothers?" "We are near our death," said they. "Let us rise up," he said, "and give three shouts upon the hill, for I see the signs of death coming on us." "We are not able to do that," said they. Then Brian rose up and raised each of them with one hand, and he shedding blood heavily all the time, until they gave the three shouts.

After that Brian brought them with him to the boat, and they were travelling the sea for a long time, but at last Brian said: "I see Beinn Edair and our father's dun, and Teamhair of the Kings." "We would have our fill of health if we could see that," said the others; "and for the love of your good name, brother," they said, "raise up our heads on your breast till we see Ireland again, and life or death will be the same to us after that. And O Brian," they said, "Flame of Valour without treachery, we would sooner death to bring ourselves away, than to see you with wounds upon your body, and with no physician to heal you."

Then they came to Beinn Edair, and from that they went on to their father's house, and Brian said to Tuireann: "Go, dear father, to Teamhair, and give this spit to Lugh, and bring the skin that has healing in it for our relief. Ask it from him for the sake of friendship," he said, "for we are of the one blood, and let him not give hardness for hardness. And O dear father," he said, "do not be long on your journey, or you will not find us alive before you."

Then Tuireann went to Teamhair, and he found Lugh of the Long Hand before him, and he gave him the spit, and he asked the skin of him to heal his children, and Lugh said he would not give it And Tuireann came back to them and told them he had not got the skin. And Brian said: "Bring me with you to Lugh, to see would I get it from him."

So they went to Lugh, and Brian asked the skin of him. And Lugh said he would not give it, and that if they would give him the breadth of the earth in gold for it, he would not take it from them, unless he was sure their death would come on them in satisfaction for the deed they had done.

When Brian heard that, he went to the place his two brothers were, and he lay down between them, and his life went out from him, and out from the other two at the same time. And their father cried and lamented over his three beautiful sons, that had the making of a king of Ireland in each of them, and his strength left him and he died; and they were buried in the one grave.

CHAPTER III. THE GREAT BATTLE OF MAGH TUIREADH

Aند it was not long after Lugh had got the fine from the sons of Tuireann that the Fomor came and landed at Scetne.

The whole host of the Fomor were come this time, and their king, Balor, of the Strong Blows and of the Evil Eye, along with them; and Bres, and Indech, son of De Domnann, a king of the Fomor, and Elathan, son of Lobos, and Goll and Ingol, and Octriallach, son of Indech, and Elathan, son of Delbaeth.

Then Lugh sent the Dagda to spy out the Fomor, and to delay them till such time as the men of Ireland would come to the battle.

So the Dagda went to their camp, and he asked them for a delay, and they said he might have that. And then to make sport of him, the Fomor made broth for him, for he had a great love for broth. So they filled the king's cauldron with four times twenty gallons of new milk, and the same of meal and fat, and they put in goats and sheep and pigs along with that, and boiled all together, and then they poured it all out into a great hole in the ground. And they called him to it then, and told him he should eat his fill, the way the Fomor would not be reproached for want of hospitality the way Bres was. "We will make an end of you if you leave any part of it after you," said Indech, son of De Domnann.

So the Dagda took the ladle, and it big enough for a man and a woman to lie in the bowl of it, and he took out bits with it, the half of a salted pig, and a quarter of lard a bit would be. "If the broth tastes as well as the bits taste, this is good food," he said. And he went on putting the full of the ladle into his mouth till the hole was empty; and when all was gone he put down his hand and scraped up all that was left among the earth and the gravel.

Sleep came on him then after eating the broth, and the Fomor were laughing at him, for his belly was the size of the cauldron of a great house. But he rose up after a while, and, heavy as he was, he made his way home; and indeed his dress was no way sightly, a cape to the hollow of the elbows, and a brown coat, long in the breast and short behind, and on his feet brogues of horse hide, with the hair outside, and in his hand a wheeled fork it would take eight men to carry, so that the track he left after him was deep enough for the boundary ditch of a province. And on his way he saw the Battle-Crow, the Morrigu, washing herself in the river Unius of Connacht, and one of her two feet at Ullad Echne, to the south of the water, and the other at Loscuinn, to the north of the water, and her hair hanging in nine loosened locks. And she said to the Dagda, that she would bring the heart's blood of Indech, son of De Domnann, that had threatened him, to the men of Ireland.

And while he was away Lugh had called together the Druids, and smiths, and physicians, and law-makers, and chariot-drivers of Ireland, to make plans for the battle.

And he asked the great magician Mathgen what could he do to help them. "It is what I can do," said Mathgen, "through my power I can throw down all the mountains of Ireland on the Fomor, until their tops will be rolling on the ground. And the twelve chief mountains of Ireland will bring you their help," he said, "and will fight for you: Slieve Leag and Denda Ulad, and Bennai Boirche and Bri Ruri, and Slieve Bladma and Slieve Snechtae, and Slieve Mis and Blai-Slieve, and Nemthann and Slieve Macca Belgodon, and Segois and Cruachan Aigle."

Then he asked the cup-bearers what help they could give. "We will put a strong thirst on the Fomor," they said, "and then we will bring the twelve chief lochs of Ireland before them, and however great their thirst may be, they will find no water in them: Derc-Loch, Loch Luimnech, Loch Orbsen, Loch Righ, Loch Mescdhae, Loch Cuan, Loch Laeig, Loch Echach, Loch Febail, Loch Decket, Loch Riach, Mor-Loch. And we will go," they said, "to the twelve chief rivers of Ireland: the Buas, the Boinn, the Banna, the Nem, the Laoi, the Sionnan, the Muaid, the Sligech, the Samair, the Fionn, the Ruirtech, the Siuir; and they will all be hidden away from the Fomor the way they will not find a drop in them. But as for the men of Ireland," they said, "there will be drink for them if they were to be in the battle to the end of seven years."

And Figol, son of Mamos, the Druid, was asked then what he would do, and he said: "It is what I will do, I will cause three showers of fire to pour on the faces of the army of the Fomor, and I will take from them two-thirds of their bravery and their strength, and I will put sickness on their bodies, and on the bodies of their horses. But as to the men of Ireland," he said, "every breath they breathe will be an increase of strength and of bravery to them; and if they are seven years in the battle they will never be any way tired."

Then Lugh asked his two witches, Bechulle and Dianan: "What power can you bring to the battle?" "It is easy to say that," they said. "We will put enchantment on the trees and the stones and the sods of the earth, till they become an armed host against the Fomor, and put terror on them and put them to the rout."

Then Lugh asked Carpre, the poet, son of Etain, what could he do. "It is not hard to say that," said Carpre. "I will make a satire on them at sunrise, and the wind from the north, and I on a hill-top and my back to a thorn-tree, and a stone and a thorn in my hand. And with that satire," he said, "I will put shame on them and enchantment, the way they will not be able to stand against fighting men."

Then he asked Goibniu the Smith what would he be able to do. "I will do this," he said. "If the men of Ireland stop in the battle to the end of seven years, for every sword that is broken and for every spear that is lost from its shaft, I will put a new one in its place. And no spear-point that will be made by my hand," he said, "will ever miss its mark; and no man it touches will ever taste life again. And that is more than Dolb, the smith of the Fomor, can do," he said.

"And you, Credne," Lugh said then to his worker in brass, "what help can you give to our men in the battle?" "It is not hard to tell that," said Credne, "rivets for their spears and hilts for their swords and bosses and rims for their shields, I will supply them all."

"And you, Luchta," he said then to his carpenter, "what will you do?" "I will give them all they want of shields and of spear shafts," said Luchta.

Then he asked Diancecht, the physician, what would he do, and it is what he said: "Every man that will be wounded there, unless his head is struck off, or his brain or his marrow cut through, I will make him whole and sound again for the battle of the morrow."

Then the Dagda said: "Those great things you are boasting you will do, I will do them all with only myself." "It is you are the good god!" said they, and they all gave a great shout of laughter.

Then Lugh spoke to the whole army and put strength in them, so that each one had the spirit in him of a king or a great lord.

Then when the delay was at an end, the Fomor and the men of Ireland came on towards one another till they came to the plain of Magh Tuireadh. That now was not the same Magh Tuireadh where the first battle was fought, but it was to the north, near Ess Dara.

And then the two armies threatened one another. "The men of Ireland are daring enough to offer battle to us," said Bres to Indech, son of De Domnann. "I give my word," said Indech, "it is in small pieces their bones will be, if they do not give in to us and pay their tribute."

Now the Men of Dea had determined not to let Lugh go into the battle, because of the loss his death would be to them; and they left nine of their men keeping a watch on him.

And on the first day none of the kings or princes went into the battle, but only the common fighting men, and they fierce and proud enough.

And the battle went on like that from day to day with no great advantage to one or the other side. But there was wonder on the Fomor on account of one thing. Such of their own weapons as were broken or blunted in the fight lay there as they were, and such of their own men as were killed showed no sign of life on the morrow; but it was not so with the Tuatha de Danaan, for if their men were killed or their weapons were broken to-day, they were as good as before on the morrow.

And this is the way that happened. The well of Slaine lay to the west of Magh Tuireadh to the east of Loch Arboch. And Diancecht and his son Octruil and his daughter Airmed used to be singing spells over the well and to be putting herbs in it; and the men that were wounded to death in the battle would be brought to the well and put into it as dead men, and they would come out of it whole and sound, through the power of the spells. And not only were they healed, but there was such fire put into them that they would be quicker in the fight than they were before.

And as to the arms, it is the way they were made new every day. Goibniu the Smith used to be in the forge making swords and spears, and he would make a spear-head by three turns, and then Luchta the Carpenter would make the shaft by three cuts, and the third cut was a finish, and would set it in the ring of the spear.

And when the spear-heads were stuck in the side of the forge, he would throw the shaft and the rings the way they would go into the spear-head and want no more setting. And then Credne the Brazier would make the rivets by three turns and would cast the rings of the spears to them, and with that they were ready and were set together.

And all this went against the Fomor, and they sent one of their young men to spy about the camp and to see could he find out how these things were done. It was Ruadan, son of Bres and of Brigit daughter of the Dagda they sent, for he was a son and grandson of the Tuatha de Danaan. So he went and saw all that was done, and came back to the Fomor.

And when they heard his story it is what they thought, that Goibniu the Smith was the man that hindered them most. And they sent Ruadan back again, and bade him make an end of him.

So he went back again to the forge, and he asked Goibniu would he give him a spear-head. And then he asked rivets of Credne, and a shaft of the carpenter, and all was given to him as he asked. And there was a woman there, Cron, mother to Fianlug, grinding the spears.

And after the spear being given to Ruadan, he turned and threw it at Goibniu, that it wounded him. But Goibniu pulled it out and made a cast of it at Ruadan, that it went through him and he died; and Bres, his father, and the army of the Fomor, saw him die. And then Brigit came and keened her son with shrieking and with crying.

And as to Goibniu, he went into the well and was healed. But after that Octriallach, son of Indech, called to the Fomor and bade each man of them bring a stone of the stones of Drinnes and throw them into the well of Slane. And they did that till the well was dried up, and a cairn raised over it, that is called Octriallach's Cairn.

And it was while Goibniu was making spear-heads for the battle of Magh Tuireadh, a charge was brought against his wife. And it was seen that it was heavy news to him, and that jealousy came on him. And it is what he did, there was a spear-shaft in his hand when he heard the story, Nes its name was; and he sang spells over the spear-shaft, and any one that was struck with that spear afterwards, it would burn him up like fire.

And at last the day of the great battle came, and the Fomor came out of their camp and stood in strong ranks. And there was not a leader or a fighting man of them was without good armour to his skin, and a helmet on his head, a broad spear in his right hand, a heavy sword in his belt, a strong shield on his shoulder. And to attack the army of the Fomor that day was to strike the head against a rock, or to go up fighting against a fire.

And the Men of Dea rose up and left Lugh and his nine comrades keeping him, and they went on to the battle; and Midhir was with them, and Bodb Dearg and Diancecht. And Badb and Macha and the Morrigu called out that they would go along with them.

And it was a hard battle was fought, and for a while it was going against the Tuatha de Danaan; and Nuada of the Silver Hand, their King, and Macha, daughter of Emmass, fell by Balor, King of the Fomor. And Cass-mail fell by Octriallach, and the Dagda got a dreadful wound from a casting spear that was thrown by Ceithlenn, wife of Balor.

But when the battle was going on, Lugh broke away from those that were keeping him, and rushed out to the front of the Men of Dea. And then there was a fierce battle fought, and Lugh was heartening the men of Ireland to fight well, the way they would not be in bonds any longer. For it was better for them, he said, to die protecting their own country than to live under bonds and under tribute any longer. And he sang a song of courage to them, and the hosts gave a great shout as they went into battle, and then they met together, and each of them began to attack the other.

And there was great slaughter, and laying low in graves, and many comely men fell there in the stall of death. Pride and shame were there side by side, and hardness and red anger, and there was red blood on the white skin of young fighting men. And the dashing of spear against shield, and sword against sword, and the shouting of the fighters, and the whistling of casting spears and the rattling of scabbards was like harsh thunder through the battle. And many slipped in the blood that was under their feet, and they fell, striking their heads one against another; and the river carried away bodies of friends and enemies together.

Then Lugh and Balor met in the battle, and Lugh called out reproaches to him; and there was anger on Balor, and he said to the men that were with him: "Lift up my eyelid till I see this chatterer that is talking to me." Then they raised Balor's eyelid, but Lugh made a cast of his red spear at him, that brought the eye out through the back of his head, so that it was towards his own army it fell, and three times nine of the Fomor died when they looked at it. And if Lugh had not put out that eye when he did, the whole of Ireland would have been burned in one flash. And after this, Lugh struck his head off.

And as for Indech, son of De Domnann, he fell and was crushed in the battle, and blood burst from his mouth, and he called out for Leat Glas, his poet, as he lay there, but he was not able to help him. And then the Morrigu came into the battle, and she was heartening the Tuatha de Danaan to fight the battle well; and, as she had promised the Dagda, she took the full of her two hands of Indech's blood, and gave it to the armies that were waiting at the ford of Unius; and it was called the Ford of Destruction from that day.

And after that it was not a battle any more, but a rout, and the Fomor were beaten back to the sea. And Lugh and his comrades were following them, and they came up with Bres, son of Elathan, and no guard with him, and he said: "It is better for you to spare my life than to kill me. And if you spare me now," he said, "the cows of Ireland will never go dry." "I will ask an advice about that from our wise men," said Lugh. So he told Maeltine Mor-Brethach, of the Great Judgments, what Bres was after saying. But Maeltine said: "Do not spare him for that, for he has no power over their offspring, though he has power so long as they are living."

Then Bres said: "If you spare me, the men of Ireland will reap a harvest of corn every quarter." But Maeltine said: "The spring is for ploughing and sowing, and the beginning of summer for the strength of corn, and the beginning of autumn for its ripeness, and the winter for using it."

"That does not save you," said Lugh then to Bres. But then to make an excuse for sparing him, Lugh said: "Tell us what is the best way for the men of Ireland to plough and to sow and to reap."

"Let their ploughing be on a Tuesday, and their casting seed into the field on a Tuesday, and their reaping on a Tuesday," said Bres. So Lugh said that would do, and he let him go free after that.

It was in this battle Ogma found Orna, the sword of Tethra, a king of the Fomor, and he took it from its sheath and cleaned it. And when the sword was taken out of the sheath, it told all the deeds that had been done by it, for there used to be that power in swords.

And Lugh and the Dagda and Ogma followed after the Fomor, for they had brought away the Dagda's harp with them, that was called Uaitne. And they came to a feasting-house, and in it they found Bres and his father Elathan, and there was the harp hanging on the wall. And it was in that harp the Dagda had bound the music, so that it would not sound till he would call to it. And sometimes it was called Dur-da-Bla, the Oak of Two Blossoms, and sometimes Coir-cethar-chuin, the Four-Angled Music.

And when he saw it hanging on the wall it is what he said: "Come summer, come winter, from the mouth of harps and bags and pipes." Then the harp sprang from the wall, and came to the Dagda, and it killed nine men on its way.

And then he played for them the three things harpers understand, the sleepy tune, and the laughing tune, and the crying tune. And when he played the crying tune, their tearful women cried, and then he played the laughing tune, till their women and children laughed; and then he played the sleepy tune, and all the hosts fell asleep. And through that sleep the three went away through the Fomor that would have been glad to harm them. And when all was over, the Dagda brought out the heifer he had got as wages from Bres at the time he was making his dun. And she called to her calf, and at the sound of her call all the cattle of Ireland the Fomor had brought away as tribute, were back in their fields again.

And Ce, the Druid of Nuada of the Silver Hand, was wounded in the battle, and he went southward till he came to Carn Corrslebe. And there he sat down to rest, tired with his wounds and with the fear that was on him, and the journey. And he saw a smooth plain before him, and it full of flowers, and a great desire came on him to reach to that plain, and he went on till he came to it, and there he died. And when his grave was made there, a lake burst out over it and over the whole plain, and it was given the name of Loch Ce. And there were but four men of the Fomor left in Ireland after the battle, and they used to be going through the country, spoiling corn and milk and fruit, and whatever came from the sea, till they were driven out one Samhain night by the Morrigu and by Angus Og, that the Fomor might never be over Ireland again.

And after the battle was won, and the bodies were cleared away, the Morrigu gave out the news of the great victory to the hosts and to the royal heights of Ireland and to its chief rivers and its invers, and it is what she said: "Peace up to the skies, the skies down to earth, the earth under the skies; strength to every one."

And as to the number of men that fell in the battle, it will not be known till we number the stars of the sky, or flakes of snow, or the dew on the grass, or grass under the feet of cattle, or the horses of the Son of Lir in a stormy sea.

And Lugh was made king over the Men of Dea then, and it was at Nas he had his court.

And while he was king, his foster-mother Taillte, daughter of Magh Mor, the Great Plain, died. And before her death she bade her husband Duach the Dark, he that built the Fort of the Hostages in Teamhair, to clear away the wood of Cuan, the way there could be a gathering of the people around her grave. So he called to the men of Ireland to cut down the wood with their wide-bladed knives and bill-hooks and hatchets, and within a month the whole wood was cut down.

And Lugh buried her in the plain of Midhe, and raised a mound over her, that is to be seen to this day. And he ordered fires to be kindled, and keening to be made, and games and sports to be held in the summer of every year out of respect to her. And the place they were held got its name from her, that is Taillten.

And as to Lugh's own mother, that was tall beautiful Ethlinn, she came to Teamhair after the battle of Magh Tuireadh, and he gave her in marriage to Tadg, son of Nuada. And the children that were born to them were Muirne, mother of Finn, the Head of the Fianna of Ireland, and Tuiren, that was mother of Bran.

CHAPTER IV. THE HIDDEN HOUSE OF LUGH

And after Lugh had held the kingship for a long time, the Dagda was made king in his place.

And Lugh went away out of Ireland, and some said he died at Uisnech, the place where the five provinces meet, and the first place there was ever a fire kindled in Ireland. It was by Mide, son of Brath, it was kindled, for the sons of Nemed, and it was burning through six years, and it was from that fire every chief fire was kindled in Ireland.

But Lugh was seen again in Ireland at the time Conchubar and the Men of the Red Branch went following white birds southward to the Boinn at the time of Cuchulain's birth. And it was he came and kept watch over Cuchulain in his three days' sleep at the time of the War for the Bull of Cuailgne.

And after that again he was seen by Conn of the Hundred Battles, and this is the way that happened.

Conn was in Teamhair one time, and he went up in the early morning to the Rath of the Kings at the rising of the sun, and his three Druids with him, Maol and Bloc and Bhuice; and his three poets, Ethain and Corb and Cesarn. And the reason he had for going up there with them every day, was to look about on every side, the way if any men of the Sidhe would come into Ireland they would not come unknown to him. And on this day he chanced to stand upon a stone that was in the rath, and the stone screamed under his feet, that it was heard all over Teamhair and as far as Bregia.

Then Conn asked his chief Druid how the stone came there, and what it screamed for. And the Druid said he would not answer that till the end of fifty-three days. And at the end of that time, Conn asked him again, and it is what the Druid said: "The Lia Fail is the name of the stone; it is out of Falias it was brought, and it is in Teamhair it was set up, and in Teamhair it will stay for ever. And as long as there is a king in Teamhair it is here will be the gathering place for games, and if there is no king to come to the last day of the gathering, there will be hardness in that year. And when the stone screamed under your feet," he said, "the number of the screams it gave was a foretelling of the number of kings of your race that would come after you. But it is not I myself will name them for you," he said.

And while they were in the same place, there came a great mist about them and a darkness, so that they could not know what way they were going, and they heard the noise of a rider coming towards them. "It would be a great grief to us," said Conn, "to be brought away into a strange country." Then the rider threw three spears at them, and every one came faster than the other. "It is the wounding of a king indeed," said the Druids, "any one to cast at Conn of Teamhair."

The rider stopped casting his spears on that, and he came to them and bade Conn welcome, and asked him to come to his house. They went on then till they came to a beautiful plain, and there they saw a king's rath, and a golden tree at its door, and inside the rath a grand house with a roof of white bronze. So they went into the house, and the rider that had come to meet them was there before them, in his royal seat, and there had never been seen a man like him in Teamhair for comeliness or for beauty, or the wonder of his face.

And there was a young woman in the house, having a band of gold on her head, and a silver vessel with hoops of gold beside her, and it full of red ale, and a golden bowl on its edge, and a golden cup at its mouth. She said then to the master of the house: "Who am I to serve drink to?" "Serve it to Conn of the Hundred Battles," he said, "for he will gain a hundred battles before he dies." And after that he bade her to pour out the ale for Art of the Three Shouts, the son of Conn; and after that he went through the names of all the kings of Ireland that would come after Conn, and he told what would be the length of their lifetime. And the young woman left the vessel with Conn, and the cup and the bowl, and she gave him along with that the rib of an ox and of a hog; twenty-four feet was the length of the ox-rib.

And the master of the house told them the young woman was the Kingship of Ireland for ever. "And as for myself," he said, "I am Lugh of the Long Hand, son of Ethlinn."

BOOK THREE: THE COMING OF THE GAEL.

CHAPTER I. THE LANDING

It is not known, now, for what length of time the Tuatha de Danaan had the sway over Ireland, and it is likely it was a long time they had it, but they were put from it at last.

It was at Inver Slane, to the north of Leinster, the sons of Gaedhal of the Shining Armour, the Very Gentle, that were called afterwards the Sons of the Gael, made their first attempt to land in Ireland to avenge Ith, one of their race that had come there one time and had met with his death.

It is under the leadership of the sons of Miled they were, and it was from the south they came, and their Druids had told them there was no country for them to settle in till they would come to that island in the west. "And if you do not get possession of it yourselves," they said, "your children will get possession of it."

But when the Tuatha de Danaan saw the ships coming, they flocked to the shore, and by their enchantments they cast such a cloud over the whole island that the sons of Miled were confused, and all they could see was some large thing that had the appearance of a pig.

And when they were hindered from landing there by enchantments, they went sailing along the coast till at last they were able to make a landing at Inver Sceine in the west of Munster.

From that they marched in good order as far as Slieve Mis. And there they were met by a queen of the Tuatha de Danaan, and a train of beautiful women attending on her, and her Druids and wise men following her. Amergin, one of the sons of Miled, spoke to her then, and asked her name, and she said it was Banba, wife of

Mac Cuill, Son of the Hazel.

They went on then till they came to Slieve Eibhline, and there another queen of the Tuatha de Danaan met them, and her women and her Druids after her, and they asked her name, and she said it was Fodhla, wife of Mac Cecht, Son of the Plough.

They went on then till they came to the hill of Uisnech, and there they saw another woman coming towards them. And there was wonder on them while they were looking at her, for in the one moment she would be a wide-eyed most beautiful queen, and in another she would be a sharp-beaked, grey-white crow. She came on to where Eremon, one of the sons of Miled, was, and sat down before him, and he asked her who was she, and she said: "I am Eriu, wife of Mac Greine, Son of the Sun."

And the names of those three queens were often given to Ireland in the after time.

The Sons of the Gael went on after that to Teamhair, where the three sons of Cermait Honey-Mouth, son of the Dagda, that had the kingship between them at that time held their court. And these three were quarrelling with one another about the division of the treasures their father had left, and the quarrel was so hot it seemed likely it would come to a battle in the end.

And the Sons of the Gael wondered to see them quarrelling about such things, and they having so fruitful an island, where the air was so wholesome, and the sun not too strong, or the cold too bitter, and where there was such a plenty of honey and acorns, and of milk, and of fish, and of corn, and room enough for them all.

Great grandeur they were living in, and their Druids about them, at the palace of Teamhair. And Amergin went to them, and it is what he said, that they must give up the kingship there and then, or they must leave it to the chance of a battle. And he said he asked this in revenge for the death of Ith, of the race of the Gael, that had come to their court before that time, and that had been killed by treachery.

When the sons of Cermait Honey-Mouth heard Amergin saying such fierce words, there was wonder on them, and it is what they said, that they were not willing to fight at that time, for their army was not ready. "But let you make an offer to us," they said, "for we see well you have good judgment and knowledge. But if you make an offer that is not fair," they said, "we will destroy you with our enchantments."

At that Amergin bade the men that were with him to go back to Inver Sceine, and to hurry again into their ships with the rest of the Sons of the Gael, and to go out the length of nine waves from the shore. And then he made his offer to the Tuatha de Danaan, that if they could hinder his men from landing on their island, he and all his ships would go back again to their own country, and would never make any attempt to come again; but that if the Sons of the Gael could land on the coast in spite of them, then the Tuatha de Danaan should give up the kingship and be under their sway.

The Tuatha de Danaan were well pleased with that offer, for they thought that by the powers of their enchantments over the winds and the sea, and by their arts, they would be well able to keep them from ever setting foot in the country again.

So the Sons of the Gael did as Amergin bade them and they went back into their ship and drew up their anchors, and moved out to the length of nine waves from the shore. And as soon as the Men of Dea saw they had left the land, they took to their enchantments and spells, and they raised a great wind that scattered the ships of the Gael, and drove them from one another. But Amergin knew it was not a natural storm was in it, and Arranan, son of Miled, knew that as well, and he went up in the mast of his ship to look about him. But a great blast of wind came against him, and he fell back into the ship and died on the moment. And there was great confusion on the Gael, for the ships were tossed to and fro, and had like to be lost. And the ship that Donn, son of Miled, was in command of was parted from the others by the dint of the storm, and was broken in pieces, and he himself and all with him were drowned, four-and-twenty men and women in all. And Ir, son of Miled, came to his death in the same way, and his body was cast on the shore, and it was buried in a small island that is now called Sceilg Michill. A brave man Ir was, leading the Sons of the Gael to the front of every battle, and their help and their shelter in battle, and his enemies were in dread of his name.

And Heremon, another of the sons of Miled, with his share of the ships, was driven to the left of the island, and it is hardly he got safe to land. And the place where he landed was called Inver Colpa, because Colpa of the Sword, another of the sons of Miled, was drowned there, and he trying to get to land. Five of the sons of Miled in all were destroyed by the storm and the winds the Men of Dea had raised by their enchantments, and there were but three of them left, Heber, and Heremon, and Amergin.

And one of them, Donn, before he was swept into the sea, called out: "It is treachery our knowledgeable men are doing on us, not to put down this wind." "There is no treachery," said Amergin, his brother. And he rose up then before them, and whatever enchantment he did on the winds and the sea, he said these words along with it:

"That they that are tossing in the great wide food-giving sea may reach now to the land.

"That they may find a place upon its plains, its mountains, and its valleys; in its forests that are full of nuts and of all fruits; on its rivers and its streams, on its lakes and its great waters.

"That we may have our gatherings and our races in this land; that there may be a king of our own in Teamhair; that it may be the possession of our many kings.

"That the sons of Miled may be seen in this land, that their ships and their boats may find a place there.

"This land that is now under darkness, it is for it we are asking; let our chief men, let their learned wives, ask that we may come to the noble woman, great Eriu."

After he had said this, the wind went down and the sea was quiet again on the moment.

And those that were left of the sons of Miled and of the Sons of the Gael landed then at Inver Sceine.

And Amergin was the first to put his foot on land, and when he stood on the shore of Ireland, it is what he said:

"I am the wind on the sea;
I am the wave of the sea;
I am the bull of seven battles;
I am the eagle on the rock;
I am a flash from the sun;
I am the most beautiful of plants;
I am a strong wild boar;

I am a salmon in the water;
I am a lake in the plain;
I am the word of knowledge;
I am the head of the spear in battle;
I am the god that puts fire in the head;
Who spreads light in the gathering on the hills?
Who can tell the ages of the moon?
Who can tell the place where the sun rests?"

CHAPTER II. THE BATTLE OF TAILLTIN

And three days after the landing of the Gael, they were attacked by Eriu, wife of Mac Greine, Son of the Sun, and she having a good share of men with her. And they fought a hard battle, and many were killed on both sides. And this was the first battle fought between the Sons of the Gael and the Men of Dea for the kingship of Ireland.

It was in that battle Fais, wife of Un, was killed in a valley at the foot of the mountain, and it was called after her, the Valley of Fais. And Scota, wife of Miled, got her death in the battle, and she was buried in a valley on the north side of the mountain near the sea. But the Sons of the Gael lost no more than three hundred men, and they beat back the Men of Dea and killed a thousand of them. And Eriu was beaten back to Tailltin, and as many of her men as she could hold together; and when she came there she told the people how she had been worsted in the battle, and the best of her men had got their death. But the Gael stopped on the battle-field, and buried their dead, and they gave a great burial to two of their Druids, Aer and Eithis, that were killed in the fight.

And after they had rested for a while, they went on to Inver Colpa in Leinster, and Heremon and his men joined them there. And then they sent messengers to the three kings of Ireland, the three sons of Cermait Honey-Mouth, and bade them to come out and fight a battle that would settle the ownership of the country once for all.

So they came out, and the best of the fighters of the Tuatha de Danaan with them, to Tailltin. And there they attacked one another, and the Sons of the Gael remembered the death of Ith, and there was great anger on them, and they fell on the Men of Dea to avenge him, and there was a fierce battle fought. And for a while neither side got the better of the other, but at the last the Gael broke through the army of the Men of Dea and put them to the rout, with great slaughter, and drove them out of the place. And their three kings were killed in the rout, and the three queens of Ireland, Eriu and Fodhla and Banba. And when the Tuatha de Danaan saw their leaders were dead they fell back in great disorder, and the Sons of the Gael followed after them. But in following them they lost two of their best leaders, Cuailgne, son of Breagan, at Slieve Cuailgne, and Fuad, his brother, at Slieve Fuad. But they were no way daunted by that, but followed the Men of Dea so hotly that they were never able to bring their army together again, but had to own themselves beaten, and to give up the country to the Gael.

And the leaders, the sons of Miled, divided the provinces of Ireland between them. Heber took the two provinces of Munster, and he gave a share of it to Amergin; and Heremon got Leinster and Connacht for his share, and Ulster was divided between Eimhir, son of Ir, son of Miled, and some others of their chief men. And it was of the sons of Eimhir, that were called the Children of Rudraighe, and that lived in Emain Macha for nine hundred years, some of the best men of Ireland came; Fergus, son of Rogh, was of them, and Conall Cearnach, of the Red Branch of Ulster.

And from the sons of Ith, the first of the Gael to get his death in Ireland, there came in the after time Fathadh Canaan, that got the sway over the whole world from the rising to the setting sun, and that took hostages of the streams and the birds and the languages.

And it is what the poets of Ireland used to be saying, that every brave man, good at fighting, and every man that could do great deeds and not be making much talk about them, was of the Sons of the Gael; and that every skilled man that had music and that did enchantments secretly, was of the Tuatha de Danaan. But they put a bad name on the Firbolgs and the men of Domnand and the Gaileoin, for lies and for big talk and injustice. But for all that there were good fighters among them, and Ferdiad, that made so good a stand against Cuchulain, in the war for the Bull of Cuailgne was one of them. And the Gaileoin fought well in the same war; but the men of Ireland had no great liking for them, and their Druids drove them out of the country afterwards.

BOOK FOUR: THE EVER-LIVING LIVING ONES.

CHAPTER I. BODB DEARG

But as to the Tuatha de Danaan after they were beaten, they would not go under the sway of the sons of Miled, but they went away by themselves. And because Manannan, son of Lir, understood all enchantments, they left it to him to find places for them where they would be safe from their enemies. So he chose out the most beautiful of the hills and valleys of Ireland for them to settle in; and he put hidden walls about them, that no man could see through, but they themselves could see through them and pass through them.

And he made the Feast of Age for them, and what they drank at it was the ale of Goibniu the Smith, that kept whoever tasted it from age and from sickness and from death. And for food at the feast he gave them his own swine, that though they were killed and eaten one day, would be alive and fit for eating again the next day, and that would go on in that way for ever.

And after a while they said: "It would be better for us one king to be over us, than to be scattered the way we are through the whole of Ireland."

Now the men among them that had the best chance of getting the kingship at that time were Bodb Dearg, son of the Dagda; and Ilbrech of Ess Ruadh; and Lir of Sidhe Fionnachaidh, the Hill of the White Field, on Slieve Fuad; and Midhir the Proud of Bri Leith, and Angus Og, son of the Dagda; but he did not covet the kingship at all, but would sooner be left as he was. Then all the chief men but those five went into council together, and it is what they agreed, to give the kingship to Bodb Dearg, for the sake of his father, for his own sake, and because he was the eldest among the children of the Dagda.

It was in Sidhe Femen Bodb Dearg had his house, and he put great enchantments about it. Cliach, the Harper of the King of the Three Rosses in Connacht, went one time to ask one of his daughters in marriage, and he stayed outside the place through the whole length of a year, playing his harp, and able to get no nearer to Bodb or to his daughter. And he went on playing till a lake burst up under his feet, the lake that is on the top of a mountain, Loch Bel Sead.

It was Bodb's swineherd went to Da Derga's Inn, and his squealing pig along with him, the night Conaire, the High King of Ireland, met with his death; and it was said that whatever feast that swineherd would go to, there would blood be shed before it was over.

And Bodb had three sons, Angus, and Artrach, and Aedh. And they used often to be living among men in the time of the Fianna afterwards. Artrach had a house with seven doors, and a free welcome for all that came, and the king's son of Ireland, and of Alban, used to be coming to Angus to learn the throwing of spears and darts; and troops of poets from Alban and from Ireland used to be with Aedh, that was the comeliest of Bodb's sons, so that his place used to be called "The Rath of Aedh of the Poets." And indeed it was a beautiful rath at that time, with golden-yellow apples in it and crimson-pointed nuts of the wood. But after the passing away of the Fianna, the three brothers went back to the Tuatha de Danaan.

And Bodb Dearg was not always in his own place, but sometimes he was with Angus at Brugh na Boinn.

Three sons of Lugaidh Menn, King of Ireland, Eochaid, and Fiacha, and Ruide, went there one time, for their father refused them any land till they would win it for themselves. And when he said that, they rose with the ready rising of one man, and went and sat down on the green of Brugh na Boinn, and fasted there on the Tuatha de Danaan, to see if they could win some good thing from them.

And they were not long there till they saw a young man, quiet and with pleasant looks, coming towards them, and he wished them good health, and they answered him the same way. "Where are you come from?" they asked him then. "From the rath beyond, with the many lights," he said. "And I am Bodb Dearg, son of the Dagda," he said, "and come in with me now to the rath."

So they went in, and supper was made ready for them, but they did not use it. Bodb Dearg asked them then why was it they were using nothing. "It is because our father has refused land to us," said they; "and there are in Ireland but the two races, the Sons of the Gael and the Men of Dea, and when the one failed us we are come to the other."

Then the Men of Dea consulted together. And the chief among them was Midhir of the Yellow Hair, and it is what he said: "Let us give a wife to every one of these three men, for it is from a wife that good or bad fortune comes."

So they agreed to that, and Midhir's three daughters, Doirenn, and Aife, and Aillbhe, were given to them. Then Midhir asked Bodb to say what marriage portion should be given to them. "I will tell you that," said Bodb. "We are three times fifty sons of kings in this hill; let every king's son give three times fifty ounces of red gold. And I myself," he said, "will give them along with that, three times fifty suits of clothing of all colours." "I will give them a gift," said a young man of the Tuatha de Danaan, from Rachlainn in the sea. "A horn I will give them, and a vat. And there is nothing wanting but to fill the vat with pure water, and it will turn into mead, fit to drink, and strong enough to make drunken. And into the horn," he said, "you have but to put salt water from the sea, and it will turn into wine on the moment." "A gift to them from me," said Lir of Sidhe Fionnachaidh, "three times fifty swords, and three times fifty well-riveted long spears." "A gift from me," said Angus Og, son of the Dagda, "a rath and a good town with high walls, and with bright sunny houses, and with wide houses, in whatever place it will please them between Rath Chobtaige and Teamhair." "A gift to them from me," said Aine, daughter of Modharn, "a woman-cook that I have, and there is **geasa** on her not to refuse food to any; and according as she serves it out, her store fills up of itself again." "Another gift to them from me," said Bodb Dearg, "a good musician that I have, Fertuinne, son of Trogain; and although there were women in the sharpest pains of childbirth, and brave men wounded early in the day, in a place where there were saws going through wood, they would sleep at the sweetness of the music he makes. And whatever house he may be in, the people of the whole country round will hear him."

So they stopped in Brugh na Boinne three days and three nights, and when they left it, Angus bade them bring away from the oak-wood three apple-trees, one in full bloom, and one shedding its blossom, and the third covered with ripe fruit.

They went then to their own dun that was given them, and it is a good place they had there, and a troop of young men, and great troops of horses and of greyhounds; and they had three sorts of music that comely kings liked to be listening to, the music of harps and of lutes, and the chanting of Trogain's son; and there were three great sounds, the tramping on the green, and the uproar of racing, and the lowing of cattle; and three other sounds, the grunting of good pigs with the fat thick on them, and the voices of the crowd on the green lawn, and the noise of men drinking inside the house. And as to Eochaid, it was said of him that he never took a step backwards in flight, and his house was never without music or drinking of ale. And it was said of Fiacha that there was no man of his time braver than himself, and that he never said a word too much. And as to Ruide, he never refused any one, and never asked anything at all of any man.

And when their lifetime was over, they went back to the Tuatha de Danaan, for they belonged to them through their wives, and there they have stopped ever since.

And Bodb Dearg had a daughter, Scathniamh, the Flower of Brightness, that gave her love to Caoilte in the time of the Fianna; and they were forced to part from one another, and they never met again till the time Caoilte was, old and withered, and one of the last that was left of the Fianna. And she came to him out of the cave of Cruachan, and asked him for the bride-price he had promised her, and that she was never able to come and ask for till then. And Caoilte went to a cairn that was near and that was full up of gold, that was wages earned by Conan Maol and hidden there, and he gave the gold to Bodb Dearg's daughter. And the people that were there wondered to see the girl so young and comely, and Caoilte so grey and bent and withered. "There is no wonder in that," said Caoilte, "for I am of the sons of Miled that wither and fade away, but she is of the Tuatha de Danaan that never change and that never die."

CHAPTER II. THE DAGDA

And it was at Brugh na Boinne the Dagda, the Red Man of all Knowledge, had his house. And the most noticeable things in it were the Hall of the Morrigu, and the Bed of the Dagda, and the Birthplace of Cermait Honey-Mouth, and the Prison of the Grey of Macha that was Cuchulain's horse afterwards. And there was a little hill by the house that was called the Comb and the Casket of the Dagda's wife; and another that was called the Hill of Dabilla, that was the little hound belonging to Boann. And the Valley of the Mata was there, the Sea-Turtle that could suck down a man in armour.

And it is likely the Dagda put up his cooking oven there, that Druimne, son of Luchair, made for him at Teamhair. And it is the way it was, the axle and the wheel were of wood, and the body was iron, and there were twice nine wheels in its axle, that it might turn the faster; and it was as quick as the quickness of a stream in turning, and there were three times nine spits from it, and three times nine pots. And it used to lie down with the cinders and to rise to the height of the roof with the flame.

The Dagda himself made a great vat one time for Ainge, his daughter, but she was not well satisfied with it, for it would not stop from dripping while the sea was in flood, though it would not lose a drop during the ebb-tide. And she gathered a bundle of twigs to make a new vat for herself, but Gaible, son of Nuada of the Silver Hand, stole it from her and hurled it away. And in the place where it fell a beautiful wood grew up, that was called Gaible's Wood.

And the Dagda had his household at Brugh na Boinne, and his steward was Dichu, and Len Linfiaclach was the smith of the Brugh. It was he lived in the lake, making the bright vessels of Fand, daughter of Flidhais; and every evening when he left off work he would make a cast of the anvil eastward to Indeoin na Dese, the

Anvil of the Dese, as far as the Grave End. Three showers it used to cast, a shower of fire, and a shower of water, and a shower of precious stones of pure purple.

But Tuirbe, father of Goibniu the Smith, used to throw better again, for he would make a cast of his axe from Tulach na Bela, the Hill of the Axe, in the face of the flood tide, and he would put his order on the sea, and it would not come over the axe.

And Corann was the best of the harpers of the household; he was harper to the Dagda's son, Diancecht. And one time he called with his harp to Cailcheir, one of the swine of Debrann. And it ran northward with all the strength of its legs, and the champions of Connacht were following after it with all their strength of running, and their hounds with them, till they got as far as Ceis Corain, and they gave it up there, all except Niall that went on the track of the swine till he found it in the oak-wood of Tarba, and then it made away over the plain of Ai, and through a lake. And Niall and his hound were drowned in following it through the lake. And the Dagda gave Corann a great tract of land for doing his harping so well.

But however great a house the Dagda had, Angus got it away from him in the end, through the help of Manannan, son of Lir. For Manannan bade him to ask his father for it for the length of a day and a night, and that he by his art would take away his power of refusing. So Angus asked for the Brugh, and his father gave it to him for a day and a night. But when he asked it back again, it is what Angus said, that it had been given to him for ever, for the whole of life and time is made up of a day and a night, one following after the other.

So when the Dagda heard that he went away and his people and his household with him, for Manannan had put an enchantment on them all.

But Dichu the Steward was away at the time, and his wife and his son, for they were gone out to get provisions for a feast for Manannan and his friends. And when he came back and knew his master was gone, he took service with Angus.

And Angus stopped in Brugh na Boinne, and some say he is there to this day, with the hidden walls about him, drinking Goibniu's ale and eating the pigs that never fail.

As to the Dagda, he took no revenge, though he had the name of being revengeful and quick in his temper. And some say it was at Teamhair he made his dwelling-place after that, but wherever it was, a great misfortune came on him.

It chanced one time Corrgenn, a great man of Connacht, came to visit him, and his wife along with him. And while they were there, Corrgenn got it in his mind that there was something that was not right going on between his wife and Aedh, one of the sons of the Dagda. And great jealousy and anger came on him, and he struck at the young man and killed him before his father's face.

Every one thought the Dagda would take Corrgenn's life then and there in revenge for his son's life. But he would not do that, for he said if his son was guilty, there was no blame to be put on Corrgenn for doing what he did. So he spared his life for that time, but if he did, Corrgenn did not gain much by it. For the punishment he put on him was to take the dead body of the young man on his back, and never to lay it down till he would find a stone that would be its very fit in length and in breadth, and that would make a gravestone for him; and when he had found that, he could bury him in the nearest hill.

So Corrgenn had no choice but to go, and he set out with his load; but he had a long way to travel before he could find a stone that would fit, and it is where he found one at last, on the shore of Loch Feabhail. So then he left the body up on the nearest hill, and he went down and raised the stone and brought it up and dug a grave and buried the Dagda's son. And it is many an Ochone! he gave when he was putting the stone over him, and when he had that done he was spent, and he dropped dead there and then.

And the Dagda brought his two builders, Garbhan and Imheall, to the place, and he bade them build a rath there round the grave. It was Garbhan cut the stones and shaped them, and Imheall set them all round the house till the work was finished, and then he closed the top of the house with a slab. And the place was called the Hill of Aileac, that is, the Hill of Sighs and of a Stone, for it was tears of blood the Dagda shed on account of the death of his son.

CHAPTER III. ANGUS OG

And as to Angus Og, son of the Dagda, sometimes he would come from Brugh na Boinn and let himself be seen upon the earth.

It was a long time after the coming of the Gael that he was seen by Cormac, King of Teamhair, and this is the account he gave of him.

He was by himself one day in his Hall of Judgment, for he used to be often reading the laws and thinking how he could best carry them out. And on a sudden he saw a stranger, a very comely young man, at the end of the hall; and he knew on the moment it was Angus Og, for he had often heard his people talking of him, but he himself used to be saying he did not believe there was any such person at all. And when his people came back to the hall, he told them how he had seen Angus himself, and had talked with him, and Angus had told him his name, and had foretold what would happen him in the future. "And he was a beautiful young man," he said, "with high looks, and his appearance was more beautiful than all beauty, and there were ornaments of gold on his dress; in his hand he held a silver harp with strings of red gold, and the sound of its strings was sweeter than all music under the sky; and over the harp were two birds that seemed to be playing on it. He sat beside me pleasantly and played his sweet music to me, and in the end he foretold things that put drunkenness on my wits."

The birds, now, that used to be with Angus were four of his kisses that turned into birds and that used to be coming about the young men of Ireland, and crying after them. "Come, come," two of them would say, and "I go, I go," the other two would say, and it was hard to get free of them. But as to Angus, even when he was in his young youth, he used to be called the Frightener, or the Disturber; for the plough teams of the world, and every sort of cattle that is used by men, would make away in terror before him.

And one time he appeared in the shape of a land-holder to two men, Ribh and Eocho, that were looking for a place to settle in. The first place they chose was near Bregia on a plain that was belonging to Angus; and it was then he came to them, leading his horse in his hand, and told them they should not stop there. And they said they could not carry away their goods without horses. Then he gave them his horse, and bade them to put all they had a mind to on that horse and he would carry it, and so he did. But the next place they chose was Magh Find, the Fine Plain, that was the playing ground of Angus and of Midhir. And that time Midhir came to them in the same way and gave them a horse to put their goods on, and he went on with them as far as Magh Dairbthenn.

And there were many women loved Angus, and there was one Enghi, daughter of Elcmair, loved him though she had not seen him. And she went one time looking for him to the gathering for games between Cletech and Sidhe in Broga; and the bright troops of the Sidhe used to come to that gathering every Samhain evening, bringing a moderate share of food with them, that is, a nut. And the sons of Derc came from the north, out of Sidhe Findabrach, and they went round about the young men and women without their knowledge and they brought away Elcmair's daughter. There were great lamentations made then, and the name the place got was Cnoguba, the Nut Lamentation, from the crying there was at that gathering.

And Derbrenn, Eochaid Fedlech's daughter, was another that was loved by Angus, and she had six fosterlings, three boys and three girls. But the mother of the boys, Dalb Garb, the Rough, put a spell on them she made from a gathering of the nuts of Caill Ochuid, that turned them into swine.

And Angus gave them into the care of Buichet, the Hospitaller of Leinster, and they stopped a year with him. But at the end of that time there came a longing On Buichet's wife to eat a bit of the flesh of one of them. So she gathered a hundred armed men and a hundred hounds to take them. But the pigs made away, and went to Brugh na Boinn, to Angus, and he bade them welcome, and they asked him to give them his help. But he said he could not do that till they had shaken the Tree of Tarbga, and eaten the salmon of Inver Umaill.

So they went to Glascarn, and stopped a year in hiding with Derbrenn. And then they shook the Tree of Tarbga, and they went on towards Inver Umaill. But Maeve gathered the men of Connacht to hunt them, and they all fell but one, and their heads were put in a mound, and it got the name of Duma Selga, the Mound of the Hunting.

And it was in the time of Maeve of Cruachan that Angus set his love on Caer Ormaith, of the Province of Connacht, and brought her away to Brugh na Boinn.

CHAPTER IV. THE MORRIGU

As to the Morrigu, the Great Queen, the Crow of Battle, where she lived after the coming of the Gael is not known, but before that time it was in Teamhair she lived. And she had a great cooking-spit there, that held three sorts of food on it at the one time: a piece of raw meat, and a piece of dressed meat, and a piece of butter. And the raw was dressed, and the dressed was not burned, and the butter did not melt, and the three together on the spit.

Nine men that were outlaws went to her one time and asked for a spit to be made for themselves. And they brought it away with them, and it had nine ribs in it, and every one of the outlaws would carry a rib in his hand wherever he would go, till they would all meet together at the close of day. And if they wanted the spit to be high, it could be raised to a man's height, and at another time it would not be more than the height of a fist over the fire, without breaking and without lessening.

And Mechi, the son the Morrigu had, was killed by Mac Cecht on Magh Mechi, that till that time had been called Magh Fertaige. Three hearts he had, and it is the way they were, they had the shapes of three serpents through them. And if Mechi had not met with his death, those serpents in him would have grown, and what they left alive in Ireland would have wasted away. And Mac Cecht burned the three hearts on Magh Luathad, the Plain of Ashes, and he threw the ashes into the stream; and the rushing water of the stream stopped and boiled up, and every creature in it died.

And the Morrigu used often to be meddling in Ireland in Cuchulain's time, stirring up wars and quarrels. It was she came and roused up Cuchulain one time when he was but a lad, and was near giving in to some enchantment that was used against him. "There is not the making of a hero in you," she said to him, "and you lying there under the feet of shadows." And with that Cuchulain rose up and struck off the head of a shadow that was standing over him, with his hurling stick. And the time Conchubar was sending out Finched to rouse up the men of Ulster at the time of the war for the Bull of Cuailgne, he bade him to go to that terrible fury, the Morrigu, to get help for Cuchulain. And she had a dispute with Cuchulain one time he met her, and she bringing away a cow from the Hill of Cruachan; and another time she helped Talchinem, a Druid of the household of Conaire Mor, to bring away a bull his wife had set her mind on. And indeed she was much given to meddling with cattle, and one time she brought away a cow from Odras, that was of the household of the cow-chief of Cormac Hua Cuined, and that was going after her husband with cattle. And the Morrigu brought the cow away with her to the Cave of Cruachan, and the Hill of the Sidhe. And Odras followed her there till sleep fell on her in the oak-wood of Falga; and the Morrigu awoke her and sang spells over her, and made of her a pool of water that went to the river that flows to the west of Slieve Buane.

And in the battle of Magh Rath, she fluttered over Congal Claen in the shape of a bird, till he did not know friend from foe. And after that again at the battle of Cluantarbh, she was flying over the head of Murchadh, son of Brian; for she had many shapes, and it was in the shape of a crow she would sometimes fight her battles.

And if it was not the Morrigu, it was Badb that showed herself in the battle of Dunbolg, where the men of Ireland were fighting under Aedh, son of Niall; and Brigit was seen in the same battle on the side of the men of Leinster.

CHAPTER V. AINE

And as to Aine, that some said was a daughter of Manannan, but some said was the Morrigu herself, there was a stone belonging to her that was called Cathair Aine. And if any one would sit on that stone he would be in danger of losing his wits, and any one that would sit on it three times would lose them for ever. And people whose wits were astray would make their way to it, and mad dogs would come from all parts of the country, and would flock around it, and then they would go into the sea to Aine's place there. But those that did cures by herbs said she had power over the whole body; and she used to give gifts of poetry and of music, and she often gave her love to men, and they called her the Leanan Sidhe, the Sweet-heart of the Sidhe.

And it was no safe thing to offend Aine, for she was very revengeful. Oilioll Oluim, a king of Ireland, killed her brother one time, and it is what she did, she made a great yew-tree by enchantment beside the river Maigh in Luimnech, and she put a little man in it, playing sweet music on a harp. And Oilioll's son was passing the river with his step-brother, and they saw the tree and heard the sweet music from it. And first they quarrelled as to which of them would have the little harper, and then they quarrelled about the tree, and they asked a judgment from Oilioll, and he gave it for his own son. And it was the bad feeling about that judgment that led to the battle of Magh Mucruimhe, and Oilioll and his seven sons were killed there, and so Aine got her revenge.

CHAPTER VI. AOIBHELL

And Aoibhell, another woman of the Sidhe, made her dwelling-place in Craig Liath, and at the time of the battle of Cluantarbh she set her love on a young man of Munster, Dubhlaing ua Artigan, that had been sent away in disgrace by the King of Ireland. But before the battle he came back to join with Murchadh, the king's son, and to fight for the Gael. And Aoibhell came to stop him; and when he would not stop with her she put a Druid covering about him, the way no one could see him.

And he went where Murchadh was fighting, and he made a great attack on the enemies of Ireland, and struck them down on every side. And Murchadh looked around him, and he said; "It seems to me I hear the sound of the blows of Dubhlaing ua Artigan, but I do not see himself." Then Dubhlaing threw off the Druid covering that was about him, and he said: "I will not keep this covering upon me when you cannot see me through it. And come now across the plain to where Aoibhell is," he said, "for she can give us news of the battle."

So they went where she was, and she bade them both to quit the battle, for they would lose their lives in it. But Murchadh said to her, "I will tell you a little true story," he said; "that fear for my own body will never make me change my face. And if we fall," he said, "the strangers will fall with us; and it is many a man will fall by my own hand, and the Gael will be sharing their strong places." "Stop with me, Dubhlaing," she said then, "and you will have two hundred years of happy life with myself." "I will not give up Murchadh," he said, "or my own good name, for silver or gold." And there was anger on Aoibhell when he said that, and she said: "Murchadh will fall, and you yourself will fall, and your proud blood will be on the plain to-morrow." And they went back into the battle, and got their death there.

And it was Aoibhell gave a golden harp to the son of Meardha the time he was getting his learning at the school of the Sidhe in Connacht and that he heard his father had got his death by the King of Lochlann. And whoever heard the playing of that harp would not live long after it. And Meardha's son went where the three sons of the King of Lochlann were, and played on his harp for them, and they died.

It was that harp Cuchulain heard the time his enemies were gathering against him at Muirthemne, and he knew by it that his life was near its end.

CHAPTER VII. MIDHIR AND ETAIN

And Midhir took a hill for himself, and his wife Fuamach was with him there, and his daughter, Bri. And Leith, son of Celtchar of Cualu, was the most beautiful among the young men of the Sidhe of Ireland at that time, and he loved Bri, Midhir's daughter. And Bri went out with her young girls to meet him one time at the Grave of the Daughters beside Teamhair. And Leith came and his young men along with him till he was on the Hill of the After Repentance. And they could not come nearer to one another because of the slingers on Midhir's hill that were answering one another till their spears were as many as a swarm of bees on a day of beauty. And Cochlan, Leith's servant, got a sharp wound from them and he died.

Then the girl turned back to Midhir's hill, and her heart broke in her and she died. And Leith said: "Although I am not let come to this girl, I will leave my name with her." And the hill was called Bri Leith from that time.

After a while Midhir took Etain Echraide to be his wife. And there was great jealousy on Fuamach, the wife he had before, when she saw the love that Midhir gave to Etain, and she called to the Druid, Bresal Etarlaim to help her, and he put spells on Etain the way Fuamach was able to drive her away.

And when she was driven out of Bri Leith, Angus Og, son of the Dagda, took her into his keeping; and when Midhir asked her back, he would not give her up, but he brought her about with him to every place he went. And wherever they rested, he made a sunny house for her, and put sweet-smelling flowers in it, and he made invisible walls about it, that no one could see through and that could not be seen.

But when news came to Fuamach that Etain was so well cared by Angus, anger and jealousy came on her again, and she searched her mind for a way to destroy

Etain altogether.

And it is what she did, she persuaded Midhir and Angus to go out and meet one another and to make peace, for there had been a quarrel between them ever since the time Etain was sent away. And when Angus was away from Brugh na Boinn, Fuamach went and found Etain there, in her sunny house. And she turned her with Druid spells into a fly, and then she sent a blast of wind into the house, that swept her away through the window.

But as to Midhir and Angus, they waited a while for Fuamach to come and join them. And when she did not come they were uneasy in their minds, and Angus hurried back to Brugh na Boinn. And when he found the sunny house empty, he went in search of Fuamach, and it was along with Etarlaim, the Druid, he found her, and he struck her head off there and then.

And for seven years Etain was blown to and fro through Ireland in great misery. And at last she came to the house of Etar, of Inver Cechmaine, where there was a feast going on, and she fell from a beam of the roof into the golden cup that was beside Etar's wife. And Etar's wife drank her down with the wine, and at the end of nine months she was born again as Etar's daughter.

And she had the same name as before, Etain; and she was reared as a king's daughter, and there were fifty young girls, daughters of princes, brought up with her to keep her company.

And it happened one day Etain and all the rest of the young girls were out bathing in the bay at Inver Cechmaine, and they saw from the water a man, with very high looks, coming towards them over the plain, and he riding a bay horse with mane and tail curled. A long green cloak he had on him, and a shirt woven with threads of red gold, and a brooch of gold that reached across to his shoulders on each side. And he had on his back a shield of silver with a rim of gold and a boss of gold, and in his hand a sharp-pointed spear covered with rings of gold from heel to socket. Fair yellow hair he had, coming over his forehead, and it bound with a golden band to keep it from loosening.

And when he came near them he got down from his horse, and sat down on the bank, and it is what he said:

"It is here Etain is to-day, at the Mound of Fair Women. It is among little children is her life on the strand of Inver Cechmaine.

"It is she healed the eye of the king from the well of Loch da Lig; it is she was swallowed in a heavy drink by the wife of Etar.

"Many great battles will happen for your sake to Echaid of Midhe; destruction will fall upon the Sidhe, and war on thousands of men."

And when he had said that, he vanished, and no one knew where he went. And they did not know the man that had come to them was Midhir of Bri Leith.

And when Etain was grown to be a beautiful young woman, she was seen by Eochaid Feidlech, High King of Ireland, and this is the way that happened.

He was going one time over the fair green of Bri Leith, and he saw at the side of a well a woman, with a bright comb of gold and silver, and she washing in a silver basin having four golden birds on it, and little bright purple stones set in the rim of the basin. A beautiful purple cloak she had, and silver fringes to it, and a gold brooch; and she had on her a dress of green silk with a long hood, embroidered in red gold, and wonderful clasps of gold and silver on her breasts and on her shoulder. The sunlight was falling on her, so that the gold and the green silk were shining out. Two plaits of hair she had, four locks in each plait, and a bead at the point of every lock, and the colour of her hair was like yellow flags in summer, or like red gold after it is rubbed.

There she was, letting down her hair to wash it, and her arms out through the sleeve-holes of her shift. Her soft hands were as white as the snow of a single night, and her eyes as blue as any blue flower, and her lips as red as the berries of the rowan-tree, and her body as white as the foam of a wave. The bright light of the moon was in her face, the highness of pride in her eyebrows, a dimple of delight in each of her cheeks, the light of wooing in her eyes, and when she walked she had a step that was steady and even like the walk of a queen.

And Eochaid sent his people to bring her to him, and he asked her name, and she told him her name was Etain, daughter of Etar, King of the Riders of the Sidhe. And Eochaid gave her his love, and he paid the bride-price, and brought her home to Teamhair as his wife, and there was a great welcome before her there.

And after a while there was a great feast made at Teamhair, and all the chief men of Ireland came to it, and it lasted from the fortnight before Samhain to the fortnight after it. And King Eochaid's brother Ailell, that was afterwards called Ailell Anglonach, of the Only Fault, came to the feast. And when he saw his brother's wife Etain, he fell in love with her on the moment, and all through the length of the feast he was not content unless he could be looking at her. And a woman, the daughter of Luchta Lamdearg, of the Red Hand, took notice of it, and she said: "What far thing are you looking at, Ailell? It is what I think, that to be looking the way you are doing is a sign of love." Then Ailell checked himself, and did not look towards Etain any more.

But when the feast was at an end, and the gathering broken up, great desire and envy came on Ailell, so that he fell sick, and they brought him to a house in Teffia. And he stopped there through the length of a year, and he was wasting away, but he told no one the cause of his sickness. And at the end of the year, Eochaid came to visit his brother, and he passed his hand over his breast, and Ailell let a groan. "What way are you?" said Eochaid then. "Are you getting any easier, for you must not let this illness come to a bad end." "By my word," said Ailell, "it is not easier I am, but worse and worse every day and every night." "What is it ails you?" said Eochaid. "And what is it that is coming against you." "By my word, I cannot tell you that," said Ailell. "I will bring one here that will know the cause of your sickness," said the king.

With that he sent Fachtna, his own physician, to Ailell; and when he came he passed his hand over Ailell's heart, and at that he groaned again. "This sickness will not be your death," said Fachtna then; "and I know well what it comes from. It is either from the pains of jealousy, or from love you have given, and that you have not found a way out of." But there was shame on Ailell, and he would not confess to the physician that what he said was right. So Fachtna went away then and left him.

As to King Eochaid, he went away to visit all the provinces of Ireland that were under his kingship, and he left Etain after him, and it is what he said: "Good Etain," he said, "take tender care of Ailell so long as he is living; and if he should die from us, make a sodded grave for him, and raise a pillar stone over it, and write his name on it in Ogham." And with that he went away on his journey.

One day, now, Etain went into the house where Ailell was lying in his sickness, and they talked together, and then she made a little song for him, and it is what she said:

"What is it ails you, young man, for it is a long time you are wasted with this sickness, and it is not the hardness of the weather has stopped your light footstep."

And Ailell answered her in the same way, and he said: "I have good cause for my hurt; the music of my own harp does not please me; there is no sort of food is pleasant to me, and so I am wasted away." Then Etain said: "Tell me what is it ails you, for I am a woman that is wise. Tell me is there anything that would cure you, the way I may help you to it?" And Ailell answered her: "O kind, beautiful woman, it is not good to tell a secret to a woman, but sometimes it may be known through the eyes." And Etain said: "Though it is bad to tell a secret, yet it ought to be told now, or how can help be given to you?" And Ailell answered: "My blessing on you, fair-haired Etain. It is not fit I am to be spoken with; my wits have been no good help to me; my body is a rebel to me. All Ireland knows, O king's wife, there is sickness in my head and in my body." And Etain said: "If there is a woman of the fair-faced women of Ireland tormenting you this way, she must come to you here if it pleases you; and it is I myself will woo her for you," she said.

Then Ailell said to her: "Woman, it would be easy for you yourself to put my sickness from me. And my desire," he said, "is a desire that is as long as a year; but it is love given to an echo, the spending of grief on a wave, a lonely fight with a shadow, that is what my love and my desire have been to me."

And it is then Etain knew what was the sickness that was on him, and it was a heavy trouble to her.

But she came to him every day to tend him, and to make ready his food, and to pour water over his hands, and all she could do she did for him, for it was a grief to her, he to wither away and to be lost for her sake. And at last one day she said to him: "Rise up, Ailell, son of a king, man of high deeds, and I will do your healing."

Then he put his arms about her, and she kissed him, and she said: "Come at the morning of to-morrow at the break of day to the house outside the dun, and I will give you all your desire."

That night Ailell lay without sleep until the morning was at hand. And at the very time he should have risen to go to her, it was at that time his sleep settled down upon him, and he slept on till the full light of day.

But Etain went to the house outside the dun, and she was not long there when she saw a man coming towards her having the appearance of Ailell, sick and tired and worn. But when he came near and she looked closely at him, she saw it was not Ailell that was in it. Then he went away, and after she had waited a while, she herself went back into the dun.

And it was then Ailell awoke, and when he knew the morning had passed by, he would sooner have had death than life, and he fretted greatly. And Etain came in then, and he told her what had happened him. And she said: "Come to-morrow to the same place."

But the same thing happened the next day. And when it happened on the third day, and the same man came to meet Etain, she said to him: "It is not you at all I come to meet here, and why is it that you come to meet me? And as to him I came to meet," she said, "indeed it is not for gain or through lightness I bade him come to me, but to heal him of the sickness he is lying under for my sake." Then the man said: "It would be more fitting for you to come to meet me than any other one. For in the time long ago," he said, "I was your first husband, and your first man." "What is it you are saying," she said, "and who are you yourself?" "It is easy to tell that," he said; "I am Midhir of Bri Leith." "And what parted us if I was your wife?" said Etain. "It was through Fuamach's sharp jealousy and through the spells of Bresal Etarlaim, the Druid, we were parted. And will you come away with me now?" he said. But Etain said: "It is not for a man whose kindred is unknown I will give up the High King of Ireland." And Midhir said: "Surely it was I myself put that great desire for you on Ailell, and it was I hindered him from going to meet you, the way you might keep your good name."

And when she went back to Ailell's house, she found his sickness was gone from him, and his desire. And she told him all that had happened, and he said: "It has turned out well for us both: I am well of my sickness and your good name is not lessened." "We give thanks to our gods for that," said Etain, "for we are well pleased to have it so."

And just at that time Eochaid came back from his journey, and they told him the whole story, and he was thankful to his wife for the kindness she had showed to Ailell.

It was a good while after that, there was a great fair held at Teamhair, and Etain was out on the green looking at the games and the races. And she saw a rider coming towards her, but no one could see him but herself; and when he came near she saw he had the same appearance as the man that came and spoke with her and her young girls the time they were out in the sea at Inver Cechmaine. And when he came up to her he began to sing words to her that no one could hear but herself. And it is what he said:

"O beautiful woman, will you come with me to the wonderful country that is mine? It is pleasant to be looking at the people there, beautiful people without any blemish; their hair is of the colour of the flag-flower, their fair body is as white as snow, the colour of the foxglove is on every cheek. The young never grow old there; the fields and the flowers are as pleasant to be looking at as the blackbird's eggs; warm, sweet streams of mead and of wine flow through that country; there is no care and no sorrow on any person; we see others, but we ourselves are not seen.

"Though the plains of Ireland are beautiful, it is little you would think of them after our great plain; though the ale of Ireland is heady, the ale of the great country is still more heady. O beautiful woman, if you come to my proud people it is the flesh of pigs newly killed I will give you for food; it is ale and new milk I will give you for drink; it is feasting you will have with me there; it is a crown of gold you will have upon your hair, O beautiful woman!

"And will you come there with me, Etain?" he said. But Etain said she would not leave Eochaid the High King. "Will you come if Eochaid gives you leave?" Midhir said then. "I will do that," said Etain.

One day, after that time, Eochaid the High King was looking out from his palace at Teamhair, and he saw a strange man coming across the plain. Yellow hair he had, and eyes blue and shining like the flame of a candle, and a purple dress on him, and in his hand a five-pronged spear and a shield having gold knobs on it.

He came up to the king, and the king bade him welcome. "Who are you yourself?" he said; "and what are you come for, for you are a stranger to me?" "If I am a stranger to you, you are no stranger to me, for I have known you this long time," said the strange man. "What is your name?" said the king. "It is nothing very great," said he; "I am called Midhir of Bri Leith." "What is it brings you here?" said Eochaid. "I am come to play a game of chess with you," said the stranger. "Are you a good player?" said the king. "A trial will tell you that," said Midhir. "The chessboard is in the queen's house, and she is in her sleep at this time," said Eochaid. "That is no matter," said Midhir, "for I have with me a chess-board as good as your own." And with that he brought out his chessboard, and it made of silver, and precious stones shining in every corner of it. And then he brought out the chessmen, and they made of gold, from a bag that was of shining gold threads.

"Let us play now," said Midhir. "I will not play without a stake," said the king. "What stake shall We play for?" said Midhir. "We can settle that after the game is over," said the king.

They played together then, and Midhir was beaten, and it is what the king asked of him, fifty brown horses to be given to him. And then they played the second time, and Midhir was beaten again, and this time the king gave him four hard things to do: to make a road over Moin Lamraide, and to clear Midhe of stones, and to cover the district of Tethra with rushes, and the district of Darbrech with trees.

So Midhir brought his people from Bri Leith to do those things, and it is hard work they had doing them. And Eochaid used to be out watching them, and he took notice that when the men of the Sidhe yoked their oxen, it was by the neck and the shoulder they used to yoke them, and not by the forehead and the head. And it was after Eochaid taught his people to yoke them that way, he was given the name of Eochaid Airem, that is, of the Plough.

And when all was done, Midhir came to Eochaid again, looking thin and wasted enough with the dint of the hard work he had been doing, and he asked Eochaid to play the third game with him. Eochaid agreed, and it was settled as before, the stake to be settled by the winner. It was Midhir won the game that time, and when the king asked him what he wanted, "It is Etain, your wife, I want," said he. "I will not give her to you," said the king. "All I will ask then," said Midhir, "is to put my arms about her and to kiss her once." "You may do that," said the king, "if you will wait to the end of a month." So Midhir agreed to that, and went away for that time.

At the end of the month he came back again, and stood in the great hall at Teamhair, and no one had ever seen him look so comely as he did that night. And Eochaid had all his best fighting men gathered in the hall, and he shut all the doors of the palace when he saw Midhir come in, for fear he would try to bring away Etain by force.

"I am come to be paid what is due to me," said Midhir. "I have not been thinking of it up to this time," said Eochaid, and there was anger on him. "You promised me Etain, your wife," said Midhir. The redness of shame came on Etain when she heard that, but Midhir said: "Let there be no shame on you, Etain, for it is through the length of a year I have been asking your love, and I have offered you every sort of treasure and riches, and you refused to come to me till such a time as your husband would give you leave." "It is true I said that," said Etain, "I will go if Eochaid gives me up to you." "I will not give you up," said Eochaid; "I will let him do no more than put his arms about you in this place, as was promised him." "I will do that," said Midhir.

With that he took his sword in his left hand, and he took Etain in his right arm and kissed her. All the armed men in the house made a rush at him then, but he rose up through the roof bringing Etain with him, and when they rushed out of the house to follow him, all they could see was two swans high up in the air, linked together by a chain of gold.

There was great anger on Eochaid then, and he went and searched all through Ireland, but there were no tidings of them to be had, for they were in the houses of the Sidhe.

It was to the Brugh of Angus on the Boinn they went first, and after they had stopped there a while they went to a hill of the Sidhe in Connacht. And there was a serving-maid with Etain at that time, Cruachan Croderg her name was, and she said to Midhir: "Is this your own place we are in?" "It is not," said Midhir; "my own place is nearer to the rising of the sun." She was not well pleased to stop there when she heard that, and Midhir said to quiet her: "It is your own name will be put on this place from this out." And the hill was called the Hill of Cruachan from that time.

Then they went to Bri Leith; and Etain's daughter Esa came to them there, and she brought a hundred of every sort of cattle with her, and Midhir fostered her for seven years. And all through that time Eochaid the High King was making a search for them.

But at last Codal of the Withered Breast took four rods of yew and wrote Oghams on them, and through them and through his enchantments he found out that Etain was with Midhir in Bri Leith.

So Eochaid went there, and made an attack on the place, and he was for nine years besieging it, and Midhir was driving him away. And then his people began digging through the hill; and when they were getting near to where Etain was, Midhir sent three times twenty beautiful women, having all of them the appearance of Etain, and he bade the king choose her out from among them. And the first he chose was his own daughter Esa. But then Etain called to him, and he knew her, and he brought her home to Teamhair.

And Eochaid gave his daughter Esa her choice of a place for herself. And she chose it, and made a rath there, that got the name of Rath Esa. And from it she could see three notable places, the Hill of the Sidhe in Broga, and the Hill of the Hostages in Teamhair, and Dun Crimthain on Beinn Edair.

But there was great anger on Midhir and his people because of their hill being attacked and dug into. And it was in revenge for that insult they brought Conaire, High King of Ireland, that was grandson of Eochaid and of Etain, to his death afterwards at Da Derga's Inn.

CHAPTER VIII. MANANNAN

Now as to Manannan the Proud, son of Lir, after he had made places for the rest of the Tuatha de Danaan to live in, he went away out of Ireland himself. And some said he was dead, and that he got his death by Uillenn Faebarderg, of the Red Edge, in battle. And it is what they said, that the battle was fought at Magh Cuilenn, and that Manannan was buried standing on his feet, and no sooner was he buried than a great lake burst up under his feet in the place that was a red bog till that time. And the lake got the name of Loch Orbson, from one of the names of Manannan. And it was said that red Badb was glad and many women were sorry at that battle.

But he had many places of living, and he was often heard of in Ireland after. It was he sent a messenger to Etain, mother of Conaire the High King, the time she was hidden in the cowherd's house. And it was he brought up Deirdre's children in Emhain of the Apple Trees, and it was said of that place, "a house of peace is the hill of the Sidhe of Emhain." And it was he taught Diarmuid of the Fianna the use of weapons, and it was he taught Cuchulain the use of the Gae Bulg, and some say it was he was Deirdre's father, and that he brought Conchubar, king of Ulster, to the place she was hidden, and he running with the appearance of a hare before the hounds of the men of Ulster to bring them there.

And it is what they say, that the time Conchubar had brought the sons of Usnach to Emain Macha, and could not come at them to kill them because of their bravery, it was to Manannan he went for help. And Manannan said he would give him no help, for he had told him at the time he brought Deirdre away that she would be the cause of the breaking up of his kingdom, and he took her away in spite of him. But Conchubar asked him to put blindness for a while on the sons of Usnach, or the whole army would be destroyed with their blows. So after a while he consented to that. And when the sons of Usnach came out again against the army of Ulster, the blindness came on them, and it was at one another they struck, not seeing who was near them, and it was by one another's hands they fell. But more say Manannan had no hand in it, and that it was Cathbad, the Druid, put a sea about them and brought them to their death by his enchantments.

And some say Culain, the Smith, that gave his name to Cuchulain afterwards, was Manannan himself, for he had many shapes.

Anyway, before Culain came to Ulster, he was living in the Island of Falga, that was one of Manannan's places. And one time before Conchubar came into the kingdom, he went to ask advice of a Druid, and the Druid bade him to go to the Island of Falga and to ask Culain, the smith he would find there, to make arms for him. So Conchubar did so, and the smith promised to make a sword and spear and shield for him.

And while he was working at them Conchubar went out one morning early to walk on the strand, and there he saw a sea-woman asleep on the shore. And he put bonds on her in her sleep, the way she would not make her escape. But when she awoke and saw what had happened, she asked him to set her free. "And I am Tiabhal," she said, "one of the queens of the sea. And bid Culain," she said, "that is making your shield for you, to put my likeness on it and my name about it. And whenever you will go into a battle with that shield the strength of your enemies will lessen, and your own strength and the strength of your people will increase."

So Conchubar let her go, and bade the smith do as she had told him. And when he went back to Ireland he got the victory wherever he brought that shield.

And he sent for Culain then, and offered him a place on the plains of Muirthemne. And whether he was or was not Manannan, it is likely he gave Cuchulain good teaching the time he stopped with him there after killing his great dog.

Manannan had good hounds one time, but they went hunting after a pig that was destroying the whole country, and making a desert of it. And they followed it till they came to a lake, and there it turned on them, and no hound of them escaped alive, but they were all drowned or maimed. And the pig made for an island then, that got the name of Muc-inis, the Pigs Island afterwards; and the lake got the name of Loch Conn, the Lake of the Hounds.

And it was through Manannan the wave of Tuaig, one of the three great waves of Ireland, got its name, and this is the way that happened.

There was a young girl of the name of Tuag, a fosterling of Conaire the High King, was reared in Teamhair, and a great company of the daughters of the kings of Ireland were put about her to protect her, the way she would be kept for a king's asking. But Manannan sent Fer Ferdiad, of the Tuatha de Danaan, that was a pupil of his own and a Druid, in the shape of a woman of his own household, and he went where Tuag was, and sang a sleep-spell over her, and brought her away to Inver Glas. And there he laid her down while he went looking for a boat, that he might bring her away in her sleep to the Land of the Ever-Living Women. But a wave of the flood-tide came over the girl, and she was drowned, and Manannan killed Fer Ferdiad in his anger.

And one time Manannan's cows came up out of the sea at Baile Cronin, three of them, a red, and a white, and a black, and the people that were there saw them standing on the strand for a while, as if thinking, and then they all walked up together, side by side, from the strand. And at that time there were no roads in Ireland, and there was great wonder on the people when they saw a good wide road ready before the three cows to walk on. And when they got about a mile from the sea they parted; the white cow went to the north-west, towards Luimnech, and the red cow went to the south-west, and on round the coast of Ireland, and the black cow went to the north-east, towards Lis Mor, in the district of Portlairge, and a road opened before each of them, that is to be seen to this day.

And some say it was Manannan went to Finn and the Fianna in the form of the Gilla Decair, the Bad Servant, and brought them away to Land-under-Wave. Anyway, he used often to go hunting with them on Cnoc Aine, and sometimes he came to their help.

CHAPTER IX. MANANNAN AT PLAY

And it was he went playing tricks through Ireland a long time after that again, the time he got the name of O'Donnell's Kern. And it is the way it happened, Aodh Dubh O'Donnell was holding a feast one time in Bel-atha Senaig, and his people were boasting of the goodness of his house and of his musicians.

And while they were talking, they saw a clown coming towards them, old striped clothes he had, and puddle water splashing in his shoes, and his sword sticking out naked behind him, and his ears through the old cloak that was over his head, and in his hand he had three spears of hollywood scorched and blackened.

He wished O'Donnell good health, and O'Donnell did the same to him, and asked where did he come from. "It is where I am," he said, "I slept last night at Dun Monaidhe, of the King of Alban; I am a day in Ile, a day in Cionn-tire, a day in Rachlainn, a day in the Watchman's Seat in Slieve Fuad; a pleasant, rambling, wandering man I am, and it is with yourself I am now, O'Donnell," he said. "Let the gate-keeper be brought to me," said O'Donnell. And when the gate-keeper came, he asked was it he let in this man, and the gate-keeper said he did not, and that he never saw him before. "Let him off, O'Donnell," said the stranger, "for it was as easy for me to come in, as it will be to me to go out again." There was wonder on them all then, any man to have come into the house without passing the gate.

The musicians began playing their music then, and all the best musicians of the country were there at the time, and they played very sweet tunes on their harps. But the strange man called out: "By my word, O'Donnell, there was never a noise of hammers beating on iron in any bad place was so bad to listen to as this noise your people are making."

With that he took a harp, and he made music that would put women in their pains and wounded men after a battle into a sweet sleep, and it is what O'Donnell said: "Since I first heard talk of the music of the Sidhe that is played in the hills and under the earth below us, I never heard better music than your own. And it is a very sweet player you are," he said. "One day I am sweet, another day I am sour," said the clown.

Then O'Donnell bade his people to bring him up to sit near himself. "I have no mind to do that," he said; "I would sooner be as I am, an ugly clown, making sport for high-up people." Then O'Donnell sent him down clothes, a hat and a striped shirt and a coat, but he would not have them. "I have no mind," he said, "to let high-up people be making a boast of giving them to me."

They were afraid then he might go from them, and they put twenty armed horsemen and twenty men on foot to hold him back from leaving the house, and as many more outside at the gate, for they knew him not to be a man of this world. "What are these men for?" said he. "They are to keep you here," said O'Donnell. "By my word, it is not with you I will be eating my supper to-morrow," he said, "but at Cnoc Aine, where Seaghan, Son of the Earl is, in Desmumain." "If I find you giving one stir out of yourself, between this and morning, I will knock you into a round lump there on the ground," said O'Donnell.

But at that the stranger took up the harp again, and he made the same sweet music as before. And when they were all listening to him, he called out to the men outside: "Here I am coming, and watch me well now or you will lose me." When the men that were watching the gate heard that, they lifted up their axes to strike at him, but in their haste it was at one another they struck, till they were all lying stretched in blood. Then the clown said to the gate-keeper: "Let you ask twenty cows and a hundred of free land of O'Donnell as a fee for bringing his people back to life. And take this herb," he said, "and rub it in the mouth of each man of them, and he will rise up whole and well again." So the gate-keeper did that, and he got the cows and the land from O'Donnell, and he brought all the people to life again.

Now at that time Seaghan, Son of the Earl, was holding a gathering on the green in front of his dun, and he saw the same man coming towards him, and dressed in the same way, and the water splashing in his shoes. But when he asked who was he, he gave himself the name of a very learned man, Duartane O'Duartane, and he said it was by Ess Ruadh he was come, and by Ceiscorainn and from that to Corrslieve, and to Magh Lorg of the Dagda, and into the district of Hy'Conaill Gabhra, "till I came to yourself," he said, "by Cruachan of Magh Ai." So they brought him into the house, and gave him wine for drinking and water for washing his feet, and he slept till the rising of the sun on the morrow. And at that time Seaghan, Son of the Earl, came to visit him, and he said: "It is a long sleep you had, and there is no wonder in that, and your journey so long yesterday. But I often heard of your learning in books and of your skill on the harp, and I would like to hear you this morning," he said. "I am good in those arts indeed," said the stranger. So they brought him a book, but he could not read a word of it, and then they brought him a harp, and he could not play any tune. "It is likely your reading and your music are gone from you," said Seaghan; and he made a little rann on him, saying it was a strange thing Duartane O'Duartane that had such a great name not to be able to read a line of a book, or even to remember one. But when the stranger heard how he was being mocked at, he took up the book, and read from the top to the bottom of the page very well and in a sweet-sounding voice. And after that he took the harp and played and sang the same way he did at O'Donnell's house the day before. "It is a very sweet man of learning you are," said Seaghan. "One day I am sweet, another day I am sour," said the stranger.

They walked out together then on Cnoc Aine, but while they were talking there, the stranger was gone all of a minute, and Seaghan, Son of the Earl, could not see where he went.

And after that he went on, and he reached Sligach just at the time O'Conchubar was setting out with the men of Connacht to avenge the Connacht hag's basket on the hag of Munster. And this time he gave himself the name of the Gilla Decair, the Bad Servant. And he joined with the men of Connacht, and they went over the Sionnan westward into Munster, and there they hunted and drove every creature that could be made travel, cattle and horses and flocks, into one place, till they got the hornless bull of the Munster hag and her two speckled cows, and O'Conchubar brought them away to give to the Connacht hag in satisfaction for her basket.

But the men of Munster made an attack on them as they were going back; and the Gilla Decair asked O'Conchubar would he sooner have the cows driven, or have the Munster men checked, and he said he would sooner have the Munster men checked. So the Gilla Decair turned on them, and with his bow and twenty-four arrows he kept them back till O'Conchubar and his people were safe out of their reach in Connacht.

But he took some offence then, on account of O'Conchubar taking the first drink himself when they came to his house, and not giving it to him, that had done so much, and he took his leave and went from them on the moment.

After that he went to where Tadg O'Cealaigh was, and having his old striped clothes and his old shoes as before. And when they asked him what art he had, he said: "I am good at tricks. And if you will give me five marks I will show you a trick," he said. "I will give that," said Tadg.

With that the stranger put three rushes on the palm of his hand. "I will blow away the middle rush now," he said, "and the other two will stop as they are." So they told him to do that, and he put the tops of two of his fingers on the two outside rushes, and blew the middle one away. "There is a trick now for you, Tadg O'Cealaigh," he said then. "By my word, that is not a bad trick," said O'Cealaigh. But one of his men said: "That there may be no good luck with him that did it. And give me the half of that money now, Tadg," he said, "and I will do the same trick for you myself." "I will give you the half of what I got if you will do it," said the stranger. So the other put the rushes on his hand, but if he did, when he tried to do the trick, his two finger-tips went through the palm of his hand. "Ob-Ob-Ob!" said the stranger, "that is not the way I did the trick. But as you have lost the money," he said, "I will heal you again."

"I could do another trick for you," he said; "I could wag the ear on one side of my head and the ear on the other side would stay still." "Do it then," said O'Cealaigh. So the man of tricks took hold of one of his ears and wagged it up and down. "That is a good trick indeed," said O'Cealaigh. "I will show you another one now," he said.

With that he took from his bag a thread of silk, and gave a cast of it up into the air, that it was made fast to a cloud. And then he took a hare out of the same bag, and it ran up the thread; and then took out a little dog and laid it on after the hare, and it followed yelping on its track; and after that again he brought out a little serving-boy and bade him to follow dog and hare up the thread. Then out of another bag he had with him he brought out a beautiful, well-dressed young woman, and bade her to follow after the hound and the boy, and to take care and not let the hare be torn by the dog. She went up then quickly after them, and it was a delight to Tadg O'Cealaigh to be looking at them and to be listening to the sound of the hunt going on in the air.

All was quiet then for a long time, and then the man of tricks said: "I am afraid there is some bad work going on up there." "What is that?" said O'Cealaigh. "I am thinking," said he, "the hound might be eating the hare, and the serving-boy courting the girl." "It is likely enough they are," said O'Cealaigh. With that the stranger drew in the thread, and it is what he found, the boy making love to the girl and the hound chewing the bones of the hare. There was great anger on the man of tricks when he saw that, and he took his sword and struck the head off the boy. "I do not like a thing of that sort to be done in my presence," said Tadg O'Cealaigh. "If it did not please you, I can set all right again," said the stranger. And with that he took up the head and made a cast of it at the body, and it joined to it, and the young man stood up, but if he did his face was turned backwards. "It would be better for him to be dead than to be living like that," said O'Cealaigh. When the man of tricks heard that, he took hold of the boy and twisted his head straight, and he was as well as before.

And with that the man of tricks vanished, and no one saw where was he gone.

That is the way Manannan used to be going round Ireland, doing tricks and wonders. And no one could keep him in any place, and if he was put on a gallows itself, he would be found safe in the house after, and some other man on the gallows in his place. But he did no harm, and those that would be put to death by him, he would bring them to life again with a herb out of his bag.

And all the food he would use would be a vessel of sour milk and a few crab-apples. And there never was any music sweeter than the music he used to be playing.

CHAPTER X. HIS CALL TO BRAN

And there were some that went to Manannan's country beyond the sea, and that gave an account of it afterwards.

One time Bran, son of Febal, was out by himself near his dun, and he heard music behind him. And it kept always after him, and at last he fell asleep with the sweetness of the sound. And when he awoke from his sleep he saw beside him a branch of silver, and it having white blossoms, and the whiteness of the silver was the same as the whiteness of the blossoms.

And he brought the branch in his hand into the royal house, and when all his people were with him they saw a woman with strange clothing standing in the house.

And she began to make a song for Bran, and all the people were looking at her and listening to her, and it is what she said:

"I bring a branch of the apple-tree from Emhain, from the far island around which are the shining horses of the Son of Lir. A delight of the eyes is the plain where the hosts hold their games; curragh racing against chariot in the White Silver Plain to the south.

"There are feet of white bronze under it, shining through life and time; a comely level land through the length of the world's age, and many blossoms falling on it.

"There is an old tree there with blossoms, and birds calling from among them; every colour is shining there, delight is common, and music, in the Gentle-Voiced Plain, in the Silver Cloud Plain to the south.

"Keening is not used, or treachery, in the tilled familiar land; there is nothing hard or rough, but sweet music striking on the ear.

"To be without grief, without sorrow, without death, without any sickness, without weakness; that is the sign of Emhain; it is not common wonder that is.

"There is nothing to liken its mists to, the sea washes the wave against the land; brightness falls from its hair.

"There are riches, there are treasures of every colour in the Gentle Land, the Bountiful Land. Sweet music to be listening to; the best of wine to drink.

"Golden chariots in the Plain of the Sea, rising up to the sun with the tide; silver chariots and bronze chariots on the Plain of Sports.

"Gold-yellow horses on the strand, and crimson horses, and others with wool on their backs, blue like the colour of the sky.

"It is a day of lasting weather, silver is dropping on the land; a pure white cliff on the edge of the sea, getting its warmth from the sun.

"The host race over the Plain of Sports; it is beautiful and not weak their game is; death or the ebbing of the tide will not come to them in the Many-Coloured Land.

"There will come at sunrise a fair man, lighting up the level lands; he rides upon the plain that is beaten by the waves, he stirs the sea till it is like blood.

"An army will come over the clear sea, rowing to the stone that is in sight, that a hundred sounds of music come from.

"It sings a song to the army; it is not sad through the length of time; it increases music with hundreds singing together; they do not look for death or the ebb-tide.

"There are three times fifty far islands in the ocean to the west of us, and every one of them twice or three times more than Ireland.

"It is not to all of you I am speaking, though I have made all these wonders known. Let Bran listen from the crowd of the world to all the wisdom that has been told him.

"Do not fall upon a bed of sloth; do not be overcome by drunkenness; set out on your voyage over the clear sea, and you may chance to come to the Land of Women."

With that the woman went from them, and they did not know where she went. And she brought away her branch with her, for it leaped into her hand from Bran's hand, and he had not the strength to hold it.

Then on the morrow Bran set out upon the sea, and three companies of nine along with him; and one of his foster-brothers and comrades was set over each company of nine.

And when they had been rowing for two days and two nights, they saw a man coming towards them in a chariot, over the sea. And the man made himself known to them, and he said that he was Manannan, son of Lir.

And then Manannan spoke to him in a song, and it is what he said:

"It is what Bran thinks, he is going in his curragh over the wonderful, beautiful clear sea; but to me, from far off in my chariot, it is a flowery plain he is riding on.

"What is a clear sea to the good boat Bran is in, is a happy plain with many flowers to me in my two-wheeled chariot.

"It is what Bran sees, many waves beating across the clear sea; it is what I myself see, red flowers without any fault.

"The sea-horses are bright in summer-time, as far as Bran's eyes can reach; there is a wood of beautiful acorns under the head of your little boat.

"A wood with blossom and with fruit, that has the smell of wine; a wood without fault, without withering, with leaves of the colour of gold.

"Let Bran row on steadily, it is not far to the Land of Women; before the setting of the sun you will reach Emhain, of many-coloured hospitality."

With that Bran went from him; and after a while he saw an island, and he rowed around it, and there was a crowd on it, wondering at them, and laughing; and they were all looking at Bran and at his people, but they would not stop to talk with them, but went on giving out gusts of laughter. Bran put one of his men on the island then, but he joined with the others, and began to stare the same way as the men of the island. And Bran went on rowing round about the island; and whenever they went past his own man, his comrades would speak to him, but he would not answer them, but would only stare and wonder at them. So they went away and left him on that island that is called the Island of Joy.

It was not long after that they reached to the Land of Women. And they saw the chief one of the women at the landing-place, and it is what she said: "Come hither to land, Bran, son of Febal, it is welcome your coming is." But Bran did not dare to go on shore. Then the woman threw a ball of thread straight to him, and he caught it in his hand, and it held fast to his palm, and the woman kept the thread in her own hand, and she pulled the curragh to the landing-place.

On that they went into a grand house, where there was a bed for every couple, three times nine beds. And the food that was put on every dish never came to an end, and they had every sort of food and of drink they wished for.

And it seemed to them they were only a year there when the desire of home took hold on one of them, Nechtan, son of Collbrain, and his kinsmen were begging and praying Bran to go back with him to Ireland. The woman said there would be repentance on them if they went; but in spite of that they set out in the end. And the woman said to them not to touch the land when they would come to Ireland, and she bade them to visit and to bring with them the man they left in the Island of Joy.

So they went on towards Ireland till they came to a place called Srub Bruin. And there were people on the strand that asked them who they were that were coming over the sea. And Bran said: "I am Bran, son of Febal." But the people said: "We know of no such man, though the voyage of Bran is in our very old stories."

Then Nechtan, son of Collbrain, made a leap out of the curragh, and no sooner did he touch the shore of Ireland than he was a heap of ashes, the same as if he had been in the earth through hundreds of years.

And then Bran told the whole story of his wanderings to the people, from the beginning. And after that he bade them farewell, and his wanderings from that time are not known.

CHAPTER XI. HIS THREE CALLS TO CORMAC

And another that went to Manannan's country was Cormac, grandson of Conn, King of Teamhair, and this is the way it happened. He was by himself in Teamhair one time, and he saw an armed man coming towards him, quiet, with high looks, and having grey hair; a shirt ribbed with gold thread next his skin, broad shoes of white bronze between his feet and the ground, a shining branch, having nine apples of red gold, on his shoulder. And it is delightful the sound of that branch was, and no one on earth would keep in mind any want, or trouble, or tiredness, when that branch was shaken for him; and whatever trouble there might be on him, he would forget it at the sound.

Then Cormac and the armed man saluted one another, and Cormac asked where did he come from. "I come," he said, "from a country where there is nothing but truth, and where there is neither age nor withering away, nor heaviness, nor sadness, nor jealousy nor envy, nor pride." "That is not so with us," said Cormac, "and I would be well pleased to have your friendship," he said. "I am well pleased to give it," said the stranger. "Give me your branch along with it," said Cormac. "I will give it," said the stranger, "if you will give me the three gifts I ask in return." "I will give them to you indeed," said Cormac.

Then the strange man left the branch and went away, and Cormac did not know where was he gone to.

He went back then into the royal house, and there was wonder on all the people when they saw the branch. And he shook it at them, and it put them all asleep from that day to the same time on the morrow.

At the end of a year the strange man came back again, and he asked for the first of his three requests. "You will get it," said Cormac. "I will take your daughter, Aille, to-day," said the stranger.

So he brought away the girl with him, and the women of Ireland gave three loud cries after the king's daughter. But Cormac shook the branch at them, until it put away sorrow from them, and put them all into their sleep.

That day month the stranger came again, and he brought Cormac's son, Carpre Lifecar, away with him. There was crying and lamenting without end in Teamhair after the boy, and on that night no one ate or slept, and they were all under grief and very downhearted. But when Cormac shook the branch their sorrow went from them.

Then the stranger came the third time, and Cormac asked him what did he want. "It is your wife, Ethne, I am asking this time," he said. And he went away then, bringing Ethne, the queen, along with him.

But Cormac would not bear that, and he went after them, and all his people were following him. But in the middle of the Plain of the Wall, a thick mist came on them, and when it was gone, Cormac found himself alone on a great plain. And he saw a great dun in the middle of the plain, with a wall of bronze around it, and in the dun a house of white silver, and it half thatched with the white wings of birds. And there was a great troop of the Riders of the Sidhe all about the house, and their arms full of white birds' wings for thatching. But as soon as they would put on the thatch, a blast of wind would come and carry it away again.

Then he saw a man kindling a fire, and he used to throw a thick oak-tree upon it. And when he would come back with a second tree, the first one would be burned out. "I will be looking at you no longer," Cormac said then, "for there is no one here to tell me your story, and I think I could find good sense in your meanings if I understood them," he said.

Then he went on to where there was another dun, very large and royal, and another wall of bronze around it, and four houses within it. And he went in and saw a great king's house, having beams of bronze and walls of silver, and its thatch of the wings of white birds. And then he saw on the green a shining well, and five streams flowing from it, and the armies drinking water in turn, and the nine lasting purple hazels of Buan growing over it. And they were dropping their nuts into the water, and the five salmon would catch them and send their husks floating down the streams. And the sound of the flowing of those streams is sweeter than any music that men sing.

Then he went into the palace, and he found there waiting for him a man and a woman, very tall, and having clothes of many colours. The man was beautiful as to shape, and his face wonderful to look at; and as to the young woman that was with him, she was the loveliest of all the women of the world, and she having yellow hair and a golden helmet. And there was a bath there, and heated stones going in and out of the water of themselves, and Cormac bathed himself in it.

"Rise up, man of the house," the woman said after that, "for this is a comely traveller is come to us; and if you have one kind of food or meat better than another, let it be brought in." The man rose up then and he said: "I have but seven pigs, but I could feed the whole world with them, for the pig that is killed and eaten to-day, you will find it alive again to-morrow."

Another man came into the house then, having an axe in his right hand, and a log in his left hand, and a pig behind him.

"It is time to make ready," said the man of the house, "for we have a high guest with us to-day."

Then the man struck the pig and killed it, and he cut the logs and made a fire and put the pig on it in a cauldron. "It is time for you to turn it," said the master of the house after a while. "There would be no use doing that," said the man, "for never and never will the pig be boiled until a truth is told for every quarter of it." "Then let you tell yours first," said the master of the house. "One day," said the man, "I found another man's cows in my land, and I brought them with me into a cattle pound. The owner of the cows followed me, and he said he would give me a reward to let the cows go free. So I gave them back to him, and he gave me an axe, and when a pig is to be killed, it is with the axe it is killed, and the log is cut with it, and there is enough wood to boil the pig, and enough for the palace besides. And that is not all, for the log is found whole again in the morning. And from that time till now, that is the way they are."

"It is true indeed that story is," said the man of the house.

They turned the pig in the cauldron then, and but one quarter of it was found to be cooked. "Let us tell another true story," they said. "I will tell one," said the master of the house. "Ploughing time had come, and when we had a mind to plough that field outside, it is the way we found it, ploughed, and harrowed, and sowed with wheat. When we had a mind to reap it, the wheat was found in the haggard, all in one thatched rick. We have been using it from that day to this, and it is no bigger and no less."

Then they turned the pig, and another quarter was found to be ready. "It is my turn now," said the woman. "I have seven cows," she said, "and seven sheep. And the milk of the seven cows would satisfy the whole of the men of the world, if they were in the plain drinking it, and it is enough for all the people of the Land of Promise, and it is from the wool of the seven sheep all the clothes they wear are made." And at that story the third quarter of the pig was boiled.

"If these stories are true," said Cormac to the man of the house, "you are Manannan, and this is Manannan's wife; for no one on the whole ridge of the world owns these treasures but himself. It was to the Land of Promise he went to look for that woman, and he got those seven cows with her."

They said to Cormac that it was his turn now. So Cormac told them how his wife, and his son, and his daughter, had been brought away from him, and how he himself had followed them till he came to that place.

And with that the whole pig was boiled, and they cut it up, and Cormac's share was put before him. "I never used a meal yet," said he, "having two persons only in my company." The man of the house began singing to him then, and put him asleep. And when he awoke, he saw fifty armed men, and his son, and his wife, and his daughter, along with them. There was great gladness and courage on him then, and ale and food were given out to them all. And there was a gold cup put in the hand of the master of the house, and Cormac was wondering at it, for the number of the shapes on it, and for the strangeness of the work. "There is a stranger thing yet about it," the man said; "let three lying words be spoken under it, and it will break into three, and then let three true words be spoken under it, and it will be as good as before." So he said three lying words under it, and it broke in three pieces. "It is best to speak truth now under it," he said, "and to mend it. And I give my word, Cormac," he said, "that until to-day neither your wife or your daughter has seen the face of a man since they were brought away from you out of Teamhair, and that your son has never seen the face of a woman." And with that the cup was whole again on the moment. "Bring away your wife and your children with you now," he said, "and this cup along with them, the way you will have it for judging between truth and untruth. And I will leave the branch with you for music and delight, but on the day of your death they will be taken from you again." "And I myself," he said, "am Manannan, son of Lir, King of the Land of Promise, and I brought you here by enchantments that you might be with me to-night in friendship.

"And the Riders you saw thatching the house," he said, "are the men of art and poets, and all that look for a fortune in Ireland, putting together cattle and riches. For when they go out, all that they leave in their houses goes to nothing, and so they go on for ever.

"And the man you saw kindling the fire," he said, "is a young lord that is more liberal than he can afford, and every one else is served while he is getting the feast ready, and every one else profiting by it.

"And the well you saw is the Well of Knowledge, and the streams are the five streams through which all knowledge goes. And no one will have knowledge who does not drink a draught out of the well itself or out of the streams. And the people of many arts are those who drink from them all."

And on the morning of the morrow, when Cormac rose up, he found himself on the green of Teamhair, and his wife, and his son, and his daughter, along with him, and he having his branch and his cup. And it was given the name of Cormac's Cup, and it used to judge between truth and falsehood among the Gael. But it was not left in Ireland after the night of Cormac's death, as Manannan had foretold him.

CHAPTER XII. CLIODNA'S WAVE

And it was in the time of the Fianna of Ireland that Ciabhan of the Curling Hair, the king of Ulster's son, went to Manannan's country.

Ciabhan now was the most beautiful of the young men of the world at that time, and he was as far beyond all other kings' sons as the moon is beyond the stars. And Finn liked him well, but the rest of the Fianna got to be tired of him because there was not a woman of their women, wed or unwed, but gave him her love. And Finn had to send him away at the last, for he was in dread of the men of the Fianna because of the greatness of their jealousy.

So Ciabhan went on till he came to the Strand of the Cairn, that is called now the Strand of the Strong Man, between Dun Sobairce and the sea. And there he saw a curragh, and it having a narrow stern of copper. And Ciabhan got into the curragh, and his people said: "Is it to leave Ireland you have a mind, Ciabhan?" "It is indeed," he said, "for in Ireland I get neither shelter or protection." He bade farewell to his people then, and he left them very sorrowful after him, for to part with him was like the parting of life from the body.

And Ciabhan went on in the curragh, and great white shouting waves rose up about him, every one of them the size of a mountain; and the beautiful speckled salmon that are used to stop in the sand and the shingle rose up to the sides of the curragh, till great dread came on Ciabhan, and he said: "By my word, if it was on land I was I could make a better fight for myself"

And he was in this danger till he saw a rider coming towards him on a dark grey horse having a golden bridle, and he would be under the sea for the length of nine waves, and he would rise with the tenth wave, and no wet on him at all. And he said: "What reward would you give to whoever would bring you out of this great danger?" "Is there anything in my hand worth offering you?" said Ciabhan. "There is," said the rider, "that you would give your service to whoever would give you his help." Ciabhan agreed to that, and he put his hand into the rider's hand.

With that the rider drew him on to the horse, and the curragh came on beside them till they reached to the shore of Tir Tairngaire, the Land of Promise. They got off the horse there, and came to Loch Luchra, the Lake of the Dwarfs, and to Manannan's city, and a feast was after being made ready there, and comely serving-boys were going round with smooth horns, and playing on sweet-sounding harps till the whole house was filled with the music.

Then there came in clowns, long-snouted, long-heeled, lean and bald and red, that used to be doing tricks in Manannan's house. And one of these tricks was, a man of them to take nine straight willow rods, and to throw them up to the rafters of the house, and to catch them again as they came down, and he standing on one leg, and having but one hand free. And they thought no one could do that trick but themselves, and they were used to ask strangers to do it, the way they could see them fail.

So this night when one of them had done the trick, he came up to Ciabhan, that was beyond all the Men of Dea or the Sons of the Gael that were in the house, in shape and in walk and in name, and he put the nine rods in his hand. And Ciabhan stood up and he did the feat before them all, the same as if he had never learned to do any other thing.

Now Gebann, that was a chief Druid in Manannan's country, had a daughter, Cliodna of the Fair Hair, that had never given her love to any man. But when she saw Ciabhan she gave him her love, and she agreed to go away with him on the morrow.

And they went down to the landing-place and got into a curragh, and they went on till they came to Teite's Strand in the southern part of Ireland. It was from Teite Brec the Freckled the strand got its name, that went there one time for a wave game, and three times fifty young girls with her, and they were all drowned in that place.

And as to Ciabhan, he came on shore, and went looking for deer, as was right, under the thick branches of the wood; and he left the young girl in the boat on the strand.

But the people of Manannan's house came after them, having forty ships. And

Iuchnu, that was in the curragh with Cliodna, did treachery, and he played music to her till she lay down in the boat and fell asleep. And then a great wave came up on the strand and swept her away.

And the wave got its name from Cliodna of the Fair Hair, that will be long remembered.

CHAPTER XIII. HIS CALL TO CONNLA

And it is likely it was Manannan sent his messenger for Connla of the Red Hair the time he went away out of Ireland, for it is to his country Connla was brought; and this is the way he got the call.

It chanced one day he was with his father Conn, King of Teamhair, on the Hill of Uisnach, and he saw a woman having wonderful clothing coming towards him. "Where is it you come from?" he asked her. "I come," she said, "from Tir-nam-Beo, the Land of the Ever-Living Ones, where no death comes. We use feasts that are lasting," she said, "and we do every kind thing without quarrelling, and we are called the people of the Sidhe." "Who are you speaking to, boy?" said Conn to him then, for no one saw the strange woman but only Connla. "He is speaking to a high woman that death or old age will never come to," she said. "I am asking him to come to Magh Mell, the Pleasant Plain where the triumphant king is living, and there he will be a king for ever without sorrow or fret. Come with me, Connla of the Red Hair," she said, "of the fair freckled neck and of the ruddy cheek; come with me, and your body will not wither from its youth and its comeliness for ever."

They could all hear the woman's words then, though they could not see her, and it is what Conn said to Coran his Druid: "Help me, Coran, you that sing spells of the great arts. There is an attack made on me that is beyond my wisdom and beyond my power, I never knew so strong an attack since the first day I was a king. There is an unseen figure fighting with me; she is using her strength against me to bring away my beautiful son; the call of a woman is bringing him away from the hands of the king."

Then Coran, the Druid, began singing spells against the woman of the Sidhe, the way no one would hear her voice, and Connla could not see her any more. But when she was being driven away by the spells of the Druid, she threw an apple to

Connla.

And through the length of a month from that time, Connla used no other food nor drink but that apple, for he thought no other food or drink worth the using. And for all he ate of it, the apple grew no smaller, but was whole all the while. And there was great trouble on Connla on account of the woman he had seen.

And at the end of a month Connla was at his father's side in Magh Archomnim, and he saw the same woman coming towards him, and it is what she said: "It is a high place indeed Connla has among dying people, and death before him. But the Ever-Living Living Ones," she said, "are asking you to take the sway over the people of Tethra, for they are looking at you every day in the gatherings of your country among your dear friends."

When Conn, the king, heard her voice, he said to his people: "Call Coran, the Druid to me, for I hear the sound of the woman's voice again." But on that she said: "O Conn, fighter of a hundred, it is little love and little respect the wonderful tribes of Traig Mor, the Great Strand, have for Druids; and where its law comes, it scatters the spells on their lips."

Then Conn looked to his son Connla to see what he would say, and Connla said: "My own people are dearer to me than any other thing, yet sorrow has taken hold of me because of this woman." Then the woman spoke to him again, and it is what she said: "Come now into my shining ship, if you will come to the Plain of Victory. There is another country it would not be worse for you to look for; though the bright sun is going down, we shall reach to that country before night. That is the country that delights the mind of every one that turns to me. There is no living race in it but women and girls only."

And when the woman had ended her song, Connla made a leap from his people into the shining boat, and they saw him sailing away from them far off and as if in a mist, as far as their eyes could see. It is away across the sea they went, and they have never come back again, and only the gods know where was it they went.

CHAPTER XIV. TADG IN MANANNAN'S ISLANDS

And another that went to the Land of the Ever-Living Ones, but that came back again, was Tadg, son of Cian, son of Olioll; and this is the way that happened.

It was one time Tadg was going his next heir's round, into the west of Munster, and his two brothers, Airnelach and Eoghan, along with him. And Cathmann, son of Tabarn, that was king of the beautiful country of Fresen that lay to the south-east of the Great Plain, was searching the sea for what he could find just at that time, and nine of his ships with him. And they landed at Beire do Bhunadas, to the west of Munster, and the country had no stir in it, and so they slipped ashore, and no one took notice of them till all were surrounded, both men and cattle. And Tadg's wife Liban, daughter of Conchubar Abratrudh of the Red Brows, and his two brothers, and a great many of the people of Munster, were taken by the foreigners and brought away to the coasts of Fresen. And Cathmann took Liban to be his own wife, and he put hardship on Tadg's two brothers: Eoghan he put to work a common ferry across a channel of the coast, and Airnelach to cut firing and to keep up fires for all the people; and all the food they got was barley seed and muddy water.

And as to Tadg himself, it was only by his courage and the use of his sword he made his escape, but there was great grief and discouragement on him, his wife and his brothers to have been brought away. But he had forty of his fighting men left that had each killed a man of the foreigners, and they had brought one in alive. And this man told them news of the country he came from. And when Tadg heard that, he made a plan in his own head, and he gave orders for a curragh to be built that would be fit for a long voyage. Very strong it was, and forty ox-hides on it of hard red leather, that was after being soaked in bark. And it was well fitted with masts, and oars, and pitch, and everything that was wanting. And they put every sort of meat, and drink, and of clothes in it, that would last them through the length of a year.

When all was ready, and the curragh out in the tide, Tadg said to his people: "Let us set out now on the high sea, looking for our own people that are away from us this long time."

They set out then over the stormy, heavy flood, till at last they saw no land before them or behind them, but only the hillsides of the great sea. And farther on again they heard the singing of a great flock of unknown birds; and pleasant white-bellied salmon were leaping about the curragh on every side, and seals, very big and dark, were coming after them, breaking through the shining wash of the oars; and great whales after them again, so that the young men liked to be looking at them, for they were not used to see the like before.

They went on rowing through twenty days and twenty nights, and at the end of that time they got sight of a high land, having a smooth coast. And when they reached it they all landed, and they pulled up the curragh and lit their fires, and food was given out to them, and they were not long making an end of it. They made beds for themselves then on the beautiful green grass, and enjoyed their sleep till the rising of the sun on the morrow.

Tadg rose up then and put on his arms, and went out, and thirty of his men along with him, to search the whole island.

They went all through it, but they found no living thing on it, man or beast, but only flocks of sheep. And the size of the sheep was past all telling, as big as horses they were, and the whole island was filled with their wool. And there was one great flock beyond all the others, all of very big rams, and one of them was biggest of all, nine horns he had, and he charged on Tadg's chief men, attacking them and butting at them.

There was vexation on them then, and they attacked him again, and there was a struggle between them. And at the first the ram broke through five of their shields. But Tadg took his spear that there was no escape from, and made a lucky cast at the ram and killed him. And they brought the ram to the curragh and made it ready for the young men to eat, and they stopped three nights on the island, and every night it was a sheep they had for their food. And they gathered a good share of the wool and put it in the curragh because of the wonder and the beauty of it.

And they found the bones of very big men on the island, but whether they died of sickness or were killed by the rams they did not know.

They left that island then and went forward till they found two strange islands where there were great flocks of wonderful birds, like blackbirds, and some of them the size of eagles or of cranes, and they red with green heads on them, and the eggs they had were blue and pure crimson. And some of the men began eating the eggs, and on the moment feathers began to grow out on them. But they went bathing after that, and the feathers dropped off them again as quick as they came.

It was the foreigner they had with them gave them the course up to this time, for he had been on the same track before. But now they went on through the length of six weeks and never saw land, and he said then, "We are astray on the great ocean that has no boundaries." Then the wind with its sharp voice began to rise, and there was a noise like the tramping of feet in the sea, and it rose up into great mountains hard to climb, and there was great fear on Tadg's people, for they had never seen the like. But he began to stir them up and to rouse them, and he bade them to meet the sea like men. "Do bravery," he said, "young men of Munster, and fight for your lives against the waves that are rising up and coming at the sides of the curragh." Tadg took one side of the curragh then and his men took the other side, and he was able to pull it round against the whole twenty-nine of them, and to bale it out and keep it dry along with that. And after a while they got a fair wind and put up their sail, the way less water came into the curragh, and then the sea went down and lay flat and calm, and there were strange birds of many shapes singing around them in every part. They saw land before them then, with a good coast, and with that courage and gladness came on them.

And when they came nearer to the land they found a beautiful inver, a river's mouth, with green hills about it, and the bottom of it sandy and as bright as silver, and red-speckled salmon in it, and pleasant woods with purple tree-tops edging the stream. "It is a beautiful country this is," said Tadg, "and it would be happy for him that would be always in it; and let you pull up the ship now," he said, "and dry it out."

A score of them went forward then into the country, and a score stopped to mind the curragh. And for all the cold and discouragement and bad weather they had gone through, they felt no wish at all for food or for fire, but the sweet smell of the crimson branches in the place they were come to satisfied them. They went on through the wood, and after a while they came to an apple garden having red apples in it, and leafy oak-trees, and hazels yellow with nuts. "It is a wonder to me," said Tadg, "to find summer here, and it winter time in our own country."

It was a delightful place they were in, but they went on into another wood, very sweet smelling, and round purple berries in it, every one of them bigger than a man's head, and beautiful shining birds eating the berries, strange birds they were, having white bodies and purple heads and golden beaks. And while they were eating the berries they were singing sweet music, that would have put sick men and wounded men into their sleep.

Tadg and his men went farther on again till they came to a great smooth flowery plain with a dew of honey over it, and three steep hills on the plain, having a very strong dun on every one of them. And when they got to the nearest hill they found a white-bodied woman, the best of the women of the whole world, and it is what she said: "Your coming is welcome, Tadg, son of Cian, and there will be food and provision for you as you want it."

"I am glad of that welcome," said Tadg; "and tell me now, woman of sweet words," he said, "what is that royal dun on the hill, having walls of white marble around it?" "That is the dun of the royal line of the kings of Ireland, from Heremon, son of Miled, to Conn of the Hundred Battles, that was the last to go into it." "What is the name of this country?" Tadg said then. "It is Inislocha, the Lake Island," she said, "and there are two kings over it, Rudrach and Dergcroche, sons of Bodb." And then she told Tadg the whole story of Ireland, to the time of the coming of the Sons of the Gael. "That is well," said Tadg then, "and you have good knowledge and learning. And tell me now," he said, "who is living in that middle dun that has the colour of gold?" "It is not myself will tell you that," she said, "but go on to it yourself and you will get knowledge of it." And with that she went from them into the dun of white marble.

Tadg and his men went on then till they came to the middle dun, and there they found a queen of beautiful shape, and she wearing a golden dress. "Health to you, Tadg," she said. "I thank you for that," said Tadg. "It is a long time your coming on this journey was foretold," she said. "What is your name?" he asked then. "I am Cesair," she said, "the first that ever reached Ireland. But since I and the men that were with me came out of that dark, unquiet land, we are living for ever in this country."

"Tell me, woman," said Tadg, "who is it lives in that dun having a wall of gold about it?" "It is not hard to tell that," she said, "every king, and every chief man, and every noble person that was in a high place of all those that had power in Ireland, it is in that dun beyond they are; Parthalon and Nemed, Firbolgs and Tuatha de Danaan." "It is good knowledge and learning you have," said Tadg. "Indeed I have good knowledge of the history of the world," she said, "and this island," she said, "is the fourth paradise of the world; and as to the others, they are Inis Daleb to the south, and Inis Ercandra to the north, and Adam's Paradise in the east of the world." "Who is there living in that dun with the silver walls?" said Tadg then. "I will not tell you that, although I have knowledge of it," said the woman; "but go to the beautiful hill where it is, and you will get knowledge of it."

They went on then to the third hill, and on the top of the hill was a very beautiful resting-place, and two sweethearts there, a boy and a girl, comely and gentle. Smooth hair they had, shining like gold, and beautiful green clothes of the one sort, and any one would think them to have had the same father and mother. Gold chains they had around their necks, and bands of gold above those again. And Tadg spoke to them: "O bright, comely children," he said, "it is a pleasant place you have here." And they answered him back, and they were praising his courage and his strength and his wisdom, and they gave him their blessing.

And it is how the young man was, he had a sweet-smelling apple, having the colour of gold, in his hand, and he would eat a third part of it, and with all he would eat, it would never be less. And that was the food that nourished the two of them, and neither age or sorrow could touch them when once they had tasted it.

"Who are you yourself?" Tadg asked him then. "I am son to Conn of the Hundred Battles," he said. "Is it Connla you are?" said Tadg. "I am indeed," said the young man, "and it is this girl of many shapes that brought me here." And the girl said: "I have given him my love and my affection, and it is because of that I brought him to this place, the way we might be looking at one another for ever, and beyond that we have never gone."

"That is a beautiful thing and a strange thing," said Tadg, "and a thing to wonder at. And who is there in that grand dun with the silver walls?" he said. "There is no one at all in it," said the girl. "What is the reason of that?" said Tadg. "It is for the kings that are to rule Ireland yet," she said; "and there will be a place in it for yourself, Tadg. And come now," she said, "till you see it."

The lovers went on to the dun, and it is hardly the green grass was bent under their white feet. And Tadg and his people went along with them.

They came then to the great wonderful house that was ready for the company of the kings; it is a pleasant house that was, and any one would like to be in it. Walls of white bronze it had, set with crystal and with carbuncles, that were shining through the night as well as through the day.

Tadg looked out from the house then, and he saw to one side of him a great sheltering apple-tree, and blossoms and ripe fruit on it. "What is that apple tree beyond?" said Tadg. "It is the fruit of that tree is food for the host in this house," said the woman. "And it was an apple of that apple-tree brought Connla here to me; a good tree it is, with its white-blossomed branches, and its golden apples that would satisfy the whole house."

And then Connla and the young girl left them, and they saw coming towards them a troop of beautiful women. And there was one among them was most beautiful of all, and when she was come to them she said: "A welcome to you, Tadg." "I thank you for that welcome," said Tadg; "and tell me," he said, "who are you yourself?" "I am Cliodna of the Fair Hair," she said, "daughter of Gebann, son of Treon, of the Tuatha de Danaan, a sweetheart of Ciabhan of the Curling Hair; and it is from me Cliodna's wave on the coast of Munster got its name; and I am a long time now in this island, and it is the apples of that tree you saw that we use for food." And Tadg was well pleased to be listening to her talk, but after a while he said: "It is best for us to go on now to look for our people." "We will be well pleased if you stop longer with us," said the woman.

And while she was saying those words they saw three beautiful birds coming to them, one of them blue and his head crimson, and one was crimson and his head green, and the third was speckled and his head the colour of gold, and they lit on the great apple-tree, and every bird of them ate an apple, and they sang sweet music then, that would put sick men into their sleep.

"Those birds will go with you," Cliodna said then; "they will give you guidance on your way, and they will make music for you, and there will be neither sorrow or sadness on you, by land or by sea, till you come to Ireland. And bring away this beautiful green cup with you," she said, "for there is power in it, and if you do but pour water into it, it will be turned to wine on the moment. And do not let it out of your hand," she said, "but keep it with you; for at whatever time it will escape from you, your death will not be far away. And it is where you will meet your death, in the green valley at the side of the Boinn; and it is a wandering wild deer will give you a wound, and after that, it is strangers will put an end to you. And I myself will bury your body, and there will be a hill over it, and the name it will get is Croidhe Essu."

They went out of the shining house then, and Cliodna of the Fair Hair went with them to the place they had left their ship, and she bade their comrades a kindly welcome; and she asked them how long had they been in that country. "It seems to us," they said, "we are not in it but one day only." "You are in it through the whole length of a year," said she, "and through all that time you used neither food nor drink. But however long you would stop here," she said, "cold or hunger would never come on you." "It would be a good thing to live this way always," said Tadg's people when they heard that. But he himself said: "It is best for us to go on and to look for our people. And we must leave this country, although it is displeasing to us to leave it."

Then Cliodna and Tadg bade farewell to one another, and she gave her blessing to him and to his people. And they set out then over the ridges of the sea; and they were downhearted after leaving that country until the birds began to sing for them, and then their courage rose up, and they were glad and light-hearted.

And when they looked back they could not see the island they had come from, because of a Druid mist that came on it and hid it from them.

Then by the leading of the birds they came to the country of Fresen, and they were in a deep sleep through the whole voyage. And then they attacked the foreigners and got the better of them, and Tadg killed Cathmann, the king, after a hard fight; and Liban his wife made no delay, and came to meet her husband and her sweetheart, and it is glad she was to see him.

And after they had rested a while they faced the sea again, and Tadg and his wife Liban, and his two brothers, and a great many other treasures along with them, and they came home to Ireland safely at the last.

CHAPTER XV. LAEGAIRE IN THE HAPPY PLAIN

And another that went to visit Magh Mell, the Happy Plain, was Laegaire, son of the King of Connacht, Crimthan Cass.

He was out one day with the king, his father, near Loch na-n Ean, the Lake of Birds, and the men of Connacht with them, and they saw a man coming to them through the mist. Long golden-yellow hair he had, and it streaming after him, and at his belt a gold-hilted sword, and in his hand two five-barbed darts, a gold-rimmed shield on his back, a five-folded crimson cloak about his shoulders.

"Give a welcome to the man that is coming towards you," said Laegaire, that had the best name of all the men of Connacht, to his people. And to the stranger he said: "A welcome to the champion we do not know."

"I am thankful to you all," said he.

"What is it you are come for, and where are you going?" said Laegaire then.

"I am come to look for the help of fighting men," said the stranger. "And my name," he said, "is Fiachna, son of Betach, of the men of the Sidhe; and it is what ails me, my wife was taken from my pillow and brought away by Eochaid, son of Sal. And we fought together, and I killed him, and now she is gone to a brother's son of his, Goll, son of Dalbh, king of a people of Magh Mell. Seven battles I gave him, but they all went against me; and on this very day there is another to be fought, and I am come to ask help. And to every one that deserves it, I will give a good reward of gold and of silver for that help."

And it is what he said:

"The most beautiful of plains is the Plain of the Two Mists; it is not far from this; it is a host of the men of the Sidhe full of courage are stirring up pools of blood upon it.

"We have drawn red blood from the bodies of high nobles; many women are keening them with cries and with tears.

"The men of the host in good order go out ahead of their beautiful king; they march among blue spears, white troops of fighters with curled hair.

"They scatter the troops of their enemies, they destroy every country they make an attack on; they are beautiful in battle, a host with high looks, rushing, avenging.

"It is no wonder they to have such strength: every one of them is the son of a king and a queen; manes of hair they have of the colour of gold.

"Their bodies smooth and comely; their eyes blue and far-seeing; their teeth bright like crystal, within their thin red lips.

"White shields they have in their hands, with patterns on them of white silver; blue shining swords, red horns set with gold.

"They are good at killing men in battle; good at song-making, good at chess-playing.

"The most beautiful of plains is the Plain of the Two Mists; the men of the Sidhe are stirring up pools of blood on it; it is not far from this place."

"It would be a shameful thing not to give our help to this man," said Laegaire.

Fiachna, son of Betach, went down into the lake then, for it was out of it he had come, and Laegaire went down into it after him, and fifty fighting men along with him.

They saw a strong place before them then, and a company of armed men, and Goll, son of Dalbh, at the head of them.

"That is well," said Laegaire, "I and my fifty men will go out against this troop." "I will answer you," said Goll, son of Dalbh.

The two fifties attacked one another then, and Goll fell, but Laegaire and his fifty escaped with their lives and made a great slaughter of their enemies, that not one of them made his escape.

"Where is the woman now?" said Laegaire. "She is within the dun of Magh Mell, and a troop of armed men keeping guard about it," said Fiachna. "Let you stop here, and I and my fifty will go there," said Laegaire.

So he and his men went on to the dun, and Laegaire called out to the men that were about it: "Your king has got his death, your chief men have fallen, let the woman come out, and I will give you your own lives." The men agreed to that, and they brought the woman out. And when she came out she made this complaint:

"It is a sorrowful day that swords are reddened for the sake of the dear dead body of Goll, son of Dalbh. It was he that loved me, it was himself I loved, it is little Laegaire Liban cares for that.

"Weapons were hacked and were split by Goll; it is to Fiachna, son of Betach, I must go; it is Goll son of Dalbh, I loved."

And that complaint got the name of "The Lament of the Daughter of Eochaid the Dumb."

Laegaire went back with her then till he put her hand in Fiachna's hand. And that night Fiachna's daughter, Deorgreine, a Tear of the Sun, was given to Laegaire as his wife, and fifty other women were given to his fifty fighting men, and they stopped with them there to the end of a year.

And at the end of that time, Laegaire said: "Let us go and ask news of our own country." "If you have a mind to go," said Fiachna, "bring horses with you; but whatever happens," he said, "do not get off from them."

So they set out then; and when they got back to Ireland, they found a great gathering of the whole of the men of Connacht that were keening them.

And when the men of Connacht saw them coming they rose up to meet them, and to bid them welcome. But Laegaire called out: "Do not come to us, for it is to bid you farewell we are here." "Do not go from us again," said Crimthan, his father, "and I will give you the sway over the three Connachts, their silver and their gold, their horses and their bridles, and their beautiful women, if you will not go from us."

And it is what Laegaire said: "In the place we are gone to, the armies move from kingdom to kingdom, they listen to the sweet-sounding music of the Sidhe, they drink from shining cups, we talk with those we love, it is beer that falls instead of rain.

"We have brought from the dun of the Pleasant Plain thirty cauldrons, thirty drinking horns; we have brought the complaint that was sung by the Sea, by the daughter of Eochaid the Dumb.

"There is a wife for every man of the fifty; my own wife to me is the Tear of the Sun; I am made master of a blue sword; I would not give for all your whole kingdom one night of the nights of the Sidhe."

With that Laegaire turned from them, and went back to the kingdom. And he was made king there along with Fiachna, son of Betach, and his daughter, and he did not come out of it yet.

BOOK FIVE: THE FATE OF THE CHILDREN OF LIR

Now at the time when the Tuatha de Danaan chose a king for themselves after the battle of Tailltin, and Lir heard the kingship was given to Bodb Dearg, it did not please him, and he left the gathering without leave and with no word to any one; for he thought it was he himself had a right to be made king. But if he went away himself, Bodb was given the kingship none the less, for not one of the five begrudged it to him but only Lir, And it is what they determined, to follow after Lir, and to burn down his house, and to attack himself with spear and sword, on account of his not giving obedience to the king they had chosen. "We will not do that," said Bodb Dearg, "for that man would defend any place he is in; and besides that," he said, "I am none the less king over the Tuatha de Danaan, although he does not submit to me."

All went on like that for a good while, but at last a great misfortune came on Lir, for his wife died from him after a sickness of three nights. And that came very hard on Lir, and there was heaviness on his mind after her. And there was great talk of the death of that woman in her own time.

And the news of it was told all through Ireland, and it came to the house of Bodb, and the best of the Men of Dea were with him at that time. And Bodb said: "If Lir had a mind for it," he said, "my help and my friendship would be good for him now, since his wife is not living to him. For I have here with me the three young girls of the best shape, and the best appearance, and the best name in all Ireland, Aobh, Aoife, and Ailbhe, the three daughters of Oilell of Aran, my own three nurselings." The Men of Dea said then it was a good thought he had, and that what he said was true.

Messages and messengers were sent then from Bodb Dearg to the place Lir was, to say that if he had a mind to join with the Son of the Dagda and to acknowledge his lordship, he would give him a foster-child of his foster-children. And Lir thought well of the offer, and he set out on the morrow with fifty chariots from Sidhe Fionnachaidh; and he went by every short way till he came to Bodb's dwelling-place at Loch Dearg, and there was a welcome before him there, and all the people were merry and pleasant before him, and he and his people got good attendance that night.

And the three daughters of Oilell of Aran were sitting on the one seat with Bodb Dearg's wife, the queen of the Tuatha de Danaan, that was their foster-mother. And Bodb said: "You may have your choice of the three young girls, Lir." "I cannot say," said Lir, "which one of them is my choice, but whichever of them is the eldest, she is the noblest, and it is best for me to take her." "If that is so," said Bodb, "it is Aobh is the eldest, and she will be given to you, if it is your wish." "It is my wish," he said. And he took Aobh for his wife that night, and he stopped there for a fortnight, and then he brought her away to his own house, till he would make a great wedding-feast.

And in the course of time Aobh brought forth two children, a daughter and a son, Fionnuala and Aodh their names were. And after a while she was brought to bed again, and this time she gave birth to two sons, and they called them Fiachra and Conn. And she herself died at their birth. And that weighed very heavy on Lir, and only for the way his mind was set on his four children he would have gone near to die of grief.

The news came to Bodb Dearg's place, and all the people gave out three loud, high cries, keening their nursling. And after they had keened her it is what Bodb Dearg said: "It is a fret to us our daughter to have died, for her own sake and for the sake of the good man we gave her to, for we are thankful for his friendship and his faithfulness. However," he said, "our friendship with one another will not be broken, for I will give him for a wife her sister Aoife."

When Lir heard that, he came for the girl and married her, and brought her home to his house. And there was honour and affection with Aoife for her sister's children; and indeed no person at all could see those four children without giving them the heart's love.

And Bodb Dearg used often to be going to Lir's house for the sake of those children; and he used to bring them to his own place for a good length of time, and then he would let them go back to their own place again. And the Men of Dea were at that time using the Feast of Age in every hill of the Sidhe in turn; and when they came to Lir's hill those four children were their joy and delight, for the beauty of their appearance; and it is where they used to sleep, in beds in sight of their father Lir. And he used to rise up at the break of every morning, and to lie down among his children.

But it is what came of all this, that a fire of jealousy was kindled in Aoife, and she got to have a dislike and a hatred of her sister's children.

Then she let on to have a sickness, that lasted through nearly the length of a year. And the end of that time she did a deed of jealousy and cruel treachery against the children of Lir.

And one day she got her chariot yoked, and she took the four children in it, and they went forward towards the house of Bodb Dearg; but Fionnuala had no mind to go with her, for she knew by her she had some plan for their death or their destruction, and she had seen in a dream that there was treachery against them in Aoife's mind. But all the same she was not able to escape from what was before her.

And when they were on their way Aoife said to her people: "Let you kill now," she said, "the four children of Lir, for whose sake their father has given up my love, and I will give you your own choice of a reward out of all the good things of the world." "We will not do that indeed," said they; "and it is a bad deed you have thought of, and harm will come to you out of it."

And when they would not do as she bade them, she took out a sword herself to put an end to the children with; but she being a woman and with no good courage, and with no great strength in her mind, she was not able to do it.

They went on then west to Loch Dairbhreach, the Lake of the Oaks, and the horses were stopped there. And Aoife bade the children of Lir to go out and bathe in the lake, and they did as she bade them. And as soon as Aoife saw them out in the lake she struck them with a Druid rod, and put on them the shape of four swans, white and beautiful. And it is what she said: "Out with you, children of the king, your luck is taken away from you for ever; it is sorrowful the story will be to your friends; it is with flocks of birds your cries will be heard for ever."

And Fionnuala said: "Witch, we know now what your name is, you have struck us down with no hope of relief; but although you put us from wave to wave, there are times when we will touch the land. We shall get help when we are seen; help, and all that is best for us; even though we have to sleep upon the lake, it is our minds will be going abroad early."

And then the four children of Lir turned towards Aoife, and it is what Fionnuala said: "It is a bad deed you have done, Aoife, and it is a bad fulfilling of friendship, you to destroy us without cause; and vengeance for it will come upon you, and you will fall in satisfaction for it, for your power for our destruction is not greater than the power of our friends to avenge it on you; and put some bounds now," she said, "to the time this enchantment is to stop on us." "I will do that," said Aoife, "and it is worse for you, you to have asked it of me. And the bounds I set to your time are this, till the Woman from the South and the Man from the North will come together. And since you ask to hear it of me," she said, "no friends and no power that you have will be able to bring you out of these shapes you are in through the length of your lives, until you have been three hundred years on Loch Dairbhreach, and three hundred years on Sruth na Maoile between Ireland and Alban, and three hundred years at Irrus Domnann and Inis Gluaire; and these are to be your journeys from this out," she said.

But then repentance came on Aoife, and she said: "Since there is no other help for me to give you now, you may keep your own speech; and you will be singing sweet music of the Sidhe, that would put the men of the earth to sleep, and there will be no music in the world equal to it; and your own sense and your own nobility will stay with you, the way it will not weigh so heavy on you to be in the shape of birds. And go away out of my sight now, children of Lir," she said, "with your white faces, with your stammering Irish. It is a great curse on tender lads, they to be driven out on the rough wind. Nine hundred years to be on the water, it is a long time for any one to be in pain; it is I put this on you through treachery, it is best for you to do as I tell you now.

"Lir, that got victory with so many a good cast, his heart is a kernel of death in him now; the groaning of the great hero is a sickness to me, though it is I that have well earned his anger."

And then the horses were caught for Aoife, and the chariot yoked for her, and she went on to the palace of Bodb Dearg, and there was a welcome before her from the chief people of the place. And the son of the Dagda asked her why she did not bring the children of Lir with her. "I will tell you that," she said. "It is because Lir has no liking for you, and he will not trust you with his children, for fear you might keep them from him altogether."

"I wonder at that," said Bodb Dearg, "for those children are dearer to me than my own children." And he thought in his own mind it was deceit the woman was doing on him, and it is what he did, he sent messengers to the north to Sidhe Fionnachaidh. And Lir asked them what did they come for. "On the head of your children," said they. "Are they not gone to you along with Aoife?" he said. "They are not," said they; "and Aoife said it was yourself would not let them come."

It is downhearted and sorrowful Lir was at that news, for he understood well it was Aoife had destroyed or made an end of his children. And early in the morning of the morrow his horses were caught, and he set out on the road to the southwest. And when he was as far as the shore of Loch Dairbhreach, the four children saw the horses coming towards them, and it is what Fionnuala said: "A welcome to the troop of horses I see coming near to the lake; the people they are bringing are strong, there is sadness on them; it is us they are following, it is for us they are looking; let us move over to the shore, Aodh, Fiachra, and comely Conn. Those that are coming can be no others in the world but only Lir and his household."

Then Lir came to the edge of the lake, and he took notice of the swans having the voice of living people, and he asked them why was it they had that voice.

"I will tell you that, Lir," said Fionnuala. "We are your own four children, that are after being destroyed by your wife, and by the sister of our own mother, through the dint of her jealousy." "Is there any way to put you into your own shapes again?" said Lir. "There is no way," said Fionnuala, "for all the men of the world could not help us till we have gone through our time, and that will not be," she said, "till the end of nine hundred years."

When Lir and his people heard that, they gave out three great heavy shouts of grief and sorrow and crying.

"Is there a mind with you," said Lir, "to come to us on the land, since you have your own sense and your memory yet?" "We have not the power," said Fionnuala, "to live with any person at all from this time; but we have our own language, the Irish, and we have the power to sing sweet music, and it is enough to satisfy the whole race of men to be listening to that music. And let you stop here to-night," she said, "and we will be making music for you."

So Lir and his people stopped there listening to the music of the swans, and they slept there quietly that night. And Lir rose up early on the morning of the morrow and he made this complaint:--

"It is time to go out from this place. I do not sleep though I am in my lying down. To be parted from my dear children, it is that is tormenting my heart.

"It is a bad net I put over you, bringing Aoife, daughter of Oilell of Aran, to the house. I would never have followed that advice if I had known what it would bring upon me.

"O Fionnuala, and comely Conn, O Aodh, O Fiachra of the beautiful arms; it is not ready I am to go away from you, from the border of the harbour where you are."

Then Lir went on to the palace of Bodb Dearg, and there was a welcome before him there; and he got a reproach from Bodb Dearg for not bringing his children along with him. "My grief!" said Lir. "It is not I that would not bring my children along with me; it was Aoife there beyond, your own foster-child and the sister of their mother, that put them in the shape of four white swans on Loch Dairbhreach, in the sight of the whole of the men of Ireland; but they have their sense with them yet, and their reason, and their voice, and their Irish."

Bodb Dearg gave a great start when he heard that, and he knew what Lir said was true, and he gave a very sharp reproach to Aoife, and he said: "This treachery will be worse for yourself in the end, Aoife, than to the children of Lir. And what shape would you yourself think worst of being in?" he said.

"I would think worst of being a witch of the air," she said. "It is into that shape I will put you now," said Bodb. And with that he struck her with a Druid wand, and she was turned into a witch of the air there and then, and she went away on the wind in that shape, and she is in it yet, and will be in it to the end of life and time.

As to Bodb Dearg and the Tuatha de Danaan they came to the shore of Loch Dairbhreach, and they made their camp there to be listening to the music of the swans.

And the Sons of the Gael used to be coming no less than the Men of Dea to hear them from every part of Ireland, for there never was any music or any delight heard in Ireland to compare with that music of the swans. And they used to be telling stories, and to be talking with the men of Ireland every day, and with their teachers and their fellow-pupils and their friends. And every night they used to sing very sweet music of the Sidhe; and every one that heard that music would sleep sound and quiet whatever trouble or long sickness might be on him; for every one that heard the music of the birds, it is happy and contented he would be after it.

These two gatherings now of the Tuatha de Danaan and of the Sons of the Gael stopped there around Loch Dairbhreach through the length of three hundred years. And it is then Fionnuala said to her brothers: "Do you know," she said, "we have spent all we have to spend of our time here, but this one night only."

And there was great sorrow on the sons of Lir when they heard that, for they thought it the same as to be living people again, to be talking with their friends and their companions on Loch Dairbhreach, in comparison with going on the cold, fretful sea of the Maoil in the north.

And they came early on the morrow to speak with their father and with their foster-father, and they bade them farewell, and Fionnuala made this complaint:--

"Farewell to you, Bodb Dearg, the man with whom all knowledge is in pledge. And farewell to our father along with you, Lir of the Hill of the White Field.

"The time is come, as I think, for us to part from you, O pleasant company; my grief it is not on a visit we are going to you.

"From this day out, O friends of our heart, our comrades, it is on the tormented course of the Maoil we will be, without the voice of any person near us.

"Three hundred years there, and three hundred years in the bay of the men of Domnann, it is a pity for the four comely children of Lir, the salt waves of the sea to be their covering by night.

"O three brothers, with the ruddy faces gone from you, let them all leave the lake now, the great troop that loved us, it is sorrowful our parting is."

After that complaint they took to flight, lightly, airily, till they came to Sruth na Maoile between Ireland and Alban. And that was a grief to the men of Ireland, and they gave out an order no swan was to be killed from that out, whatever chance there might be of killing one, all through Ireland.

It was a bad dwelling-place for the children of Lir they to be on Sruth na Maoile. When they saw the wide coast about them, they were filled with cold and with sorrow, and they thought nothing of all they had gone through before, in comparison to what they were going through on that sea.

Now one night while they were there a great storm came on them, and it is what Fionnuala said: "My dear brothers," she said, "it is a pity for us not to be making ready for this night, for it is certain the storm will separate us from one another. And let us," she said, "settle on some place where we can meet afterwards, if we are driven from one another in the night."

"Let us settle," said the others, "to meet one another at Carraig na Ron, the Rock of the Seals, for we all have knowledge of it."

And when midnight came, the wind came on them with it, and the noise of the waves increased, and the lightning was flashing, and a rough storm came sweeping down, the way the children of Lir were scattered over the great sea, and the wideness of it set them astray, so that no one of them could know what way the others went. But after that storm a great quiet came on the sea, and Fionnuala was alone on Sruth na Maoile; and when she took notice that her brothers were wanting she was lamenting after them greatly, and she made this complaint:--

"It is a pity for me to be alive in the state I am; it is frozen to my sides my wings are; it is little that the wind has not broken my heart in my body, with the loss of Aodh.

"To be three hundred years on Loch Dairbhreach without going into my own shape, it is worse to me the time I am on Sruth na Maoile.

"The three I loved, Och! the three I loved, that slept under the shelter of my feathers; till the dead come back to the living I will see them no more for ever.

"It is a pity I to stay after Fiachra, and after Aodh, and after comely Conn, and with no account of them; my grief I to be here to face every hardship this night."

She stopped all night there upon the Rock of the Seals until the rising of the sun, looking out over the sea on every side till at last she saw Conn coming to her, his feathers wet through and his head hanging, and her heart gave him a great welcome; and then Fiachra came wet and perished and worn out, and he could not say a word they could understand with the dint of the cold and the hardship he had gone through. And Fionnuala put him under her wings, and she said: "We would be well off now if Aodh would but come to us."

It was not long after that, they saw Aodh coming, his head dry and his feathers beautiful, and Fionnuala gave him a great welcome, and she put him in under the feathers of her breast, and Fiachra under her right wing and Conn under her left wing, the way she could put her feathers over them all. "And Och! my brothers," she said, "this was a bad night to us, and it is many of its like are before us from this out."

They stayed there a long time after that, suffering cold and misery on the Maoil, till at last a night came on them they had never known the like of before, for frost and snow and wind and cold. And they were crying and lamenting the hardship of their life, and the cold of the night and the greatness of the snow and the hardness of the wind. And after they had suffered cold to the end of a year, a worse night again came on them, in the middle of winter. And they were on Carraig na Ron, and the water froze about them, and as they rested on the rock, their feet and their wings and their feathers froze to the rock, the way they were not able to move from it. And they made such a hard struggle to get away, that they left the skin of their feet and their feathers and the tops of their wings on the rock after them.

"My grief, children of Lir," said Fionnuala, "it is bad our state is now, for we cannot bear the salt water to touch us, and there are bonds on us not to leave it; and if the salt water goes into our sores," she said, "we will get our death." And she made this complaint:--

"It is keening we are to-night; without feathers to cover our bodies; it is cold the rough, uneven rocks are under our bare feet.

"It is bad our stepmother was to us the time she played enchantments on us, sending us out like swans upon the sea.

"Our washing place is on the ridge of the bay, in the foam of flying manes of the sea; our share of the ale feast is the salt water of the blue tide.

"One daughter and three sons; it is in the clefts of the rocks we are; it is on the hard rocks we are, it is a pity the way we are."

However, they came on to the course of the Maoil again, and the salt water was sharp and rough and bitter to them, but if it was itself, they were not able to avoid it or to get shelter from it. And they were there by the shore under that hardship till such time as their feathers grew again, and their wings, and till their sores were entirely healed. And then they used to go every day to the shore of Ireland or of Alban, but they had to come back to Sruth na Maoile every night.

Now they came one day to the mouth of the Banna, to the north of Ireland, and they saw a troop of riders, beautiful, of the one colour, with well-trained pure white horses under them, and they travelling the road straight from the south-west.

"Do you know who those riders are, sons of Lir?" said Fionnuala.

"We do not," they said; "but it is likely they might be some troop of the Sons of the Gael, or of the Tuatha de Danaan."

They moved over closer to the shore then, that they might know who they were, and when the riders saw them they came to meet them until they were able to hold talk together.

And the chief men among them were two sons of Bodb Dearg, Aodh Aithfhiosach, of the quick wits, and Fergus Fithchiollach, of the chess, and a third part of the Riders of the Sidhe along with them, and it was for the swans they had been looking for a long while before that, and when they came together they wished one another a kind and loving welcome.

And the children of Lir asked for news of all the Men of Dea, and above all of Lir, and Bodb Dearg and their people.

"They are well, and they are in the one place together," said they, "in your father's house at Sidhe Fionnachaidh, using the Feast of Age pleasantly and happily, and with no uneasiness on them, only for being without yourselves, and without knowledge of what happened you from the day you left Loch Dairbhreach."

"That has not been the way with us," said Fionnuala, "for we have gone through great hardship and uneasiness and misery on the tides of the sea until this day."

And she made this complaint:--

"There is delight to-night with the household of Lir! Plenty of ale with them and of wine, although it is in a cold dwelling-place this night are the four children of the king.

"It is without a spot our bedclothes are, our bodies covered over with curved feathers; but it is often we were dressed in purple, and we drinking pleasant mead.

"It is what our food is and our drink, the white sand and the bitter water of the sea; it is often we drank mead of hazel-nuts from round four-lipped drinking cups.

"It is what our beds are, bare rocks out of the power of the waves; it is often there used to be spread out for us beds of the breast-feathers of birds.

"Though it is our work now to be swimming through the frost and through the noise of the waves, it is often a company of the sons of kings were riding after us to the Hill of Bodb.

"It is what wasted my strength, to be going and coming over the current of the Maoil the way I never was used to, and never to be in the sunshine on the soft grass.

"Fiachra's bed and Conn's bed is to come under the cover of my wings on the sea. Aodh has his place under the feathers of my breast, the four of us side by side.

"The teaching of Manannan without deceit, the talk of Bodb Dearg on the pleasant ridge; the voice of Angus, his sweet kisses; it is by their side I used to be without grief."

After that the riders went on to Lir's house, and they told the chief men of the Tuatha de Danaan all the birds had gone through, and the state they were in. "We have no power over them," the chief men said, "but we are glad they are living yet, for they will get help in the end of time."

As to the children of Lir, they went back towards their old place in the Maoil, and they stopped there till the time they had to spend in it was spent. And then Fionnuala said: "The time is come for us to leave this place. And it is to Irrus Domnann we must go now," she said, "after our three hundred years here. And indeed there will be no rest for us there, or any standing ground, or any shelter from the storms. But since it is time for us to go, let us set out on the cold wind, the way we will not go astray."

So they set out in that way, and left Sruth na Maoile behind them, and went to the point of Irrus Domnann, and there they stopped, and it is a life of misery and a cold life they led there. And one time the sea froze about them that they could not move at all, and the brothers were lamenting, and Fionnuala was comforting them, for she knew there would help come to them in the end.

And they stayed at Irrus Domnann till the time they had to spend there was spent. And then Fionnuala said: "The time is come for us to go back to Sidhe Fionnachaidh, where our father is with his household and with all our own people."

"It pleases us well to hear that," they said.

So they set out flying through the air lightly till they came to Sidhe Fionnachaidh; and it is how they found the place, empty before them, and nothing in it but green hillocks and thickets of nettles, without a house, without a fire, without a hearthstone. And the four pressed close to one another then, and they gave out three sorrowful cries, and Fionnuala made this complaint:--

"It is a wonder to me this place is, and it without a house, without a dwelling-place. To see it the way it is now, Ochone! it is bitterness to my heart.

"Without dogs, without hounds for hunting, without women, without great kings; we never knew it to be like this when our father was in it.

"Without horns, without cups, without drinking in the lighted house; without young men, without riders; the way it is to-night is a foretelling of sorrow.

"The people of the place to be as they are now, Ochone! it is grief to my heart! It is plain to my mind to-night the lord of the house is not living.

"Och, house where we used to see music and playing and the gathering of people! I think it a great change to see it lonely the way it is to-night.

"The greatness of the hardships we have gone through going from one wave to another of the sea, we never heard of the like of them coming on any other person.

"It is seldom this place had its part with grass and bushes; the man is not living that would know us, it would be a wonder to him to see us here."

However, the children of Lir stopped that night in their father's place and their grandfather's, where they had been reared, and they were singing very sweet music of the Sidhe. And they rose up early on the morning of the morrow and went to Inis Gluaire, and all the birds of the country gathered near them on Loch na-n Ean, the Lake of the Birds. And they used to go out to feed every day to the far parts of the country, to Inis Geadh and to Accuill, the place Donn, son of Miled, and his people that were drowned were buried, and to all the western islands of Connacht, and they used to go back to Inis Gluaire every night.

It was about that time it happened them to meet with a young man of good race, and his name was Aibric; and he often took notice of the birds, and their singing was sweet to him and he loved them greatly, and they loved him. And it is this young man that told the whole story of all that had happened them, and put it in order.

And the story he told of what happened them in the end is this.

It was after the faith of Christ and blessed Patrick came into Ireland, that Saint Mochaomhog came to Inis Gluaire. And the first night he came to the island, the children of Lir heard the voice of his bell, ringing near them. And the brothers started up with fright when they heard it "We do not know," they said, "what is that weak, unpleasing voice we hear."

"That is the voice of the bell of Mochaomhog," said Fionnuala; "and it is through that bell," she said, "you will be set free from pain and from misery."

They listened to that music of the bell till the matins were done, and then they began to sing the low, sweet music of the Sidhe.

And Mochaomhog was listening to them, and he prayed to God to show him who was singing that music, and it was showed to him that the children of Lir were singing it. And on the morning of the morrow he went forward to the Lake of the Birds, and he saw the swans before him on the lake, and he went down to them at the brink of the shore. "Are you the children of Lir?" he said.

"We are indeed," said they.

"I give thanks to God for that," said he, "for it is for your sakes I am come to this island beyond any other island, and let you come to land now," he said, "and give your trust to me, that you may do good deeds and part from your sins."

They came to the land after that, and they put trust in Mochaomhog, and he brought them to his own dwelling-place, and they used to be hearing Mass with him. And he got a good smith and bade him make chains of bright silver for them, and he put a chain between Aodh and Fionnuala, and a chain between Conn and Fiachra. And the four of them were raising his heart and gladdening his mind, and no danger and no distress that was on the swans before put any trouble on them now.

Now the king of Connacht at that time was Lairgnen, son of Colman, son of Cobthach, and Deoch, daughter of Finghin, was his wife. And that was the coming together of the Man from the North and the Woman from the South, that Aoife had spoken of.

And the woman heard talk of the birds, and a great desire came on her to get them, and she bade Lairgnen to bring them to her, and he said he would ask them of Mochaomhog.

And she gave her word she would not stop another night with him unless he would bring them to her. And she set out from the house there and then. And Lairgnen sent messengers after her to bring her back, and they did not overtake her till she was at Cill Dun. She went back home with them then, and Lairgnen sent messengers to ask the birds of Mochaomhog, and he did not get them.

There was great anger on Lairgnen then, and he went himself to the place Mochaomhog was, and he asked was it true he had refused him the birds. "It is true indeed," said he. At that Lairgnen rose up, and he took hold of the swans, and pulled them off the altar, two birds in each hand, to bring them away to Deoch. But no sooner had he laid his hand on them than their bird skins fell off, and what was in their place was three lean, withered old men and a thin withered old woman, without blood or flesh.

And Lairgnen gave a great start at that, and he went out from the place. It is then Fionnuala said to Mochaomhog: "Come and baptize us now, for it is short till our death comes; and it is certain you do not think worse of parting with us than we do of parting with you. And make our grave afterwards," she said, "and lay Conn at my right side and Fiachra on my left side, and Aodh before my face, between my two arms. And pray to the God of Heaven," she said, "that you may be able to baptize us."

The children of Lir were baptized then, and they died and were buried as Fionnuala had desired; Fiachra and Conn one at each side of her, and Aodh before her face. And a stone was put over them, and their names were written in Ogham, and they were keened there, and heaven was gained for their souls.

And that is the fate of the children of Lir so far.

PART TWO: THE FIANNA.

BOOK ONE: FINN, SON OF CUMHAL.

CHAPTER I. THE COMING OF FINN

At the time Finn was born his father Cumhal, of the sons of Baiscne, Head of the Fianna of Ireland, had been killed in battle by the sons of Morna that were fighting with him for the leadership. And his mother, that was beautiful long-haired Muirne, daughter of Tadg, son of Nuada of the Tuatha de Danaan and of Ethlinn, mother of Lugh of the Long Hand, did not dare to keep him with her; and two women, Bodhmall, the woman Druid, and Liath Luachra, came and brought him away to care him.

It was to the woods of Slieve Bladhma they brought him, and they nursed him secretly, because of his father's enemies, the sons of Morna, and they kept him there a long time.

And Muirne, his mother, took another husband that was king of Carraighe; but at the end of six years she came to see Finn, going through every lonely place till she came to the wood, and there she found the little hunting cabin, and the boy asleep in it, and she lifted him up in her arms and kissed him, and she sang a little sleepy song to him; and then she said farewell to the women, and she went away again.

And the two women went on caring him till he came to sensible years; and one day when he went out he saw a wild duck on the lake with her clutch, and he made a cast at her that cut the wings off her that she could not fly, and he brought her back to the cabin, and that was his first hunt.

And they gave him good training in running and leaping and swimming. One of them would run round a tree, and she having a thorn switch, and Finn after her with another switch, and each one trying to hit at the other; and they would leave him in a field, and hares along with him, and would bid him not to let the hares quit the field, but to keep before them whichever way they would go; and to teach him swimming they would throw him into the water and let him make his way out.

But after a while he went away with a troop of poets, to hide from the sons of Morna, and they hid him in the mountain of Crotta Cliach; but there was a robber in Leinster at that time, Fiacuil, son of Codhna, and he came where the poets were in Fidh Gaible and killed them all. But he spared the child and brought him to his own house, that was in a cold marsh. But the two women, Bodhmall and Liath, came looking for him after a while, and Fiacuil gave him up to them, and they brought him back to the same place he was before.

He grew up there, straight and strong and fair-haired and beautiful. And one day he was out in Slieve Bladhma, and the two women along with him, and they saw before them a herd of the wild deer of the mountain. "It is a pity," said the old women, "we not to be able to get a deer of those deer." "I will get one for you," said Finn; and with that he followed after them, and caught two stags of them and brought them home to the hunting cabin. And after that he used to be hunting for them every day. But at last they said to him: "It is best for you to leave us now, for the sons of Morna are watching again to kill you."

So he went away then by himself, and never stopped till he came to Magh Life, and there he saw young lads swimming in a lake, and they called to him to swim against them. So he went into the lake, and he beat them at swimming. "Fair he is and well shaped," they said when they saw him swimming, and it was from that time he got the name of Finn, that is, Fair. But they got to be jealous of his strength, and he went away and left them.

He went on then till he came to Loch Lein, and he took service there with the King of Finntraigh; and there was no hunter like him, and the king said: "If Cumhal had left a son, you would be that son."

He went from that king after, and he went into Carraighe, and there he took service with the king, that had taken his mother Muirne for his wife. And one day they were playing chess together, and he won seven games one after another.

"Who are you at all?" said the king then. "I am a son of a countryman of the Luigne of Teamhair," said Finn. "That is not so," said the king, "but you are the son that Muirne my wife bore to Cumhal. And do not stop here any longer," he said, "that you may not be killed under my protection."

From that he went into Connacht looking for his father's brother, Crimall, son of Trenmor; and as he was going on his way he heard the crying of a lone woman. He went to her, and looked at her, and tears of blood were on her face. "Your face is red with blood, woman," he said. "I have reason for it," said she, "for my only son is after being killed by a great fighting man that came on us." And Finn followed after the big champion and fought with him and killed him. And the man he killed was the same man that had given Cumhal his first wound in the battle where he got his death, and had brought away his treasure-bag with him.

Now as to that treasure-bag, it is of a crane skin it was made, that was one time the skin of Aoife, the beautiful sweetheart of Ilbrec, son of Manannan, that was put into the shape of a crane through jealousy. And it was in Manannan's house it used to be, and there were treasures kept in it, Manannan's shirt and his knife, and the belt and the smith's hook of Goibniu, and the shears of the King of Alban, and the helmet of the King of Lochlann, and a belt of the skin of a great fish, and the bones of Asal's pig that had been brought to Ireland by the sons of Tuireann. All those treasures would be in the bag at full tide, but at the ebbing of the tide it would be empty. And it went from Manannan to Lugh, son of Ethlinn, and after that to Cumhal, that was husband to Muirne, Ethlinn's daughter.

And Finn took the bag and brought it with him till he found Crimall, that was now an old man, living in a lonely place, and some of the old men of the Fianna were with him, and used to go hunting for him. And Finn gave him the bag, and told him his whole story.

And then he said farewell to Crimall, and went on to learn poetry from Finegas, a poet that was living at the Boinn, for the poets thought it was always on the brink of water poetry was revealed to them. And he did not give him his own name, but he took the name of Deimne. Seven years, now, Finegas had stopped at the Boinn, watching the salmon, for it was in the prophecy that he would eat the salmon of knowledge that would come there, and that he would have all knowledge after. And when at the last the salmon of knowledge came, he brought it to where Finn was, and bade him to roast it, but he bade him not to eat any of it. And when Finn brought him the salmon after a while he said: "Did you eat any of it at all, boy?" "I did not," said Finn; "but I burned my thumb putting down a blister that rose on the skin, and after doing that, I put my thumb in my mouth." "What is your name, boy?" said Finegas. "Deimne," said he. "It is not, but it is Finn your name is, and it is to you and not to myself the salmon was given in the prophecy." With that he gave Finn the whole of the salmon, and from that time Finn had the knowledge that came from the nuts of the nine hazels of wisdom that grow beside the well that is below the sea.

And besides the wisdom he got then, there was a second wisdom came to him another time, and this is the way it happened. There was a well of the moon belonging to Beag, son of Buan, of the Tuatha de Danaan, and whoever would drink out of it would get wisdom, and after a second drink he would get the gift of foretelling. And the three daughters of Beag, son of Buan, had charge of the well, and they would not part with a vessel of it for anything less than red gold. And one day Finn chanced to be hunting in the rushes near the well, and the three women ran out to hinder him from coming to it, and one of them that had a vessel of the water in her hand, threw it at him to stop him, and a share of the water went into his mouth. And from that out he had all the knowledge that the water of that well could give.

And he learned the three ways of poetry; and this is the poem he made to show he had got his learning well:--

"It is the month of May is the pleasant time; its face is beautiful; the blackbird sings his full song, the living wood is his holding, the cuckoos are singing and ever singing; there is a welcome before the brightness of the summer.

"Summer is lessening the rivers, the swift horses are looking for the pool; the heath spreads out its long hair, the weak white bog-down grows. A wildness comes on the heart of the deer; the sad restless sea is asleep.

"Bees with their little strength carry a load reaped from the flowers; the cattle go up muddy to the mountains; the ant has a good full feast.

"The harp of the woods is playing music; there is colour on the hills, and a haze on the full lakes, and entire peace upon every sail.

"The corncrake is speaking, a loud-voiced poet; the high lonely waterfall is singing a welcome to the warm pool, the talking of the rushes has begun.

"The light swallows are darting; the loudness of music is around the hill; the fat soft mast is budding; there is grass on the trembling bogs.

"The bog is as dark as the feathers of the raven; the cuckoo makes a loud welcome; the speckled salmon is leaping; as strong is the leaping of the swift fighting man.

"The man is gaining; the girl is in her comely growing power; every wood is without fault from the top to the ground, and every wide good plain.

"It is pleasant is the colour of the time; rough winter is gone; every plentiful wood is white; summer is a joyful peace.

"A flock of birds pitches in the meadow; there are sounds in the green fields, there is in them a clear rushing stream.

"There is a hot desire on you for the racing of horses; twisted holly makes a leash for the hound; a bright spear has been shot into the earth, and the flag-flower is golden under it.

"A weak lasting little bird is singing at the top of his voice; the lark is singing clear tidings; May without fault, of beautiful colours.

"I have another story for you; the ox is lowing, the winter is creeping in, the summer is gone. High and cold the wind, low the sun, cries are about us; the sea is quarrelling.

"The ferns are reddened and their shape is hidden; the cry of the wild goose is heard; the cold has caught the wings of the birds; it is the time of ice-frost, hard, unhappy."

And after that, Finn being but a young lad yet, made himself ready and went up at Samhain time to the gathering of the High King at Teamhair. And it was the law at that gathering, no one to raise a quarrel or bring out any grudge against another through the whole of the time it lasted. And the king and his chief men, and Goll, son of Morna, that was now Head of the Fianna, and Caoilte, son of Ronan, and Conan, son of Morna, of the sharp words, were sitting at a feast in the great house of the Middle Court; and the young lad came in and took his place among them, and none of them knew who he was.

The High King looked at him then, and the horn of meetings was brought to him, and he put it into the boy's hand, and asked him who was he.

"I am Finn, son of Cumhal," he said, "son of the man that used to be head over the Fianna, and king of Ireland; and I am come now to get your friendship, and to give you my service."

"You are son of a friend, boy," said the king, "and son of a man I trusted."

Then Finn rose up and made his agreement of service and of faithfulness to the king; and the king took him by the hand and put him sitting beside his own son, and they gave themselves to drinking and to pleasure for a while.

Every year, now, at Samhain time, for nine years, there had come a man of the Tuatha de Danaan out of Sidhe Finnachaidh in the north, and had burned up Teamhair. Aillen, son of Midhna, his name was, and it is the way he used to come, playing music of the Sidhe, and all the people that heard it would fall asleep. And when they were all in their sleep, he would let a flame of fire out of his mouth, and would blow the flame till all Teamhair was burned.

The king rose up at the feast after a while, and his smooth horn in his hand, and it is what he said: "If I could find among you, men of Ireland, any man that would keep Teamhair till the break of day to-morrow without being burned by Aillen, son of Midhna, I would give him whatever inheritance is right for him to have, whether it be much or little."

But the men of Ireland made no answer, for they knew well that at the sound of the sweet pitiful music made by that comely man of the Sidhe, even women in their pains and men that were wounded would fall asleep.

It is then Finn rose up and spoke to the King of Ireland. "Who will be your sureties that you will fulfil this?" he said. "The kings of the provinces of Ireland," said the king, "and Cithruadh with his Druids." So they gave their pledges, and Finn took in hand to keep Teamhair safe till the breaking of day on the morrow.

Now there was a fighting man among the followers of the King of Ireland, Fiacha, son of Conga, that Cumhal, Finn's father, used to have a great liking for, and he said to Finn: "Well, boy," he said, "what reward would you give me if I would bring you a deadly spear, that no false cast was ever made with?" "What reward are you asking of me?" said Finn. "Whatever your right hand wins at any time, the third of it to be mine," said Fiacha, "and a third of your trust and your friendship to be mine." "I will give you that," said Finn. Then Fiacha brought him the spear, unknown to the sons of Morna or to any other person, and he said: "When you will hear the music of the Sidhe, let you strip the covering off the head of the spear and put it to your forehead, and the power of the spear will not let sleep come upon you."

Then Finn rose up before all the men of Ireland, and he made a round of the whole of Teamhair. And it was not long till he heard the sorrowful music, and he stripped the covering from the head of the spear, and he held the power of it to his forehead. And Aillen went on playing his little harp, till he had put every one in their sleep as he was used; and then he let a flame of fire out from his mouth to burn Teamhair. And Finn held up his fringed crimson cloak against the flame, and it fell down through the air and went into the ground, bringing the four-folded cloak with it deep into the earth.

And when Aillen saw his spells were destroyed, he went back to Sidhe Finna-chaidh on the top of Slieve Fuad; but Finn followed after him there, and as Aillen was going in at the door he made a cast of the spear that went through his heart. And he struck his head off then, and brought it back to Teamhair, and fixed it on a crooked pole and left it there till the rising of the sun over the heights and invers of the country.

And Aillen's mother came to where his body was lying, and there was great grief on her, and she made this complaint:--

"Ochone! Aillen is fallen, chief of the Sidhe of Beinn Boirche; the slow clouds of death are come on him. Och! he was pleasant, Och! he was kind. Aillen, son of Midhna of Slieve Fuad.

"Nine times he burned Teamhair. It is a great name he was always looking for, Ochone, Ochone, Aillen!"

And at the breaking of day, the king and all the men of Ireland came out upon the lawn at Teamhair where Finn was. "King," said Finn, "there is the head of the man that burned Teamhair, and the pipe and the harp that made his music. And it is what I think," he said, "that Teamhair and all that is in it is saved."

Then they all came together into the place of counsel, and it is what they agreed, the headship of the Fianna of Ireland to be given to Finn. And the king said to Goll, son of Morna: "Well, Goll," he said, "is it your choice to quit Ireland or to put your hand in Finn's hand?" "By my word, I will give Finn my hand," said Goll.

And when the charms that used to bring good luck had done their work, the chief men of the Fianna rose up and struck their hands in Finn's hand, and Goll, son of Morna, was the first to give him his hand the way there would be less shame on the rest for doing it.

And Finn kept the headship of the Fianna until the end; and the place he lived in was Almhuin of Leinster, where the white dun was made by Nuada of the Tuatha de Danaan, that was as white as if all the lime in Ireland was put on it, and that got its name from the great herd of cattle that died fighting one time around the well, and that left their horns there, speckled horns and white.

And as to Finn himself, he was a king and a seer and a poet; a Druid and a knowledgeable man; and everything he said was sweet-sounding to his people. And a better fighting man than Finn never struck his hand into a king's hand, and whatever any one ever said of him, he was three times better. And of his justice it used to be said, that if his enemy and his own son had come before him to be judged, it is a fair judgment he would have given between them. And as to his generosity it used to be said, he never denied any man as long as he had a mouth to eat with, and legs to bring away what he gave him; and he left no woman without her bride-price, and no man without his pay; and he never promised at night what he would not fulfil on the morrow, and he never promised in the day what he would not fulfil at night, and he never forsook his right-hand friend. And if he was quiet in peace he was angry in battle, and Oisin his son and Osgar his son's son followed him in that. There was a young man of Ulster came and claimed kinship with them one time, saying they were of the one blood. "If that is so," said Oisin, "it is from the men of Ulster we took the madness and the angry heart we have in battle." "That is so indeed," said Finn.

CHAPTER II. FINN'S HOUSEHOLD

And the number of the Fianna of Ireland at that time was seven score and ten chief men, every one of them having three times nine righting men under him. And every man of them was bound to three things, to take no cattle by oppression, not to refuse any man, as to cattle or riches; no one of them to fall back before nine fighting men. And there was no man taken into the Fianna until his tribe and his kindred would give securities for him, that even if they themselves were all killed he would not look for satisfaction for their death. But if he himself would harm others, that harm was not to be avenged on his people. And there was no man taken into the Fianna till he knew the twelve books of poetry. And before any man was taken, he would be put into a deep hole in the ground up to his middle, and he having his shield and a hazel rod in his hand. And nine men would go the length of ten furrows from him and would cast their spears at him at the one time. And if he got a wound from one of them, he was not thought fit to join with the Fianna. And after that again, his hair would be fastened up, and he put to run through the woods of Ireland, and the Fianna following after him to try could they wound him, and only the length of a branch between themselves and himself when they started. And if they came up with him and wounded him, he was not let join them; or if his spears had trembled in his hand, or if a branch of a tree had undone the plaiting of his hair, or if he had cracked a dry stick under his foot, and he running. And they would not take him among them till he had made a leap over a stick the height of himself, and till he had stooped under one the height of his knee, and till he had taken a thorn out from his foot with his nail, and he running his fastest. But if he had done all these things, he was of Finn's people.

It was good wages Finn and the Fianna got at that time; in every district a townland, in every house the fostering of a pup or a whelp from Samhain to Beltaine, and a great many things along with that. But good as the pay was, the hardships and the dangers they went through for it were greater. For they had to hinder the strangers and robbers from beyond the seas, and every bad thing, from coming into Ireland. And they had hard work enough in doing that.

And besides the fighting men, Finn had with him his five Druids, the best that ever came into the west, Cainnelsciath, of the Shining Shield, one of them was, that used to bring down knowledge from the clouds in the sky before Finn, and that could foretell battles. And he had his five wonderful physicians, four of them belonging to Ireland, and one that came over the sea from the east. And he had his five high poets and his twelve musicians, that had among them Daighre, son of Morna, and Suanach, son of Senshenn, that was Finn's teller of old stories, the sweetest that ever took a harp in his hand in Ireland or in Alban. And he had his three cup-bearers and his six door-keepers and his horn-players and the stewards of his house and his huntsman, Comhrag of the five hundred hounds, and his serving-men that were under Garbhcronan, of the Rough Buzzing; and a great troop of others along with them.

And there were fifty of the best sewing-women in Ireland brought together in a rath on Magh Feman, under the charge of a daughter of the King of Britain, and they used to be making clothing for the Fianna through the whole of the year. And three of them, that were a king's daughters, used to be making music for the rest on a little silver harp; and there was a very great candlestick of stone in the middle of the rath, for they were not willing to kindle a fire more than three times in the year for fear the smoke and the ashes might harm the needlework.

And of all his musicians the one Finn thought most of was Cnu Deireoil, the Little Nut, that came to him from the Sidhe.

It was at Slieve-nam-ban, for hunting, Finn was the time he came to him. Sitting down he was on the turf-built grave that is there; and when he looked around him he saw a small little man about four feet in height standing on the grass. Light yellow hair he had, hanging down to his waist, and he playing music on his harp. And the music he was making had no fault in it at all, and it is much that the whole of the Fianna did not fall asleep with the sweetness of its sound. He came up then, and put his hand in Finn's hand. "Where do you come from, little one, yourself and your sweet music?" said Finn. "I am come," he said, "out of the place of the Sidhe in

Slieve-nam-ban, where ale is drunk and made; and it is to be in your company for a while I am come here." "You will get good rewards from me, and riches and red gold," said Finn, "and my full friendship, for I like you well." "That is the best luck ever came to you, Finn," said all the rest of the Fianna, for they were well pleased to have him in their company. And they gave him the name of the Little Nut; and he was good in speaking, and he had so good a memory he never forgot anything he heard east or west; and there was no one but must listen to his music, and all the Fianna liked him well. And there were some said he was a son of Lugh Lamh-Fada, of the Long Hand.

And the five musicians of the Fianna were brought to him, to learn the music of the Sidhe he had brought from that other place; for there was never any music heard on earth but his was better. These were the three best things Finn ever got, Bran and Sceolan that were without fault, and the Little Nut from the House of the Sidhe in Slieve-nam-ban.

CHAPTER III. BIRTH OF BRAN.

This, now, is the story of the birth of Bran.

Finn's mother, Muirne, came one time to Almhuin, and she brought with her Tuiren, her sister. And Iollan Eachtach, a chief man of the Fianna of Ulster, was at Almhuin at the time, and he gave his love to Tuiren, and asked her in marriage, and brought her to his own house. But before they went, Finn made him gave his word he would bring her back safe and sound if ever he asked for her, and he bade him find sureties for himself among the chief men of the Fianna. And Iollan did that, and the sureties he got were Caoilte and Goll and Lugaidh Lamha, and it was Lugaidh gave her into the hand of Iollan Eachtach.

But before Iollan made that marriage, he had a sweetheart of the Sidhe, Uchtdealb of the Fair Breast; and there came great jealousy on her when she knew he had taken a wife. And she took the appearance of Finn's woman-messenger, and she came to the house where Tuiren was, and she said: "Finn sends health and long life to you, queen, and he bids you to make a great feast; and come with me now," she said, "till I speak a few words with you, for there is hurry on me."

So Tuiren went out with her, and when they were away from the house the woman of the Sidhe took out her dark Druid rod from under her cloak and gave her a blow of it that changed her into a hound, the most beautiful that was ever seen. And then she went on, bringing the hound with her, to the house of Fergus Fionnliath, king of the harbour of Gallimh. And it is the way Fergus was, he was the most unfriendly man to dogs in the whole world, and he would not let one stop in the same house with him. But it is what Uchtdealb said to him: "Finn wishes you life and health, Fergus, and he says to you to take good care of his hound till he comes himself; and mind her well," she said, "for she is with young, and do not let her go hunting when her time is near, or Finn will be no way thankful to you." "I wonder at that message," said Fergus, "for Finn knows well there is not in the world a man has less liking for dogs than myself. But for all that," he said, "I will not refuse Finn the first time he sent a hound to me."

And when he brought the hound out to try her, she was the best he ever knew, and she never saw the wild creature she would not run down; and Fergus took a great liking for hounds from that out.

And when her time came near, they did not let her go hunting any more, and she gave birth to two whelps.

And as to Finn, when he heard his mother's sister was not living with Iollan Eachtach, he called to him for the fulfilment of the pledge that was given to the Fianna. And Iollan asked time to go looking for Tuiren, and he gave his word that if he did not find her, he would give himself up in satisfaction for her. So they agreed to that, and Iollan went to the hill where Uchtdealb was, his sweetheart of the Sidhe, and told her the way things were with him, and the promise he had made to give himself up to the Fianna. "If that is so," said she, "and if you will give me your pledge to keep me as your sweetheart to the end of your life, I will free you from that danger." So Iollan gave her his promise, and she went to the house of Fergus Fionnliath, and she brought Tuiren away and put her own shape on her again, and gave her up to Finn. And Finn gave her to Lugaidh Lamha that asked her in marriage.

And as to the two whelps, they stopped always with Finn, and the names he gave them were Bran and Sceolan.

CHAPTER IV. OISIN'S MOTHER.

It happened one time Finn and his men were coming back from the hunting, a beautiful fawn started up before them, and they followed after it, men and dogs, till at last they were all tired and fell back, all but Finn himself and Bran and Sceolan. And suddenly as they were going through a valley, the fawn stopped and lay down on the smooth grass, and Bran and Sceolan came up with it, and they did not harm it at all, but went playing about it, licking its neck and its face.

There was wonder on Finn when he saw that, and he went on home to Almhuin, and the fawn followed after him playing with the hounds, and it came with them into the house at Almhuin. And when Finn was alone late that evening, a beautiful young woman having a rich dress came before him, and she told him it was she herself was the fawn he was after hunting that day. "And it is for refusing the love of Fear Doirche, the Dark Druid of the Men of Dea," she said, "I was put in this shape. And through the length of three years," she said, "I have lived the life of a wild deer in a far part of Ireland, and I am hunted like a wild deer. And a serving-man of the Dark Druid took pity on me," she said, "and he said that if I was once within the dun of the Fianna of Ireland, the Druid would have no more power over me. So I made away, and I never stopped through the whole length of a day till I came into the district of Almhuin. And I never stopped then till there was no one after me but only Bran and Sceolan, that have human wits; and I was safe with them, for they knew my nature to be like their own."

Then Finn gave her his love, and took her as his wife, and she stopped in Almhuin. And so great was his love for her, he gave up his hunting and all the things he used to take pleasure in, and gave his mind to no other thing but herself.

But at last the men of Lochlann came against Ireland, and their ships were in the bay below Beinn Edair, and they landed there.

And Finn and the battalions of the Fianna went out against them, and drove them back. And at the end of seven days Finn came back home, and he went quickly over the plain of Almhuin, thinking to see Sadbh his wife looking out from the dun, but there was no sign of her. And when he came to the dun, all his people came out to meet him, but they had a very downcast look. "Where is the flower of Almhuin, beautiful gentle Sadbh?" he asked them. And it is what they said: "While you were away fighting, your likeness, and the likeness of Bran and of Sceolan appeared before the dun, and we thought we heard the sweet call of the Dord Fiann. And Sadbh, that was so good and so beautiful, came out of the house," they said, "and she went out of the gates, and she would not listen to us, and we could not stop her." "Let me go meet my love," she said, "my husband, the father of the child that is not born." And with that she went running out towards the shadow of yourself that was before her, and that had its arms stretched out to her. But no sooner did she touch it than she gave a great cry, and the shadow lifted up a hazel rod, and on the moment it was a fawn was standing on the grass. Three times she turned and made for the gate of the dun, but the two hounds the shadow had with him went after her and took her by the throat and dragged her back to him. "And by your hand of valour, Finn," they said, "we ourselves made no delay till we went out on the plain after her. But it is our grief, they had all vanished, and there was not to be seen woman, or fawn or Druid, but we could hear the quick tread of feet on the hard plain, and the howling of dogs. And if you would ask every one of us in what quarter he heard those sounds, he would tell you a different one."

When Finn heard that, he said no word at all, but he struck his breast over and over again with his shut hands. And he went then to his own inside room, and his people saw him no more for that day, or till the sun rose over Magh Life on the morrow.

And through the length of seven years from that time, whenever he was not out fighting against the enemies of Ireland, he went searching and ever searching in every far corner for beautiful Sadbh. And there was great trouble on him all the time, unless he might throw it off for a while in hunting or in battle. And through all that time he never brought out to any hunting but the five hounds he had most trust in, Bran and Sceolan and Lomaire and Brod and Lomluath, the way there would be no danger for Sadbh if ever he came on her track.

But after the end of seven years, Finn and some of his chief men were hunting on the sides of Beinn Gulbain, and they heard a great outcry among the hounds, that were gone into some narrow place. And when they followed them there, they saw the five hounds of Finn in a ring, and they keeping back the other hounds, and in the middle of the ring was a young boy, with high looks, and he naked and having long hair. And he was no way daunted by the noise of the hounds, and did not look at them at all, but at the men that were coming up. And as soon as the fight was stopped Bran and Sceolan went up to the little lad, and whined and licked him, that any one would think they had forgotten their master. Finn and the others came up to him then, and put their hands on his head, and made much of him. And they brought him to their own hunting cabin, and he ate and drank with them, and before long he lost his wildness and was the same as themselves. And as to Bran and Sceolan, they were never tired playing about him.

And it is what Finn thought, there was some look of Sadbh in his face, and that it might be he was her son, and he kept him always beside him. And little by little when the boy had learned their talk, he told them all he could remember. He used to be with a deer he loved very much, he said, and that cared and sheltered him, and it was in a wide place they used to be, having hills and valleys and streams and woods in it, but that was shut in with high cliffs on every side, that there was no way of escape from it. And he used to be eating fruits and roots in the summer, and in the winter there was food left for him in the shelter of a cave. And a dark-looking man used to be coming to the place, and sometimes he would speak to the deer softly and gently, and sometimes with a loud angry voice. But whatever way he spoke, she would always draw away from him with the appearance of great dread on her, and the man would go away in great anger. And the last time he saw the deer, his mother, the dark man was speaking to her for a long time, from softness to anger. And at the end he struck her with a hazel rod, and with that she was forced to follow him, and she looking back all the while at the child, and crying after him that any one would pity her. And he tried hard to follow after her, and made every attempt, and cried out with grief and rage, but he had no power to move, and when he could hear his mother no more he fell on the grass and his wits went from him. And when he awoke it is on the side of the hill he was, where the hounds found him. And he searched a long time for the place where he was brought up, but he could not find it.

And the name the Fianna gave him was Oisin, and it is he was their maker of poems, and their good fighter afterwards.

CHAPTER V. THE BEST MEN OF THE FIANNA

And while Oisin was in his young youth, Finn had other good men along with him, and the best of them were Goll, son of Morna, and Caoilte, son of Ronan, and Lugaidh's Son.

As to Goll, that was of Connacht, he was very tall and light-haired, and some say he was the strongest of all the Fianna. Finn made a poem in praise of him one time when some stranger was asking what sort he was, saying how hardy he was and brave in battle, and as strong as a hound or as the waves, and with all that so kind and so gentle, and open-handed and sweet-voiced, and faithful to his friends.

And the chessboard he had was called the Solustairtech, the Shining Thing, and some of the chessmen were made of gold, and some of them of silver, and each one of them was as big as the fist of the biggest man of the Fianna; and after the death of Goll it was buried in Slieve Baune.

And as to Caoilte, that was a grey thin man, he was the best runner of them all. And he did a good many great deeds; a big man of the Fomor he killed one time, and he killed a five-headed giant in a wheeling door, and another time he made an end of an enchanted boar that no one else could get near, and he killed a grey stag that had got away from the Fianna through twenty-seven years. And another time he brought Finn out of Teamhair, where he was kept by force by the High King, because of some rebellion the Fianna had stirred up. And when Caoilte heard Finn had been brought away to Teamhair, he went out to avenge him. And the first he killed was Cuireach, a king of Leinster that had a great name, and he brought his head up to the hill that is above Buadhmaic. And after that he made a great rout through Ireland, bringing sorrow into every house for the sake of Finn, killing a man in every place, and killing the calves with the cows.

And every door the red wind from the east blew on, he would throw it open, and go in and destroy all before him, setting fire to the fields, and giving the wife of one man to another.

And when he came to Teamhair, he came to the palace, and took the clothes off the door-keeper, and he left his own sword that was worn thin in the king's sheath, and took the king's sword that had great power in it. And he went into the palace then in the disguise of a servant, to see how he could best free Finn.

And when evening came Caoilte held the candle at the king's feast in the great hall, and after a while the king said: "You will wonder at what I tell you, Finn, that the two eyes of Caoilte are in my candlestick." "Do not say that," said Finn, "and do not put reproach on my people although I myself am your prisoner; for as to Caoilte," he said, "that is not the way with him, for it is a high mind he has, and he only does high deeds, and he would not stand serving with a candle for all the gold of the whole world."

After that Caoilte was serving the King of Ireland with drink, and when he was standing beside him he gave out a high sorrowful lament. "There is the smell of Caoilte's skin on that lament," said the king. And when Caoilte saw he knew him he spoke out and he said: "Tell me what way I can get freedom for my master." "There is no way to get freedom for him but by doing one thing," said the king, "and that is a thing you can never do. If you can bring me together a couple of all the wild creatures of Ireland," he said, "I will give up your master to you then."

When Caoilte heard him say that he made no delay, but he set out from Teamhair, and went through the whole of Ireland to do that work for the sake of Finn. It is with the flocks of birds he began, though they were scattered in every part, and from them he went on to the beasts. And he gathered together two of every sort, two ravens from Fiodh da Bheann; two wild ducks from Loch na Seillein; two foxes from Slieve Cuilinn; two wild oxen from Burren; two swans from blue Dobhran; two owls from the wood of Faradhruim; two polecats from the branchy wood on the side of Druim da Raoin, the Ridge of the Victories; two gulls from the strand of Loch Leith; four woodpeckers from white Brosna; two plovers from Carraigh Dhain; two thrushes from Leith Lomard; two wrens from Dun Aoibh; two herons from Corrain Cleibh; two eagles from Carraig of the stones; two hawks from Fiodh Chonnach; two sows from Loch Meilghe; two water-hens from Loch Erne; two moor-hens from Monadh Maith; two sparrow-hawks from Dubhloch; two stonechats from Magh Cuillean; two tomtits from Magh Tuallainn; two swallows from Sean Abhla; two cormorants from Ath Cliath; two wolves from Broit Cliathach; two blackbirds from the Strand of the Two Women; two roebucks from Luachair Ire; two pigeons from Ceas Chuir; two nightingales from Leiter Ruadh; two starlings from green-sided Teamhair; two rabbits from Sith Dubh Donn; two wild pigs from Cluaidh Chuir; two cuckoos from Drom Daibh; two lapwings from Leanain na Furraich; two woodcocks from Craobh Ruadh; two hawks from the Bright Mountain; two grey mice from Luimneach; two otters from the Boinn; two larks from the Great Bog; two bats from the Cave of the Nuts; two badgers from the province of Ulster; two landrail from the banks of the Sionnan; two wagtails from Port Lairrge; two curlews from the harbour of Gallimh; two hares from Muirthemne; two deer from Sith Buidhe; two peacocks from Magh Mell; two cormorants from Ath Cliath; two eels from Duth Dur; two goldfinches from Slieve na-n Eun; two birds of slaughter from Magh Bhuilg; two bright swallows from Granard; two redbreasts from the Great Wood; two rock-cod from Cala Chairge; two sea-pigs from the great sea; two wrens from Mios an Chuil; two salmon from Eas Mhic Muirne; two clean deer from Gleann na Smoil; two cows from Magh Mor; two cats from the Cave of Cruachan; two sheep from bright Sidhe Diobhlain; two pigs of the pigs of the son of Lir; a ram and a crimson sheep from Innis.

And along with all these he brought ten hounds of the hounds of the Fianna, and a horse and a mare of the beautiful horses of Manannan.

And when Caoilte had gathered all these, he brought them to the one place. But when he tried to keep them together, they scattered here and there from him; the raven went away southward, and that vexed him greatly, but he overtook it again in Gleann da Bheann, beside Loch Lurcan. And then his wild duck went away from him, and it was not easy to get it again, but he followed it through every stream to grey Accuill till he took it by the neck and brought it back, and it no way willing.

And indeed through the length of his life Caoilte remembered well all he went through that time with the birds, big and little, travelling over hills and ditches and striving to bring them with him, that he might set Finn his master free.

And when he came to Teamhair he had more to go through yet, for the king would not let him bring them in before morning, but gave him a house having nine doors in it to put them up in for the night. And no sooner were they put in than they raised a loud screech all together, for a little ray of light was coming to them through fifty openings, and they were trying to make their escape. And if they were not easy in the house, Caoilte was not easy outside it, watching every door till the rising of the sun on the morrow.

And when he brought out his troop, the name the people gave them was "Caoilte's Rabble," and there was no wonder at all in that.

But all the profit the King of Ireland got from them was to see them together for that one time. For no sooner did Finn get his freedom than the whole of them scattered here and there, and no two of them went by the same road out of Teamhair.

And that was one of the best things Caoilte, son of Ronan, ever did. And another time he ran from the wave of Cliodna in the south to the wave of Rudraige in the north. And Colla his son was a very good runner too, and one time he ran a race backwards against the three battalions of the Fianna for a chessboard. And he won the race, but if he did, he went backward over Beinn Edair into the sea.

And very good hearing Caoilte had. One time he heard the King of the Luigne of Connacht at his hunting, and Blathmec that was with him said, "What is that hunt, Caoilte?" "A hunt of three packs of hounds," he said, "and three sorts of wild creatures before them. The first hunt," he said, "is after stags and large deer and the second hunt is after swift small hares, and the third is a furious hunt after heavy boars." "And what is the fourth hunt, Caoilte?" said Blathmec. "It is the hunting of heavy-sided, low-bellied badgers." And then they heard coming after the hunt the shouts of the lads and of the readiest of the men and the serving-men that were best at carrying burdens. And Blathmec went out to see the hunting, and just as Caoilte had told him, that was the way it was.

And he understood the use of herbs, and one time he met with two women that were very downhearted because their husbands had gone from them to take other wives. And Caoilte gave them Druid herbs, and they put them in the water of a bath and washed in it, and the love of their husbands came back to them, and they sent away the new wives they had taken.

And as to Lugaidh's Son, that was of Finn's blood, and another of the best men of the Fianna, he was put into Finn's arms as a child, and he was reared up by

Duban's daughter, that had reared eight hundred fighting men of the Fianna, till his twelfth year, and then she gave him all he wanted of arms and of armour, and he went to Chorraig Conluain and the mountains of Slieve Bladhma, where Finn and the Fianna were at that time.

And Finn gave him a very gentle welcome, and he struck his hand in Finn's hand, and made his agreement of service with him. And he stopped through the length of a year with the Fianna; but he was someway sluggish through all that time, so that under his leading not more than nine of the Fianna got to kill so much as a boar or a deer. And along with that, he used to beat both his servants and his hounds.

And at last the three battalions of the Fianna went to where Finn was, at the Point of the Fianna on the edge of Loch Lein, and they made their complaint against Lugaidh's Son, and it is what they said: "Make your choice now, will you have us with you, or will you have Lugaidh's Son by himself."

Then Lugaidh's Son came to Finn, and Finn asked him, "What is it has put the whole of the Fianna against you?" "By my word," said the lad, "I do not know the reason, unless it might be they do not like me to be doing my feats and casting my spears among them."

Then Finn gave him an advice, and it is what he said: "If you have a mind to be a good champion, be quiet in a great man's house; be surly in the narrow pass. Do not beat your hound without a cause; do not bring a charge against your wife without having knowledge of her guilt; do not hurt a fool in fighting, for he is without his wits. Do not find fault with high-up persons; do not stand up to take part in a quarrel; have no dealings with a bad man or a foolish man. Let two-thirds of your gentleness be showed to women and to little children that are creeping on the floor, and to men of learning that make the poems, and do not be rough with the common people. Do not give your reverence to all; do not be ready to have one bed with your companions. Do not threaten or speak big words, for it is a shameful thing to speak stiffly unless you can carry it out afterwards. Do not forsake your lord so long as you live; do not give up any man that puts himself under your protection for all the treasures of the world. Do not speak against others to their lord, that is not work for a good man. Do not be a bearer of lying stories, or a tale-bearer that is always chattering. Do not be talking too much; do not find fault hastily; however brave you may be, do not raise factions against you. Do not be going to drinking-houses, or finding fault with old men; do not meddle with low people; this is right conduct I am telling you. Do not refuse to share your meat; do not have a niggard for your friend; do not force yourself on a great man or give him occasion to speak against you. Hold fast to your arms till the hard fight is well ended. Do not give up your opportunity, but with that follow after gentleness."

That was good advice Finn gave, and he was well able to do that; for it was said of him that he had all the wisdom of a little child that is busy about the house, and the mother herself not understanding what he is doing; and that is the time she has most pride in him.

And as to Lugaidh's Son, that advice stayed always with him, and he changed his ways, and after a while he got a great name among the poets of Ireland and of Alban, and whenever they would praise Finn in their poems, they would praise him as well.

And Aoife, daughter of the King of Lochlann, that was married to Mal, son of Aiel, King of Alban, heard the great praise the poets were giving to Lugaidh's Son, and she set her love on him for the sake of those stories.

And one time Mal her husband and his young men went hunting to Slieve-mor-Monaidh in the north of Alban. And when he was gone Aoife made a plan in her sunny house where she was, to go over to Ireland, herself and her nine foster-sisters. And they set out and went over the manes of the sea till they came to Beinn Edair, and there they landed.

And it chanced on that day there was a hunting going on, from Slieve Bladhma to Beinn Edair. And Finn was in his hunting seat, and his fosterling, brown-haired Duibhruinn, beside him. And the little lad was looking about him on every side, and he saw a ship coming to the strand, and a queen with modest looks in the ship, and nine women along with her. They landed then, and they came up to where Finn was, bringing every sort of present with them, and Aoife sat down beside him. And Finn asked news of her, and she told him the whole story, and how she had given her love to Lugaidh's Son, and was come over the sea looking for him; and Finn made her welcome.

And when the hunting was over, the chief men of the Fianna came back to where Finn was, and every one asked who was the queen that was with him. And

Finn told them her name, and what it was brought her to Ireland. "We welcome her that made that journey," said they all; "for there is not in Ireland or in Alban a better man than the man she is come looking for, unless Finn himself."

And as to Lugaidh's Son, it was on the far side of Slieve Bladhma he was hunting that day, and he was the last to come in. And he went into Finn's tent, and when he saw the woman beside him he questioned Finn the same as the others had done, and Finn told him the whole story. "And it is to you she is come," he said; "and here she is to you out of my hand, and all the war and the battles she brings with her; but it will not fall heavier on you," he said, "than on the rest of the Fianna."

And she was with Lugaidh's Son a month and a year without being asked for. But one day the three battalions of the Fianna were on the Hill of the Poet in Leinster, and they saw three armed battalions equal to themselves coming, against them, and they asked who was bringing them. "It is Mal, son of Aiel, is bringing them," said Finn, "to avenge his wife on the Fianna. And it is a good time they are come," he said, "when we are gathered together at the one spot."

Then the two armies went towards one another, and Mal, son of Aiel, took hold of his arms, and three times he broke through the Fianna, and every time a hundred fell by him. And in the middle of the battle he and Lugaidh's Son met, and they fought against one another with spear and sword. And whether the fight was short or long, it was Mal fell by Lugaidh's Son at the last.

And Aoife stood on a hill near by, as long as the battle lasted. And from that out she belonged to Lugaidh's Son, and was a mother of children to him.

BOOK TWO: FINN'S HELPERS

CHAPTER I. THE LAD OF THE SKINS

Besides all the men Finn had in his household, there were some that would come and join him from one place or another. One time a young man wearing a dress of skins came to Finn's house at Almhuin, and his wife along with him, and he asked to take service with Finn.

And in the morning, as they were going to their hunting, the Lad of the Skins said to Finn: "Let me have no one with me but myself, and let me go into one part of the country by myself, and you yourself with all your men go to another part." "Is it on the dry ridges you will go," said Finn, "or is it in the deep bogs and marshes, where there is danger of drowning?" "I will go in the deep boggy places," said he.

So they all went out from Almhuin, Finn and the Fianna to one part, and the Lad of the Skins to another part, and they hunted through the day. And when they came back at evening, the Lad of the Skins had killed more than Finn and all his men together.

When Finn saw that, he was glad to have so good a servant. But Conan said to him: "The Lad of the Skins will destroy ourselves and the whole of the Fianna of Ireland unless you will find some way to rid yourself of him." "I never had a good man with me yet, Conan," said Finn, "but you wanted me to put him away; and how could I put away a man like that?" he said. "The way to put him away," said Conan, "is to send him to the King of the Floods to take from him the great cauldron that is never without meat, but that has always enough in it to feed the whole world. And let him bring that cauldron back here with him to Almhuin," he said.

So Finn called to the Lad of the Skins, and he said: "Go from me now to the

King of the Floods and get the great cauldron that is never empty from him, and bring it here to me." "So long as I am in your service I must do your work," said the Lad of the Skins. With that he set out, leaping over the hills and valleys till he came to the shore of the sea. And then he took up two sticks and put one of them across the other, and a great ship rose out of the two sticks. The Lad of the Skins went into the ship then, and put up the sails and set out over the sea, and he heard nothing but the whistling of eels in the sea and the calling of gulls in the air till he came to the house of the King of the Floods. And at that time there were hundreds of ships waiting near the shore; and he left his ship outside them all, and then he stepped from ship to ship till he stood on land.

There was a great feast going on at that time in the king's house, and the Lad of the Skins went up to the door, but he could get no farther because of the crowd. So he stood outside the door for a while, and no one looked at him, and he called out at last: "This is a hospitable house indeed, and these are mannerly ways, not to ask a stranger if there is hunger on him or thirst." "That is true," said the king; "and give the cauldron of plenty now to this stranger," he said, "till he eats his fill."

So his people did that, and no sooner did the Lad of the Skins get a hold of the cauldron than he made away to the ship and put it safe into it. But when he had done that he said: "There is no use in taking the pot by my swiftness, if I do not take it by my strength." And with that he turned and went to land again. And the whole of the men of the army of the King of the Floods were ready to fight; but if they were, so was the Lad of the Skins, and he went through them and over them all till the whole place was quiet.

He went back to his ship then and raised the sails and set out again for Ireland, and the ship went rushing back to the place where he made it. And when he came there, he gave a touch of his hand to the ship, and there was nothing left of it but the two sticks he made it from, and they lying on the strand before him, and the cauldron of plenty with them. And he took up the cauldron on his back, and brought it to Finn, son of Cumhal, at Almhuin. And Finn gave him his thanks for the work he had done.

One day, now, Finn was washing himself at the well, and a voice spoke out of the water, and it said: "You must give back the cauldron, Finn, to the King of the Floods, or you must give him battle in place of it."

Finn told that to the Lad of the Skins, but the answer he got from him was that his time was up, and that he could not serve on time that was past. "But if you want me to go with you," he said, "let you watch my wife, that is Manannan's daughter, through the night; and in the middle of the night, when she will be combing her hair, any request you make of her, she cannot refuse it. And the request you will make is that she will let me go with you to the King of the Floods, to bring the cauldron to his house and to bring it back again."

So Finn watched Manannan's daughter through the night, and when he saw her combing her hair, he made his request of her. "I have no power to refuse you," she said; "but you must promise me one thing, to bring my husband back to me, alive or dead. And if he is alive," she said, "put up a grey-green flag on the ship coming back; but if he is dead, put up a red flag."

So Finn promised to do that, and he himself and the Lad of the Skins set out together for the dun of the King of the Floods, bringing the cauldron with them.

No sooner did the king see them than he gave word to all his armies to make ready. But the Lad of the Skins made for them and overthrew them, and he went into the king's dun, and Finn with him, and they overcame him and brought away again the cauldron that was never empty.

But as they were going back to Ireland, they saw a great ship coming towards them. And when the Lad of the Skins looked at the ship, he said: "I think it is an old enemy of my own is in that ship, that is trying to bring me to my death, because of my wife that refused him her love." And when the ship came alongside, the man that was in it called out: "I know you well, and it is not by your dress I know you, son of the King of the Hills." And with that he made a leap on to the ship, and the two fought a great battle together, and they took every shape; they began young like two little boys, and fought till they were two old men; they fought from being two young pups until they were two old dogs; from being two young horses till they were two old horses. And then they began to fight in the shape of birds, and it is in that shape they killed one another at the last. And Finn threw the one bird into the water, but the other, that was the Lad of the Skins, he brought with him in the ship. And when he came in sight of Ireland, he raised a red flag as he had promised the woman.

And when he came to the strand, she was there before him, and when she saw

Finn, she said: "It is dead you have brought him back to me." And Finn gave her the bird, and she asked was that what she was to get in the place of her husband. And she was crying over the bird, and she brought it into a little boat with her, and she bade Finn to push out the boat to sea.

And he pushed it out, and it was driven by wind and waves till at last she saw two birds flying, having a dead one between them. And the two living birds let down the dead one on an island; and it was not long till it rose up living, and the three went away together.

And when Manannan's daughter saw that, she said: "There might be some cure for my man on the island, the way there was for that dead bird."

And the sea brought the boat to the island, and she went searching around, but all she could find was a tree having green leaves. "It might be in these leaves the cure is," she said; and she took some of the leaves and brought them to where the Lad of the Skins was, and put them about him. And on that moment he stood up as well and as sound as ever he was.

They went back then to Ireland, and they came to Almhuin at midnight, and the Lad of the Skins knocked at the door, and he said: "Put me out my wages." "There is no man, living or dead, has wages on me but the Lad of the Skins," said Finn; "and I would sooner see him here to-night," he said, "than the wages of three men." "If that is so, rise up and you will see him," said he.

So Finn rose up and saw him, and gave him a great welcome, and paid him his wages.

And after that he went away and his wife with him to wherever his own country was; but there were some said he was gone to the country of his wife's father, Manannan, Son of the Sea.

CHAPTER II. BLACK, BROWN, AND GREY

Finn was hunting one time near Teamhair of the Kings, and he saw three strange men coming towards him, and he asked what were their names. "Dubh and Dun and Glasan, Black, Brown, and Grey, are our names," they said, "and we are come to find Finn, son of Cumhal, Head of the Fianna, and to take service with him."

So Finn took them into his service, and when evening came he said: "Let each one of you watch through a third part of the night." And there was a trunk of a tree there, and he bade them make three equal parts of it, and he gave a part to each of the three men, and he said: "When each one of you begins his watch, let him set fire to his own log, and as long as the wood burns let him watch."

Then they drew lots, and the lot fell to Dubh to go on the first watch. So he set fire to his log, and he went out around the place, and Bran with him. He went farther and farther till at last he saw a bright light, and when he came to the place where it was, he saw a large house. He went inside, and there was a great company of very strange-looking men in it, and they drinking out of a single cup. One of the men, that seemed to be the highest, gave the cup to the man nearest him; and after he had drunk his fill he passed it on to the next, and so on to the last. And while it was going round, he said: "This is the great cup that was taken from Finn, son of Cumhal, a hundred years ago, and however many men may be together, every man of them can drink his fill from it, of whatever sort of drink he has a mind for."

Dubh was sitting near the door, on the edge of the crowd, and when the cup came to him he took a drink from it, and then he slipped away in the dark, bringing it with him. And when he came to the place where Finn was, his log was burned out.

Then it was the turn of Dun to go out, for the second lot had fallen on him, and he put a light to his log, and went out, and Bran with him.

He walked on through the night till he saw a fire that was shining from a large house, and when he went in he saw a crowd of men, and they fighting. And a very old man that was in a high place above the rest called out: "Stop fighting now, for I have a better gift for you than the one you lost to-night." And with that he drew a knife out of his belt and held it up, and said: "This is the wonderful knife, the small knife of division, that was stolen from Finn, son of Cumhal, a hundred years ago; and you have but to cut on a bone with that knife and you will get your fill of the best meat in the world." Then he gave the knife to the man nearest him, and a bare bone with it, and the man began to cut, and there came off the bone slices of the best meat in the world.

The knife and the bone were sent round then from man to man till they came to Dun, and as soon as he had the knife in his hand he slipped out unknown and hurried back, and he had just got to the well where Finn was, when his part of the log burned out.

Then Glasan lighted his log and went out on his watch till he came to the house, the same way the others did. And he looked in and he saw the floor full of dead bodies, and he thought to himself: "There must be some great wonder here. And if I lie down on the floor and put some of the bodies over me," he said, "I will be able to see all that happens."

So he lay down and pulled some of the bodies over him, and he was not long there till he saw an old hag coming into the house, having one leg and one arm and one upper tooth, that was long enough to serve her in place of a crutch. And when she came inside the door she took up the first dead body she met with, and threw it aside, for it was lean. And as she went on, she took two bites out of every fat body she met with, and threw away every lean one.

She had her fill of flesh and blood before she came to Glasan, and she dropped down on the floor and fell asleep, and Glasan thought that every breath she drew would bring down the roof on his head. He rose up then and looked at her, and wondered at the bulk of her body. And at last he drew his sword and hit her a slash that killed her; but if he did, three young men leaped out of her body. And Glasan made a stroke that killed the first of them, and Bran killed the second, but the third made his escape.

Glasan made his way back then, and just when he got to where Finn was, his log of wood was burned out, and the day was beginning to break.

And when Finn rose up in the morning he asked news of the three watchers, and they gave him the cup and the knife and told him all they had seen, and he gave great praise to Dubh and to Dun; but to Glasan he said: "It might have been as well for you to have left that old hag alone, for I am in dread the third young man may bring trouble on us all."

It happened at the end of twenty-one years, Finn and the Fianna were at their hunting in the hills, and they saw a Red-Haired Man coming towards them, and he spoke to no one, but came and stood before Finn. "What is it you are looking for?" said Finn. "I am looking for a master for the next twenty-one years," he said. "What wages are you asking?" said Finn. "No wages at all, but only if I die before the twenty-one years are up, to bury me on Inis Caol, the Narrow Island." "I will do that for you," said Finn.

So the Red-Haired Man served Finn well through the length of twenty years. But in the twenty-first year he began to waste and to wither away, and he died.

And when he was dead, the Fianna were no way inclined to go to Inis Caol to bury him. But Finn said he would break his word for no man, and that he himself would bring his body there. And he took an old white horse that had been turned loose on the hills, and that had got younger and not older since it was put out, and he put the body of the Red-Haired Man on its back, and let it take its own way, and he himself followed it, and twelve men of the Fianna.

And when they came to Inis Caol they saw no trace of the horse or of the body. And there was an open house on the island, and they went in. And there were seats for every man of them inside, and they sat down to rest for a while.

But when they tried to rise up it failed them to do it, for there was enchantment on them. And they saw the Red-Haired Man standing before them in that moment.

"The time is come now," he said, "for me to get satisfaction from you for the death of my mother and my two brothers that were killed by Glasan in the house of the dead bodies." He began to make an attack on them then, and he would have made an end of them all, but Finn took hold of the Dord Fiann, and blew a great blast on it.

And before the Red-Haired Man was able to kill more than three of them, Diarmuid, grandson of Duibhne, that had heard the sound of the Dord Fiann, came into the house and made an end of him, and put an end to the enchantment. And Finn, with the nine that were left of the Fianna, came back again to Almhuin.

CHAPTER III. THE HOUND

One day the three battalions of the Fianna came to Magh Femen, and there they saw three young men waiting for them, having a hound with them; and there was not a colour in the world but was on that hound, and it was bigger than any other hound.

"Where do you come from, young men?" said Finn. "Out of the greater Iruath in the east," said they; "and our names are Dubh, the Dark, and Agh, the Battle, and Ilar, the Eagle." "What is it you came for?" "To enter into service, and your friendship," said they. "What good will it do us, you to be with us?" said Finn. "We are three," said they, "and you can make a different use of each one of us." "What uses are those?" said Finn. "I will do the watching for all the Fianna of Ireland and of Alban," said one of them. "I will take the weight of every fight and every battle that will come to them, the way they can keep themselves in quiet," said the second. "I will meet every troublesome thing that might come to my master," said the third; "and let all the wants of the world be told to me and I will satisfy them. And I have a pipe with me," he said; "and all the men of the world would sleep at the sound of it, and they in their sickness. And as to the hound," he said, "as long as there are deer in Ireland he will get provision for the Fianna every second night. And I myself," he said, "will get it on the other nights." "What will you ask of us to be with us like that?" said Finn. "We will ask three things," they said: "no one to come near to the place where we have our lodging after the fall of night; nothing to be given out to us, but we to provide for ourselves; and the worst places to be given to us in the hunting." "Tell me by your oath now," said Finn, "why is it you will let no one see you after nightfall?" "We have a reason," said they; "but do not ask it of us, whether we are short or long on the one path with you. But we will tell you this much," they said, "every third night, one of us three is dead and the other two are watching him, and we have no mind for any one to be looking at us."

So Finn promised that; but if he did there were some of the Fianna were not well pleased because of the ways of those three men, living as they did by themselves, and having a wall of fire about them, and they would have made an end of them but for Finn protecting them.

About that time there came seven men of poetry belonging to the people of Cithruadh, asking the fee for a poem, three times fifty ounces of gold and the same of silver to bring back to Cithruadh at Teamhair. "Whatever way we get it, we must find some way to get that," said a man of the Fianna. Then the three young men from Iruath said: "Well, men of learning," they said, "would you sooner get the fee for your poem to-night or to-morrow?" "To-morrow will be time enough," said they.

And the three young men went to the place where the hound had his bed a little way off from the rath, and the hound threw out of his mouth before them the three times fifty ounces of gold and three times fifty of silver, and they gave them to the men of poetry, and they went away.

Another time Finn said: "What can the three battalions of the Fianna do to-night, having no water?" And one of the men of Iruath said: "How many drinking-horns are with you?" "Three hundred and twelve," said Caoilte. "Give me the horns into my hand," said the young man, "and whatever you will find in them after that, you may drink it." He filled the horns then with beer and they drank it, and he did that a second and a third time; and with the third time of filling they were talkative and their wits confused. "This is a wonderful mending of the feast," said Finn. And they gave the place where all that happened the name of the Little Rath of Wonders.

And one time after that again there came to Finn three bald red clowns, holding three red hounds in their hands, and three deadly spears. And there was poison on their clothes and on their hands and their feet, and on everything they touched. And Finn asked them who were they. And they said they were three sons of Uar, son of Indast of the Tuatha de Danaan; and it was by a man of the Fianna, Caoilte son of Ronan, their father was killed in the battle of the Tuatha de Danaan on Slieve nan Ean, the Mountain of Birds, in the east. "And let Caoilte son of Ronan give us the blood-fine for him now," they said. "What are your names?" said Finn. "Aincel and Digbail and Espaid; Ill-wishing and Harm and Want are our names. And what answer do you give us now, Finn?" they said. "No one before me ever gave a blood-fine for a man killed in battle, and I will not give it," said Finn. "We will do revenge and robbery on you so," said they. "What revenge is that?" said Finn. "It is what I will do," said Aincel, "if I meet with two or three or four of the Fianna, I will take their feet and their hands from them." "It is what I will do," said Digbail, "I will not leave a day without loss of a hound or a serving-boy or a fighting man to the Fianna of Ireland." "And I myself will be always leaving them in want of people, or of a hand, or of an eye," said Espaid. "Without we get some help against them," said Caoilte, "there will not be one of us living at the end of a year." "Well," said Finn, "we will make a dun and stop here for a while, for I will not be going through Ireland and these men following after me, till I find who are the strongest, themselves or ourselves."

So the Fianna made little raths for themselves all about Slieve Mis, and they stopped there through a month and a quarter and a year. And through all that time the three red bald-headed men were doing every sort of hurt and harm upon them.

But the three sons of the King of Iruath came to speak with Finn, and it is what they said: "It is our wish, Finn, to send the hound that is with us to go around you three times in every day, and however many may be trying to hurt or to rob you, they will not have power to do it after that. But let there be neither fire nor arms nor any other dog in the house he goes into," they said. "I will let none of these things go into the one house with him," said Finn, "and he will go safe back to you." So every day the hound would be sent to Finn, having his chain of ridges of red gold around his neck, and he would go three times around Finn, and three times he would put his tongue upon him. And to the people that were nearest to the hound when he came into the house it would seem like as if a vat of mead was being strained, and to others there would come the sweet smell of an apple garden.

And every harm and sickness the three sons of Uar would bring on the Fianna, the three sons of the King of Iruath would take it off them with their herbs and their help and their healing.

And after a while the High King of Ireland came to Slieve Mis with a great, troop of his men, to join with Finn and the Fianna. And they told the High King the whole story, and how the sons of Uar were destroying them, and the three sons of the King of Iruath were helping them against them. "Why would not the men that can do all that find some good spell that would drive the sons of Uar out of Ireland?" said the High King.

With that Caoilte went looking for the three young men from Iruath and brought them to the High King. "These are comely men," said the High King, "good in their shape and having a good name. And could you find any charm, my sons," he said, "that will drive out these three enemies that are destroying the Fianna of Ireland?" "We would do that if we could find those men near us," said they; "and it is where they are now," they said, "at Daire's Cairn at the end of the raths." "Where are Garb-Cronan, the Rough Buzzing One, and Saltran of the Long Heel?" said Finn. "Here we are, King of the Fianna," said they. "Go out to those men beyond, and tell them I will give according to the judgment of the King of Ireland in satisfaction for their father." The messengers went out then and brought them in, and they sat down on the bank of the rath.

Then the High King said: "Rise up, Dubh, son of the King of Iruath, and command these sons of Uar with a spell to quit Ireland." And Dubh rose up, and he said: "Go out through the strength of this spell and this charm, you three enemies of the Fianna, one-eyed, lame-thighed, left-handed, of the bad race. And go out on the deep bitter sea," he said, "and let each one of you strike a blow of his sword on the head of his brothers. For it is long enough you are doing harm and destruction on the King of the Fianna, Finn, son of Cumhal."

With that the hound sent a blast of wind under them that brought them out into the fierce green sea, and each of them struck a blow on the head of the others. And that was the last that was seen of the three destroying sons of Uar, Aincel and Digbail and Espaid.

But after the time of the Fianna, there came three times in the one year, into West Munster, three flocks of birds from the western sea having beaks of bone and fiery breath, and the wind from their wings was as cold as a wind of spring. And the first time they came was at reaping time, and every one of them brought away an ear of corn from the field. And the next time they came they did not leave apple on tree, or nut on bush, or berry on the rowan; and the third time they spared no live thing they could lift from the ground, young bird or fawn or silly little child. And the first day they came was the same day of the year the three sons of Uar were put out in the sea.

And when Caoilte, that was one of the last of the Fianna, and that was living yet, heard of them, he remembered the sons of Uar, and he made a spell that drove them out into the sea again, and they perished there by one another.

It was about the length of a year the three sons of the King of Iruath stopped with Finn. And at the end of that time Donn and Dubhan, two sons of the King of Ulster, came out of the north to Munster. And one night they kept watch for the Fianna, and three times they made a round of the camp. And it is the way the young men from Iruath used to be, in a place by themselves apart from the Fianna, and their hound in the middle between them; and at the fall of night there used a wall of fire to be around them, the way no one could look at them.

And the third time the sons of the King of Ulster made the round of the camp, they saw the fiery wall, and Donn said: "It is a wonder the way those three young men are through the length of a year now, and their hound along with them, and no one getting leave to look at them."

With that he himself and his brother took their arms in their hands, and went inside the wall of fire, and they began looking at the three men and at the hound. And the great hound they used to see every day at the hunting was at this time no bigger than a lap-dog that would be with a queen or a high person. And one of the young men was watching over the dog, and his sword in his hand, and another of them was holding a vessel of white silver to the mouth of the dog; and any drink any one of the three would ask for, the dog would put it out of his mouth into the vessel.

Then one of the young men said to the hound: "Well, noble one and brave one and just one, take notice of the treachery that is done to you by Finn." When the dog heard that he turned to the King of Ulster's sons, and there rose a dark Druid wind that blew away the shields from their shoulders and the swords from their sides into the wall of fire. And then the three men came out and made an end of them; and when that was done the dog came and breathed on them, and they turned to ashes on the moment, and there was never blood or flesh or bone of them found after.

And the three battalions of the Fianna divided themselves into companies of nine, and went searching through every part of Ireland for the King of Ulster's two sons.

And as to Finn, he went to Teamhair Luachra, and no one with him but the serving-lads and the followers of the army. And the companies of nine that were looking for the King of Ulster's sons came back to him there in the one night; but they brought no word of them, if they were dead or living.

But as to the three sons of the King of Iruath and the hound that was with them, they were seen no more by Finn and the Fianna.

CHAPTER IV. RED RIDGE

There was another young man came and served Finn for a while; out of Connacht he came, and he was very daring, and the Red Ridge was the name they gave him. And he all but went from Finn one time, because of his wages that were too long in coming to him. And the three battalions of the Fianna came trying to quiet him, but he would not stay for them. And at the last Finn himself came, for it is a power he had, if he would make but three verses he would quiet any one. And it is what he said: "Daring Red Ridge," he said, "good in battle, if you go from me to-day with your great name it is a good parting for us. But once at Rath Cro," he said, "I gave you three times fifty ounces in the one day; and at Cam Ruidhe I gave you the full of my cup of silver and of yellow gold. And do you remember," he said, "the time we were at Rath Ai, when we found the two women, and when we ate the nuts, myself and yourself were there together."

And after that the young man said no more about going from him.

And another helper came to Finn one time he was fighting at a ford, and all his weapons were used or worn with the dint of the fight. And there came to him a daughter of Mongan of the Sidhe, bringing him a flat stone having a chain of gold to it. And he took the stone and did great deeds with it. And after the fight the stone fell into the ford, that got the name of Ath Liag Finn.

And that stone will never be found till the Woman of the Waves will find it, and will bring it to land on a Sunday morning; and on that day seven years the world will come to an end.

BOOK THREE: THE BATTLE OF THE WHITE STRAND.

CHAPTER I. THE ENEMIES OF IRELAND

Of all the great battles the Fianna fought to keep the foreigners out of Ireland, the greatest was the one that was fought at Finntraigh the White Strand, in Munster; and this is the whole story of it, and of the way the Fianna came to have so great a name.

One time the enemies of Ireland gathered together under Daire Donn, High King of the Great World, thinking to take Ireland and to put it under tribute.

The King of Greece was of them, and the King of France, and the King of the Eastern World, and Lughman of the Broad Arms, King of the Saxons, and Fiacha of the Long Hair, King of the Gairean, and Tor the son of Breogan, King of the Great Plain, and Sligech, son of the King of the Men of Cepda, and Comur of the Crooked Sword, King of the Men of the Dog-Heads, and Caitchenn, King of the Men of the Cat-Heads, and Caisel of the Feathers, King of Lochlann, and Madan of the Bent Neck, son of the King of the Marshes, and three kings from the rising of the sun in the east, and Ogarmach, daughter of the King of Greece, the best woman-warrior that ever came into the world, and a great many other kings and great lords.

The King of the World asked then: "Who is there can give me knowledge of the harbours of Ireland?" "I will do that for you, and I will bring you to a good harbour," said Glas, son of Bremen, that had been put out of Ireland by Finn for doing some treachery.

Then the armies set out in their ships, and they were not gone far when the wind rose and the waves, and they could hear nothing but the wild playing of the sea-women, and the screams of frightened birds, and the breaking of ropes and of sails. But after a while, when the wind found no weakness in the heroes, it rose from them and went up into its own high place. And then the sea grew quiet and the waves grew tame and the harbours friendly, and they stopped for a while at an island that was called the Green Rock. But the King of the World said then: "It is not a harbour like this you promised me, Glas, son of Dremen, but a shore of white sand where my armies could have their fairs and their gatherings the time they would not be fighting." "I know a harbour of that sort in the west of Ireland," said Glas, "the Harbour of the White Strand in Corca Duibhne." So they went into their ships again, and went on over the sea towards Ireland.

CHAPTER II. CAEL AND CREDHE

Now as to Finn, when it was shown to him that the enemies of Ireland were coming, he called together the seven battalions of the Fianna. And the place where they gathered was on the hill that was called Fionntulach, the White Hill, in Munster. They often stopped on that hill for a while, and spear-shafts with spells on them were brought to them there, and they had every sort of thing for food, beautiful blackberries, haws of the hawthorn, nuts of the hazels of Cenntire, tender twigs of the bramble bush, sprigs of wholesome gentian, watercress at the beginning of summer. And there would be brought to their cooking-pots birds out of the oak-woods, and squirrels from Berramain, and speckled eggs from the cliffs, and salmon out of Luimnech, and eels of the Sionnan, and woodcocks of Fidhrinne, and otters from the hidden places of the Doile, and fish from the coasts of Buie and Beare, and dulse from the bays of Cleire.

And as they were going to set out southwards, they saw one of their young men, Gael, grandson of Nemhnain, coming towards them. "Where are you come from, Cael?" Finn asked him. "From Brugh na Boinne," said he. "What were you asking there?" said Finn. "I was asking to speak with Muirenn, daughter of Derg, that was my own nurse," said he. "For what cause?" said Finn. "It was about a high marriage and a woman of the Sidhe that was showed to me in a dream; Credhe it was I saw, daughter of the King of Ciarraighe Luachra." "Do you know this, Cael," said Finn, "that she is the greatest deceiver of all the women of Ireland; and there is hardly a precious thing in Ireland but she has coaxed it away to her own great dun." "Do you know what she asks of every man that comes asking for her?" said Cael. "I know it," said Finn; "she will let no one come unless he is able to make a poem setting out the report of her bowls and her horns and her cups, her grand vessels and all her palaces." "I have all that ready," said Cael; "it was given to me by my nurse,

Muirenn, daughter of Derg."

They gave up the battle then for that time, and they went on over every hilly place and every stony place till they came to Loch Cuire in the west; and they came to the door of the hill of the Sidhe and knocked at it with the shafts of their long gold-socketted spears. And there came young girls having yellow hair to the windows of the sunny houses; and Credhe herself, having three times fifty women with her, came out to speak with them. "It is to ask you in marriage we are come," said Finn. "Who is it is asking for me?" said she. "It is Cael, the hundred-killer, grandson of Nemhnain, son of the King of Leinster in the east." "I have heard talk of him, but I have never seen him," said Credhe. "And has he any poem for me?" she said. "I have that," said Cael, and he rose up then and sang his poem:

"A journey I have to make, and it is no easy journey, to the house of Credhe against the breast of the mountain, at the Paps of Dana; it is there I must be going through hardships for the length of seven days. It is pleasant her house is, with men and boys and women, with Druids and musicians, with cup-bearer and door-keeper, with horse-boy that does not leave his work, with distributer to share food; and Credhe of the Fair Hair having command over them all.

"It would be delightful to me in her dun, with coverings and with down, if she has but a mind to listen to me.

"A bowl she has with juice of berries in it to make her eyebrows black; crystal vats of fermenting grain; beautiful cups and vessels. Her house is of the colour of lime; there are rushes for beds, and many silken coverings and blue cloaks; red gold is there, and bright drinking-horns. Her sunny house is beside Loch Cuire, made of silver and yellow gold; its ridge is thatched without any fault, with the crimson wings of birds. The doorposts are green, the lintel is of silver taken in battle. Credhe's chair on the left is the delight of delights, covered with gold of Elga; at the foot of the pleasant bed it is, the bed that was made of precious stones by Tuile in the east. Another bed there is on the right, of gold and silver, it is made without any fault, curtains it has of the colour of the foxglove, hanging on rods of copper.

"The people of her house, it is they have delight, their cloaks are not faded white, they are not worn smooth; their hair is fair and curling. Wounded men in their blood would sleep hearing the birds of the Sidhe singing in the eaves of the sunny house.

"If I have any thanks to give to Credhe, for whom the cuckoo calls, she will get better praise than this; if this love-service I have done is pleasing to her, let her not delay, let her say, 'Your coming is welcome to me.'

"A hundred feet there are in her house, from one corner to another; twenty feet fully measured is the width of her great door; her roof has its thatch of the wings of blue and yellow birds, the border of her well is of crystals and carbuncles.

"There is a vat there of royal bronze; the juice of pleasant malt is running from it; over the vat is an apple-tree with its heavy fruit; when Credhe's horn is filled from the vat, four apples fall into it together.

"She that owns all these things both at low water and at flood, Credhe from the Hill of the Three Peaks, she is beyond all the women of Ireland by the length of a spear-cast.

"Here is this song for her, it is no sudden bride-gift it is, no hurried asking; I bring it to Credhe of the beautiful shape, that my coming may be very bright to her."

Then Credhe took him for her husband, and the wedding-feast was made, and the whole of the Fianna stopped there through seven days, at drinking and pleasure, and having every good thing.

CHAPTER III. CONN CRITHER

Finn now, when he had turned from his road to go to Credhe's house, had sent out watchmen to every landing-place to give warning when the ships of the strangers would be in sight. And the man that was keeping watch at the White Strand was Conn Crither, son of Bran, from Teamhair Luachra.

And after he had been a long time watching, he was one night west from the Round Hill of the Fianna that is called Cruachan Adrann, and there he fell asleep. And while he was in his sleep the ships came; and what roused him was the noise of the breaking of shields and the clashing of swords and of spears, and the cries of women and children and of dogs and horses that were under flames, and that the strangers were making an attack on.

Conn Crither started up when he heard that, and he said: "It is great trouble has come on the people through my sleep; and I will not stay living after this," he said, "for Finn and the Fianna of Ireland to see me, but I will rush into the middle of the strangers," he said, "and they will fall by me till I fall by them."

He put on his suit of battle then and ran down towards the strand. And on the way he saw three women dressed in battle clothes before him, and fast as he ran he could not overtake them. He took his spear then to make a cast of it at the woman was nearest him, but she stopped on the moment, and she said: "Hold your hand and do not harm us, for we are not come to harm you but to help you." "Who are you yourselves?" said Conn Crither. "We are three sisters," she said, "and we are come from Tir nan Og, the Country of the Young, and we have all three given you our love, and no one of us loves you less than the other, and it is to give you our help we are come." "What way will you help me?" said Conn. "We will give you good help," she said, "for we will make Druid armies about you from stalks of grass and from the tops of the watercress, and they will cry out to the strangers and will strike their arms from their hands, and take from them their strength and their eyesight. And we will put a Druid mist about you now," she said, "that will hide you from the armies of the strangers, and they will not see you when you make an attack on them. And we have a well of healing at the foot of Slieve Iolair, the Eagle's Mountain," she said, "and its waters will cure every wound made in battle. And after bathing in that well you will be as whole and as sound as the day you were born. And bring whatever man you like best with you," she said, "and we will heal him along with you."

Conn Crither gave them his thanks for that, and he hurried on to the strand. And it was at that time the armies of the King of the Great Plain were taking spoils from Traigh Moduirn in the north to Finntraighe in the south. And Conn Crither came on them, and the Druid army with him, and he took their spoils from them, and the Druid army took their sight and their strength from them, and they were routed, and they made away to where the King of the Great Plain was, and Conn Crither followed, killing and destroying. "Stop with me, king-hero," said the King of the Great Plain, "that I may fight with you on account of my people, since there is not one of them that turns to stand against you."

So the two set their banners in the earth and attacked one another, and fought a good part of the day until Conn Crither struck off the king's head. And he lifted up the head, and he was boasting of what he had done. "By my word," he said, "I will not let myself be parted from this body till some of the Fianna, few or many, will come to me."

CHAPTER IV. GLAS, SON OF BREMEN

The King of the World heard that, and he said: "It is a big word that man is saying," he said; "and rise up now, Glas, son of Dremen, and see which of the Fianna of Ireland it is that is saying it."

Glas left the ship then, and he went to where Conn Crither was, and he asked who was he. "I am Conn Crither, son of Bran, from Teamhair Luachra," said he. "If that is so," said Glas, "you are of the one blood with myself, for I am Glas, son of Bremen from Teamhair Luachra." "It is not right for you to come fighting against me from those foreigners, so," said Conn. "It is a pity indeed," said Glas; "and but for Finn and the Fianna driving me from them, I would not fight against you or against one of themselves for all the treasures of the whole world." "Do not say that," said Conn, "for I swear by my hand of valour," he said, "if you had killed Finn's own son and the sons of his people along with him, you need not be in dread of him if only you came under his word and his protection." "I think indeed the day is come for me to fight beside you," said Glas, "and I will go back and tell that to the King of the World."

He went back then to where the king was, and the king asked him which of the men of the Fianna was in it. "It is a kinsman of my own is in it, High King," said Glas; "and it is weak my heart is, he to be alone, and I have a great desire to go and help him." "If you go," said the King of the World, "it is what I ask you, to come and to tell me every day how many of the Fianna of Ireland have fallen by me; and if a few of my own men should fall," he said, "come and tell me who it was they fell by." "It is what I ask you," said Glas, "not to let your armies land till the Fianna come to us, but to let one man only come to fight with each of us until that time," he said.

So two of the strangers were sent against them that day, and they got their death by Glas and by Conn Crither. Then they asked to have two men sent against each of them, and that was done; and three times nine fell by them before night. And Conn Crither was covered with wounds after the day, and he said to Glas: "Three women came to me from the Country of the Young, and they promised to put me in a well of healing for my wounds. And let you watch the harbour to-night," he said, "and I will go look for them." So he went to them, and they bathed him in the well of healing, and he was whole of his wounds.

And as to Glas, son of Dremen, he went down to the harbour, and he said: "O King of the World," he said, "there is a friend of mine in the ships, Madan of the Bent Neck, son of the King of the Marshes; and it is what he said in the great world in the east, that he himself would be enough to take Ireland for you, and that he would bring it under tribute to you by one way or another. And I ask you to let him come alone against me to-night, till we see which of us will fight best for Ireland."

So Madan came to the land, and the two attacked one another, and made a very hard fight; but as it was not in the prophecy that Glas would find his death there, it was the son of the King of the Marshes that got his death by him.

And not long after that Conn Crither came back to Glas, and he gave Glas great praise for all he had done.

CHAPTER V. THE HELP OF THE MEN OF DEA

hen Taistellach that was one of Finn's messengers came to the White Strand asking news; and Conn bade him go back to where Finn was and tell him the way things were. But Taistellach would not go until he had wetted his sword in the blood of one of the enemies of Ireland, the same as the others had done. And he sent a challenge to the ships, and Coimhleathan, a champion that was very big and tall, came and fought with him on the strand, and took him in his arms to bring him back living to the ship of the High King; but Taistellach struck his head off in the sea and brought it back to land.

"Victory and blessing be with you!" said Conn Crither. "And go now to-night," he said, "to the house of Bran, son of Febal my father at Teamhair Luachra, and bid him to gather all the Tuatha de Danaan to help us; and go on to-morrow to the Fianna of Ireland." So Taistellach went on to Bran's house, and he told him the whole story and gave him the message.

Then Bran, son of Febal, went out to gather the Tuatha de Danaan, and he went to Dun Sesnain in Ui Conall Gabra, where they were holding a feast at that time. And there he found three of the best young men of the Tuatha de Danaan, Ilbrec the Many Coloured, son of Manannan, and Nemanach the Pearly, son of Angus Og, and Sigmall, grandson of Midhir, and they made him welcome and bade him to stop with them. "There is a greater thing than this for you to do, Men of Dea," said Bran; and he told them the whole story, and the way Conn Crither his son was. "Stop with me to-night," said Sesnan, "and my son Dolb will go to Bodb Dearg, son of the Dagda, and gather in the Tuatha de Danaan to us."

So he stopped there, and Dolb, son of Sesnan, went to Sidhe Bean Finn above Magh Femen, and Bodb Dearg was there at that time, and Dolb gave him his message. "Young man," said Bodb Dearg, "we are no way bound to help the men of Ireland out of that strait." "Do not say that," said Dolb, "for there is not a king's son or a prince or a leader of the Fianna of Ireland without having a wife or a mother or a foster-mother or a sweetheart of the Tuatha de Danaan; and it is good help they have given you every time you were in want of it." "I give my word," said Bodb Dearg, "it is right to give a good answer to so good a messenger." With that he sent word to the Tuatha de Danaan in every place where they were, and they gathered to him. And from that they went on to Dun Sesnain, and they stopped there through the night And they rose up in the morning and put on their shirts of the dearest silk and their embroidered coats of rejoicing, and they took their green shields and their swords and their spears. And their leaders at that time besides Bodb Dearg were Midhir of Bri Leith, and Lir of Sidhe Finnachaidh, and Abarthach, son of Ildathach, and Ilbrec, son of Manannan, and Fionnbhar of Magh Suil, and Argat Lamh, the Silver Hand, from the Sionnan, and the Man of Sweet Speech from the Boinn.

And the whole army of them came into Ciarraighe Luachra, and to red-haired Slieve Mis, and from that to the harbour of the White Strand. "O Men of Dea," said Abarthach then, "let a high mind and high courage rise within you now in the face of the battle. For the doings of every one among you," he said, "will be told till the end of the world; and let you fulfil now the big words you have spoken in the drinking-houses." "Rise up, Glas, son of Dremen," said Bodb Dearg then, "and tell out to the King of the World that I am come to do battle." Glas went then to the King of the World. "Are those the Fianna of Ireland I see?" said the king. "They are not," said Glas, "but another part of the men of Ireland that do not dare to be on the face of the earth, but that live in hidden houses under the earth, and it is to give warning of battle from them I am come." "Who will answer the Tuatha de Danaan for me?" said the King of the World. "We will go against them," said two of the kings that were with him, Comur Cromchenn, King of the Men of the Dog-Heads, and Caitchenn, King of the Men of the Cat-Heads. And they had five red-armed battalions with them, and they went to the shore like great red waves. "Who is there to match with the King of the Dog-Heads for me?" said Bodb Dearg. "I will go against him," said Lir of Sidhe Finnachaidh, "though I heard there is not in the world a man with stronger hands than himself." "Who will be a match for the King of the Cat-Heads?" said Bodb Dearg. "I will be a match for him," said Abarthach, son of Ildathach.

So Lir and the King of the Dog-Heads attacked one another, and they made a hard fight; but after a while Lir was getting the worst of it. "It is a pity the way Lir is," said Bodb Dearg; "and let some of you rise up and help him," he said. Then Ilbrec, son of Manannan, went to his help; but if he did, he got a wound himself and could do nothing. Then Sigmal, grandson of Midhir, went to his help, and after him the five sons of Finnaistucan, and others of the Men of Dea, but they were all driven off by the King of the Dog-Heads. But at that time Abarthach had made an end of the King of the Cat-Heads, and he rose on his spear, and made a leap, and came down between Lir and his enemy. "Leave off now and look on at the fight," he said to Lir, "and leave it to me and the foreigner." With that he took his sword in his left hand and made a thrust with his spear in through the king's armour. And as the king was raising up his shield, he struck at him with the sword that was in his left hand, and cut off both his legs at the knees, and the king let fall his shield then, and Abarthach struck off his head. And the two kings being dead, their people broke away and ran, but the Men of Dea followed them and made an end of them all; but if they did, they lost a good many of their own men.

CHAPTER VI. THE MARCH OF THE FIANNA

Ana Finn and the Fianna were at the house of Credhe yet, and they saw Taistellach coming towards them. It was the custom, now, with Finn when he sent any one looking for news, that it was to himself it was to be told first, the way that if he got bad news he would let on not to mind it; and if it was good news he got, he would have the satisfaction of telling it himself. So Taistellach told him how the foreigners were come to the harbour of the White Strand.

Then Finn turned to his chief men, and he said: "Fianna of Ireland, there never came harm or danger to Ireland to be put aside this great danger that is come against us now. And you get great tribute and great service from the chief men of Ireland," he said, "and if you take that from them it is right for you to defend them now."

And the Fianna all said they would not go back one step from the defence of Ireland. And as to Credhe, she gave every one of them a battle dress, and they were taking leave of her, and Finn said: "Let the woman come along with us till we know is it good or bad the end of this journey will be." So she came with them, bringing a great herd of cattle; and through the whole length of the battle, that lasted a year and a day, she had new milk for them, and it was to her house the wounded were brought for healing.

Then the Fianna set out, and they went to the borders of Ciarraighe Luachra and across by the shores of the Bannlid with their left hand to Slieve Mis, and they made shelters for themselves that night, and kindled fires.

But Caoilte and Oisin and Lugaidh's Son said to one another they would go on to the harbour, the way they would have time to redden their hands in the blood of the foreigners before the rest of the Fianna would come.

And at that time the King of the World bade some of his chief men to go on shore and to bring him back some spoils. So they went to land and they gave out a great shout, and the people of the ships gave out a great shout at the same time. "I swear by the oath my people swear by," said Caoilte, "I have gone round the whole world, but I never heard so many voices together in the one place." And with that he himself and Oisin and Lugaidh's Son made an attack on the strangers, and struck great blows at them. And when Conn Crither and Glas, son of Bremen, heard the noise of those blows, they knew they were struck by some of the Fianna of Ireland, and they came and joined with them, and did great destruction on the strangers, till there was not one left of all that had come to land.

CHAPTER VII. THE FIRST FIGHTERS

And in the morning they saw Finn and all his people coming to the rath that is above the harbour. "My father Finn," said Oisin than, "let us fight now with the whole of the foreigners altogether." "That is not my advice," said Finn, "for the number of their armies is too great for us, and we could not stand against them. But we will send out every day," he said, "some son of a king or of a leader against some king of the kings of the world that is equal in blood to ourselves. And let none of you redden your arms," he said, "but against a king or a chief man at first, for when a king is fallen, his people will be more inclined to give way. And who will give out a challenge of battle from me now?" he said. "I will do that," said the son of Cuban, leader of the Fianna of Munster. "Do not go, my son," said Finn, "for it is not showed to me that you will have good luck in the battle, and I never sent out any man to fight without I knew he would come back safe to me." "Do not say that," said Cuban's son, "for I would not for the treasure of the whole world go back from a fight on account of a bad foretelling. And as it is my own country they have done their robbery in first," he said, "I will defend it for you." "It is sorrowful I am for that," said Finn, "for whichever of the kings of the world will meet you to-day, yourself and himself will fall together."

Then Glas, son of Dremen, gave out a challenge of fight from Cuban's son, and the King of Greece answered it. And the two fought hand to hand, and the King of Greece made a great cast of his thick spear at Cuban's son, that went through his body and broke his back in two. But he did not take that blow as a gift, but he paid for it with a strong cast of his own golden spear that went through the ringed armour of the King of Greece. And those two fell together, sole to sole, and lip to lip. "There is grief on me, Cuban's son to have fallen," said Finn, "for no one ever went from his house unsatisfied; and a man that I would not keep, or the High King of Ireland would not keep for a week, he would keep him in his house through the length of a year. And let Follamain, his son, be called to me now," he said, "and I will give him his father's name and place."

They stopped there then till the next morning. "Who will go and fight to-day?" said Finn then. "I will do that," said Goll Garb, son of the King of Alban and of the daughter of Goll, son of Morna.

So he put on his battle dress, and there came against him the three kings from the rising of the sun in the east, and their three battalions with them. And Goll Garb rushed among their men, and wounded and maimed and destroyed them, and blinded their eyes for ever, so that their wits went from them, and they called to him to stop his deadly sword for a while. So he did that; and it is what they agreed to take their three kings and to give them over to Goll Garb that he might stop doing destruction with his sword.

"Who will go out and fight to-day?" said Finn, on the morning of the morrow. "I will go," said Oisin, "and the chief men of the sons of Baiscne with me; for we get the best share of all the pleasant things of Ireland, and we should be first to defend her." "I will answer that challenge," said the King of France, "for it is against Finn I am come to Ireland, on account of my wife that he brought away from me; and these men will fall by me now," he said, "and Finn himself at the last; for when the branches of a tree are cut off, it is not hard to cut down the tree itself."

So the King of France and Oisin met one another at the eastern end of the strand, and they struck their banners of soft silk into the green hill, and bared their swords and made a quick attack on one another. And at one time the king struck such a great blow that he knocked a groan out of Oisin. But for all that he was worsted in the end, and great fear came on him, like the fear of a hundred horses at the sound of thunder, and he ran from Oisin, and he rose like a swallow, that his feet never touched the earth at all; and he never stopped till he came to Gleann na-n Gealt, the Valley of Wild Men. And ever since that time, people that have lost their wits make for that valley; and every mad person in Ireland, if he had his way, would go there within twenty-four hours.

And there rose great cries of lamentation from the armies of the World when they saw him going from them, and the Fianna of Ireland raised great shouts of joy.

And when the night was coming on, it is what Finn said: "It is sad and gloomy the King of the World is to-night; and it is likely he will make an attack on us. And which of you will keep watch over the harbour through the night?" he said. "I will," said Oisin, "with the same number that was fighting along with me to-day; for it is not too much for you to fight for the Fianna of Ireland through a day and a night," he said.

So they went down to the harbour, and it was just at that time the King of the World was saying, "It seems to me, men of the World, that our luck of battle was not good to-day. And let a share of you rise up now," he said, "and make an attack on the Fianna of Ireland." Then there rose up the nine sons of Garb, King of the Sea of Icht, that were smiths, and sixteen hundred of their people along with them, and they all went on shore but Dolar Durba that was the eldest of them. And the sons of Baiscne were ready for them, and they fought a great battle till the early light of the morrow. And not one of them was left alive on either side that could hold a weapon but only Oisin and one of the sons of Garb. And they made rushes at one another, and threw their swords out of their hands, and closed their arms about one another, and wrestled together, so that it was worth coming from the east to the west of the world to see the fight of those two. Then the foreigner gave a sudden great fall to Oisin, to bring him into the sea, for he was a great swimmer, and he thought to get the better of him there. And Oisin thought it would not be worthy of him to refuse any man his place of fighting. So they went into the water together, and they were trying to drown one another till they came to the sand and the gravel of the clear sea. And it was a torment to the heart of the Fianna, Oisin to be in that strait. "Rise up, Fergus of the Sweet Lips," said Finn then, "and go praise my son and encourage him." So Fergus went down to the edge of the sea, and he said: "It is a good fight you are making, Oisin, and there are many to see it, for the armies of the whole world are looking at you, and the Fianna of Ireland. And show now," he said, "your ways and your greatness, for you never went into any place but some woman of high beauty or some king's daughter set her love on you." Then Oisin's courage increased, and anger came on him and he linked his hands behind the back of the foreigner and put him down on the sand under the sea with his face upwards, and did not let him rise till the life was gone from him. And he brought the body to shore then, and struck off his head and brought it to the Fianna.

But there was great grief and anger on Dolar Durba, the eldest of the sons of Garb, that had stopped in the ship, and he made a great oath that he would have satisfaction for his brothers. And he went to the High King, and he said: "I will go alone to the strand, and I will kill a hundred men every day till I have made an end of the whole of the armies of Ireland; and if any one of your own men comes to interfere with me," he said, "I will kill him along with them."

The next morning Finn asked who would lead the battle that day. "I will," said Dubhan, son of Donn. "Do not," said Finn, "but let some other one go."

But Dubhan went to the strand, and a hundred men along with him; and there was no one there before him but Dolar Durba, and he said he was there to fight with the whole of them. And Dubhan's men gave a great shout of laughter when they heard that; but Dolar Durba rushed on them, and he made an end of the whole hundred, without a man of them being able to put a scratch on him. And then he took a hurling stick and a ball, and he threw up the ball and kept it in the air with the hurl from the west to the east of the strand without letting it touch the ground at all. And then he put the ball on his right foot and kicked it high into the air, and when it was coming down he gave it a kick of his left foot and kept it in the air like that, and he rushing like a blast of March wind from one end of the strand to the other. And when he had done that he walked up and down on the strand making great boasts, and challenging the men of Ireland to do the like of those feats. And every day he killed a hundred of the men that were sent against him.

CHAPTER VIII. THE KING OF ULSTER'S SON

Now it chanced at that time that news of the great battle that was going on reached to the court of the King of Ulster. And the king's son, that was only twelve years of age, and that was the comeliest of all the young men of Ireland, said to his father: "Let me go to help Finn, son of Cumhal, and his men." "You are not old enough, or strong enough, boy; your bones are too soft," said the king. And when the boy went on asking, his father shut him up in some close place, and put twelve young men, his foster-brothers, in charge of him.

There was great anger on the young lad then, and he said to his foster-brothers: "It is through courage and daring my father won a great name for himself in his young youth, and why does he keep me from winning a name for myself? And let you help me now," he said, "and I will be a friend to you for ever." And he went on talking to them and persuading them till he got round them all, and they agreed to go with him to join Finn and the Fianna. And when the king was asleep, they went into the house where the arms were kept, and every lad of them brought away with him a shield and a sword and a helmet and two spears and two greyhound whelps. And they went across Ess Ruadh in the north, and through Connacht of many tribes, and through Caille an Chosanma, the Woods of Defence, that were called the choice of every king and the true honour of every poet, and into Ciarraighe, and so on to the White Strand.

And when they came there Dolar Durba was on the strand, boasting before the men of Ireland. And Oisin was rising up to go against him, for he said he would sooner die fighting with him than see the destruction he was doing every day on his people. And all the wise men and the fighting men and the poets and the musicians of the Fianna gave a great cry of sorrow when they heard Oisin saying that.

And the King of Ulster's son went to Finn and stood before him and saluted him, and Finn asked who was he, and where did he come from. "I am the son of the King of Ulster," he said; "and I am come here, myself and my twelve foster-brothers, to give you what help we can." "I give you a welcome," said Finn.

Just then they heard the voice of Dolar Durba, very loud and boastful. "Who is that I hear?" said the king's son. "It is a man of the foreigners asking for a hundred of my men to go and meet him," said Finn.

Now, when the twelve foster-brothers heard that, they said no word but went down to the strand, unknown to the king's son and to Finn.

"You are not a grown man," said Conan; "and neither yourself or your comrades are fit to face any fighting man at all." "I never saw the Fianna of Ireland till this day," said the young lad; "but I know well that you are Conan Maol, that never says a good word of any man. And you will see now," he said, "if I am in dread of that man on the strand, or of any man in the world, for I will go out against him by myself."

But Finn kept him back and was talking with him; but then Conan began again, and he said: "It is many men Dolar Durba has made an end of, and there was not a man of all those that could not have killed a hundred of the like of you every day."

When the king's son heard that, there was great anger on him, and he leaped up, and just then Dolar Durba gave a great shout on the strand. "What is he giving, that shout for?" said the king's son. "He is shouting for more men to come against him," said Conan, "for he is just after killing your twelve comrades." "That is a sorrowful story," said the king's son.

And with that he took hold of his arms, and no one could hold him or hinder him, and he rushed down to the strand where Dolar Durba was. And all the armies of the strangers gave a great shout of laughter, for they thought all Finn's men had been made an end of, when he sent a young lad like that against their best champion. And when the boy heard that, his courage grew the greater, and he fell on Dolar Durba and gave him many wounds before he knew he was attacked at all. And they fought a very hard fight together, till their shields and their swords were broken in pieces. And that did not stop the battle, but they grappled together and fought and wrestled that way, till the tide went over them and drowned them both. And when the sea went over them the armies on each side gave out a great sorrowful cry.

And after the ebb-tide on the morrow, the two bodies were found cold and quiet, each one held fast by the other. But Dolar Durba was beneath the king's son, so they knew it was the young lad was the best and had got the victory. And they buried him, and put a flag-stone over his grave, and keened him there.

CHAPTER IX. THE HIGH KING'S SON

Then Finn said he would send a challenge himself to Daire Bonn, the King of the Great World. But Caoilte asked leave to do that day's fighting himself. And Finn said he would agree to that if he could find enough of men to go with him. And he himself gave him a hundred men, and Oisin did the same, and so on with the rest. And he gave out his challenge, and it was the son of the King of the Great Plain that answered it. And while they were in the heat of the fight, a fleet of ships came into the harbour, and Finn thought they were come to help the foreigners. But Oisin looked at them, and he said: "It is seldom your knowledge fails you, Finn, but those are friends of our own: Fiachra, son of the King of the Fianna of the Bretons, and Duaban Donn, son of the King of Tuathmumain with his own people."

And when those that were in the ships came on shore, they saw Caoilte's banner going down before the son of the King of the Great Plain. And they all went hurrying on to his help, and between them they made an end of the king's son and of all his people.

"Who will keep watch to-night?" said Finn then. "We will," said the nine Garbhs of the Fianna, of Slieve Mis, and Slieve Cua, and Slieve Clair, and Slieve Crot, and Slieve Muice, and Slieve Fuad, and Slieve Atha Moir, and Dun Sobairce and Dundealgan.

And they were not long watching till they saw the King of the Men of Dregan coming towards them, and they fought a fierce battle; and at the end of the night there were left standing but three of the Garbhs, and the King of the Men of Dregan. And they fought till their wits were gone from them; and those four fell together, sole against sole, and lip against lip.

And the fight went on from day to day, and from week to week, and there were great losses on both sides. And when Fergus of the Sweet Lips saw that so many of the Fianna were fallen, he asked no leave but went to Teamhair of the Kings, where the High King of Ireland was, and he told him the way it was with Finn and his people. "That is good," said the High King, "Finn to be in that strait; for there is no labouring man dares touch a pig or a deer or a salmon if he finds it dead before him on account of the Fianna; and there is no man but is in dread to go from one place to another without leave from Finn, or to take a wife till he knows if she has a sweetheart among the Fianna of Ireland. And it is often Finn has given bad judgments against us," he said, "and it would be better for us the foreigners to gain the day than himself."

Then Fergus went out to the lawn where the High King's son was playing at ball. "It is no good help you are giving to Ireland," said Fergus then, "to be playing a game without lasting profit, and strangers taking away your country from you." And he was urging him and blaming him, and great shame came on the young man, and he threw away the stick and went through the people of Teamhair and brought together all the young men, a thousand and twenty of them that were in it. And they asked no leave and no advice from the High King, but they set out and went on till they came to Finntraigh. And Fergus went to where Finn was, and told him the son of the High King of Ireland was come with him; and all the Fianna rose up before the young man and bade him welcome. And Finn said: "Young man," he said, "we would sooner see you coming at a time when there would be musicians and singers and poets and high-up women to make pleasure for you than at the time we are in the straits of battle the way we are now." "It is not for playing I am come," said the young man, "but to give you my service in battle." "I never brought a lad new to the work into the breast of battle," said Finn, "for it is often a lad coming like that finds his death, and I would not wish him to fall through me." "I give my word," said the young man, "I will do battle with them on my own account if I may not do it on yours." Then Fergus of the Fair Lips went out to give a challenge of battle from the son of the High King of Ireland to the King of the World.

"Who will answer the King of Ireland's son for me?" said the King of the World. "I will go against him," said Sligech, King of the Men of Cepda; and he went on shore, and his three red battalions with him. And the High King's son went against them, and his comrades were near him, and they were saying to him: "Take a good heart now into the fight, for the Fianna will be no better pleased if it goes well with you than if it goes well with the foreigner." And when the High King's son heard that, he made a rush through the army of the foreigners, and began killing and overthrowing them, till their chief men were all made an end of. Then Sligech their king came to meet him, very angry and destroying, and they struck at one another and made a great fight, but at the last the King of Ireland's son got the upper hand, and he killed the King of the Men of Cepda and struck off his head.

CHAPTER X. THE KING OF LOCHLANN AND HIS SONS

And the fighting went on from day to day, and at last Finn said to Fergus of the Sweet Lips: "Go out, Fergus, and see how many of the Fianna are left for the fight to-day." And Fergus counted them, and he said: "There is one battalion only of the Fianna left in good order; but there are some of the men of it," he said, "are able to fight against three, and some that are able to fight against nine or thirty or a hundred." "If that is so," said Finn, "rise up and go to where the King of the World is, and bid him to come out to the great battle."

So Fergus went to the King of the World, and it is the way he was, on his bed listening to the music of harps and pipes. "King of the World," said Fergus, "it is long you are in that sleep; and that is no shame for you," he said, "for it will be your last sleep. And the whole of the Fianna are gone out to their place of battle," he said, "and let you go out and answer them." "In my opinion," said the King of the World, "there is not a man of them is able to fight against me; and how many are there left of the Fianna of Ireland?" "One battalion only that is in good order," said Fergus. "And how many of the armies of the World are there left?" he said. "Thirty battalions came with me to Ireland; and there are twenty of them fallen by the Fianna, and what is left of them is ten red battalions in good order. And there are eight good fighters of them," he said, "that would put down the men of the whole world if they were against me; that is, myself, and Conmail my son, and Ogarmach, the daughter of the King of Greece, that is the best hand in battle of the whole world after myself, and Finnachta of the Teeth, the chief of my household, and the King of Lochlann, Caisel Clumach of the Feathers, and his three sons, Tocha, and Forne of the Broad Shoulders, and Mongach of the Sea."

"I swear by the oath of my people," said the King of Lochlann then, "if any man of the armies goes out against the Fianna before myself and my three sons, we will not go at all, for we would not get the satisfaction we are used to, unless our swords get their fill of blood." "I will go out against them alone," said Forne, the youngest son of the King of Lochlann. With that he put on his battle suit, and he went among the Fianna of Ireland, and a red-edged sword in each of his hands. And he destroyed those of their young men that were sent against him, and he made the strand narrow with their bodies.

And Finn saw that, and it was torment to his heart, and danger of death and loss of wits to him, and he was encouraging the men of Ireland against Forne. And Fergus of the True Lips stood up, and it is what he said: "Fianna of Ireland," he said, "it is a pity the way you are under hardship and you defending Ireland. And one man is taking her from you to-day," he said, "and you are like no other thing but a flock of little birds looking for shelter in a bush from a hawk that is after them. And it is going into the shelter of Finn and Oisin and Caoilte you are," he said; "and not one of you is better than another, and none of you sets his face against the foreigner." "By my oath," said Oisin, "all that is true, and no one of us tries to do better than another keeping him off." "There is not one of you is better than another," said Fergus. Then Oisin gave out a great shout against the King of Lochlann's son. "Stop here with me, king's son," he said, "until I fight with you for the Fianna." "I give my word it is short the delay will be," said Forne.

Then he himself and Oisin made an attack on one another, and it seemed for a while that the battle was going against Oisin. "By my word, Man of Poetry," said Finn then to Fergus of the True Lips, "it is a pity the way you sent my son against the foreigner. And rise up and praise him and hearten him now," he said. So Fergus went down to where the fight was, and he said: "There is great shame on the Fianna, Oisin, seeing you so low in this fight; and there is many a foot messenger and many a horsemen from the daughters of the kings and princes of Ireland looking at you now," he said. And great courage rose in Oisin then, and he drove his spear through the body of Forne, the King of Lochlann's son. And he himself came back to the Fianna of Ireland.

Then the armies of the World gave out a great cry, keening Forne; and there was anger and not fear on his brothers, for they thought it no right thing he to have fallen by a man of the Fianna. And Tocha, the second son of the King of Lochlann, went on shore to avenge his brother. And he went straight into the middle of the Fianna, and gave his sword good feeding on their bodies, till they broke away before him and made no stand till Lugaidh's Son turned round against him. And those two fought a great fight, till their swords were bent and their spears crumbled away, and they lost their golden shields. And at the last Lugaidh's Son made a stroke of his sword that cut through the foreigner's sword, and then he made another stroke that cut his heart in two halves. And he came back high and proud to the Fianna.

Then the third son of the King of Lochlann, Mongach of the Sea, rose up, and all the armies rose up along with him. "Stop here, Men of the World," he said, "for it is not you but myself that has to go and ask satisfaction for the bodies of my brothers." So he went on shore; and it is the way he was, with a strong iron flail in his hand having seven balls of pure iron on it, and fifty iron chains, and fifty apples on every chain, and fifty deadly thorns on every apple. And he made a rush through the Fianna to break them up entirely and to tear them into strings, and they gave way before him. And great shame came on Fidach, son of the King of the Bretons, and he said: "Come here and praise me, Fergus of the True Lips, till I go out and fight with the foreigner." "It is easy to praise you, son," said Fergus, and he was praising him for a long time.

Then the two looked at one another and used fierce, proud words. And then Mongach of the Sea raised his iron flail and made a great blow at the King of the Bretons' son. But he made a quick leap to one side and gave him a blow of his sword that cut off his two hands at the joint; and he did not stop at that, but made a blow at his middle that cut him into two halves. But as he fell, an apple of the flail with its deadly thorns went into Fidach's comely mouth and through his brain, and it was foot to foot those two fell, and lip to lip.

And the next that came to fight on the strand was the King of Lochlann himself, Caisel of the Feathers. And he came to the battle having his shield on his arm; and it is the way the shield was, that was made for him by the smith of the Fomor, there were red flames coming from it; and if it was put under the sea itself, not one of its flames would stop blazing. And when he had that shield on his arm no man could come near him.

And there was never such destruction done on the men of Ireland as on that day, for the flames of fire that he sent from his shield went through the bodies of men till they blazed up like a splinter of oak that was after hanging through the length of a year in the smoke of a chimney; and any one that would touch the man that was burning would catch fire himself. And every other harm that ever came into Ireland before was small beside this.

Then Finn said: "Lift up your hands, Fianna of Ireland, and give three shouts of blessing to whoever will hinder this foreigner." And the Fianna gave those three shouts; and the King of Lochlann gave a great laugh when he heard them. And Druimderg, grandson of the Head of the Fianna of Ulster, was near him, and he had with him a deadly spear, the Croderg, the Red-Socketed, that came down from one to another of the sons of Rudraighe. And he looked at the King of Lochlann, and he could see no part of him without armour but his mouth that was opened wide, and he laughing at the Fianna. Then Druimderg made a cast with the Croderg that hit him in the open mouth, and he fell, and his shield fell along with its master, and its flame went out. And Druimderg struck the head from his body, and made great boasts of the things he had done.

CHAPTER XI. LABRAN'S JOURNEY

It is then Fergus of the True Lips set out again and went through the length of Ireland till he came to the house of Tadg, son of Nuada, that was grandfather to Finn. And there was great grief on Muirne, Finn's mother, and on Labran of the Long Hand her brother, and on all her people, when they knew the great danger he was in. And Tadg asked his wife who did she think would escape with their lives from the great fighting at the White Strand. "It is a pity the way they are there," said she; "for if all the living men of the world were on one side, Daire Donn, the King of the World, would put them all down; for there are no weapons in the world that will ever be reddened on him. And on the night he was born, the smith of the Fomor made a shield and a sword, and it is in the prophecy that he will fall by no other arms but those. And it is to the King of the Country of the Fair Men he gave them to keep, and it is with him they are now." "If that is so," said Tadg, "you might be able to get help for Finn, son of Cumhal, the only son of your daughter. And bid Labran Lamfada to go and ask those weapons of him," he said. "Do not be asking me," said she, "to go against Daire Donn that was brought up in my father's house." But after they had talked for a while, they went out on the lawn, and they sent Labran looking for the weapons in the shape of a great eagle.

And he went on from sea to sea, till at noon on the morrow he came to the dun of the King of the Country of the Fair Men; and he went in his own shape to the dun and saluted the king, and the king bade him welcome, and asked him to stop with him for a while. "There is a thing I want more than that," said Labran, "for the wife of a champion of the Fianna has given me her love, and I cannot get her without fighting for her; and it is the loan of that sword and that shield you have in your keeping I am come asking now," he said.

There were seven rooms, now, in the king's house that opened into one another, and on the first door was one lock, and on the second two locks, and so on to the door of the last room that had seven locks; and it was in that the sword and the shield that were made by the smith of the Fomor were kept. And they were brought out and were given to Labran, and stalks of luck were put with them, and they were bound together with shield straps. Then Labran of the Long Hand went back across the seas again, and he reached his father's dun between the crowing of the cock and the full light of day; and the weakness of death came on him. "It is a good message you are after doing, my son," said Tadg, "and no one ever went that far in so short a time as yourself." "It is little profit that is to me," said Labran, "for I am not able to bring them to Finn in time for the fight to-morrow."

But just at that time one of Tadg's people saw Aedh, son of Aebinn, that was as quick as the wind over a plain till the middle of every day, and after that, there was no man quicker than he was. "You are come at a good time," said Tadg. And with that he gave him the sword and the shield to bring to Finn for the battle.

So Aedh, son of Aebinn, went with the swiftness of a hare or of a fawn or a swallow, till at the rising of the day on the morrow he came to the White Strand. And just at that time Fergus of the True Lips was rousing up the Fianna for the great fight, and it is what he said: "Fianna of Ireland," he said, "if there was the length of seven days in one day, you would have work to fill it now; for there never was and there never will be done in Ireland a day's work like the work of to-day."

Then the Fianna of Ireland rose up, and they saw Aedh, son of Aebinn, coming towards them with his quick running, and Finn asked news from him. "It is from the dun of Tadg, son of Nuada, I am come," he said, "and it is to yourself I am sent, to ask how it is you did not redden your weapons yet upon the King of the World." "I swear by the oath of my people," said Finn, "if I do not redden my weapons on him, I will crush his body within his armour." "I have here for you, King of the Fianna," said Aedh then, "the deadly weapons that will bring him to his death; and it was Labran of the Long Hand got them for you through his Druid arts." He put them in Finn's hand then, and Finn took the coverings off them, and there rose from them flashes of fire and deadly bubbles; and not one of the Fianna could stay looking at them, but it put great courage into them to know they were with Finn. "Rise up now," said Finn to Fergus of the True Lips, "and go where the King of the World is, and bid him to come out to the place of the great fight."

CHAPTER XII. THE GREAT FIGHT

Then the King of the World came to the strand, and all his armies with him; and all that were left of the Fianna went out against them, and they were like thick woods meeting one another, and they made great strokes, and there were swords crashing against bones, and bodies that were hacked, and eyes that were blinded, and many a mother was left without her son, and many a comely wife without her comrade.

Then the creatures of the high air answered to the battle, foretelling the destruction that would be done that day; and the sea chattered of the losses, and the waves gave heavy shouts keening them, and the water-beasts roared to one another, and the rough hills creaked with the danger of the battle, and the woods trembled mourning the heroes, and the grey stones cried out at their deeds, and the wind sobbed telling them, and the earth shook, foretelling the slaughter; and the cries of the grey armies put a blue cloak over the sun, and the clouds were dark; and the hounds and the whelps and the crows, and the witches of the valley, and the powers of the air, and the wolves of the forests, howled from every quarter and on every side of the armies, urging them against one another.

It was then Conan, son of Morna, brought to mind that himself and his kindred had done great harm to the sons of Baiscne, and he had a wish to do some good thing for them on account of that, and he raised up his sword and did great deeds.

And Finn was over the battle, encouraging the Fianna; and the King of the World was on the other side encouraging the foreigners. "Rise up now, Fergus," said Finn, "and praise Conan for me that his courage may be the greater, for it is good work he is doing on my enemies." So Fergus went where Conan was, and at that time he was heated with the dust of the fight, and he was gone outside to let the wind go about him.

"It is well you remember the old quarrel between the sons of Morna and the sons of Baiscne, Conan," said Fergus; "and you would be ready to go to your own death if it would bring harm on the sons of Baiscne," he said. "For the love of your good name, Man of Poetry," said Conan, "do not be speaking against me without cause, and I will do good work on the foreigners when I get to the battle again." "By my word," said Fergus, "that would be a good thing for you to do." He sang a verse of praise for him then, and Conan went back into the battle, and his deeds were not worse this time than they were before. And Fergus went back to where Finn was.

"Who is best in the battle now?" said Finn. "Duban, son of Cas, a champion of your own people," said Fergus, "for he never gives but the one stroke to any man, and no man escapes with his life from that stroke, and three times nine and eighty men have fallen by him up to this time." And Duban Donn, great-grandson of the King of Tuathmumhain, was there listening to him, and it is what he said: "By my oath, Fergus," he said, "all you are saying is true, for there is not a son of a king or of a lord is better in the battle than Duban, son of Cas; and I will go to my own death if I do not go beyond him." With that he went rushing through the battle like flames over a high hill that is thick with furze. Nine times he made a round of the battle, and he killed nine times nine in every round.

"Who is best in the battle now?" said Finn, after a while. "It is Duban Donn that is after going from us," said Fergus. "For there has been no one ahead of him since he was in his seventh year, and there is no one ahead of him now." "Rise up and praise him that his courage may be the greater," said Finn. "It is right to praise him," said Fergus, "and the foreigners running before him on every side as they would run from a heavy drenching of the sea." So Fergus praised him for a while, and he went back then to Finn.

"Who is best in the battle now?" said Finn. "It is Osgar is best in it now," said Fergus, "and he is fighting alone against two hundred Franks and two hundred of the men of Gairian, and the King of the Men of Gairian himself. And all these are beating at his shield," he said, "and not one of them has given him a wound but he gave him a wound back for it." "What way is Caoilte, son of Ronan?" said Finn. "He is in no great strait after the red slaughter he has made," said Fergus. "Go to him then," said Finn, "and bid him to keep off a share of the foreigners from Osgar." So Fergus went to him. "Caoilte," he said, "it is great danger your friend Osgar is in under the blows of the foreigners, and let you rise up and give him some help," he said.

Caoilte went then to the place where Osgar was, and he gave a straight blow of his sword at the man who was nearest him, that made two halves of him. Osgar raised his head then and looked at him. "It is likely, Caoilte," he said, "you did not dare redden your sword on any one till you struck down a man that was before my sword. And it is a shame for you," he said, "all the men of the great world and the Fianna of Ireland to be in the one battle, and you not able to make out a fight for yourself without coming to take a share of my share of the battle. And I give my oath," he said, "I would be glad to see you put down in your bed of blood on account of that thing." Caoilte's mind changed when he heard that, and he turned again to the army of the foreigners with the redness of anger on his white face; and eighty fighting men fell in that rout.

"What way is the battle now?" said Finn. "It is a pity," said Fergus, "there never came and there never will come any one that can tell the way it is now. For by my word," he said, "the tree-tops of the thickest forest in the whole of the western world are not closer together than the armies are now. For the bosses of their shields are in one another's hands. And there is fire coming from the edges of their swords," he said, "and blood is raining down like a shower on a day of harvest; and there were never so many leaves torn by the wind from a great forest as there are locks of long golden hair, and of black curled hair, cut off by sharp weapons, blowing into the clouds at this time. And there is no person could tell one man from another, now," he said, "unless it might be by their voices." With that he went into the very middle of the fight to praise and to hearten the men of the Fianna.

"Who is first in the battle now, Fergus?" said Finn, when he came back to him. "By my oath, it is no friend of your own is first in it," said Fergus, "for it is Daire Donn, the King of the World; and it is for you he is searching through the battle," he said, "and three times fifty of his own people were with him. But two of the men of your Fianna fell on them," he said, "Cairell the Battle Striker, and Aelchinn of Cruachan, and made an end of them. But they were not able to wound the King of the World," he said, "but the two of them fell together by him."

Then the King of the World came towards Finn, and there was no one near him but Arcallach of the Black Axe, the first that ever brought a wide axe into Ireland.

"I give my word," said Arcallach, "I would never let Finn go before me into any battle." He rose up then and made a terrible great blow of his axe at the king, that went through his royal crown to the hair of his head, but that did not take a drop of blood out of him, for the edge of the axe turned and there went balls of fire over the plain from that blow. And the King of the World struck back at Arcallach, and made two halves of him.

Then Finn and the King of the World turned on one another. And when the king saw the sword and the shield in Finn's hand, he knew those were the weapons that were to bring him to his death, and great dread came on him, and his comeliness left him, and his fingers were shaking, and his feet were unsteady, and the sight of his eyes was weakened.

And then the two fought a great fight, striking at one another like two days of judgment for the possession of the world.

But the king, that had never met with a wound before, began to be greatly weakened in the fight. And Finn gave great strokes that broke his shield and his sword, and that cut off his left foot, and at the last he struck off his head. But if he did, he himself fell into a faint of weakness with the dint of the wounds he had got.

Then Finnachta of the Teeth, the first man of the household of the King of the World, took hold of the royal crown of the king, and brought it where Conmail his son was, and put it on his head.

"That this may bring you success in many battles, my son," he said. And he gave him his father's weapons along with it; and the young man went through the battle looking for Finn, and three fifties of the men of the Fianna fell by him. Then Goll Garbh the Rough, son of the King of Alban, saw him and attacked him, and they fought a hard fight. But the King of Albain's son gave him a blow under the shelter of the shield, in his left side, that made an end of him.

Finnachta of the Teeth saw that, and he made another rush at the royal crown, and brought it to where Ogarmach was, the daughter of the King of Greece. "Put on that crown, Ogarmach," he said, "as it is in the prophecy the world will be owned by a woman; and it will never be owned by any woman higher than yourself," he said.

She went then to look for Finn in the battle, and Fergus of the True Lips saw her, and he went where Finn was. "O King of the Fianna," he said then, "bring to mind the good fight you made against the King of the World and all your victories before that; for it is a great danger is coming to you now," he said, "and that is Ogarmach, daughter of the King of Greece."

With that the woman-fighter came towards him. "O Finn," she said, "it is little satisfaction you are to me for all the kings and lords that have fallen by you and by your people; but for all that," she said, "there is nothing better for me to get than your own self and whatever is left of your people." "You will not get that," said Finn, "for I will lay your head in its bed of blood the same as I did to every other one." Then those two attacked one another like as if there had risen to smother one another the flooded wave of Cliodna, and the seeking wave of Tuaigh, and the big brave wave of Rudraighe. And though the woman-warrior fought for a long time, a blow from Finn reached to her at last and cut through the royal crown, and with a second blow he struck her head off. And then he fell himself in his bed of blood, and was the same as dead, but that he rose again.

And the armies of the World and the Fianna of Ireland were fallen side by side there, and there were none left fit to stand but Cael, son of Crimthan of the Harbours, and the chief man of the household of the King of the World, Finnachta of the Teeth. And Finnachta went among the dead bodies and lifted up the body of the King of the World and brought it with him to his ship, and he said: "Fianna of Ireland," he said, "although it is bad this battle was for the armies of the World, it was worse for yourselves; and I am going back to tell that in the East of the World," he said. Finn heard him saying that, and he lying on the ground in his blood, and the best men of the sons of Baiscne about him, and he said: "It is a pity I not to have found death before I heard the foreigner saying those words. And nothing I myself have done, or the Fianna of Ireland, is worth anything since there is left a man of the foreigners alive to go back into the great world again to tell that story. And is there any one left living near me?" he said. "I am," said Fergus of the True Lips. "What way is the battle now?" said Finn. "It is a pity the way it is," said Fergus, "for, by my word," he said, "since the armies met together to-day, no man of the foreigners or of the men of Ireland took a step backward from one another till they all fell foot to foot, and sole to sole. And there is not so much as a blade of grass or a grain of sand to be seen," he said, "with the bodies of fighting men that are stretched on them; and there is no man of the two armies that is not stretched in that bed of blood, but only the chief man of the household of the King of the World, and your own foster-son, Cael, son of Crimthan of the Harbours." "Rise up and go to him," said Finn. So Fergus went where Cael was, and asked what way was he. "It is a pity the way I am," said Cael, "for I swear by my word that if my helmet and my armour were taken from me, there is no part of my body but would fall from the other; and by my oath," he said, "it is worse to me to see that man beyond going away alive than I myself to be the way I am. And I leave my blessing to you, Fergus," he said; "and take me on your back to the sea till I swim after the foreigner, and it is glad I would be the foreigner to fall by me before the life goes out from my body." Fergus lifted him up then and brought him to the sea, and put him swimming after the foreigner. And Finnachta waited for him to reach the ship, for he thought he was one of his own people. And Cael raised himself up when he came beside the ship, and Finnachta stretched out his hand to him. And Cael took hold of it at the wrist, and clasped his fingers round it, and gave a very strong pull at him, that brought him over the side. Then their hands shut across one another's bodies, and they went down to the sand and the gravel of the clear sea.

CHAPTER XIII. CREDHE'S LAMENT

Then there came the women and the musicians and the singers and the physicians of the Fianna of Ireland to search out the kings and the princes of the Fianna, and to bury them; and every one that might be healed was brought to a place of healing.

And Credhe, wife of Cael, came with the others, and went looking through the bodies for her comely comrade, and crying as she went. And as she was searching, she saw a crane of the meadows and her two nestlings, and the cunning beast the fox watching the nestlings; and when the crane covered one of the birds to save it, he would make a rush at the other bird, the way she had to stretch herself out over the birds; and she would sooner have got her own death by the fox than her nestlings to be killed by him. And Credhe was looking at that, and she said: "It is no wonder I to have such love for my comely sweetheart, and the bird in that distress about her nestlings."

Then she heard a stag in Druim Ruighlenn above the harbour, that was making great lamentations for his hind from place to place, for they had been nine years together, and had lived in the wood at the foot of the harbour, Fidh Leis, and Finn had killed the hind, and the stag was nineteen days without tasting grass or water, lamenting after the hind. "It is no shame for me," said Credhe, "I to die for grief after Cael, since the stag is shortening his life sorrowing after the hind."

Then she met with Fergus of the True Lips. "Have you news of Cael for me, Fergus?" she said. "I have news," said Fergus, "for he and the last man that was left of the foreigners, Finnachta Fiaclach, are after drowning one another in the sea."

And at that time the waves had put Cael back on the strand, and the women and the men of the Fianna that were looking for him raised him up, and brought him to the south of the White Strand.

And Credhe came to where he was, and she keened him and cried over him, and she made this complaint:--

"The harbour roars, O the harbour roars, over the rushing race of the Headland of the Two Storms, the drowning of the hero of the Lake of the Two Dogs, that is what the waves are keening on the strand.

"Sweet-voiced is the crane, O sweet-voiced is the crane in the marshes of the Ridge of the Two Strong Men; it is she cannot save her nestlings, the wild dog of two colours is taking her little ones.

"Pitiful the cry, pitiful the cry the thrush is making in the Pleasant Ridge, sorrowful is the cry of the blackbird in Leiter Laeig.

"Sorrowful the call, O sorrowful the call of the deer in the Ridge of Two Lights; the doe is lying dead in Druim Silenn, the mighty stag cries after her.

"Sorrowful to me, O sorrowful to me the death of the hero that lay beside me; the son of the woman of the Wood of the Two Thickets, to be with a bunch of grass under his head.

"Sore to me, O sore to me Cael to be a dead man beside me, the waves to have gone over his white body; it is his pleasantness that has put my wits astray.

"A woeful shout, O a woeful shout the waves are making on the strand; they that took hold of comely Cael, a pity it is he went to meet them.

"A woeful crash, O a woeful crash the waves are making on the strand to the north, breaking against the smooth rock, crying after Cael now he is gone.

"A sorrowful fight, O a sorrowful fight, the sea is making with the strand to the north; my beauty is lessened; the end of my life is measured.

"A song of grief, O a song of grief is made by the waves of Tulcha Leis; all I had is gone since this story came to me. Since the son of Crimthann is drowned I will love no one after him for ever; many a king fell by his hand; his shield never cried out in the battle."

After she had made that complaint, Credhe laid herself down beside Cael and died for grief after him. And they were put in the one grave, and it was Caoilte raised the stone over them.

And after that great battle of the White Strand, that lasted a year and a day, there was many a sword and shield left broken, and many a dead body lying on the ground, and many a fighting man left with a foolish smile on his face.

And the great name that was on the armies of the World went from them to the Fianna of Ireland; and they took the ships and the gold and the silver and all the spoils of the armies of the World. And from that time the Fianna had charge of the whole of Ireland, to keep it from the Fomor and from any that might come against it.

And they never lost power from that time until the time of their last battle, the sorrowful battle of Gabhra.

BOOK FOUR: HUNTINGS AND ENCHANTMENTS.

CHAPTER I. THE KING OF BRITAIN'S SON

Arthur, son of the King of Britain, came one time to take service with Finn, and three times nine men along with him. And they went hunting one day on Beinn Edair, and Finn took his place on the Cairn of the Fianna between the hill and the sea, and Arthur took his stand between the hunt and the sea, the way the deer would not escape by swimming.

And while Arthur was there he took notice of three of Finn's hounds, Bran, and Sceolan and Adhnuall, and he made a plan in his mind to go away across the sea, himself and his three nines, bringing those three hounds along with him. So he did that, and he himself and his men brought away the hounds and crossed the sea, and the place where they landed was Inver Mara Gamiach on the coast of Britain. And after they landed, they went to the mountain of Lodan, son of Lir, to hunt on it.

And as to the Fianna, after their hunting was done they gathered together on the hill; and as the custom was, all Finn's hounds were counted. Three hundred full-grown hounds he had, and two hundred whelps; and it is what the poets used to say, that to be counting them was like counting the branches on a tree.

Now on this day when they were counted, Bran and Sceolan and Adhnuall were missing; and that was told to Finn. He bade his people to search again through the three battalions of the Fianna, but search as they would, the hounds were not to be found.

Then Finn sent for a long-shaped basin of pale gold, and water in it, and he put his face in the water, and his hand over his face, and it was showed him what had happened, and he said: "The King of Britain's son has brought away the hound. And let nine men be chosen out to follow after them," he said. So nine men were chosen out, Diarmuid, grandson of Duibhne; Goll, son of Morna; Oisin, son of Finn; Faolan, the friend of the hounds, son of a woman that had come over the sea to give her love to Finn; Ferdoman, son of Bodb Dearg; two sons of Finn, Raighne Wide Eye and Cainche the Crimson-Red; Glas, son of Enchered Bera, with Caoilte and Lugaidh's Son. And their nine put their helmets on their heads, and took their long spears in their hands, and they felt sure they were a match for any four hundred men from the east to the west of the world.

They set out then, till they came to the mountain of Lodan, son of Lir; and they were not long there till they heard talk of men that were hunting in that place.

Arthur of Britain and his people were sitting on a hunting mound just at that time, and the nine men of the Fianna made an attack on them and killed all of them but Arthur, that Goll, son of Morna, put his two arms about and saved from death. Then they turned to go back to Ireland, bringing Arthur with them, and the three hounds. And as they were going, Goll chanced to look around him and he saw a dark-grey horse, having a bridle with fittings of worked gold. And then he looked to the left and saw a bay mare that was not easy to get hold of, and it having a bridle of silver rings and a golden bit. And Goll took hold of the two, and he gave them into Oisin's hand, and he gave them on to Diarmuid.

They went back to Finn then, bringing his three hounds with them, and the King of Britain's son as a prisoner; and Arthur made bonds with Finn, and was his follower till he died.

And as to the horse and the mare, they gave them to Finn; and the mare bred eight times, at every birth eight foals, and it is of that seed came all the horses of the fair Fianna of the Gael, for they had used no horses up to that time.

And that was not the only time Finn was robbed of some of his hounds. For there was a daughter of Roman was woman-Druid to the Tuatha de Danaan, and she set her love on Finn. But Finn said, so long as there was another woman to be found in the world, he would not marry a witch. And one time, three times fifty of Finn's hounds passed by the hill where she was; and she breathed on the hounds and shut them up in the hill, and they never came out again. It was to spite Finn she did that, and the place got the name of Duma na Conn, the Mound of the Hounds.

And as to Adhnuall, one of the hounds Finn thought most of, and that was brought back from the King of Britain's son, this is the way he came to his death afterwards.

There was a great fight one time between the Fianna and Macoon, son of Macnia, at some place in the province of Leinster, and a great many of the Fianna were killed. And the hound Adhnuall went wandering northward from the battle and went astray; and three times he went round the whole of Ireland, and then he came back to the place of the battle, and to a hill where three young men of the Fianna that had fallen there were buried after their death, and three daughters of a King of Alban that had died for love of them. And when Adhnuall came to that hill, he gave three loud howls and he stretched himself out and died.

CHAPTER II. THE CAVE OF CEISCORAN

Finn called for a great hunt one time on the plains of Magh Chonaill and in the forest parts of Cairbre of the Nuts. And he himself went up to the top of Ceiscoran, and his two dogs Bran and Sceolan with him.

And the Fianna were shouting through the whole country where they were hunting, the way the deer were roused in their wild places and the badgers in their holes, and foxes in their wanderings, and birds on the wing.

And Conaran, son of Imidd, of the Tuatha de Danaan, had the sway in Ceiscoran at that time, and when he heard the shouting and the cry of the hounds all around, he bade his three daughters that had a great share of enchantments, to do vengeance on Finn for his hunting.

The three women went then to the opening of a cave that was in the hills, and there they sat down together, and they put three strong enchanted hanks of yarn on crooked holly-sticks, and began to reel them off outside the cave.

They were not long there till Finn and Conan came towards them, and saw the three ugly old hags at their work, their coarse hair tossed, their eyes red and bleary, their teeth sharp and crooked, their arms very long, their nails like the tips of cows' horns, and the three spindles in their hands.

Finn and Conan passed through the hanks of yarn to get a better look at the hags. And no sooner had they done that, than a deadly trembling came on them and a weakness, and the bold hags took hold of them and put them in tight bonds.

Two other men of the Fianna came up then, and the sons of Menhann along with them, and they went through the spindles to where Finn and Conan were, and their strength went from them in the same way, and the hags tied them fast and carried them into the cave.

They were not long there till Caoilte and Lugaidh's Son came to the place, and along with them the best men of the sons of Baiscne. The sons of Morna came as well, and no sooner did they see the hanks than their strength and their bravery went out of them the same as it went from the others.

And in the end the whole number of them, gentle and simple, were put in bonds by the hags, and brought into the cave. And there began at the mouth of the cave a great outcry of hounds calling for their masters that had left them there. And there was lying on the hillside a great heap of deer, and wild pigs, and hares, and badgers, dead and torn, that were brought as far as that by the hunters that were tied up now in the cave.

Then the three women came in, having swords in their hands, to the place where they were lying, to make an end of them. But first they looked out to see was there ever another man of the Fianna to bring in and to make an end of with the rest. And they saw coming towards them a very tall man that was Goll, son of Morna, the Flame of Battle. And when the three hags saw him they went to meet him, and they fought a hard battle with him. And great anger came on Goll, and he made great strokes at the witches, and at the last he raised up his sword, and with one blow he cut the two that were nearest him through and through.

And then the oldest of the three women wound her arms about Goll, and he beheading the two others, and he turned to face her and they wrestled together, till at last Goll gave her a great twist and threw her on the ground. He tied her fast then with the straps of a shield, and took his sword to make an end of her. But the hag said: "O champion that was never worsted, strong man that never went back in battle, I put my body and my life under the protection of your bravery. And it is better for you," she said, "to get Finn and the Fianna safe and whole than to have my blood; and I swear by the gods my people swear by," she said, "I will give them back to you again."

With that Goll set her free, and they went together into the hill where the Fianna were lying. And Goll said: "Loose off the fastenings first from Fergus of the True Lips and from the other learned men of the Fianna; and after that from Finn, and Oisin, and the twenty-nine sons of Morna, and from all the rest."

She took off the fastenings then, and the Fianna made no delay, but rose up and went out and sat down on the side of the hill. And Fergus of the Sweet Lips looked at Goll, son of Morna, and made great praises of him, and of all that he had done.

CHAPTER III. DONN SON OF MIDHIR

One time the Fianna were at their hunting at the island of Toraig to the north of Ireland, and they roused a fawn that was very wild and beautiful, and it made for the coast, and Finn and six of his men followed after it through the whole country, till they came to Slieve-nam-Ban. And there the fawn put down its head and vanished into the earth, and none of them knew where was it gone to.

A heavy snow began to fall then that bent down the tops of the trees like a willow-gad, and the courage and the strength went from the Fianna with the dint of the bad weather, and Finn said to Caoilte: "Is there any place we can find shelter to-night?" Caoilte made himself supple then, and went over the elbow of the hill southward.

And when he looked around him he saw a house full of light, with cups and horns and bowls of different sorts in it. He stood a good while before the door of the house, that he knew to be a house of the Sidhe, thinking would it be best go in and get news of it, or to go back to Finn and the few men that were with him. And he made up his mind to go into the house, and there he sat down on a shining chair in the middle of the floor; and he looked around him, and he saw, on the one side, eight-and-twenty armed men, each of them having a well-shaped woman beside him. And on the other side he saw six nice young girls, yellow-haired, having shaggy gowns from their shoulders. And in the middle there was another young girl sitting in a chair, and a harp in her hand, and she playing on it and singing. And every time she stopped, a man of them would give her a horn to drink from, and she would give it back to him again, and they were all making mirth around her.

She spoke to Caoilte then. "Caoilte, my life," she said, "give us leave to attend on you now." "Do not," said Caoilte, "for there is a better man than myself outside,

Finn, son of Cumhal, and he has a mind to eat in this house to-night." "Rise up, Caoilte, and go for Finn," said a man of the house then; "for he never refused any man in his own house, and he will get no refusal from us."

Caoilte went back then to Finn, and when Finn saw him he said: "It is long you are away from us, Caoilte, for from the time I took arms in my hands I never had a night that put so much hardship on me as this one."

The six of them went then into the lighted house and their shields and their arms with them. And they sat down on the edge of a seat, and a girl having yellow hair came and brought them to a shining seat in the middle of the house, and the newest of every food, and the oldest of every drink was put before them. And when the sharpness of their hunger and their thirst was lessened, Finn said: "Which of you can I question?" "Question whoever you have a mind to," said the tallest of the men that was near him. "Who are you yourself then?" said Finn, "for I did not think there were so many champions in Ireland, and I not knowing them."

"Those eight-and-twenty armed men you see beyond," said the tall man, "had the one father and mother with myself; and we are the sons of Midhir of the Yellow Hair, and our mother is Fionnchaem, the fair, beautiful daughter of the King of the Sidhe of Monaid in the east. And at one time the Tuatha de Danaan had a gathering, and gave the kingship to Bodb Dearg, son of the Dagda, at his bright hospitable place, and he began to ask hostages of myself and of my brothers; but we said that till all the rest of the Men of Dea had given them, we would not give them. Bodb Dearg said then to our father: 'Unless you will put away your sons, we will wall up your dwelling-place on you.' So the eight-and-twenty brothers of us came out to look for a place for ourselves; and we searched all Ireland till we found this secret hidden place, and we are here ever since. And my own name," he said, "is Donn, son of Midhir. And we had every one of us ten hundred armed men belonging to himself, but they are all worn away now, and only the eight-and-twenty of us left." "What is it is wearing you away?" said Finn. "The Men of Dea," said Donn, "that come three times in every year to give battle to us on the green outside." "What is the long new grave we saw on the green outside?" said Finn. "It is the grave of Diangalach, a man of enchantments of the Men of Dea; and that is the greatest loss came on them yet," said Donn; "and it was I myself killed him," he said. "What loss came next to that?" said Finn. "All the Tuatha de Danaan had of jewels and riches and treasures, horns and vessels and cups of pale gold, we took from them at the one time." "What was the third greatest loss they had?" said Finn. "It was Fethnaid, daughter of Feclach, the woman-harper of the Tuatha de Danaan, their music and the delight of their minds," said Donn.

"And to-morrow," he said, "they will be coming to make an attack on us, and there is no one but myself and my brothers left; and we knew we would be in danger, and that we could make no stand against them. And we sent that bare-headed girl beyond to Toraig in the North in the shape of a foolish fawn, and you followed her here. It is that girl washing herself, and having a green cloak about her, went looking for you.

"And the empty side of the house," he said, "belonged to our people that the Men of Dea have killed."

They spent that night in drinking and in pleasure. And when they rose up in the morning of the morrow, Donn, son of Midhir, said to Finn, "Come out with me now on the lawn till you see the place where we fight the battles every year." They went out then and they looked at the graves and the flag-stones, and Donn said: "It is as far as this the Men of Dea come to meet us." "Which of them come here?" said Finn.

"Bodb Dearg with his seven sons," said Donn; "and Angus Og, son of the Dagda, with his seven sons; and Finnbharr of Cnoc Medha with his seventeen sons; Lir of Sidhe Fionnachaidh with his twenty-seven sons and their sons; Tadg, son of Nuada, out of the beautiful hill of Almhuin; Donn of the Island and Donn of the Vat; the two called Glas from the district of Osraige; Dobhran Dubthaire from the hill of Liamhain of the Smooth Shirt; Aedh of the Island of Rachrainn in the north; Ferai and Aillinn and Lir and Fainnle, sons of Eogobal, from Cnoc Aine in Munster; Cian and Coban and Conn, three sons of the King of Sidhe Monaid in Alban; Aedh Minbhreac of Ess Ruadh with his seven sons; the children of the Morrigu, the Great Queen, her six-and-twenty women warriors, the two Luaths from Magh Life; Derg and Drecan out of the hill of Beinn Edair in the east; Bodb Dearg himself with his great household, ten hundred ten score and ten. Those are the chief leaders of the Tuatha de Danaan that come to destroy our hill every year."

Finn went back into the hill then, and told all that to his people.

"My people," he said, "it is in great need and under great oppression the sons of

Midhir are, and it is into great danger we are come ourselves. And unless we make a good fight now," he said, "it is likely we will never see the Fianna again."

"Good Finn," every one of them said then, "did you ever see any drawing-back in any of us that you give us that warning?" "I give my word," said Finn, "if I would go through the whole world having only this many of the Fianna of Ireland along with me, I would not know fear nor fright. And good Donn," he said, "is it by day or by night the Men of Dea come against you?" "It is at the fall of night they come," said Donn, "the way they can do us the most harm."

So they waited till night came on, and then Finn said: "Let one of you go out now on the green to keep watch for us, the way the Men of Dea will not come on us without word or warning."

And the man they set to watch was not gone far when he saw five strong battalions of the Men of Dea coming towards him. He went back then to the hill and he said: "It is what I think, that the troops that are come against us this time and are standing now around the grave of the Man of Enchantments are a match for any other fighting men."

Finn called to his people then, and he said: "These are good fighters are come against you, having strong red spears. And let you all do well now in the battle. And it is what you have to do," he said, "to keep the little troop of brothers, the sons of Midhir, safe in the fight; for it would be a treachery to friendship any harm to come on them, and we after joining them; and myself and Caoilte are the oldest among you, and leave the rest of the battle to us."

Then from the covering time of evening to the edge of the morning they fought the battle. And the loss of the Tuatha de Danaan was no less a number than ten hundred ten score and ten men. Then Bodb Dearg and Midhir and Fionnbhar said to one another: "What are we to do with all these? And let Lir of Sidhe Fionnach-aidh give us an advice," they said, "since he is the oldest of us." And Lir said: "It is what I advise, let every one carry away his friends and his fosterlings, his sons and his brothers, to his own place. And as for us that stop here," he said, "let a wall of fire be made about us on the one side, and a wall of water on the other side." Then the Men of Dea put up a great heap of stones, and brought away their dead; and of all the great slaughter that Finn and his men and the sons of Midhir had made, there was not left enough for a crow to perch upon.

And as to Finn and his men, they went back into the hill, hurt and wounded and worn-out.

And they stopped in the hill with the sons of Midhir through the whole length of a year, and three times in the year the Men of Dea made an attack on the hill, and a battle was fought.

And Conn, son of Midhir, was killed in one of the battles; and as to the Fianna, there were so many wounds on them that the clothing was held off from their bodies with bent hazel sticks, and they lying in their beds, and two of them were like to die. And Finn and Caoilte and Lugaidh's Son went out on the green, and Caoilte said: "It was a bad journey we made coming to this hill, to leave two of our comrades after us." "It is a pity for whoever will face the Fianna of Ireland," said Lugaidh's Son, "and he after leaving his comrades after him." "Whoever will go back and leave them, it will not be myself," said Finn. Then Bonn, son of Midhir, came to them. "Good Donn," said Finn, "have you knowledge of any physician that can cure our men?" "I only know one physician could do that," said Donn; "a physician the Tuatha de Danaan have with them. And unless a wounded man has the marrow of his back cut through, he will get relief from that physician, the way he will be sound at the end of nine days." "How can we bring that man here," said Finn, "for those he is with are no good friends to us?" "He goes out every morning at break of day," said Donn, "to gather healing herbs while the dew is on them." "Find some one, Donn," said Caoilte, "that will show me that physician, and, living or dead, I will bring him with me."

Then Aedh and Flann, two of the sons of Midhir, rose up. "Come with us, Caoilte," they said, and they went on before him to a green lawn with the dew on it; and when they came to it they saw a strong young man armed and having a cloak of the wool of the seven sheep of the Land of Promise, and it full of herbs of healing he was after gathering for the Men of Dea that were wounded in the battle. "Who is that man?" said Caoilte. "That is the man we came looking for," said Aedh. "And mind him well now," he said, "that he will not make his escape from us back to his own people."

They ran at him together then, and Caoilte took him by the shoulders and they brought him away with them to the ford of the Slaine in the great plain of Leinster, where the most of the Fianna were at that time; and a Druid mist rose up about them that they could not be seen.

And they went up on a little hill over the ford, and they saw before them four young men having crimson fringed cloaks and swords with gold hilts, and four good hunting hounds along with them. And the young man could not see them because of the mist, but Caoilte saw they were his own two sons, Colla and Faolan, and two other young men of the Fianna, and he could hear them talking together, and saying it was a year now that Finn, son of Cumhal, was gone from them. "And what will the Fianna of Ireland do from this out," said one of them, "without their lord and their leader?" "There is nothing for them to do," said another, "but to go to Teamhair and to break up there, or to find another leader for themselves." And there was heavy sorrow on them for the loss of their lord; and it was grief to Caoilte to be looking at them.

And he and the two sons of Midhir went back then by the Lake of the Two Birds to Slieve-nam Ban, and they went into the hill.

And Finn and Donn gave a great welcome to Luibra, the physician, and they showed him their two comrades that were lying in their wounds. "Those men are brothers to me," said Donn, "and tell me how can they be cured?" Luibra looked then at their wounds, and he said: "They can be cured if I get a good reward." "You will get that indeed," said Caoilte; "and tell me now," he said, "how long will it take to cure them?" "It will take nine days," said Luibra. "It is a good reward you will get," said Caoilte, "and this is what it is, your own life to be left to you. But if these young men are not healed," he said, "it is my own hand will strike off your head."

And within nine days the physician had done a cure on them, and they were as well and as sound as before.

And it was after that time the High King sent a messenger to bring the Fianna to the Feast of Teamhair. And they all gathered to it, men and women, boys and heroes and musicians. And Goll, son of Morna, was sitting at the feast beside the king. "It is a great loss you have had, Fianna of Ireland," said the king, "losing your lord and your leader, Finn, son of Cumhal." "It is a great loss indeed," said Goll.

"There has no greater loss fallen on Ireland since the loss of Lugh, son of Eth-ne," said the king. "What orders will you give to the Fianna now, king?" said Goll. "To yourself, Goll," said the king, "I will give the right of hunting over all Ireland till we know if the loss of Finn is lasting." "I will not take Finn's place," said Goll, "till he has been wanting to us through the length of three years, and till no person in Ireland has any hope of seeing him again."

Then Ailbe of the Freckled Face said to the king: "What should these seventeen queens belonging to Finn's household do?" "Let a safe, secret sunny house be given to every one of them," said the king; "and let her stop there and her women with her, and let provision be given to her for a month and a quarter and a year till we have knowledge if Finn is alive or dead."

Then the king stood up, and a smooth drinking-horn in his hand, and he said: "It would be a good thing, men of Ireland, if any one among you could get us news of Finn in hills or in secret places, or in rivers or invers, or in any house of the Sidhe in Ireland or in Alban."

With that Berngal, the cow-owner from the borders of Slieve Fuad, that was divider to the King of Ireland, said: "The day Finn came out from the north, following after a deer of the Sidhe, and his five comrades with him, he put a sharp spear having a shining head in my hand, and a hound's collar along with it, and he bade me to keep them till he would meet me again in the same place." Berngal showed the spear and the collar then to the king and to Goll, and they looked at them and the king said: "It is a great loss to the men of Ireland the man is that owned this collar and this spear. And were his hounds along with him?" he said. "They were," said Berngal; "Bran and Sceolan were with Finn, and Breac and Lainbhui with Caoilte, and Conuall and Comrith with Lugaidh's Son."

The High King called then for Fergus of the True Lips, and he said: "Do you know how long is Finn away from us?" "I know that well," said Fergus; "it is a month and a quarter and a year since we lost him. And indeed it is a great loss he is to the Fianna of Ireland," he said, "himself and the men that were with him." "It is a great loss indeed," said the king, "and I have no hope at all of finding those six that were the best men of Ireland or of Alban."

And then he called to Cithruadh, the Druid, and he said: "It is much riches and many treasures Finn gave you, and tell us now is he living or is he dead?" "He is living," said Cithruadh then. "But as to where he is, I will give no news of that," he said, "for he himself would not like me to give news of it." There was great joy among them when they heard that, for everything Cithruadh had ever foretold had come true. "Tell us when will he come back?" said the king. "Before the Feast of

Teamhair is over," said the Druid, "you will see the Leader of the Fianna drinking at it."

And as to Finn and his men, they stopped in the House of the Two Birds till they had taken hostages for Donn, son of Midhir, from the Tuatha de Danaan. And on the last day of the Feast of Teamhair they came back to their people again.

And from that time out the Fianna of Ireland had not more dealings with the people living in houses than they had with the People of the Gods of Dana.

CHAPTER IV. THE HOSPITALITY OF CUANNA'S HOUSE

It happened one day Finn and Oisin and Caoilte and Diarmuid and Lugaidh's Son went up on the top of Cairn Feargall, and their five hounds with them, Bran and Sceolan, Sear Dubh, Luath Luachar and Adhnuall. And they were not long there till they saw a giant coming towards them, very tall and rough and having an iron fork on his back and a squealing pig between the prongs of the fork. And there was a beautiful eager young girl behind the giant, shoving him on before her. "Let some one go speak with those people," said Finn. So Diarmuid went towards them, but they turned away before he came to them. Then Finn and the rest rose up and went after them, but before they came to the giant and the girl, a dark Druid mist rose up that hid the road. And when the mist cleared away, Finn and the rest looked about them, and they saw a good light-roofed house at the edge of a ford near at hand. They went on to the house, and there was a green lawn before it, and in the lawn two wells, and on the edge of one well there was a rough iron vessel, and on the edge of the other a copper vessel. They went into the house then, and they found there a very old white-haired man, standing to the right hand of the door, and the beautiful young girl they saw before, sitting near him, and the great rough giant beside the fire, and he boiling a pig. And on the other side of the fire there was an old countryman, having dark-grey hair and twelve eyes in his head, and his twelve eyes were twelve sons of battle. And there was a ram in the house having a white belly and a very black head, and dark-blue horns and green feet. And there was a hag in the end of the house and a worn grey gown on her, and there was no one in the house but those.

And the man at the door gave them a welcome, and then the five of them sat down on the floor of the house, and their hounds along with them.

"Let great respect be shown to Finn, son of Cumhal, and to his people," said the man at the door. "It is the way I am," said the giant, "to be asking always and getting nothing." But for all that he rose up and showed respect to Finn.

Presently there came a great thirst on Finn, and no one took notice of it but Caoilte, and he began complaining greatly. "Why are you complaining, Caoilte?" said the man at the door; "you have but to go out and get a drink for Finn at which- ever of the wells you will choose." Caoilte went out then, and he brought the full of the copper vessel to Finn, and Finn took a drink from it, and there was the taste of honey on it while he was drinking, and the taste of gall on it after, so that fierce windy pains and signs of death came on him, and his appearance changed, that he would hardly be known. And Caoilte made greater complaints than he did before on account of the way he was, till the man at the door bade him to go out and to bring him a drink from the other well. So Caoilte did that, and brought in the full of the iron vessel. And Finn never went through such great hardship in any battle as he did drinking that draught, from the bitterness of it; but no sooner did he drink it than his own colour and appearance came back to him and he was as well as before, and his people were very glad when they saw that.

Then the man of the house asked was the pig ready that was in the cauldron. "It is ready," said the giant; "and leave the dividing of it to me," he said. "What way will you divide it?" said the man of the house. "I will give one hind quarter to Finn and his dogs," said the giant, "and the other hind quarter to Finn's four comrades; and the fore quarter to myself, and the chine and the rump to the old man there by the fire and the hag in the corner; and the entrails to yourself and to the young girl that is beside you." "I give my word," said the man of the house, "you have shared it well." "I give my word," said the ram, "it is a bad division to me, for you have forgotten my share in it." With that he took hold of the quarter that was before the Fianna, and brought it into a corner and began to eat it. On that the four of them at- tacked him with their swords, but with all the hard strokes they gave they could not harm him at all, for the swords slipped from his back the same as they would from a rock. "On my word it is a pity for any one that has the like of you for comrades," said the man with the twelve eyes, "and you letting a sheep bring away your food from you." With that he went up to the ram and took him by the feet and threw him out from the door that he fell on his back, and they saw him no more.

It was not long after that, the hag rose up and threw her pale grey gown over Finn's four comrades, and they turned to four old men, weak and withered, their heads hanging. When Finn saw that there came great dread on him, and the man at the door saw it, and he bade him to come over to him, and to put his head in his breast and to sleep. Finn did that, and the hag took her covering off the four men, the way that when Finn awoke they were in their own shape again, and it is well pleased he was to see that.

"Is there wonder on you, Finn?" said the man at the door, "at the ways of this house?" "I never wondered more at anything I ever saw," said Finn. "I will tell you the meaning of them, so," said the man. "As to the giant you saw first," he said, "having the squealing pig in the prongs of his fork, Sluggishness is his name; and the girl here beside me that was shoving him along is Liveliness, for liveliness pushes on sluggishness, and liveliness goes farther in the winking of an eye than the foot can travel in a year. The old man there beyond with the twelve bright eyes betokens the World, and he is stronger than any other, and he showed that when he made nothing of the ram. The ram you saw betokens the Desires of Men. The hag is Old Age, and her gown withered up your four comrades. And the two wells you drank the two draughts out of," he said, "betoken Lying and Truth; for it is sweet to people to be telling a lie, but it is bitter in the end. And as to myself," he said, "Cuanna from Innistuil is my name, and it is not here I am used to be, but I took a very great love for you, Finn, because of your wisdom and your great name, and so I put these things in your way that I might see you. And the hospitality of Cuanna's house to Finn will be the name of this story to the end of the world. And let you and your men come together now," he said, "and sleep till morning."

So they did that, and when they awoke in the morning, it is where they were, on the top of Cairn Feargall, and their dogs and their arms beside them.

CHAPTER V. CAT-HEADS AND DOG-HEADS

Nine of the Fianna set out one time, looking for a pup they wanted, and they searched through many places before they found it. All through Magh Leine they searched, and through the Valley of the Swords, and through the storm of Druim Cleibh, and it is pleasant the Plain of the Life looked after it; but not a pup could they find. Then they went searching through Durlass of the generous men, and great Teamhair and Dun Dobhran and Ceanntsaile, men and dogs searching the whole of Ireland, but not a pup could they find.

And while they were going from place to place, and their people with them, they saw the three armies of the sons of the King of Ruadhleath coming towards them. Cat-headed one army was, and the one alongside of it was Dog-headed, and the men of the third army were White-backed.

And when the Fianna saw them coming, Finn held up his shining spear, and light-hearted Caoilte gave out a great shout that was heard in Almhuin, and in Magh Leine, and in Teamhair, and in Dun Reithlein. And that shout was answered by Goll, son of Morna, and by Faolan, Finn's son that was with him, and by the Stutterers from Burren, and by the two sons of Maith Breac, and by Iolunn of the Sharp Edge, and by Cael of the Sharp Sword, that never gave his ear to tale-bearers.

It is pleasant the sound was then of the spears and the armies and of the silken banners that were raised up in the gusty wind of the morning. And as to the banners, Finn's banner, the Dealb-Greine, the Sun-Shape, had the likeness of the sun on it; and Coil's banner was the Fulang Duaraidh, that was the first and last to move in a battle; and Faolan's banner was the Coinneal Catha, the Candle of Battle; and Oisin's banner was the Donn Nimhe, the Dark Deadly One; and Caoilte's was the Lamh Dearg, the Red Hand; and Osgar's was the Sguab Gabhaidh that had a Broom of rowan branches on it, and the only thing asked when the fight was at the hottest was where that Broom was; and merry Diarmuid's banner was the Liath Loinneach, the Shining Grey; and the Craobh Fuileach, the Bloody Branch, was the banner of Lugaidh's Son. And as to Conan, it is a briar he had on his banner, because he was always for quarrels and for trouble. And it used to be said of him he never saw a man frown without striking him, or a door left open without going in through it.

And when the Fianna had raised their banners they attacked the three armies; and first of all they killed the whole of the Cat-Heads, and then they took the Dog-Heads in hand and made an end of them, and of the White-Backs along with them.

And after that they went to a little hill to the south, having a double dun on it, and it is there they found a hound they were able to get a pup from.

And by that time they had searched through the whole of Ireland, and they did not find in the whole of it a hundred men that could match their nine.

And as well as their banners, some of the Fianna had swords that had names to them, Mac an Luin, Son of the Waves, that belonged to Finn; and Ceard-nan Gallan, the Smith of the Branches, that was Oisin's; and Caoilte's Cruadh-Chosgarach, the Hard Destroying One; and Diarmuid's Liomhadoir, the Burnisher; and Osgar's Cosgarach Mhor, the Great Triumphant One.

And it is the way they got those swords: there came one time to where Finn and Caoilte and some others of the Fianna were, a young man, very big and ugly, having but one foot and one eye; a cloak of black skins he had over his shoulders, and in his hand a blunt ploughshare that was turning to red. And he told them he was Lon, son of Liobhan, one of the three smiths of the King of Lochlann. And whether he thought to go away from the Fianna, or to bring them to his smithy, he started running, and they followed after him all through Ireland, to Slieve-na-Righ, and to Luimnech, and to Ath Luain, and by the right side of Cruachan of Connacht, and to Ess Ruadh and to Beinn Edair, and so to the sea.

And wherever it was they found the smithy, they went into it, and there they found four smiths working, and every one of them having seven hands. And Finn and Caoilte and the rest stopped there watching them till the swords were made, and they brought them away with them then, and it is good use they made of them afterwards.

And besides his sword, Mac an Luin, Finn had a shield was called Sgiath Gailbhinn, the Storm Shield; and when it called out it could be heard all through Ireland.

And whether or not it was the Storm Shield, Finn had a wonderful shield that he did great deeds with, and the story of it is this:

At the time of the battle of the Great Battle of Magh Tuireadh, Lugh, after he had struck the head off Balor of the Evil Eye, hung it in the fork of a hazel-tree. And the tree split, and the leaves fell from it with the dint of the poison that dropped from the head. And through the length of fifty years that tree was a dwelling-place of crows and of ravens. And at the end of that time Manannan, son of Lir, was passing by, and he took notice of the tree that it was split and withered, and he bade his men to dig it up. And when they began to dig, a mist of poison rose up from the roots, and nine of the men got their death from it, and another nine after them, and the third nine were blinded. And Luchtaine the Carpenter made a shield of the wood of that hazel for Manannan. And after a while Manannan gave it, and a set of chessmen along with it, to Tadg, son of Nuada; and from him it came to his grandson, Finn, son of Muirne and of Cumhal.

CHAPTER VI. LOMNA'S HEAD

FINN took a wife one time of the Luigne of Midhe. And at the same time there was in his household one Lomna, a fool.

Finn now went into Tethra, hunting with the Fianna, but Lomna stopped at the house. And after a while he saw Coirpre, a man of the Luigne, go in secretly to where Finn's wife was.

And when the woman knew he had seen that, she begged and prayed of Lomna to hide it from Finn. And Lomna agreed to that, but it preyed on him to have a hand in doing treachery on Finn. And after a while he took a four-square rod and wrote an Ogham on it, and these were the words he wrote:--"An alder stake in a paling of silver; deadly night-shade in a bunch of cresses; a husband of a lewd woman; a fool among the well-taught Fianna; heather on bare Ualann of Luigne."

Finn saw the message, and there was anger on him against the woman; and she knew well it was from Lomna he had heard the story, and she sent a message to Coirpre bidding him to come and kill the fool.

So Coirpre came and struck his head off, and brought it away with him.

And when Finn came back in the evening he saw the body, and it without a head. "Let us know whose body is this," said the Fianna. And then Finn did the divination of rhymes, and it is what he said: "It is the body of Lomna; it is not by a wild boar he was killed; it is not by a fall he was killed; it is not in his bed he died; it is by his enemies he died; it is not a secret to the Luigne the way he died. And let out the hounds now on their track," he said.

So they let out the hounds, and put them on the track of Coirpre, and Finn followed them, and they came to a house, and Coirpre in it, and three times nine of his men and he cooking fish on a spit; and Lomna's head was on a spike beside the fire.

And the first of the fish that was cooked Coirpre divided between his men, but he put no bit into the mouth of the head. And then he made a second division in the same way. Now that was against the law of the Fianna, and the head spoke, and it said: "A speckled white-bellied salmon that grows from a small fish under the sea; you have shared a share that is not right; the Fianna will avenge it upon you, Coirpre." "Put the head outside," said Coirpre, "for that is an evil word for us." Then the head said from outside: "It is in many pieces you will be; it is great fires will be lighted by Finn in Luigne."

And as it said that, Finn came in, and he made an end of Coirpre, and of his men.

CHAPTER VII. ILBREC OF ESS RUADH

One time Caoilte was hunting on Beinn Gulbain, and he went on to Ess Ruadh. And when he came near the hill of the Sidhe that is there, he saw a young man waiting for him, having a crimson fringed cloak about him, and on his breast a silver brooch, and a white shield, ornamented with linked beasts of red gold, and his hair rolled in a ball at the back, and covered with a golden cup. And he had heavy green weapons, and he was holding two hounds in a silver chain.

And when Caoilte came up to him he gave him three loving kisses, and sat down beside him on the grass. "Who are you, young champion?" said Caoilte. "I am Derg, son of Eoghan of the people of Usnach," he said, "and foster-brother of your own." Caoilte knew him then, and he said: "And what is your life with your mother's people, the Tuatha de Danaan in Sidhe Aedha?" "There is nothing wanting to us there of food or of clothing," said the young man. "But for all that," he said, "I would sooner live the life of the worst treated of the serving-boys of the Fianna than the life I am living in the hill of the Sidhe." "Lonely as you are at your hunting to-day," said Caoilte, "it is often I saw you coming to the Valley of the Three Waters in the south, where the Siuir and the Beoir and the Berba come together, with a great company about you; fifteen hundred young men, fifteen hundred serving-boys, and fifteen hundred women." "That was so," said Derg; "and although myself and my gentle hound are living in the hill of the Sidhe, my mind is always on the Fianna. And I remember well the time," he said, "when you yourself won the race against Finn's lasting black horse. And come now into the hill," he said, "for the darkness of the night is coming on."

So he brought Caoilte into the hill with him, and they were set down in their right places.

It was at that time, now, there was great war between Lir of Sidhe Fionnach-aidh and Ilbrec of Ess Ruadh. There used a bird with an iron beak and a tail of fire to come every evening to a golden window of Ilbrec's house, and there he would shake himself till he would not leave sword on pillow, or shield on peg, or spear in rack, but they would come down on the heads of the people of the house; and whatever they would throw at the bird, it is on the heads of some of themselves it would fall. And the night Caoilte came in, the hall was made ready for a feast, and the bird came in again, and did the same destruction as before, and nothing they threw at him would touch him at all. "Is it long the bird has been doing this?" said Caoilte. "Through the length of a year now," said Derg, "since we went to war with Sidhe Fionnachaidh."

Then Caoilte put his hand within the rim of his shield, and he took out of it a copper rod he had, and he made a cast of it at the bird, that brought it down on the floor of the hall. "Did any one ever make a better cast than that?" said Ilbrec. "By my word," said Caoilte, "there is no one of us in the Fianna has any right to boast against another." Then Ilbrec took down a sharp spear, having thirty rivets of gold in it, from its place, and he said: "That is the Spear of Fiacha, son of Congha, and it is with that Finn made an end of Aillen, son of Midhna, that used to burn Teamhair. And keep it beside you now, Caoilte," he said, "till we see will Lir come to avenge his bird on us."

Then they took up their horns and their cups, and they were at drinking and pleasure, and Ilbrec said: "Well, Caoilte," he said, "if Lir comes to avenge his bird on us, who will you put in command of the battle?" "I will give the command to Derg there beyond," said he. "Will you take it in hand, Derg?" said the people of the hill. "I will take it," said Derg, "with its loss and its gain."

So that is how they spent the night, and it was not long in the morning till they heard blowing of horns, and rattling of chariots, and clashing of shields, and the up-roar of a great army that came all about the hill. They sent some of their people out then to see were there many in it, and they saw three brave armies of the one size. "It would be a great vexation to me," said Aedh Nimbrec, the Speckled, then, "we to get our death and Lir's people to take the hill." "Did you never hear, Aedh," said Caoilte, "that the wild boar escapes sometimes from both hounds and from wolves, and the stag in the same way goes away from the hounds with a sudden start; and what man is it you are most in dread of in the battle?" he said. "The man that is the best fighter of all the Men of Dea," said they all, "and that is Lir of Sidhe Fionnach-aidh." "The thing I have done in every battle I will not give up to-day," said Caoilte, "to meet the best man that is in it hand to hand." "The two that are next to him in fighting," they said then, "are Donn and Dubh." "I will put down those two," said Derg.

Then the host of the Sidhe went out to the battle, and the armies attacked one another with wide green spears and with little casting spears, and with great stones; and the fight went on from the rising of the day till midday. And then Caoilte and Lir met with one another, and they made a very fierce fight, and at the last Lir of Sidhe Fionnachaidh fell by the hand of Caoilte.

Then the two good champions Dubh and Donn, sons of Eirrge, determined to go on with the battle, and it is how they fought, Dubh in the front of the whole army, and Donn behind all, guarding the rear. But Derg saw that, and he put his finger into the thong of his spear and made a cast at the one that was nearest him, and it broke his back and went on into the body of the other, so that the one cast made an end of the two. And that ended the battle, and all that was left of the great army of Lir went wearing away to the north. And there was great rejoicing in the hill at Ess Ruadh, and Ilbrec took the spoils of the beaten army for his people, and to Caoilte he gave the enchanted spear of Fiacha, together with nine rich cloaks and nine long swords with hilts and guards of gold, and nine hounds for hunting. And they said farewell to one another, and Caoilte left his blessing to the people of the hill, and he brought their thanks with him. And as hard as the battle had been, it was harder again for Derg to part from his comrade, and the day he was parted from Finn and from all the Fianna was no sadder to him than this day.

It was a long time after that Caoilte went again to the hill of Ilbrec at Ess Ru-adh, and this is the way it happened.

It was in a battle at Beinn Edair in the east that Mane, son of the King of Lochlann, made a cast at him in the middle of the battle with a deadly spear. And he heard the whistling of the spear, and it rushing to him; and he lifted his shield to protect his head and his body, but that did not save him, for it struck into his thigh, and left its poison in it, so that he had to go in search of healing. And it is where he went, to the hill of the Sidhe at Ess Ruadh, to ask help of Bebind, daughter of

Elcmar of Brugh na Boinne, that had the drink of healing of the Tuatha de Danaan, and all that was left of the ale of Goibniu that she used to be giving out to them.

And Caoilte called to Cascorach the Musician, son of Caincenn, and bade him bring his harp and come along with him. And they stopped for a night in the hill of the Sidhe of Druim Nemed in Luigne of Connacht, and from that they went forward by Ess Dara, the Fall of the Oaks, and Druim Dearg na Feinne, the Red Ridge of the Fianna, and Ath Daim Glas, the Ford of the Grey Stag, and to Beinn Gulbain, and northward into the plain of Ceitne, where the Men of Dea used to pay their tribute to the Fomor; and up to the Footstep of Ess Ruadh, and the High Place of the Boys, where the boys of the Tuatha de Danaan used to be playing their hurling. And Aedh of Ess Ruadh and Ilbrec of Ess Ruadh were at the door of the hill, and they gave Caoilte a true welcome. "I am glad of that welcome," said Caoilte. And then Bebind, daughter of Elcmar of Brugh na Boinne, came out, and three times fifty comely women about her, and she sat down on the green grass and gave three loving kisses to the three, to Caoilte and to Cascorach and to Fermaise, that had come with them out of the hill of the Sidhe in Luigne of Connacht. And all the people of the hill welcomed them, and they said: "It is little your friendship would be worth if you would not come to help us and we in need of help." "It was not for bravery I was bade come," said Cascorach; "but when the right time comes I will make music for you if you have a mind to hear it." "It is not for deeds of bravery we are come," said Fermaise, "but we will give you our help if you are in need of it." Then Caoilte told them the cause of his journey. "We will heal you well," said they. And then they all went into the hill and stayed there three days and three nights at drinking and pleasure.

And indeed it was good help Caoilte and Cascorach gave them after that. For there was a woman-warrior used to come every year with the ships of the men of Lochlann to make an attack on the Tuatha de Danaan. And she had been reared by a woman that knew all enchantments, and there was no precious thing in all the hills of the Sidhe but she had knowledge of it, and would bring it away. And just at this time there came a messenger to the door of the hill with news that the harbour was full of ships, and that a great army had landed, and the woman-warrior along with it.

And it was Cascorach the Musician went out against her, having a shield he got the loan of from Donn, son of Midhir; and she used high words when she saw so young a man coming to fight with her, and he alone. But he made an end of her for all her high talk, and left her lying on the strand with the sea foam washing up to her.

And as to Caoilte, he went out in a chariot belonging to Midhir of the Yellow Hair, son of the Dagda, and a spear was given him that was called Ben-badb, the War-Woman, and he made a cast of the spear that struck the King of Lochlann, that he fell in the middle of his army, and the life went from him. And Fermaise went looking for the king's brother, Eolus, that was the comeliest of all the men of the world; and he knew him by the band of gold around his head, and his green armour, and his red shield, and he killed him with a cast of a five-pronged spear. And when the men of Lochlann saw their three leaders were gone, they went into their ships and back to their own country. And there was great joy through the whole country, both among the men of Ireland and the Tuatha de Danaan, the men of Lochlann to have been driven away by the deeds of Caoilte and Fermaise and Cascorach.

And that was not all they did, for it was at that time there came three flocks of beautiful red birds from Slieve Fuad in the north, and began eating the green grass before the hill of the Sidhe. "What birds are those?" said Caoilte. "Three flocks they are that come and destroy the green every year, eating it down to the bare flag-stones, till they leave us no place for our races," said Ilbrec. Then Caoilte and his comrades took up three stones and threw them at the flocks and drove them away. "Power and blessings to you," said the people of the Sidhe then, "that is a good work you have done. And there is another thing you can do for us," they said, "for there are three ravens come to us every year out of the north, and the time the young lads of the hill are playing their hurling, each one of the ravens carries off a boy of them. And it is to-morrow the hurling will be," they said.

So when the full light of day was come on the morrow, the whole of the Tuatha de Danaan went out to look at the hurling; and to every six men of them was given a chess-board, and a board for some other game to every five, and to every ten men a little harp, and a harp to every hundred men, and pipes that were sharp and powerful to every nine.

Then they saw the three ravens from the north coming over the sea, and they pitched on the great tree of power that was on the green, and they gave three gloomy screeches, that if such a thing could be, would have brought the dead out of the earth or the hair off the head of the listeners; and as it was, they took the courage out of the whole gathering.

Then Cascorach, son of Caincenn, took a man of the chessmen and made a cast at one of the ravens that struck his beak and his throat, and made an end of him; and Fermaise killed the second of them, and Caoilte the third of them in the same way.

"Let my cure be done now," said Caoilte, "for I have paid my fee for it, and it is time." "You have paid it indeed," said Ilbrec. "And where is Bebind, daughter of Elcmar?" he said. "I am here," said she.

"Bring Caoilte, son of Ronan, with you into some hidden place," he said, "and do his cure, and let him be well served, for he has driven every danger from the Men of Dea and from the Sons of the Gael. And let Cascorach make music for him, and let Fermaise, son of Eogabil, be watching him and guarding him and attending him."

So Elcmar's daughter went to the House of Arms, and her two sons with her, and a bed of healing was made ready for Caoilte, and a bowl of pale gold was brought to her, and it full of water. And she took a crystal vessel and put herbs into it, and she bruised them and put them in the water, and gave the bowl to Caoilte, and he drank a great drink out of it, that made him cast up the poison of the spear that was in him. Five drinks of it he took, and after that she gave him new milk to drink; but with the dint of the reaching he was left without strength through the length of three days and three nights.

"Caoilte, my life," she said then, "in my opinion you have got relief." "I have got it indeed," he said, "but that the weakness of my head is troubling me." "The washing of Flann, daughter of Flidais, will be done for you now," she said, "and the head that washing is done for will never be troubled with pain, or baldness, or weakness of sight." So that cure was done to him for a while; and the people of the hill divided themselves into three parts; the one part of their best men and great nobles, and another of their young men, and another of their women and poets, to be visiting him and making mirth with him as long as he would be on his bed of healing. And everything that was best from their hunting, it was to him they would bring it.

And one day, when Elcmar's daughter and her two sons and Cascorach and

Fermaise were with Caoilte, there was heard a sound of music coming towards them from the waters of Ess Ruadh, and any one would leave the music of the whole world for that music. And they put their harps on the corners of the pillars and went out, and there was wonder on Caoilte that they left him. And he took notice that his strength and the strength of his hands was not come to him yet, and he said: "It is many a rough battle and many a hard fight I went into, and now there is not enough strength in me so much as to go out along with the rest," and he cried tears down.

And the others came back to him then, and he asked news of them. "What was that sound of music we heard?" he said. "It was Uaine out of the hill of the Sidhe, at the Wave of Cliodna in the south," said they; "and with her the birds of the Land of Promise; and she is musician to the whole of that country. And every year she goes to visit one of the hills of the Sidhe, and it is our turn this time." Then the woman from the Land of Promise came into the house, and the birds came in along with her, and they pitched on the pillars and the beams, and thirty of them came in where Caoilte was, began singing together. And Cascorach took his harp, and whatever he would play, the birds would sing to it. "It is much music I have heard," said Caoilte, "but music so good as that I never heard before."

And after that Caoilte asked to have the healing of his thigh done, and the daughter of Elcmar gave herself to that, and all that was bad was sucked from the wound by her serving people till it was healed. And Caoilte stopped on where he was for three nights after that.

And then the people of the hill rose up and went into the stream to swim. And Caoilte said: "What ails me now not to go swim, since my health has come back to me?" And with that he went into the water. And afterwards they went back into the hill, and there was a great feast made that night.

And Caoilte bade them farewell after that, and Cascorach, but Fermaise stopped with them for a while. And the people of the hill gave good gifts to Caoilte; a fringed crimson cloak of wool from the seven sheep of the Land of Promise; and a fish-hook that was called Aicil mac Mogha, and that could not be set in any river or inver but it would take fish; and along with that they gave him a drink of remembrance, and after that drink there would be no place he ever saw, or no battle or fight he ever was in, but it would stay in his memory. "That is a good help from kinsmen and from friends," said Caoilte.

Then Caoilte and Cascorach went out from the hill, and the people of it made a great lamentation after them.

CHAPTER VIII. THE CAVE OF CRUACHAN

CAOLITE was one time at Cruachan of Connacht, and Cascorach was with him, and there he saw sitting on a heap of stones a man with very rough grey hair, having a dark brown cloak fastened with a pin of bronze, and a long stick of white hazel in his hand; and there was a herd of cattle before him in a fenced field.

Caoilte asked news of him. "I am steward to the King of Ireland," said the old man, "and it is from him I hold this land. And we have great troubles on us in this district," he said. "What troubles are those?" said Caoilte. "I have many herds of cattle," he said, "and every year at Samhain time, a woman comes out of the hill of the Sidhe of Cruachan and brings away nine of the best out of every herd. And as to my name, I am Bairnech, son of Carbh of Collamair of Bregia."

"Who was the best man that ever came out of Collamair?" said Caoilte. "I know, and the men of Ireland and of Alban know," said he, "it was Caoilte, son of Ronan. And do you know where is that man now?" he said. "I myself am that man and your own kinsman," said Caoilte.

When Bairnech heard that, he gave him a great welcome, and Caoilte gave him three kisses. "It seems to me that to-night is Samhain night," said Caoilte. "If that is so, it is to-night the woman will come to rob us," said Bernech. "Let me go to-night to the door of the hill of the Sidhe," said Cascorach. "You may do that, and bring your arms with you," said Caoilte.

So Cascorach went then, and it was not long till he saw the girl going past him out of the hill of Cruachan, having a beautiful cloak of one colour about her; a gown of yellow silk tied up with a knot between her thighs, two spears in her hands, and she not in dread of anything before her or after her.

Then Cascorach blew a blast against her, and put his finger into the thong of his spear, and made a cast at the girl that went through her, and that is the way she was made an end of by Cascorach of the Music. And then Bernech said to Caoilte: "Caoilte," he said, "do you know the other oppression that is on me in this place?" "What oppression is that?" said Caoilte. "Three she-wolves that come out of the Cave of Cruachan every year and destroy our sheep and our wethers, and we can do nothing against them, and they go back into the cave again. And it will be a good friend that will rid us of them," he said. "Well, Cascorach," said Caoilte, "do you know what are the three wolves that are robbing this man?" "I know well," said Cascorach, "they are the three daughters of Airetach, of the last of the people of oppression of the Cave of Cruachan, and it is easier for them to do their robbery as wolves than as women." "And will they come near to any one?" said Caoilte. "They will only come near to one sort," said Cascorach; "if they see the world's men having harps for music, they will come near to them." "And how would it be for me," he said, "to go to-morrow to the cairn beyond, and to bring my harp with me?"

So in the morning he rose up and went to the cairn and stopped on it, playing his harp till the coming of the mists of the evening. And while he was there he saw the three wolves coming towards him, and they lay down before him, listening to the music. But Cascerach found no way to make an attack on them, and they went back into the cave at the end of the day.

Cascorach went back then to Caoilte and told him what had happened. "Go up to-morrow to the same place," said Caoilte, "and say to them it would be better for them to be in the shape of women for listening to music than in the shape of wolves."

So on the morrow Cascorach went out to the same cairn, and set his people about it, and the wolves came there and stretched themselves to listen to the music. And Cascorach was saying to them: "If you were ever women," he said, "it would be better for you to be listening to the music as women than as wolves." And they heard that, and they threw off the dark trailing coverings that were about them, for they liked well the sweet music of the Sidhe. And when Caoilte saw them there side by side, and elbow by elbow, he made a cast of his spear, and it went through the three women, that they were like a skein of thread drawn together on the spear. And that is the way he made an end of the strange, unknown three. And that place got the name of the Valley of the Shapes of the Wolves.

CHAPTER IX. THE WEDDING AT CEANN SLIEVE

Finn and the Fianna made a great hunting one time on the hill of Torc that is over Loch Lein and Feara Mor. And they went on with their hunting till they came to pleasant green Slieve Echtge, and from that it spread over other green-topped hills, and through thick tangled woods, and rough red-headed hills, and over the wide plains of the country. And every chief man among them chose the place that was to his liking, and the gap of danger he was used to before. And the shouts they gave in the turns of the hunt were heard in the woods all around, so that they started the deer in the wood, and sent the foxes wandering, and the little red beasts climbing rocks, and badgers from their holes, and birds flying, and fawns running their best. Then they let out their angry small-headed hounds and set them hunting. And it is red the hands of the Fianna were that day, and it is proud they were of their hounds that were torn and wounded before evening.

It happened that day no one stopped with Finn but only Diorraing, son of Domhar. "Well, Diorraing," said Finn, "let you watch for me while I go asleep, for it is early I rose to-day, and it is an early rising a man makes when he cannot see the shadow of his five fingers between himself and the light of day, or know the leaves of the hazel from the leaves of the oak." With that he fell into a quiet sleep that lasted till the yellow light of the evening. And the rest of the Fianna, not knowing where he was gone, gave over the hunt.

And the time was long to Diorraing while Finn was asleep, and he roused him and told him the Fianna must have given up the hunt, for he could not hear a cry or a whistle from them. "The end of day is come," said Finn then, "and we will not follow them to-night. And go now to the wood," he said, "and bring timber and dead branches for a shelter, and I will go looking for food for the night." So Diorraing went to the wood, but he was not gone far till he saw a fine well-lighted house of the Sidhe before him on the edge of the wood near at hand, and he went back to Finn with the news. "Let us go to it," said Finn, "for we ought not to be working in this place, and people living so near at hand." They went then to the door of the house and knocked at it, and the door-keeper came to it. "Whose house is this?" said Diorraing. "It belongs to Conan of Ceann Slieve," said the door-keeper. "Tell him," said Diorraing, "there are two of the Fianna of the Gael at the door."

The door-keeper went in then and told Conan there were two men of the Fianna at the door. "The one of them," he said, "is young and strong, and quiet and fair-haired, and more beautiful than the rest of the men of the world, and he has in his hand a small-headed, white-breasted hound, having a collar of rubbed gold and a chain of old silver. And the other of them," he said, "is brown and ruddy and white-toothed, and he is leading a yellow-spotted hound by a chain of bright bronze." "It is well you have made your report of them," said Conan, "and I know them by it; for the man you spoke of first is Finn, son of Cumhal, Head of the Fianna of Ireland, and Bran in his hand; and the other is Diorraing, and Sceolan in his hand. And go now quickly and let them in," he said.

Finn and Diorraing were brought in then, and they got good attendance, and their arms were taken from them, and a grand feast was made ready that pleased them well. And the wife of Conan was at the one side of Finn, and his daughter, Finndealbh, of the Fair Shape, was at his other side. And they had a great deal of talk together, and at last, seeing her so beautiful, the colour of gold on her curled hair, and her eyes as blue as flowers, and a soft four-cornered cloak fastened at her breast with a silver pin, he asked her of Conan for his wife. "Leave asking that, Finn," said Conan, "for your own courage is not greater than the courage of the man she is promised to." "Who is that?" said Finn. "He is Fatha, son of the King of Ess Ruadh," said Conan. "Your wounds and your danger on yourself," said Diorraing; "and it would be right," he said, "that stammering tongue that gave out those words to be tied and to be shortened for ever, and a drink of death to be given to you; for if the whole of the Men of Dea," he said, "could be put into the one body, Finn would be better than them all." "Leave off, Diorraing," said Finn, "for it is not fighting I am here, but asking a wife, and I will get her whether the Men of Dea think good or bad of it." "I will not be making a quarrel with you," said Conan, "but I put you under bonds as a true hero to answer me everything I am going to ask you." "I will do that," said Finn.

With that Conan put questions to Finn as to his birth and his rearing, and the deeds he had done since he came to the Fianna, and Finn gave full answers to them all. And at last he said: "Let us go on with this no longer, but if you have musicians with you, let them be brought to us now; for it is not my custom," he said, "to be for a single night without music." "Tell me this first," said Conan, "who was it made the Dord Fiann, the Mutterer of the Fianna, and when was it made?" "I will tell you the truth of that," said Finn; "it was made in Ireland by the three sons of Cearmait Honey-Mouth; and nine men used to be sounding it, and since it came to me I have fifty men sounding it." "And tell me this," said Conan, "what is the music pleased you best of all you ever heard?" "I will tell you that," said Finn; "the time the seven battalions of the Fianna are gathered in the one place and raise their spear-shafts over their heads, and the sharp whining of the clear, cold wind goes through them, that is very sweet to me. And when the drinking-hall is set out in Almhuin, and the cup-bearers give out the bright cups to the chief men of the Fianna, that is very sweet to me; and it is sweet to me to be listening to the voice of the sea-gull and the heron, and the noise of the waves of Traig Liath, the song of the three sons of Meardha, the whistle of Lugaidh's Son, and the voice of the cuckoo in the beginning of summer, and the grunting of the pigs on the Plain of Eithne, and the shouting of laughter in Doire." And it is what he said: "The Dord in the green-topped woods, the lasting wash of the waves against the shore, the noise of the waves at Traig Liath meeting with the river of the White Trout; the three men that came to the Fianna, a man of them gentle and a man of them rough, another man of them ploughing the clouds, they were sweeter than any other thing.

"The grey mane of the sea, the time a man cannot follow its track; the swell that brings the fish to the land, it is sleep-music, its sound is sweet.

"Feargall, son of Fionn, a man that was ready-handed, it is long his leap was, it is well marked his track is; he never gave a story that did not do away with secrets; it is his voice was music of sleep to me."

And when Finn had answered all the questions so well, Conan said he would give him his daughter, and that he would have a wedding-feast ready at the end of a month.

They spent the rest of the night then in sleep; but Finn saw a dreadful vision through his sleep that made him start three times from his bed. "What makes you start from your bed, Finn?" said Diorraing. "It was the Tuatha de Danaan I saw," said he, "taking up a quarrel against me, and making a great slaughter of the Fianna."

Now as to the Fianna, they rested at Fotharladh of Moghna that night, and they were downhearted, having no tidings of Finn. And early on the morrow two of them, Bran Beag and Bran Mor, rose up and went to Mac-an-Reith, son of the Ram, that had the gift of true knowledge, and they asked him where did Finn spend the night. And Mac-an-Reith was someway unwilling to tell them, but at the last he said it was at the house of Conan of Ceann Slieve.

The two Brans went on then to Conan's house, and Finn made them welcome; but they blamed him when they heard he was taking a wife, and none of his people with him. "Bid all the Fianna to come to the feast at the end of a month," said Conan then. So Finn and Diorraing and the two Brans went back to where the Fianna were and told them all that had happened, and they went on to Almhuin.

And when they were in the drinking-hall at Almhuin that night, they saw the son of the King of Ireland coming to where they were. "It is a pity the king's son to have come," said Finn; "for he will not be satisfied without ordering everything in the hall in his own way." "We will not take his orders," said Oisin, "but we will leave the half of the hall to him, and keep the other half ourselves."

So they did that; but it happened that in the half of the house that was given up to the King of Ireland's son, there were sitting two of the Men of Dea, Failbhe Mor and Failbhe Beag; and it is what they said, that it is because they were in that side of the hall it was given up. "It is a pity," said Failbhe Beag, "this shame and this great insult to have been put on us to-night; and it is likely Finn has a mind to do more than that again to us," he said, "for he is going to bring away the woman that is promised to the third best man of the Tuatha de Danaan, and against the will of her father and mother." And these two went away early in the morning to Fionnbhar of Magh Feabhail, and told him of the insults Finn and the Fianna of Ireland had a mind to put on the Tuatha de Danaan.

And when Fionnbhar that was king over the Tuatha de Danaan heard that, he sent out messengers through the length of Ireland to gather them all to him. And there came six good battalions to him on the edge of Loch Derg Dheirc at the end of a month; and it was the same day Conan had the wedding-feast made ready for

Finn and his people.

And Finn was at Teamhair Luachra at that time, and when he heard the feast was ready, he set out to go to it. And it chanced that the most of the men he had with him at that time were of the sons of Morna. And when they were on their way, Finn said to Goll, "O Goll," he said, "I never felt any fear till now going to a feast. And there are but few of my people with me," he said; "and I know there is no good thing before me, but the Men of Dea are going to raise a quarrel against me and to kill my people." "I will defend you against anything they may do," said Goll.

They went on then to Conan's house, and there was a welcome before them, and they were brought into the drinking-hall, and Finn was put in the place beside the door, and Goll on his right and Finndeilb, of the Fair Shape, on his left, and all the rest in the places they were used to.

And as to Fionnbhar of Magh Feabhail and the Tuatha de Danaan, they put a Druid mist about themselves and went on, hidden and armed, in sixteen battalions, to the lawn before Conan's house. "It is little profit we have being here," they said then, "and Goll being with Finn against us." "Goll will not protect him this time," said Ethne, the woman-Druid, "for I will entice Finn out of the house, however well he is watched."

She went on to the house then, and took her stand before Finn outside. "Who is that before me?" she said then. "It is I myself," said Finn. "I put you under the bonds a true hero never broke," she said, "to come out to me here." When Finn heard that, he made no delay and went out to her; and for all there were so many in the house, not one of them took notice of him going, only Caoilte, and he followed him out. And at the same time the Tuatha de Danaan let out a flock of blackbirds having fiery beaks, that pitched on the breasts of all the people in the house, and burned them and destroyed them, till the young lads and the women and children of the place ran out on all sides, and the woman of the house, Conan's wife, was drowned in the river outside the dun.

But as to Ethne, the woman-Druid, she asked Finn would he run against her. "For it is to run a race against you I called you out," she said. "What length of a race?" said Finn. "From Doire da Torc, the Wood of the Two Boars, to Ath Mor, the Great Ford," she said. So they set out, but Finn got first over the ford. And Caoilte was following after them, and Finn was urging him, and he said: "It is ashamed of your running you should be, Caoilte, a woman to be going past you." On that Caoilte made a leap forward, and when he was in front of the witch he turned about and gave a blow of his sword that made two equal halves of her.

"Power and good luck to you, Caoilte!" said Finn; "for though it is many a good blow you have struck, you never struck a better one than this."

They went back then to the lawn before Conan's dun, and there they found the whole company of the Tuatha de Danaan, that had put the Druid mist off them. "It seems to me, Caoilte," said Finn, "that we are come into the middle of our enemies."

With that they turned their backs to one another, and they were attacked on all sides till groans of weakness from the unequal fight were forced from Finn. And when Goll, that was in the house, heard that, he said: "It is a pity the Tuatha de Danaan to have enticed Finn and Caoilte away from us; and let us go to their help and make no delay," he said.

Then he rushed out, and all that were there of the Fianna with him, and Conan of Ceann Slieve and his sons. And great anger came on Goll, that he looked like a tall mountain under his grey shield in the battle. And he broke through the Tuatha de Danaan till he reached to Fionnbhar their leader, and they attacked one another, cutting and wounding, till at the last Fionnbhar of Magh Feabhail fell by the strokes of Goll. And a great many others fell in that battle, and there never was a harder battle fought in Ireland, for there was no man on one side or the other had a mind to go back one step before whoever he was fighting against. For they were the two hardest fighting troops to be found in the four parts of the world, the strong, hardy Fianna of the Gael, and the beautiful Men of Dea; and they went near to being all destroyed in that battle.

But after a while they saw the rest of the Fianna that were not in the battle coming from all parts of Ireland. And when the Tuatha de Danaan saw them coming, they put the Druid mist about themselves again and made away. And clouds of weakness came on Finn himself, and on them that were with him, with the dint of the fight. And there were many men of the Fianna lost in that battle; and as to the rest, it is a long time they stopped in Almhuin of Leinster, till their wounds were entirely healed.

CHAPTER X. THE SHADOWY ONE

And indeed Finn had no great luck in going to look for a wife that time; and he had no better luck another time he asked a wife from among the Sidhe. And this is the way that happened.

It was on the mountain of Bearnas Mor he was hunting, and a great wild pig turned on the hounds of the Fianna and killed the most of them, but Bran made an attack on it then and got the best of it. And the pig began to scream, and with that a very tall man came out of the hill and he asked Finn to let the pig go free. And when he agreed to that, the man brought them into the hill of the Sidhe at Glandeirgdeis; and when they came to the door of the house he struck the pig with his Druid rod, and on the moment it changed into a beautiful young woman, and the name he called her by was Scathach, the Shadowy One.

And he made a great feast for the Fianna, and Finn asked the young girl in marriage, and the tall man, her father, said he would give her to him on that very night.

But when night came on, Scathach asked the loan of a harp, and it was brought to her. One string it had of iron, and one of bronze, and one of silver. And when the iron string would be played, it would set all the hosts of the world crying and ever crying; and when the bright bronze string would be played, it would set them all laughing from the one day to the same hour on the morrow; and when the silver string would be played, all the men of the whole world would fall into a long sleep.

And it is the sleepy silver string the Shadowy One played upon, till Finn and Bran and all his people were in their heavy sleep.

And when they awoke at the rising of the sun on the morrow, it is outside on the mountain of Bearnas they were, where they first saw the wild pig.

CHAPTER XI. FINN'S MADNESS

One time Finn and the Fianna were come to a ford of the Slaine, and they sat down for a while. And as they were sitting there they saw on the round rock up over the ford a young woman, having a dress of silk and a green cloak about her, and a golden brooch in the cloak, and the golden crown that is the sign of a queen on her head. "Fianna of Ireland," she said, "let one of you come now and speak with me."

Then Sciathbreac, of the Speckled Shield, went towards her. "Who is it you are wanting?" he said, "Finn, son of Cumhal," said she. Finn went over then to talk with her. "Who are you?" he said, "and what is it you are wanting?" "I am Daireann, daughter of Bodb Dearg, son of the Dagda," she said; "and I am come to be your wife if you will give me the bride-gift I ask." "What bride-gift is that?" said Finn. "It is your promise," said she, "I to be your only wife through the length of a year, and to have the half of your time after that." "I will not give that promise," said Finn, "to any woman of the world, and I will not give it to you," he said.

On that the young woman took a cup of white silver from under a covering, and filled it with strong drink, and she gave it to Finn. "What is this?" said Finn. "It is very strong mead," said she. Now there were bonds on Finn not to refuse anything belonging to a feast, so he took the cup and drank what was in it, and on the moment he was like one gone mad. And he turned his face towards the Fianna, and every harm and every fault and every misfortune in battle that he knew against any one of them, he sprang it on them, through the mad drunkenness the young woman had put on him.

Then the chief men of the Fianna of Ireland rose up and left the place to him, every one of them setting out for his own country, till there was no one left upon the hill but Finn and Caoilte. And Caoilte rose up and followed after them, and he said: "Fianna of Ireland," he said, "do not leave your lord and your leader through the arts and the tricks of a woman of the Sidhe." Thirteen times he went after them, bringing them back to the hill in that way. And with the end of the day and the fall of night the bitterness went from Finn's tongue; and by the time Caoilte had brought back the whole of the Fianna, his sense and his memory were come back to him, and he would sooner have fallen on his sword and got his death, than have stayed living.

And that was the hardest day's work Caoilte ever did, unless the day he brought the flock of beasts and birds to Teamhair, to ransom Finn from the High King of Ireland.

Another time Maer, wife of Bersa of Berramain, fell in love with Finn, and she made nine nuts of Segair with love charms, and sent them to Finn, and bade him eat them. "I will not," said Finn; "for they are not nuts of knowledge, but nuts of ignorance; and it is not known what they are, unless they might be an enchantment for drinking love." So he buried them a foot deep in the earth.

CHAPTER XII. THE RED WOMAN

One time the Fianna were in Almhuin with no great work to do, and there came a very misty morning, and Finn was in dread that sluggishness would come on his men, and he rose up, and he said: "Make yourselves ready, and we will go hunting to Gleann-na-Smol."

They all said the day was too misty to go hunting; but there was no use in talking: they had to do as Finn bade them. So they made themselves ready and went on towards Gleann-na-Smol; and they were not gone far when the mist lifted and the sun came shining out.

And when they were on the edge of a little wood, they saw a strange beast coming towards them with the quickness of the wind, and a Red Woman on its track. Narrow feet the beast had, and a head like the head of a boar, and long horns on it; but the rest of it was like a deer, and there was a shining moon on each of its sides.

Finn stopped, and he said: "Fianna of Ireland," he said, "did you ever see a beast like that one until now?" "We never did indeed," said they; "and it would be right for us to let out the hounds after it." "Wait a while," said Finn, "till I speak with the Red Woman; but do not let the beast go past you," he said. They thought to keep back the beast then, going before it; but they were hardly able to hinder it at all, and it went away through them.

And when the Red Woman was come up to them, Finn asked her what was the name of the beast she was following. "I do not know that," she said, "though I am on its track since I left the borders of Loch Dearg a month ago, and I never lost sight of it since then; and the two moons that are on its two sides shine through the country all around in the night time. And I must follow it till it falls," she said, "or I will lose my own life and the lives of my three sons that are the best fighting men in the whole world." "We will take the beast for you if you have a mind," said Finn. "Do not try to do that," she said, "for I myself am swifter than you are, and I cannot come up with it." "We will not let it go till we know what sort of a beast is it," said Finn. "If you yourself or your share of men go after it, I will bind you hand and foot," said she. "It is too stiff your talk is," said Finn. "And do you not know," he said, "I am Finn, son of Cumhal; and there are fourscore fighting men along with me that were never beaten yet." "It is little heed I give to yourself or your share of men," said the Red Woman; "and if my three sons were here, they would stand up against you." "Indeed it will be a bad day," said Finn, "when the threat of a woman will put fear on myself or on the Fianna of Ireland." With that he sounded his horn, and he said: "Let us all follow now, men and dogs, after that beast that we saw."

He had no sooner said that word than the woman made a great water-worm of herself, and made an attack on Finn, and she would have killed him then and there but for Bran being with him. Bran took a grip of the worm and shook it, and then it wound itself round Bran's body, and would have crushed the life out of her, but Finn thrust his sharp sword into its throat. "Keep back your hand," said the worm then, "and you will not have the curse of a lonely woman upon you." "It is what I think," said Finn, "that you would not leave me my life if you could take it from me; but go out of my sight now," he said, "and that I may never see you again."

Then she made herself into a Red Woman again, and went away into the wood.

All the Fianna were gone on the track of the beast while Finn was talking and fighting with the Red Woman; and he did not know in what place they were, but he went following after them, himself and Bran. It was late in the evening when he came up with a share of them, and they still on the track of the beast. The darkness of the night was coming on, but the two moons in the sides of the beast gave a bright light, and they never lost it from sight. They followed it on always; and about midnight they were pressing on it, and it began to scatter blood after it, and it was not long till Finn and his men were red from head to foot. But that did not hinder them, and they followed him on till they saw him going in at the foot of Cnoc-na-righ at the breaking of day.

When they came to the foot of the hill the Red Woman was standing there before them. "You did not take the beast," she said. "We did not take it, but we know where it is," said Finn.

She took a Druid rod then, and she struck a blow on the side of the hill, and on the moment a great door opened, and they heard sweet music coming from within. "Come in now," said the Red Woman, "till you see the wonderful beast." "Our clothing is not clean," said Finn, "and we would not like to go in among a company the way we are," he said.

She put a horn to her mouth and blew it, and on the moment there came ten young men to her. "Bring water for washing," she said, "and four times twenty suits of clothes, and a beautiful suit and a crown of shining stones for Finn, son of Cumhal." The young men went away then, and they came back at the end of a minute with water and with clothing.

When the Fianna were washed and dressed, the Red Woman brought them into a great hall, where there was the brightness of the sun and of the moon on every side. From that she brought them into another great room; and although Finn and his men had seen many grand things up to that time, they had never seen any sight so grand as what they saw in this place. There was a king sitting in a golden chair, having clothes of gold and of green, and his chief people were sitting around him, and his musicians were playing. And no one could know what colour were the dresses of the musicians, for every colour of the rainbow was in them. And there was a great table in the middle of the room, having every sort of thing on it, one better than another.

The king rose up and gave a welcome to Finn and to his men, and he bade them to sit down at the table; and they ate and drank their fill, and that was wanting to them after the hunt they had made. And then the Red Woman rose up, and she said: "King of the Hill, if it is your will, Finn and his men have a mind to see the wonderful beast, for they spent a long time following after it, and that is what brought them here."

The king struck a blow then on his golden chair, and a door opened behind him, and the beast came through it and stood before the king. And it stooped down before him, and it said: "I am going on towards my own country now; and there is not in the world a runner so good as myself, and the sea is the same to me as the land. And let whoever can come up with me come now," it said, "for I am going."

With that the beast went out from the hill as quick as a blast of wind, and all the people that were in it went following after it. It was not long till Finn and his men were before the rest, in the front of the hunt, gaining on the beast.

And about midday Bran made the beast turn, and then she forced it to turn a second time, and it began to put out cries, and it was not long until its strength began to flag; and at last, just at the setting of the sun, it fell dead, and Bran was at its side when it fell.

Then Finn and his men came up, but in place of a beast it was a tall man they saw lying dead before them. And the Red Woman came up at the same time, and she said: "High King of the Fianna, that is the King of the Firbolgs you have killed; and his people will put great troubles on this country in the time to come, when you yourself, Finn, and your people will be under the sod. And I myself am going now to the Country of the Young," she said, "and I will bring you with me if you have a mind to come." "We give you our thanks for that," said Finn, "but we would not give up our own country if we were to get the whole world as an estate, and the Country of the Young along with it." "That is well," said the Red Woman; "but you are going home empty after your hunt." "It is likely we will find a deer in Gleann-na-Smol," said Finn. "There is a fine deer at the foot of that tree beyond," said the Red Woman, "and I will rouse it for you." With that she gave a cry, and the deer started out and away, and Finn and his men after it, and it never stopped till it came to Gleann-na-Smol, but they could not come up with it. Then the Red Woman came to them, and she said: "I think you are tired now with following after the deer; and call your hounds off now," she said, "and I will let out my own little dog after it." So Finn sounded a little horn he had at his side, and on the moment the hounds came back to him. And then the Red Woman brought out a little hound as white as the snow of the mountains, and put it after the deer; and it was not long till it had come up with the deer and killed it, and then it came back and made a leap in under the cloak of the Red Woman. There was great wonder on Finn; but before he could ask a question of the Red Woman, she was gone out of sight. And as to the deer, Finn knew there was enchantment on it, and so he left it there after him. And it is tired and empty the Fianna were, going back to Almhuin that night.

CHAPTER XIII. FINN AND THE PHANTOMS

Finn went to a gathering one time at Aonach Clochair, and a great many of the men of Munster crowded to it. And the horses of the Fianna were brought there, and the horses of the men of Munster, and they ran races against one another.

And Fiachu, son of Eoghan, was in it; and when the games were over he gave good presents to Finn, a lasting black horse that won the three prizes of the gathering, and a chariot, and a horse for the chariot-driver, and a spear, having a deadly spell, and weapons of silver, and three comely hounds, Feirne and Derchaem and Dialath, having collars of yellow gold and chains of white bronze.

And Finn rose up and gave his thanks to Fiachu, son of Eoghan, and he and his people set out to the house of Cacher at Cluain-da-loch. And they stopped three days feasting in Cacher's house, and then Finn gave him the price of his feast and of his ale, fifty rings, and fifty horses and fifty cows.

And he himself and the Fianna went on from that over Luachair to the strand at Berramain. And Finn went trying his black horse on the strand, and Caoilte and Oisin went racing against him; but it was only folly for them to do that, for he gave a blow to his horse, and away with him to Traigh Liath and over the Plain of Health to the Old Yew of the Old Valley, and to the inver of the Flesc and the inver of the Lemain to Loch Lein, till he came to the hill of Bairnech, and Caoilte and Oisin after him.

"Night is coming on us," said Finn then; "and go look for some place where we can sleep," he said. He looked round then at the rocks on his left hand and he saw a house, and a fire shining out from it in the valley below. "I never knew of a house in this valley," he said.

"It is best for us to go see it," said Caoilte, "for there are many things we have no knowledge of."

The three went on then to the house, and they heard screams and crying from it; and when they came to the house, the people of it were very fierce and rough; and a big grey man took hold of their horses and brought them in and shut the door of the house with iron hooks. "My welcome to you, Finn of the great name," he said then; "it is a long time you were in coming here."

They sat down then on the hard boards of a bed, and the grey man kindled a fire, and he threw logs of elder-wood on it, till they went near being smothered with the smoke. They saw a hag in the house then having three heads on her lean neck; and there was on the other side a man without a head, having one eye, and it in his breast. "Rise up, you that are in the house, and make music for the King of the Fianna," said the grey man then.

With that nine bodies rose up out of the corner nearest the Fianna, and nine heads rose up on the other side of the bed, and they raised nine harsh screeches together, that no one would like to be listening to. And then the hag answered to them, and the headless man answered; and if all of that music was harsh, there was none of it that you would not wish to hear sooner than the music of the one-eyed man. And the music that was sung went near to breaking the bones of their heads; and indeed it is no sweet music that was.

Then the big grey man rose up and took the axe that was for cutting logs, and he began striking at the horses, flaying and destroying them. Then there were brought fifty pointed spits of the rowan-tree, and he put a piece of the horse's flesh on each one of the spits, and settled them on the hearth. But when he took the spits from the fire and put them before Finn, it is raw the flesh was on them yet. "Take your food away," said Finn then, "for I have never eaten meat that was raw, and I never will eat it because of being without food for one day." "If you are come into our house to refuse our food," said the grey man, "we will surely go against yourselves, Finn and Caoilte and Oisin."

With that all in the house made an attack on the three; and they were driven back into the corner, and the fire was quenched, and the fight went on through the whole night in the darkness, and but for Finn and the way he fought, they would have been put down.

And when the sun rose and lighted up the house on the morrow, a mist came into the head of each of the three, so that they fell as if dead on the floor.

But after awhile they rose up again, and there was nothing to be seen of the house or of the people of the house, but they had all vanished. And their horses were there, and they took them and went on, very weak and tired, for a long way, till they came to the strand of Berramain.

And those three that fought against them were the three Shapes out of the Valley of the Yew Tree that came to avenge their sister, Cuillen of the Wide Mouth.

Now as to Cuillen, she was a daughter of the King of Munster, and her husband was the King of Ulster's son. And they had a son that was called Fear Og, the Young Man; and there was hardly in Ireland a man so good as himself in shape and in courage and in casting a spear. And one time he joined in a game with the Fianna, and he did better than them all, and Finn gave him a great reward. And after that he went out to a hunt they made, and it was by him and by none of the Fianna the first blood was got of pig or of deer. And when they came back, a heavy sickness fell on the young man through the eyes and the envy of the Fianna, and it left him without life at the end of nine days. And he was buried under a green hill, and the shining stone he used to hold in his hand, and he doing his feats, was put over his head.

And his mother, Cuillen, came to his grave keening him every day through the length of a year. And one day she died there for grief after her son, and they put her into the same green hill.

But as to Finn, he was afraid of no earthly thing, and he killed many great serpents in Loch Cuilinn and Loch Neathach, and at Beinn Edair; and Shadow-Shapes at Loch Lein and Drom Cleib and Loch Liath, and a serpent and a cat in Ath Cliath.

CHAPTER XIV. THE PIGS OF ANGUS

Angus Og, son of the Dagda, made a feast one time at Brugh na Boinne for Finn and the Fianna of the Gael. Ten hundred of them were in it, and they wearing green clothing and crimson cloaks; and as to the people of Angus' house, it is clothing of red silk they had.

And Finn was sitting beside Angus in the beautiful house, and it is long since the like of those two were seen in Ireland. And any stranger would wonder to see the way the golden cups were going from hand to hand.

And Angus said out in a loud voice that every one could hear: "It is a better life this is than to be hunting." There was anger on Finn then, and he said: "It is a worse life than hunting to be here, without hounds, without horses, without battalions, without the shouting of armies." "Why are you talking like that, Finn?" said Angus, "for as to the hounds you have," he said, "they would not kill so much as one pig." "You have not yourself," said Finn, "and the whole host of the Tuatha de Danaan have not a pig that ever went on dry land that Bran and Sceolan would not kill." "I will send you a pig," said Angus, "that will go from you and your hounds, and that will kill them in the end."

The steward of the house called out then in a loud voice: "Let every one go now to his bed, before the lightness of drunkenness comes on you." But Finn said to his people: "Let us make ready and leave this; for we are but a few," he said, "among the Men of Dea." So they set out and went westward till they came to Slieve Fuad where the Fianna were at that time.

And through the whole length of a year after that, the Tuatha de Danaan were boasting how they would get the better of the Fianna, and the Fianna were thinking how they could do best in the hunt. And at the end of that time Angus sent messengers to Finn, asking him with great respect if he was ready to keep his word.

And Finn said he was, and the hounds were brought out, and he himself was holding Bran and Sceolan, one in each hand, and Caoilte had Adhnuall, and Oisin had Ablach, and merry Bran Beag had Lonn, and Diarmuid was holding Eachtach, and Osgar was holding Mac an Truim, and Garraidh was held by Faolan, and Rith Fada, of the Long Run, by hungry Conan.

And they were not long there with their hounds till they saw on the plain to the east a terrible herd of great pigs, every one of them the height of a deer. And there was one pig out in front of the rest was blacker than a smith's coal, and the bristles on its head were like a thicket of thorn-trees.

Then Caoilte let out Adhnuall, and she was the first to kill a pig of the herd. And then Bran made away from the leash that Finn was holding, and the pigs ran their best, but she came up with them, and took hold of a pig of them. And at that Angus said: "O Bran, fosterling of fair-haired Fergus, it is not a right thing you are doing, to kill my own son." But when Bran heard that, her ways changed and it was like an enemy she took hold of the pig, and did not let it go, and held her breath back and kept it for the Fianna.

And it was over Slieve Cua the hunt went, and Slieve Crot, and from Magh Cobha to Cruachan, and to Fionnabraic and to Finnias. And at evening when the hunt was over, there was not one pig of the whole herd without a hurt, and there were but a hundred and ten pigs left living. But if the hunt brought destruction on Angus, it brought losses on the Fianna as well, for there were ten hundred of their men missing besides serving-lads and dogs.

"Let us go to Brugh na Boinne and get satisfaction for our people," said Oisin then. "That is the advice of a man without sense," said Finn; "for if we leave these pigs the way they are, they will come to life again. And let us burn them," he said, "and throw their ashes in the sea."

Then the seven battalions of the Fianna made seven fires to every battalion; but for all they could do, they could not set fire to one pig. Then Bran, that had great sense and knowledge, went away, and she came back bringing three logs along with her, but no one knows what wood it was they came from. And when the logs were put on the fire they lit up like a candle, and it is with them the pigs were burned; and after that their ashes were thrown into the sea.

Then Oisin said again: "Let us go now to Brugh na Boinne and avenge the death of our people." So the whole of the Fianna set out for Brugh na Boinne, and every step they made could surely be heard through the whole of the skies.

And Angus sent out messengers to where Finn was, offering any one thing to him if he would spare his people. "I will take no gift at all from you, Angus of the slender body," said Finn, "so long as there is a room left in your house, north or east, without being burned." But Angus said: "Although you think bad of the loss of your fine people that you have the sway over, yet, O Finn, father of Oisin, it is sorrowful to me the loss of my own good son is. For as to the black pig that came before you on the plain," he said, "it was no common pig was in it, but my own son. And there fell along with him," he said, "the son of the King of the Narrow Sea, and the son of the King of the Sea of Gulls, and the son of Ilbhrec, son of Manannan, and seven score of the comely sons of kings and queens. And it is what destroyed my strength and my respect entirely, they to have been burned away from me in a far place. And it is a pity for you, sweet daring Bran," he said, "fosterling of Fergus of the thirty woods and plains, that you did not do something worth praise before killing your own foster-brother. And I will put a curse on you, Bran," he said, "beyond every hound in Ireland, that you will never see with your eyes any deer you may ever kill."

There was anger on Finn when he heard that, and he said: "If you put a curse on Bran, Angus, there will not be a room left, east or west, in the whole of your great house without being burned." "If you do that," said Angus, "I will put trees and stones in front of you in every battle; and I will know what number of men you have in your armies," he said, "looking at them through my ring."

Then Oisin, that was wise, said: "It is best for you to agree between yourselves now; and let us be helpful to one another," he said, "and pay whatever fines are due."

So they agreed to that, and they made peace, and gave children to be fostered by one another: a son of Finn's to Angus, and son of Angus Og to the Fianna.

But for all that, it is not very friendly to Finn Angus was afterwards, at the time he was following after Diarmuid and Grania through the whole length of Ireland.

CHAPTER XV. THE HUNT OF SLIEVE CUILINN

Finn was one time out on the green of Almhuin, and he saw what had the appearance of a grey fawn running across the plain. He called and whistled to his hounds then, but neither hound nor man heard him or came to him, but only Bran and Sceolan. He set them after the fawn, and near as they kept to her, he himself kept nearer to them, till at last they reached to Slieve Cuilinn in the province of Ulster.

But they were no sooner at the hill than the fawn vanished from them, and they did not know where was she gone, and Finn went looking for her eastward, and the two hounds went towards the west.

It was not long till Finn came to a lake, and there was sitting on the brink of it a young girl, the most beautiful he had ever seen, having hair of the colour of gold, and a skin as white as lime, and eyes like the stars in time of frost; but she seemed to be some way sorrowful and downhearted. Finn asked her did she see his hounds pass that way. "I did not see them," she said; "and it is little I am thinking of your hounds or your hunting, but of the cause of my own trouble." "What is it ails you, woman of the white hands?" said Finn; "and is there any help I can give you?" he said. "It is what I am fretting after," said she, "a ring of red gold I lost off my finger in the lake. And I put you under bonds, Finn of the Fianna," she said, "to bring it back to me out of the lake."

With that Finn stripped off his clothes and went into the lake at the bidding of the woman, and he went three times round the whole lake and did not leave any part of it without searching, till he brought back the ring. He handed it up to her then out of the water, and no sooner had he done that than she gave a leap into the water and vanished.

And when Finn came up on the bank of the lake, he could not so much as reach to where his clothes were; for on the moment he, the head and the leader of the Fianna of Ireland, was but a grey old man, weak and withered.

Bran and Sceolan came up to him then, but they did not know him, and they went on round the lake, searching after their master.

In Almhuin, now, when he was missed, Caoilte began asking after him. "Where is Finn," he said, "of the gentle rule and of the spears?" But no one knew where was he gone, and there was grief on the Fianna when they could not find him. But it is what Conan said: "I never heard music pleased me better than to hear the son of Cumhal is missing. And that he may be so through the whole year," he said, "and I myself will be king over you all." And downhearted as they were, it is hardly they could keep from laughing when they heard Conan saying that.

Caoilte and the rest of the chief men of the Fianna set out then looking for Finn, and they got word of him; and at last they came to Slieve Cuilinn, and there they saw a withered old man sitting beside the lake, and they thought him to be a fisherman. "Tell us, old man," said Caoilte, "did you see a fawn go by, and two hounds after her, and a tall fair-faced man along with them?" "I did see them," he said, "and it is not long since they left me." "Tell us where are they now?" said Caoilte. But Finn made no answer, for he had not the courage to say to them that he himself was Finn their leader, being as he was an ailing, downhearted old man, without leaping, without running, without walk, grey and sorrowful.

Caoilte took out his sword from the sheath then, and he said: "It is short till you will have knowledge of death unless you will tell us what happened those three."

Then Finn told them the whole story; and when the seven battalions of the Fianna heard him, and knew it was Finn that was in it, they gave three loud sorrowful cries. And to the lake they gave the name of Loch Doghra, the Lake of Sorrow.

But Conan of the sharp tongue began abusing Finn and all the Fianna by turns. "You never gave me right praise for my deeds, Finn, son of Cumhal," he said, "and you were always the enemy of the sons of Morna; but we are living in spite of you," he said, "and I have but the one fault to find with your shape, and that is, that it was not put on the whole of the Fianna the same as on yourself." Caoilte made at him then; "Bald, senseless Conan," he said, "I will break your mouth to the bone." But Conan ran in then among the rest of the Fianna and asked protection from them, and peace was made again.

And as to Finn, they asked him was there any cure to be found for him. "There is," he said; "for I know well the enchantment was put on me by a woman of the Sidhe, Miluchradh, daughter of Cuilinn, through jealousy of her sister Aine. And bring me to the hill that belongs to Cuilinn of Cuailgne," he said, "for he is the only one can give me my shape again."

They came around him then, and raised him up gently on their shields, and brought him on their shoulders to the hill of the Sidhe in Cuailgne, but no one came out to meet them. Then the seven battalions began digging and rooting up the whole hill, and they went on digging through the length of three nights and three days. And at the end of that time Cuilinn of Cuailgne, that some say was Manannan, son of Lir, came out of the hill, holding in his hand a vessel of red gold, and he gave the vessel into Finn's hand. And no sooner did Finn drink what was in the vessel than his own shape and his appearance came back to him. But only his hair, that used to be so fair and so beautiful, like the hair of a woman, never got its own colour again, for the lake that Cuilinn's daughter had made for Finn would have turned all the men of the whole world grey if they had gone into it.

And when Finn had drunk all that was in the vessel it slipped from his hand into the earth, that was loosened with the digging, and he saw it no more. But in the place where it went into the earth, a tree grew up, and any one that would look at the branches of that tree in the morning, fasting, would have knowledge of all that was to happen on that day.

That, now, is the way Finn came by his grey hair, through the jealousy of Miluchradh of the Sidhe, because he had not given his love to her, but to her sister Aine.

BOOK FIVE: OISIN'S CHILDREN

Now as to Oisin, that was so brave and so comely, and that could overtake a deer at its greatest speed, and see a thistle thorn on the darkest night, the wife he took was Eibhir of the plaited yellow hair, that was the foreign sweetheart of the High King of Ireland.

It is beyond the sea she lived, in a very sunny place; and her father's name was Iunsa, and her sunny house was thatched with the feathers of birds, and the doorposts were of gold, and the doors of ribbed grass. And Oisin went there looking for her, and he fought for her against the High King and against an army of the Firbolgs he had helping him; and he got the better of them all, and brought away Eibhir of the yellow hair to Ireland.

And he had a daughter that married the son of Oiliol, son of Eoghan, and of Beara, daughter of the King of Spain. It was that Eoghan was driven out of Ireland one time, and it is to Spain he went for safety. And Beara, that was daughter of the King of Spain, was very shining and beautiful, and her father had a mind to know who would be her husband, and he sent for his Druid and asked the question of him. "I can tell you that," said the Druid, "for the man that is to be her husband will come to land in Spain this very night. And let your daughter go eastward to the river Eibhear," he said, "and she will find a crimson-spotted salmon in that river, having shining clothing on him from head to tail. And let her strip that clothing off him," he said, "and make with it a shining shirt for her husband."

So Beara went to the river Eibhear, and found the golden salmon as the Druid had said, and she stripped him of his crimson clothing and made a shining shirt of it.

And as to Eoghan, the waves of the shore put a welcome before him, and he came the same night to the king's house. And the king gave him a friendly welcome; and it is what all the people said, that there was never seen a comelier man than Eoghan, or a woman more beautiful than Beara, and that it was fitting for them to come together. And Eoghan's own people said they would not be sorry for being sent away out of Ireland, if only Eoghan could get her for his wife.

And after a while the king sent his Druid to ask Eoghan why he did not ask for Beara. "I will tell you that," said Eoghan; "it would not be fitting for me to be refused a wife, and I am but an exile in this country, and I have brought no treasures or goods with me out of Ireland for giving to learned men and to poets. But for all that," he said, "the king's daughter is dear to me, and I think I have the friendship of the king."

The Druid went back with that message. "That is the answer of a king," said the King of Spain; "and bid my daughter to sit at Eoghan's right hand," he said, "and I will give her to him this very night." And when Beara, the king's daughter, heard that, she sent out her serving-maid to bring the shirt she had made for Eoghan, and he put it on him over his armour, and its shining was seen in every place; and it was from wearing that shirt he got the name of Eoghan the Bright.

And Oiliol was the first son they had; it was he that had his ear bitten off by Aine of the Sidhe in revenge for her brother, and it was his son married Oisin's daughter afterwards.

And as to Osgar, that was Oisin's son, of all the young men of the Fianna he was the best in battle. And when he was but a young child he was made much of by the whole of the Fianna, and it is for him they used to keep the marrow bones, and they did not like to put any hardship on him. And he grew up tall and idle, and no one thought he would turn out so strong as he did. And one day there was an attack made on a troop of the Fianna, and all that were in it went out to fight, but they left Osgar after them. And when he knew the fight was going on, he took a log of wood that was the first thing he could find, and attacked the enemy and made a great slaughter, and they gave way and ran before him. And from that out there was no battle he did not go into; and he was said to be the strongest of all the Fianna, though the people of Connacht said that Goll was the strongest. And he and Diarmuid, grandson of Duibhne, were comrades and dear friends; and it was Diarmuid taught him feats of arms and of skill, and chess-playing. And Oisin his father took great pride in him, and his grandfather Finn. And one time Finn was holding a feast at Almhuin, and he asked the chief men of the Fianna that were there what was the music they thought the best. "To be playing at games," said Conan, "that is the best music I ever heard;" for though Conan was a good hand against an enemy, there never was a man had less sense. "The music I like the best is to be talking with a woman," said Diarmuid. "My music is the outcry of my hounds, and they putting a deer to its last stand," said Lugaidh's Son. "The music of the woods is best to me," said Oisin; "the sound of the wind and of the cuckoo and the blackbird, and the sweet silence of the crane."

And then Osgar was asked, and he said: "The best music is the striking of swords in a battle." And it is likely he took after Finn in that, for in spite of all the sweet sounds he gave an account of the time he was at Conan's house, at Ceann Slieve, it used to be said by the Fianna that the music that was best with Finn was what happened.

This now is the way Osgar met with his wife.

One time Finn and his men came to Slieve Crot, and they saw a woman waiting there before them, having a crimson fringed cloak, and a gold brooch in it, and a band of yellow gold on her forehead. Finn asked her name, and where she came from. "Etain of the Fair Hair is my name," she said, "daughter of Aedh of the White Breast, of the hill of the Sidhe at Beinn Edair, son of Angus Og." "What is it brought you here, girl?" said Finn. "To ask a man of the Fianna of Ireland to run a race with me." "What sort of a runner are you?" said Diarmuid. "I am a good runner," said the girl; "for it is the same to me if the ground is long or short under my feet."

All of the Fianna that were there then set out to run with her, and they ran to the height over Badhamair and on to Ath Cliath, and from that on to the hill of the Sidhe at Beinn Edair.

And there was a good welcome before them, and they were brought meat and wine for drinking, and water for washing their feet. And after a while they saw a nice fair-haired girl in front of the vats, and a cup of white silver in her hand, and she giving out drink to every one. "It seems to me that is the girl came asking the Fianna to race against her at Slieve Crot," said Finn. "It is not," said Aedh of the White Breast, "for that is the slowest woman there is among us." "Who was it so?" said Finn. "It was Be-mannair, daughter of Ainceol, woman-messenger of the Tuatha de Danaan. And it is she that changes herself into all shapes; and she will take the shape of a fly, and of a true lover, and every one leaves their secret with her. And it was she outran you coming from the east," he said, "and not this other girl that was drinking and making merry here in the hall." "What is her name?" said Finn. "Etain of the Fair Hair," he said; "a daughter of my own, and a darling of the Tuatha de Danaan. And it is the way with her, she has a lover of the men of the Fianna." "That is well," said Finn; "and who is that lover?" "It is Osgar, son of Oisin," said Aedh; "and it is she herself sent her messenger for you," he said, "in her own shape, to Slieve Crot in the south. And the son of the High King of Ireland has offered a great bride-price to the Men of Dea for her," he said, "three hundreds of the land nearest to Bregia and to Midhe, and to put himself and his weight of gold into a balance, and to give it all to her. But we did not take it," he said, "since she had no mind or wish for it herself, and so we made no dealing or agreement about her." "Well," said Finn, "and what conditions will you ask of Osgar?" "Never to leave me for anything at all but my own fault," said the girl. "I will make that agreement with you indeed," said Osgar. "Give me sureties for it," said she; "give me the sureties of Goll for the sons of Morna, and of Finn, son of Cumhal, for the Fianna of Ireland."

So they gave those sureties, and the wedding-feast was made, and they stopped there for twenty nights. And at the end of that time Osgar asked Finn where would he bring his wife. "Bring her to wide Almhuin for the first seven years," said Finn.

But a while after that, in a great battle at Beinn Edair, Osgar got so heavy a wound that Finn and the Fianna were as if they had lost their wits. And when Etain of the Fair Hair came to the bed where Osgar was lying, and saw the way he was, and that the great kinglike shape he had was gone from him, greyness and darkness came on her, and she raised pitiful cries, and she went to her bed and her heart broke in her like a nut; and she died of grief for her husband and her first love.

But it was not at that time Osgar got his death, but afterwards in the battle of Gabhra.

BOOK SIX: DIARMUID.

CHAPTER I. BIRTH OF DIARMUID

Diarmuid, now, was son of Bonn, son of Duibhne of the Fianna, and his mother was Crochnuit, that was near in blood to Finn. And at the time he was born, Bonn was banished from the Fianna because of some quarrel they had with him, and Angus Og took the child from him to rear him up at Brugh na Boinne.

And after a while Crochnuit bore another son to Roc Diocain, that was Head Steward to Angus. Roc Diocain went then to Donn, and asked would he rear up his son for him, the way Angus was rearing Donn's son. But Donn said he would not take the son of a common man into his house, and it would be best for Angus to take him. So Angus took the child into Brugh na Boinne, and he and Diarmuid were reared up together.

And one day Finn was on the great Hill at Almhuin of Leinster, and no one with him but Donn and a few of the poets and learned men of the Fianna, and their hounds and dogs, and Bran Beag came in and asked did he remember there were bonds on him, not to stop in Almhuin for ten nights together. Finn asked the people about him then where would he go and be entertained for that night, and Donn said: "I will bring you to the house of Angus, son of the Dagda, where my young son is being reared."

So they went together to the house of Angus at Brugh na Boinne, and the child Diarmuid was there, and it is great love Angus had for him. And the Steward's son was with him that night, and the people of the household made as much of him as Angus made of Diarmuid; and there was great vexation on Donn when he saw that.

It chanced after a while a great fight rose between two of Finn's hounds about some broken meat that was thrown to them; and the women and the common people of the place ran from them, and the others rose up to part them from one another. And in running away, the Steward's child ran between the knees of Donn, and Donn gave the child a strong squeeze between his two knees that killed him on the moment, and he threw him under the feet of the hounds. And when the Steward came after that and found his son dead, he gave a long very pitiful cry, and he said to Finn: "There is not a man in the house to-night has suffered more than myself from this uproar, for I had but one son only, and he has been killed; and what satisfaction will I get from you for that, Finn?" he said. "Try can you find the mark of a tooth or of a nail of one of the hounds on him," said Finn, "and if you can, I will give you satisfaction for him."

So they looked at the child, and there was no scratch or mark of a tooth on him at all. Then the Steward put Finn under the destroying bonds of the Druid cave of Cruachan, to give him knowledge of who it was killed his son. And Finn asked for a chess-board, and for water to be brought to him, in a basin of pale gold, and he searched, and it was shown to him truly that it was Donn had killed the Steward's son between his two knees. When Finn knew that, he said he would take the fine on himself; but the Steward would not consent to that, but forced him to tell who was it had done him the wrong. And when he knew it was Donn had killed the child, he said: "There is no man in the house it is easier to get satisfaction from than from him, for his own son is here, and I have but to put him between my two knees, and if I let him go from me safe, I will forgive the death of my son." Angus was vexed at what the Steward said, and as to Donn, he thought to strike his head off till Finn put him back from him. Then the Steward came again, having a Druid rod with him, and he struck his own son with the rod, and he made of him a wild boar, without bristle or ear or tail, and he said: "I put you under bonds to bring Diarmuid, grandson of Duibhne, to his death; and your own life will be no longer than his life," he said. With that the wild boar rose up and ran out of the open door; and he was called afterwards the Boar of Slieve Guillion, and it was by him Diarmuid came to his death at the last.

And when Diarmuid came to his full strength he was given a place among the Fianna of Ireland; and all women loved him, and he did many great deeds, fighting with the enemies of the Fianna and of Ireland; and one time he fought a wild ox through the length of seven days and seven nights on the top of the Mountain of Happiness.

CHAPTER II. HOW DIARMUID GOT HIS LOVE-SPOT

Diarmuid and Conan and Goll and Osgar went one day hunting, and they went so far they could not get home in the evening, and they spent the first part of the night walking through the woods and pulling berries and eating them. And when it was about midnight they saw a light, and they went towards it, and they found a little house before them, and the light shining from it. They went in then, and they saw an old man there, and he bade them welcome, and he called them all by their names. And they saw no one in the house but the old man and a young girl and a cat. And the old man bade the girl to make food ready for the Fianna of Ireland, for there was great hunger on them.

And when the food was ready and put on the table, there came a great wether that was fastened up in the back of the house, and he rose up on the table where they were eating, and when they saw that, they looked at one another. "Rise up, Conan," said Goll, "and fasten that wether in the place it was before." Conan rose up and took hold of it, but the wether gave itself a shake that threw Conan under one of its feet. The rest were looking at that, and Goll said: "Let you rise up, Diarmuid, and fasten up the wether." So Diarmuid rose up and took hold of it, but it gave itself a shake the same way as before; and when Diarmuid was down it put one of its feet on him. Goll and Osgar looked at one another then, and shame came on them, a wether to have done so much as that. And Osgar got up, but the wether put him down under one of his feet, so that it had now the three men under him. Then Goll rose up and took hold of it and threw it down; but if he did, it rose up again in spite of him, and put Goll under his fourth foot.

"It is a great shame," said the old man then, "the like of that to be done to the Fianna of Ireland. And rise up now, cat," he said, "and tie the wether in the place where he was." The cat rose up then and took hold of the wether, and brought it over and tied it in its place at the end of the house.

The men rose up then, but they had no mind to go on eating, for there was shame on them at what the wether had done to them. "You may go on eating," said the old man; "and when you are done I will show you that now you are the bravest men of the world." So they ate their fill then, and the old man spoke to them, and it is what he said: "Goll," he said, "you are the bravest of all the men of the world, for you have wrestled with the world and you threw it down. The strength of the world is in the wether, but death will come to the world itself; and that is death," he said, showing them the cat.

They were talking together then, and they had their food eaten, and the old man said their beds were ready for them that they could go to sleep. The four of them went then into the one room, and when they were in their beds the young girl came to sleep in the same room with them, and the light of her beauty was shining on the walls like as if it was the light of a candle.

And when Conan saw her he went over to the side of the bed where she was.

Now, it was Youth the young girl was, and when she saw Conan coming to her: "Go back to your bed, Conan," she said; "I belonged to you once, and I will never belong to you again." Conan went back to his bed then, and Osgar had a mind to go over where she was. Then she said to him: "Where are you going?" "I am going over to yourself for a while," said he.

"Go back again, Osgar," she said; "I belonged to you once, and I will never belong to you again."

Then Diarmuid rose up to go to her: "Where are you going, Diarmuid?" she said. "I am going over to yourself for a while," said he. "O Diarmuid," she said, "that cannot be; I belonged to you once, and I can never belong to you again; but come over here to me, Diarmuid," she said, "and I will put a love-spot on you, that no woman will ever see without giving you her love." So Diarmuid went over to her, and she put her hand on his forehead, and she left the love-spot there, and no woman that ever saw him after that was able to refuse him her love.

CHAPTER III. THE DAUGHTER OF KING UNDER-WAVE

One snowy night of winter the Fianna were come into the house after their hunting. And about midnight they heard a knocking at the door, and there came in a woman very wild and ugly, and her hair hanging to her heels. She went to the place Finn was lying, and she asked him to let her in under the border of his covering. But when he saw her so strange and so ugly and so wild-looking he would not let her in. She gave a great cry then, and she went to where Oisin was, and asked him to let her shelter under the border of his covering. But Oisin refused her the same way. Then she gave another great scream, and she went over where Diarmuid was. "Let me in," she said, "under the border of your covering." Diarmuid looked at her, and he said: "You are strange-looking and wild and ugly, and your hair is down to your heels. But come in for all that," he said.

So she came in under the border of his covering.

"O Diarmuid," she said then, "I have been travelling over sea and ocean through the length of seven years, and in all that time I never got shelter any night till this night. And let me to the warmth of the fire now," she said. So Diarmuid brought her over to the fire, and all the Fianna that were sitting there went away from it seeing her so ugly and so dreadful to look at. And she was not long at the fire when she said: "Let me go under the warmth of the covering with you now." "It is asking too much you are," said Diarmuid; "first it was to come under the border you asked, and then to come to the fire, and now it is under the bed-covering with me you want to be. But for all that you may come," he said.

So she came in under the covering, and he turned a fold of it between them. But it was not long till he looked at her, and what he saw was a beautiful young woman beside him, and she asleep. He called to the others then to come over, and he said: "Is not this the most beautiful woman that ever was seen?" "She is that," they said, and they covered her up and did not awaken her.

But after a while she stirred, and she said: "Are you awake, Diarmuid?" "I am awake," he said. "Where would you like to see the best house built that ever was built?" she said. "Up there on the hillside, if I had my choice," said he, and with that he fell asleep.

And in the morning two men of the Fianna came in, and they said they were after seeing a great house up on the hill, where there was not a house before. "Rise up, Diarmuid," said the strange woman then; "do not be lying there any longer, but go up to your house, and look out now and see it," she said. So he looked out and he saw the great house that was ready, and he said: "I will go to it, if you will come along with me." "I will do that," she said, "if you will make me a promise not to say to me three times what way I was when I came to you." "I will never say it to you for ever," said Diarmuid.

They went up then to the house, and it was ready for them, with food and servants; and everything they could wish for they had it. They stopped there for three days, and when the three days were ended, she said: "You are getting to be sorrowful because you are away from your comrades of the Fianna." "I am not sorrowful indeed," said Diarmuid. "It will be best for you to go to them; and your food and your drink will be no worse when you come back than they are now," said she. "Who will take care of my greyhound bitch and her three pups if I go?" said Diarmuid. "There is no fear for them," said she.

So when he heard that, he took leave of her and went back to the Fianna, and there was a great welcome before him. But for all that they were not well pleased but were someway envious, Diarmuid to have got that grand house and her love from the woman they themselves had turned away.

Now as to the woman, she was outside the house for a while after Diarmuid going away, and she saw Finn, son of Cumhal, coming towards her, and she bade him welcome. "You are vexed with me, Queen?" he said. "I am not indeed," she said; "and come in now and take a drink of wine from me." "I will go in if I get my request," said Finn. "What request is there that you would not get?" said she. "It is what I am asking, one of the pups of Diarmuid's greyhound bitch." "That is no great thing to ask," she said; "and whichever one you choose of them you may bring it away."

So he got the pup, and he brought it away with him.

At the fall of night Diarmuid came back to the house, and the greyhound met him at the door and gave a yell when she saw him, and he looked for the pups, and one of them was gone. There was anger on him then, and he said to the woman: "If you had brought to mind the way you were when I let you in, and your hair hanging, you would not have let the pup be brought away from me." "You ought not to say that, Diarmuid," said she. "I ask your pardon for saying it," said Diarmuid. And they forgave one another, and he spent the night in the house.

On the morrow Diarmuid went back again to his comrades, and the woman stopped at the house, and after a while she saw Oisin coming towards her. She gave him a welcome, and asked him into the house, and he said he would come if he would get his request. And what he asked was another of the pups of the greyhound.

So she gave him that, and he went away bringing the pup with him. And when Diarmuid came back that night the greyhound met him, and she cried out twice. And he knew that another of the pups was gone, and he said to the greyhound, and the woman standing there: "If she had remembered the way she was when she came to me, she would not have let the pup be brought away."

The next day he went back again to the Fianna, and when he was gone, the woman saw Caoilte coming towards her, and he would not come in to take a drink from her till he had got the promise of one of the pups the same as the others.

And when Diarmuid came back that night the greyhound met him and gave three yells, the most terrible that ever were heard. There was great anger on him then, when he saw all the pups gone, and he said the third time: "If this woman remembered the way she was when I found her, and her hair down to her heels, she would not have let the pup go." "O Diarmuid, what is it you are after saying?" she said. He asked forgiveness of her then, and he thought to go into the house, but it was gone and the woman was gone on the moment, and it was on the bare ground he awoke on the morrow. There was great sorrow on him then, and he said he would search in every place till he would find her again.

So he set out through the lonely valleys, and the first thing he saw was the greyhound lying dead, and he put her on his shoulder and would not leave her because of the love he had for her. And after a while he met with a cowherd, and he asked him did he see a woman going the way. "I saw a woman early in the morning of yesterday, and she walking hard," said the cowherd. "What way was she going?" said Diarmuid. "Down that path below to the strand, and I saw her no more after that," he said.

So he followed the path she took down to the strand till he could go no farther, and then he saw a ship, and he leaned on the handle of his spear and made a light leap on to the ship, and it went on till it came to land, and then he got out and lay down on the side of a hill and fell asleep, and when he awoke there was no ship to be seen. "It is a pity for me to be here," he said, "for I see no way of getting from it again."

But after a while he saw a boat coming, and a man in the boat rowing it, and he went down and got into the boat, and brought the greyhound with him. And the boat went out over the sea, and then down below it; and Diarmuid, when he went down, found himself on a plain. And he went walking along it, and it was not long before he met with a drop of blood. He took it up and put it in a napkin. "It is the greyhound lost this," he said. And after a while he met with another drop of blood, and then with a third, and he put them in the napkin. And after that again he saw a woman, and she gathering rushes as if she had lost her wits.

He went towards her and asked her what news had she. "I cannot tell it till I gather the rushes," she said. "Be telling it while you are gathering them," said Diarmuid. "There is great haste on me," she said. "What is this place where we are?" said Diarmuid. "It is Land-under-Wave," said she. "And what use have you for the rushes when they are gathered?" "The daughter of King Under-Wave is come home," she said, "and she was for seven years under enchantment, and there is sickness on her now, and all the physicians are gathered together and none of them can do her any good, and a bed of rushes is what she finds the wholesomest." "Will you show me where the king's daughter is?" said Diarmuid. "I will do that," said the woman; "I will put you in the sheaf of rushes, and I will put the rushes under you and over you, and I will carry you to her on my back." "That is a thing you cannot do," said Diarmuid. But she put the rushes about him, and lifted him on her back, and when she got to the room she let down the bundle. "O come here to me," said the daughter of King Under-Wave, and Diarmuid went over to her, and they took one another's hands, and were very joyful at that meeting. "Three parts of my sickness is gone from me now," she said then; "but I am not well yet, and I never will be, for every time I thought of you, Diarmuid, on my journey, I lost a drop of the blood of my heart." "I have got those three drops here in this napkin," said Diarmuid, "and take them now in a drink and you will be healed of your sickness." "They would do nothing for me," she said, "since I have not the one thing in the world that I want, and that is the thing I will never get," she said. "What thing is that?" said Diarmuid. "It is the thing you will never get, nor any man in the world," she said, "for it is a long time they have failed to get it." "If it is in any place on the whole ridge of the world I will get it," said Diarmuid. "It is three draughts from the cup of the King of Magh an Ionganaidh, the Plain of Wonder," she said, "and no man ever got it or ever will get it." "Tell me where that cup is to be found," said Diarmuid, "for there are not as many men as will keep it from me on the whole ridge of the world." "That country is not far from the boundary of my father's country," she said; "but there is a little river between, and you would be sailing on that river in a ship, having the wind behind it, for a year and a day before you would reach to the Plain of Wonder."

Diarmuid set out then, and he came to the little river, and he was a good while walking beside it, and he saw no way to cross it. But at last he saw a low-sized, reddish man that was standing in the middle of the river. "You are in straits, Diarmuid, grandson of Duibhne," he said; "and come here and put your foot in the palm of my hand and I will bring you through." Diarmuid did as he bade him, and put his foot in the red man's palm, and he brought him across the river. "It is going to the King of the Plain of Wonder you are," he said, "to bring away his cup from him; and I myself will go with you."

They went on then till they came to the king's dun, and Diarmuid called out that the cup should be sent out to him, or else champions to fight with him should be sent out. It was not the cup was sent out, but twice eight hundred fighting men; and in three hours there was not one of them left to stand against him. Then twice nine hundred better fighters again were sent out against him, and within four hours there was not one of them left to stand against him. Then the king himself came out, and he stood in the great door, and he said: "Where did the man come from that has brought destruction on the whole of my kingdom?" "I will tell you that," said he; "I am Diarmuid, a man of the Fianna of Ireland." "It is a pity you not to have sent a messenger telling me that," said the king, "and I would not have spent my men upon you; for seven years before you were born it was put in the prophecy that you would come to destroy them. And what is it you are asking now?" he said. "It is the cup of healing from your own hand I am asking," said Diarmuid. "No man ever got that cup from me but yourself," said the king, "but it is easy for me to give it to you, whether or not there is healing in it."

Then the King of the Plain of Wonder gave Diarmuid the cup, and they parted from one another; and Diarmuid went on till he came to the river, and it was then he thought of the red man, that he had given no thought to while he was at the king's house. But he was there before him, and took his foot in the palm of his hand and brought him over the river. "I know where it is you are going, Diarmuid," he said then; "it is to heal the daughter of King Under-Wave that you have given your love to. And it is to a well I will give you the signs of you should go," he said, "and bring a share of the water of that well with you. And when you come where the woman is, it is what you have to do, to put that water in the cup, and one of the drops of blood in it, and she will drink it, and the same with the second drop and the third, and her sickness will be gone from her from that time. But there is another thing will be gone along with it," he said, "and that is the love you have for her."

"That will not go from me," said Diarmuid. "It will go from you," said the man; "and it will be best for you make no secret of it, for she will know, and the king will know, that you think no more of her then than of any other woman. And King Under-Wave will come to you," he said, "and will offer you great riches for healing his daughter. But take nothing from him," he said, "but ask only a ship to bring you home again to Ireland. And do you know who am I myself?" he said. "I do not know," said Diarmuid. "I am the messenger from beyond the world," he said; "and I came to your help because your own heart is hot to come to the help of another."

So Diarmuid did as he bade him, and he brought the water and the cup and the drops of blood to the woman, and she drank them, and at the third draught she was healed. And no sooner was she healed than the love he had for her was gone, and he turned away from her. "O Diarmuid," she said, "your love is gone from me." "O, it is gone indeed," said he.

Then there was music made in the whole place, and the lamenting was stopped, because of the healing of the king's daughter. And as to Diarmuid, he would take no reward and he would not stop there, but he asked for a ship to bring him home to Ireland, to Finn and the Fianna. And when he came where they were, there was a joyful welcome before him.

CHAPTER IV. THE HARD SERVANT

The Fianna went hunting one time in the two proud provinces of Munster. They went out from Almhuin by the nearest paths till they came to the Brosna river in Slieve Bladhma, and from there to the twelve mountains of Eiblinne, and on to Aine Cliach, the harp of Aine.

They scattered themselves then and hunted through the borders of the forest that is called Magh Breogain, through blind trackless places and through broken lands, over beautiful level plains and the high hills of Desmumum, under pleasant Slieve Crot and smooth Slieve na Muc, along the level banks of the blue Siuir and over the green plain of Feman and the rough plain of Eithne, and the dark woods of Belach Gabrain.

And Finn was at the side of a hill, and the chief men of the Fianna along with him, to watch the hunting; for they liked to be listening to the outcry of the hounds and the hurried cries of the boys, and the noise and the whistling and the shouts of the strong men.

Finn asked then which of the men that were with him would go and keep watch on the side of the hill where they were. And Finnbane, son of Bresel, said he would go. And he went on to the top of the hill, where he could see about him on all sides. And he was not long there till he saw coming from the east a very big man, ugly and gloomy and deformed; and it is how he was, a dark-coloured shield on his back, a wide sword on his crooked left thigh, two spears on his shoulder, a torn loose cloak over his limbs, that were as black as a quenched coal. A sulky horse he had with him that had no good appearance, bony and thin as to body, and weak in the legs, and he leading it with a rough iron halter; and it was a great wonder the head was not pulled from the horse's body, or the arms pulled out of his owner, with the sudden stands and stops and the jerks it made. And the big man was striking blows on the horse with an iron cudgel to try and knock some going out of him, and the sound of the blows was like the breaking of strong waves.

And when Finnbane saw all that, he thought to himself it would not be right to let the like of that stranger go up unknown to Finn and the Fianna, and he ran back in haste to where they were and told them all he had seen.

And when he had told his story, they saw the big man coming towards them; but as short as he was from them he was long in coming, from the badness of his walk and his going.

And when he came into Finn's presence he saluted him, and bowed his head and bent his knee, making signs of humility.

Finn raised his hand over his head then, and asked news of him, and if he was of the noble or of the mean blood of the great world. He answered that he had no knowledge who he came from, but only that he was a man of the Fomor, travelling in search of wages to the kings of the earth, "and I heard," he said, "that Finn never refused wages to any man." "I never did indeed," said Finn, "and I will not refuse you. But why is it," he said, "you are without a boy to mind your horse?" "I have a good reason for that," said the big man; "there is nothing in the world is worse to me than a boy to be with me; for it is a hundred men's share of food," he said, "that serves me for one day, and it is little enough I think it, and I would begrudge a boy to be sharing it with me." "What is the name you have?" said Finn. "The name I have is the Gilla Decair, the Hard Servant," said he. "Why did you get that name?" said Finn. "There is a good reason for that," said the big man, "for there is nothing in the world is harder to me than to do anything at all for my master, or whatever person I am with. And tell me this, Conan, son of Morna," he said, "who gets the best wages, a horseman or a man afoot?" "A horseman gets twice as much," said Conan. "Then I call you to witness, Conan," he said, "that I am a horseman, and that it was as a horseman I came to the Fianna. And give me your guarantee now, Finn, son of Cumhal, and the guarantee of the Fianna, and I will turn out my horse with your horses." "Let him out then," said Finn.

The big man pulled off the iron halter then from his horse, and it made off as hard as it could go, till it came where the horses of the Fianna were; and it began to tear and to kick and to bite at them, killing and maiming. "Take your horse out of that, big man," said Conan; "and by the earth and the sky," he said, "only it was on the guarantee of Finn and the Fianna you took the halter off him, I would let out his brains through the windows of his head; and many as is the bad prize Finn has found in Ireland," he said, "he never got one as bad as yourself." "And I swear by earth and sky as well as yourself," said the big man, "I will never bring him out of that; for I have no serving-boy to do it for me, and it is not work for me to be leading my horse by the hand."

Conan, son of Morna, rose up then and took the halter and put it on the horse, and led it back to where Finn was, and held it with his hand. "You would never have done a horse-boy's service, Conan," said Finn, "to any one of the Fianna, however far he might be beyond this Fomor. And if you will do what I advise," he said, "you will get up on the horse now, and search out with him all the hills and hollows and flowery plains of Ireland, till his heart is broken in his body in payment for the way he destroyed the horses of the Fianna."

Conan made a leap then on to the horse, and struck his heels hard into him, but with all that the horse would not stir. "I know what ails him," said Finn, "he will not stir till he has the same weight of horsemen on him as the weight of the big man."

On that thirteen men of the Fianna went up behind Conan, and the horse lay down with them and rose up again. "I think that you are mocking at my horse and at myself," said the big man; "and it is a pity for me to be spending the rest of the year with you, after all the humbugging I saw in you to-day, Finn. And I know well," he said, "that all I heard about you was nothing but lies, and there was no cause for the great name you have through the world. And I will quit you now, Finn," he said.

With that he went from them, slow and weak, dragging himself along till he had put a little hill between himself and the Fianna. And as soon as he was on the other side of it, he tucked up his cloak to his waist, and away with him, as if with the quickness of a swallow or a deer, and the rush of his going was like a blast of loud wind going over plains and mountains in spring-time.

When the horse saw his master going from him, he could not bear with it, but great as his load was he set out at full gallop following after him. And when Finn and the Fianna saw the thirteen men behind Conan, son of Morna, on the horse, and he starting off, they shouted with mocking laughter.

And when Conan found that he was not able to come down off the horse, he screeched and shouted to them not to let him be brought away with the big man they knew nothing of, and he began abusing and reproaching them. "A cloud of death over water on you, Finn," he said, "and that some son of a slave or a robber of the bad blood, one that is a worse son of a father and mother even than yourself, may take all that might protect your life, and your head along with that, unless you follow us to whatever place or island the big man will carry us to, and unless you bring us back to Ireland again."

Finn and the Fianna rose up then, and they followed the Gilla Decair over every bald hill, and through every valley and every river, on to pleasant Slieve Luachra, into the borders of Corca Duibhne; and the big man, that was up on the horse then along with Conan and the rest, faced towards the deep sea. And Liagan Luath of Luachar took hold of the horse's tail with his two hands, thinking to drag him back by the hair of it; but the horse gave a great tug, and away with him over the sea, and Liagan along with him, holding on to his tail.

It was a heavy care to Finn, those fourteen men of his people to be brought away from him, and he himself under bonds to bring them back. "What can we do now?" Oisin asked him. "What should we do, but to follow our people to whatever place or island the big man has brought them, and, whatever way we do it, to bring them back to Ireland again." "What can we do, having neither a ship or any kind of boat?" said Oisin. "We have this," said Finn, "the Tuatha de Danaan left as a gift to the children of the Gael, that whoever might have to leave Ireland for a while, had but to go to Beinn Edair, and however many would go along with him, they would find a ship that would hold them all." Finn looked towards the sea then, and he saw two strong armed men coming towards him. The first one had on his back a shield ribbed and of many colours, having shapes of strange, wonderful beasts engraved on it, and a heavy sword at his side, and two thick spears on his shoulders; a cloak of lasting crimson about him, with a gold brooch on the breast; a band of white bronze on his head, gold under each of his feet; and the other was dressed in the same way. They made no delay till they came to where Finn was, and they bowed their heads and bent their knees before him, and Finn raised his hand over their heads, and bade them to give an account of themselves. "We are sons of the King of the Eastern World," they said, "and we are come to Ireland asking to be taken into the service of Finn; for we heard there was not a man in all Ireland," they said, "would be better than yourself to judge of the skill we have." "What is your name, and what skill is that?" said Finn. "My name is Feradach, the Very Brave," he said; "and I have a carpenter's axe and a sling, and if there were so many as thirty hundred of the men of Ireland along with me in one spot, with three blows of the axe on the sling-stick I could get a ship that would hold them all. And I would ask no more help of them," he said, "than to bow down their heads while I was striking those three blows." "That is a good art," said Finn. "And tell me now," he said, "what can the other man do?" "I can do this," he said, "I can follow the track of the teal over nine ridges and nine furrows until I come on her in her bed; and it is the same to me to do it on sea as on land," he said. "That is a good art," said Finn; "and it would be a good help to us if you would come following a track with us now." "What is gone from you?" said one of the men. Finn told them then the whole story of the Hard Servant.

Then Feradach, the Very Brave, struck three blows on his sling-stick with the axe that he had, and the whole of the Fianna bowed their heads, and on the moment the whole of the bay and of the harbour was filled with ships and with fast boats. "What will we do with that many ships?" said Finn. "We will do away with all you make no use of," he said.

Caoilte rose up then and let out three great shouts, and all the Fianna of Ireland, in whatever places they were, heard them, and they thought Finn and his people to be in some kind of danger from men from beyond the sea.

They came then in small companies as they chanced to be, till they came to the stepping-stones of the Cat's Head in the western part of Corca Duibhne. And they asked news of Finn, what had happened that he called them away from their hunting, and Finn told them all that had happened. Then Finn and Oisin went into council together, and it is what they agreed; that as but fifteen of his people were brought away from Finn, he himself with fifteen others would go on their track; Oisin to be left at the head of the Fianna to guard Ireland.

And they said farewell to one another, and a grand ship was made ready for Finn and his people, and there was food put in it for using and gold for giving away. The young men and the heroes took to their seats then, and took hold of the oars, and they set out over the restless hills and the dark valleys of the great sea.

And the sea rose up and bellowed, and there was madness on the broken green waters; but to Finn and his people it was a call in the morning and a sleepy time at night to be listening to the roaring and the crooning that was ever and always about the sides of the ship.

They went on like that for three days and three nights, and saw no country or island. But at the end of that time a man of them went up into the head of the ship, and he saw out before them a great, rough grey cliff. They went on towards it then, and they saw on the edge of the cliff a high rock, round-shaped, having sides more slippery than an eel's back. And they found the track of the Hard Servant as far as to the foot of the rock.

Fergus of the True Lips said then to Diarmuid: "It is no brave thing you are doing, Diarmuid, grandson of Duibhne, to hold back like this, for it was with Manannan the Powerful, son of Lir, you were reared and got your learning, in the Land of Promise and in the coasts of the harbours, and with Angus Og, the Dagda's son. And are you without any share of their skill and their daring now," he said, "that would bring Finn and his people up this rock?"

Diarmuid's face reddened when he heard those words, and he took hold of Manannan's staves of power that were with him, and he reddened again, and he rose on the staves and gave a leap, and got a standing-place for his two feet on the overhanging rock. He looked down from that on Finn and his people, but whatever wish he had to bring them up to where he was, he was not able to do it.

He left the rock behind him then, and he was not gone far when he saw a wild tangled place before him, with thick woods that were of all he had ever walked the most leafy and the fullest of the sounds of wind and streams and birds, and of the humming of bees.

He went on walking the plain, and as he was looking about him, he saw a great tree with many twigs and branches, and a rock beside it, and a smooth-pointed drinking-horn on it, and a beautiful fresh well at its foot. And there was a great drouth on Diarmuid after the sea-journey, and he had a mind to drink a hornful of the water. But when he stooped to it he heard a great noise coming towards him, and he knew then there was enchantment in the water.

"I will drink my fill of it for all that," he said. And it was not long after that till he saw a Man of Enchantments coming towards him armed, having no friendly look. And it was in no friendly way he spoke to Diarmuid when he came up to him, but he gave him great abuse. "It is no right thing," he said, "to be walking through my thickets and to be drinking up my share of water." With that they faced one another angrily, and they fought till the end of the day.

The Enchanter thought it well to leave off fighting then, and he made a leap into the bottom of the well away from him, but there was vexation on Diarmuid to be left like that.

He looked around him then, and he saw a herd of deer coming through the scrub, and he went towards them, and threw a spear that went through the nearest stag and drove the bowels out of him. He kindled a fire then, and he cut thin bits of the flesh and put them on spits of white hazel, and that night he had his fill of meat and of the water of the well.

He rose up early on the morrow, and he found the Enchanter at the well before him. "It seems to me, Grandson of Duibhne," he said, "that it is not enough for you to be walking my scrub and my woods without killing my deer as well." With that they started again, giving one another blow for blow, thrust for thrust, and wound for wound till the end of the day came on them. And Diarmuid killed another great deer that night, and in the morning the fight began again. But in the evening, when the Enchanter was making his leap into the well, Diarmuid threw his arms about his neck, thinking to stop him, but it is what happened, he fell in himself. And when he was at the bottom of the well the Enchanter left him.

Diarmuid went then following after the Enchanter, and he found before him a beautiful wide flowery plain, and a comely royal city in the plain, and on the green before the dun he saw a great army; and when they saw Diarmuid following after the Enchanter, they left a way and a royal road for the Enchanter to pass through till he got inside the dun. And then they shut the gates, and the whole army turned on Diarmuid.

But that put no fear or cowardice on him, but he went through them and over them like a hawk would go through little birds, or a wild dog through a flock of sheep, killing all before him, till some of them made away to the woods and wastes, and another share of them through the gates of the dun, and they shut them, and the gates of the city after them. And Diarmuid, all full of hurts and wounds after the hard fight, lay down on the plain. A very strong daring champion came then and kicked at him from behind, and at that Diarmuid roused himself up, and put out his brave ready hand for his weapons.

"Wait a while, Grandson of Duibhne," the champion said then; "it is not to do you any hurt or harm I am come, but to say to you it is a bad sleeping-place for you to have, and it on your ill-wisher's lawn. And come now with me," he said, "and I will give you a better resting-place."

Diarmuid followed him then, and they went a long, long way from that, till they came to a high-topped city, and three times fifty brave champions in it, three times fifty modest women, and another young woman on a bench, with blushes in her cheeks, and delicate hands, and having a silken cloak about her, and a dress sewed with gold threads, and on her head the flowing veil of a queen.

There was a good welcome before Diarmuid for his own sake and the sake of his people, and he was put in a house of healing that was in the city, and good herbs were put to his hurts till he was smooth and sound again.

And a feast was made then, and the tables and the benches were set, and no high person was put in the place of the mean, or mean in the place of the high, but every one in his own place, according to his nobility, or his descent, or his art. Plenty of good food was brought to them then, and well-tasting strong drinks, and they spent the first part of the night in drinking, and the second part with music and delight and rejoicing of the mind, and the third part in sound sleep that lasted till the sun rose over the heavy sodded earth on the morrow.

Three days and three nights Diarmuid stopped in that city, and the best feast he ever found was given to him all through. And at the end of that time he asked what was the place he was in, and who was head of it. And the champion that brought him there told him it was Land-Under-Wave, and that the man that had fought with him was its king. "And he is an enemy of the Red Hand to me," he said. "And as to myself," he said, "I was one time getting wages from Finn, son of Cumhal, in Ireland, and I never put a year over me that pleased me better. And tell me now," he said, "what is the journey or the work that is before you?"

And Diarmuid told him the story of the Hard Servant then from beginning to end.

Now, as to Finn and his people, when they thought Diarmuid was too long away from them, they made ladders of the cords of the ship and put them against the rock, looking for him.

And after a while they found the leavings of the meat he had eaten, for Diarmuid never ate meat without leaving some after him.

Finn looked then on every side, and he saw a rider coming towards him over the plain on a dark-coloured beautiful horse, having a bridle of red gold. Finn saluted him when he came up, and the rider stooped his head and gave Finn three kisses, and asked him to go with him. They went on a long way till they came to a wide, large dwelling-place full of arms, and a great troop of armed men on the green before the fort. Three nights and three days Finn and his people stopped in the dun, and the best feast they ever got was served out to them.

At the end of that time Finn asked what country was he in, and the man that brought him there told him it was the land of Sorcha, and that he himself was its king. "And I was with yourself one time, Finn, son of Cumhal," he said, "taking your wages through the length of a year in Ireland."

Then Finn and the King of Sorcha called a great gathering of the people and a great meeting. And when it was going on they saw a woman-messenger coming to them through the crowd, and the king asked news of her. "I have news indeed," she said; "the whole of the bay and the harbour is full of ships and of boats, and there are armies all through the country robbing all before them." "I know well," said the king, "it is the High King of Greece is in it, for he has a mind to put the entire world under him, and to get hold of this country like every other." The King of Sorcha looked at Finn then, and Finn understood it was help from him he was asking, and it is what he said: "I take the protection of this country on myself so long as I am in it." He and his people rose up then, and the King of Sorcha along with them, and they went looking for the strange army. And when they came up with it they made great slaughter of its champions, and those they did not kill ran before them, and made no better stand than a flock of frightened birds, till there were hardly enough of them left to tell the story.

The High King spoke then, and it is what he said: "Who is it has done this great slaughter of my people? And I never heard before," he said, "any talk of the courage or of the doings of the men of Ireland either at this time or in the old times. But from this out," he said, "I will banish the Sons of the Gael for ever to the very ends of the earth."

But Finn and the King of Sorcha raised a green tent in view of the ships of the Greeks.

The King of the Greeks called then for help against Finn and the King of Sorcha, to get satisfaction for the shame that was put on his people. And the sons of kings of the eastern and southern world came to his help, but they could make no stand against Finn and Osgar and Oisin and Goll, son of Morna. And at the last the King of Greece brought all his people back home, the way no more of them would be put an end to.

And then Finn and the King of Sorcha called another great gathering. And while it was going on, they saw coming towards them a great troop of champions, bearing flags of many-coloured silk, and grey swords at their sides and high spears reared up over their heads. And in the front of them was Diarmuid, grandson of Duibhne.

When Finn saw him, he sent Fergus of the True Lips to ask news of him, and they told one another all that had happened.

And it would take too long to tell, and it would tire the hearers, how Finn made the Hard Servant bring home his fifteen men that he had brought away. And when he had brought them back to Ireland, the whole of the Fianna were watching to see him ride away again, himself and his long-legged horse. But while they were watching him, he vanished from them, and all they could see was a mist, and it stretching out towards the sea.

And that is the story of the Hard Servant, and of Diarmuid's adventures on the island Under-Wave.

CHAPTER V. THE HOUSE OF THE QUICKEN TREES

And it is often the Fianna would have been badly off without the help of Diarmuid. It was he came to their help the time Miodac, the son of the King of Lochlann, brought them into the enchanted House of the Quicken Trees.

It was by treachery he brought them in, giving himself out to be a poet, and making poems for Finn to make out the meaning of. A verse he made about a great army that he saw riding over the plains to victory, and robbing all before it, and the riders of it having no horses but plants and branches. "I understand that," said Finn, "it was an army of bees you saw, that was gathering riches from the flowers as it went." And another verse Miodac made was about a woman in Ireland that was swifter than the swiftest horse. "I know that," said Finn, "that woman is the River Boinn; and if she goes slow itself, she is swifter in the end than the swiftest horse, for her going never stops." And other verses he made about Angus' house at Brugh na Boinn, but Finn made them all out.

And after that he said he had a feast ready for them, and he bade them go into his House of the Quicken Trees till he would bring it. And they did that, and went in, and it was a beautiful house, having walls of every colour, and foreign coverings of every colour on the floor, and a fire that gave out a very pleasant smoke. And they sat down there, and after a while Finn said: "It is a wonder such a beautiful house to be here." "There is a greater wonder than that," said Goll; "that fire that was so pleasant when we came in is giving out now the worst stench in the world." "There is a greater wonder than that," said Glas; "the walls that were of all colours are now but rough boards joined together." "There is a greater wonder than that," said Fiacha; "where there were seven high doors to the house there is now but one little door, and it shut." "Indeed, there is a more wonderful thing than that," said Conan; "for we sat down on beautiful coverings, and now there is nothing between us and the bare ground, and it as cold as the snow of one night." And he tried to rise up, but he could not stir, or any of the rest of them, for there was enchantment that kept them where they were.

And it was the treachery of Miodac, and the spells of the Three Kings of the Island of the Floods that had brought them into that danger. And Finn knew by his divination that their enemies were gathering to make an end of them, and he said to his people there was no use in making complaints, but to sound the music of the Dord Fiann.

And some of the Fianna that were waiting for him not far off heard that sorrowful music, and came fighting against Miodac and his armies, and they fought well, but they could not stand against them. And at the last it was Diarmuid, grandson of Duibhne, that made an end of Miodac that was so treacherous, and of the Three Kings of the Island of the Floods, and took the enchantment off the floor of the House of the Rowan Trees with their blood.

And when he was freeing the Fianna, Conan called out, asking him to bring him a share of the feast Miodac had made ready for his own friends, for there was hunger on him. And when Diarmuid took no heed of him, he said: "If it was a comely woman was speaking to you, Diarmuid, you would not refuse to listen."

For if many women loved Diarmuid, there were many he himself gave his love to; and if he was often called Diarmuid the brave, or the hardy, or the comely, or the Hawk of Ess Ruadh, it is often he was called as well the friend and the coaxer of women, Diarmuid-na-man.

BOOK SEVEN: DIARMUID AND GRANIA.

CHAPTER I. THE FLIGHT FROM TEAMHAIR

Finn rose up one morning early in Almhuin of Leinster, and he sat out alone on the green lawn without a boy or a servant being with him. And Oisin followed him there, and Diorraing the Druid. "What is the cause of your early rising, Finn?" said Oisin. "It is not without cause, indeed, I rise early," said Finn, "for I am without a wife or a companion since Maighneis, daughter of Black Garraidh, died from me; for quiet sleep is not used to come to a man that is without a fitting wife." "Why would you be like that?" said Oisin, "for there is not a woman in all green Ireland you would throw a look on but we would bring her to you, willing or unwilling." "I myself could find a wife would be fitting for you," said Diorraing. "Who is that?" said Finn. "It is Grania, daughter of the High King of Ireland," said Diorraing; "and she is the woman of the best make and shape and the best speech of the women of the whole world." "By my word, Diorraing," said Finn, "there is strife and disagreement between the High King and myself this long time, and it would not be pleasing to me to get a refusal from him. And it is best for you two to go together," he said, "and to ask his daughter for me in marriage; the way that if he gives a refusal, it will be to you and not to myself he will give it." "We will go," said Oisin, "even if it is little profit we will get by it. And let no one at all know of our going," he said, "until such time as we are come back again."

After that the two bade farewell to Finn, and set out, and it is not told what they did till they came to Teamhair. The King of Ireland was holding a gathering at that time on the green of Teamhair, and the chief nobles of his people were with him. And there was a friendly welcome given to Oisin and to Diorraing, and the king put off the gathering till the next day, for he was sure it was some pressing thing had brought these two men of the Fianna to Teamhair. And Oisin went aside with him, and told him it was to ask his daughter Grania in marriage they were come from Finn, Head of the Fianna of Ireland.

The king spoke, and it is what he said: "There is not a son of a king or of a great prince, there is not a champion in Ireland my daughter has not given a refusal to, and it is on me they all lay the blame of that. And I will give you no answer at all," he said, "till you go to herself; for it is better for you to get her own answer, than to be displeased with me."

So they went together to the sunny house of the women, and the king sat down at the head of the high seat beside Grania, and he said: "Here, Grania, are two of the people of Finn, son of Cumhal, come to ask you as a wife for him, and what answer have you a mind to give them?" And it is what Grania said: "If he is a fitting son-in-law for you, why would he not be a fitting husband for me?"

They were satisfied then, and there was a feast made for them that night in Grania's sunny house, and the king settled for a meeting a fortnight from that time between himself and Finn at Teamhair.

So Oisin and Diorraing went back again to Almhuin, and told Finn their story from beginning to end. And as everything wears away, so did that time of delay.

And then Finn gathered together the seven battalions of the Fianna from every part where they were to Almhuin. And they set out in great bands and troops till they came to Teamhair.

The king was out on the green before them, and the great people of the men of Ireland, and there was a great welcome before Finn and the Fianna.

But when Grania saw grey-haired Finn, she said: "It is a great wonder it was not for Oisin Finn asked me, for he would be more fitting for me than a man that is older than my father."

But they talked together for a while, and Finn was putting questions to Grania, for she had the name of being very quick with answers. "What is whiter than snow?" he said. "The truth," said Grania. "What is the best colour?" said Finn. "The colour of childhood," said she. "What is hotter than fire?" "The face of a hospitable man when he sees a stranger coming in, and the house empty." "What has a taste more bitter than poison?" "The reproach of an enemy." "What is best for a champion?" "His doings to be high, and his pride to be low." "What is the best of jewels?" "A knife." "What is sharper than a sword?" "The wit of a woman between two men." "What is quicker than the wind?" said Finn then. "A woman's mind," said Grania. And indeed she was telling no lie when she said that. And for all their talk together she had no liking for Finn, and she felt the blood in her heart to be rising against him.

And the wedding-feast was made ready then, and they all went into the king's feasting-house in the Middle Court. And the king sat down to take his share of drinking and pleasure, and his wife at his left side, and Grania beside her again; and Finn, son of Cumhal, at the right hand of the king, and Oisin at the other side, and every other one according to his nobility and his birth.

Then Daire of the poems stood up before Grania, and sang the songs and good poems of her fathers to her. And there was sitting near to Grania a knowledgeable man, a Druid of Finn's people, and it was not long until they began to talk together. "Tell me now," said Grania, "who is that man on the right hand of Oisin?" "That is Goll, son of Morna," said the Druid, "the ready fighter." "Who is that beside Goll?" said Grania. "Osgar, son of Oisin," said the Druid. "And who is that thin-legged man beside Osgar?" "That is Caoilte, son of Ronan." "Who is that proud, hasty man beside Caoilte?" "Lugaidh's Son of the Strong Hand." "Who is that sweet-worded man," she said then, "with the dark hair, and cheeks like the rowan berry, on the left side of Oisin, son of Finn?" "That is Diarmuid, grandson of Duibhne," said the Druid, "that is the best lover of women in the whole world." "That is a good company," said Grania.

And after the feast had gone on a while, their own feast was made for the dogs outside. And the dogs began to fight with one another, and the noise was heard in the hall, and the chief men of the Fianna went to drive them away from one another.

Now Diarmuid was used to keep his cap always over the love-spot the woman had left on his forehead, for no woman could see that spot but she would give him her love. And it chanced, while he was driving the dogs apart, the cap fell from him, and Grania was looking cut at him as it fell, and great love for him came on her there and then. And she called her serving-maid to her, and bade her bring the great golden cup that held drink for nine times nine men from the sunny house.

And when the serving-maid brought the cup, she filled it with wine that had enchantment in it, and she said: "Give the cup first to Finn, and bid him take a drink from it, and tell him it is I myself sent it to him." So the serving-maid did that, and Finn took the cup and drank out of it, and no sooner did he drink than he fell into a deep sleep. And then the cup was given to the king, and the queen, and the sons of kings, and the whole company, but only Oisin and Osgar and Caoilte and Diarmuid, and Diorraing the Druid. And all that drank of it fell into the same heavy sleep.

And when they were all in their sleep, Grania rose up softly from the seat where she was, and she turned her face to Diarmuid, and she said: "Will you take my love, Diarmuid, son of Duibhne, and will you bring me away out of this house to-night?"

"I will not," said Diarmuid; "I will not meddle with the woman that is promised to Finn." "If that is so," said Grania, "I put you under Druid bonds, to bring me out of this house to-night before the awaking of Finn and of the King of Ireland from their sleep."

"It is under bad bonds you are putting me, Grania," said Diarmuid. "And why is it," he said, "that you put them on me more than on the great men and sons of kings that are in the Middle Court to-night? for there is not one of them all but is as well worthy of a woman's love as myself." "By my hand, Diarmuid, it is not without cause I laid those bonds on you," said Grania; "for I was at the door a while ago when you were parting the dogs," she said, "and my eyes fell on you, and I gave you the love there and then that I never gave to any other, and never will give for ever."

"It is a wonder you to give that love to me, and not to Finn," said Diarmuid, "for there is not in Ireland a man is a better lover of a woman than himself. And do you know this, Grania," he said, "the night Finn is in Teamhair it is he himself is the keeper of its gates. And as that is so, we cannot leave the town." "There is a side door of escape at my sunny house," said Grania, "and we will go out by it." "It is a thing I will never do," said Diarmuid, "to go out by any side door of escape at all." "That may be so," said Grania, "but I heard it said that every fighting man has leave to pass over the walls of any dun and of any strong place at all by the shafts of his spears. And I will go out through the door," she said, "and let you follow me like that."

With that she went out, and Diarmuid spoke to his people, and it is what he said, "O Oisin, son of Finn, what must I do with these bonds that are laid on me?" "You are not guilty if the bonds were laid on you," said Oisin; "and I tell you to follow Grania, and to keep yourself well out of the hands of Finn." "Osgar, son of Oisin," he said then, "what must I do with these bonds that are put on me?" "I tell you to follow Grania," said Osgar, "for it is a pitiful man that would break his bonds." "What advice do you give me, Caoilte?" said Diarmuid. "It is what I say," said Caoilte, "that I myself have a fitting wife; and that it would be better to me than all the riches of the world Grania to have given me that love." "What advice do you give me, Diorraing?" "I tell you to follow Grania," said Diorraing, "although you will get your death by it, and that is bad to me." "Is that the advice you all give me?" said Diarmuid. "It is," said Oisin, and all the rest with him. With that Diarmuid stood up and stretched out his hand for his weapons, and he said farewell to Oisin and the others, and every tear he shed was of the size of a mountain berry. He went out then to the wall of the dun, and he put the shafts of his two spears under him, and he rose with a light leap and he came down on the grassy earth outside, and Grania met him there. Then Diarmuid said: "It is a bad journey you are come on, Grania. For it would be better for you to have Finn, son of Cumhal, as a lover than myself, for I do not know any part or any western corner of Ireland that will hide you. And if I do bring you with me," he said, "it is not as a wife I will bring you, but I will keep my faith to Finn. And turn back now to the town," he said, "and Finn will never get news of what you are after doing." "It is certain I will not turn back," said Grania, "and I will never part with you till death parts us." "If that is so, let us go on, Grania," said Diarmuid.

They went on then, and they were not gone far out from the town when Grania said: "I am getting tired, indeed." "It is a good time to be tired," said Diarmuid, "and go now back again to your own house. For I swear by the word of a true champion," he said, "I will never carry yourself or any other woman to the end of life and time." "That is not what you have to do," said Grania, "for my father's horses are in a grass field by themselves, and chariots with them; and turn back now, and bring two horses of them, and I will wait in this place till you come to me again."

Diarmuid went back then for the horses, and we have no knowledge of their journey till they reached to the ford on the Sionnan, that is called now Ath-luain.

And Diarmuid said then to Grania: "It is easier to Finn to follow our track, the horses being with us." "If that is so," said Grania: "leave the horses here, and I will go on foot from this out."

Diarmuid went down to the river then, and he brought a horse with him over the ford, and left the other horse the far side of the river. And he himself and Grania went a good way with the stream westward, and they went to land at the side of the province of Connacht. And wherever they went, Diarmuid left unbroken bread after him, as a sign to Finn he had kept his faith with him.

And from that they went on to Doire-da-Bhoth, the Wood of the Two Huts. And Diarmuid cut down the wood round about them, and he made a fence having seven doors of woven twigs, and he set out a bed of soft rushes and of the tops of the birch-tree for Grania in the very middle of the wood.

CHAPTER II. THE PURSUIT

And as to Finn, son of Cumhal, I will tell out his story now.

All that were in Teamhair rose up early in the morning of the morrow, and they found Diarmuid and Grania were wanting from them, and there came a scorching jealousy and a weakness on Finn. He sent out his trackers then on the plain, and bade them to follow Diarmuid and Grania. And they followed the track as far as the ford on the Sionnan, and Finn and the Fianna followed after them, but they were not able to carry the track across the ford. And Finn gave them his word that unless they would find the track again without delay, he would hang them on each side of the ford.

Then the sons of Neamhuin went up against the stream, and they found a horse on each side of it, and then they went on with the stream westward, and they found the track going along the side of the Province of Connacht, and Finn and the Fianna of Ireland followed it on. And Finn said: "I know well where we will find Diarmuid and Grania now; it is in Doire-da-Bhoth they are." Oisin and Osgar and Caoilte and Diorraing were listening when Finn said those words. And Osgar spoke to the others, and it is what he said: "There is danger they might be there, and it would be right for us to give them some warning; and look now, Osgar, where is Bran the hound, for Finn himself is no dearer to him than Diarmuid, and bid him go now with a warning to him."

So Osgar told Bran, and Bran understood him well, and she went to the rear of the whole troop the way Finn would not see her, and she followed on the track of Diarmuid and Grania till she came to Doire-da-Bhoth, and she put her head into Diarmuid's bosom, and he in his sleep.

Diarmuid started up out of his sleep then, and he awoke Grania, and said to her: "Here is Bran, Finn's hound, and she is come with a warning to tell us Finn himself is coming." "Let us take that warning, then," said Grania, "and make your escape." "I will not take it," said Diarmuid, "for if I cannot escape Finn, I would as soon he took me now as at any other time." When Grania heard that, great fear came on her.

Bran went away from them then, and when Oisin saw her coming back, he said: "I am in dread Bran found no chance to get to Diarmuid, and we should send him some other warning. And look where is Fearghoin," he said, "Caoilte's serving-man." Now it was the way with Fearghoin, every shout he would give would be heard in the three nearest hundreds to him. So they made him give out three shouts the way Diarmuid would hear him. And Diarmuid heard him, and he said to Grania: "I hear Caoilte's serving-man, and it is with Caoilte he is, and it is along with Finn Caoilte is, and those shouts were sent as a warning to me." "Take that warning," said Grania. "I will not take it," said Diarmuid, "for Finn and the Fianna will come up with us before we leave the wood." And fear and great dread came on Grania when she heard him say that.

As for Finn, he did not leave off following the track till he came to Doire-da-Bhoth, and he sent the sons of Neamhuin to search through the wood, and they saw Diarmuid, and the woman along with him. They came back then where Finn was, and he asked them were Diarmuid and Grania in the wood? "Diarmuid is in it," they said, "and there is some woman with him, but we knew Diarmuid, and we do not know Grania." "May no good come to the friends of Diarmuid for his sake," said Finn, "and he will not quit that wood till he has given me satisfaction for everything he has done to me."

"It is jealousy has put you astray, Finn," said Oisin; "you to think Diarmuid would stop here on the plain of Maen Mhagh, and no close place in it but Doire-da-Bhoth, and you following after him." "Saying that will do you no good," said Finn, "for I knew well when I heard the three shouts Caoilte's serving-man gave out, it was you sent them to Diarmuid as a warning. And another thing," he said, "it was you sent my own hound Bran to him. But none of those things you have done will serve you, for he will not leave Doire-da-Bhoth till he gives me satisfaction for everything he has done to me, and every disgrace he has put on me." "It is great foolishness for you, Finn," said Osgar then, "to be thinking Diarmuid would stop in the middle of this plain and you waiting here to strike the head off him." "Who but himself cut the wood this way," said Finn, "and made this close sheltered place with seven woven narrow doors to it. And O Diarmuid," he said out then, "which of us is the truth with, myself or Oisin?" "You never failed from your good judgment, Finn," said Diarmuid, "and indeed I myself and Grania are here." Then Finn called to his men to go around Diarmuid and Grania, and to take them.

Now it was shown at this time to Angus Og, at Brugh na Boinne, the great danger Diarmuid was in, that was his pupil at one time, and his dear foster-son. He set out then with the clear cold wind, and did not stop in any place till he came to Doire-da-Bhoth. And he went unknown to Finn or the Fianna into the place where Diarmuid and Grania were, and he spoke kind words to Diarmuid, and he said: "What is the thing you have done, grandson of Duibhne?" "It is," said Diarmuid, "the daughter of the King of Ireland that has made her escape with me from her father and from Finn, and it is not by my will she came." "Let each of you come under a border of my cloak, so," said Angus, "and I will bring you out of the place where you are without knowledge of Finn or his people." "Bring Grania with you," said Diarmuid, "but I will never go with you; but if I am alive I will follow you before long. And if I do not," he said, "give Grania to her father, and he will do well or ill to her."

With that Angus put Grania under the border of his cloak, and brought her out unknown to Finn or the Fianna, and there is no news told of them till they came to Ros-da-Shoileach, the Headland of the Two Sallows.

And as to Diarmuid, after Angus and Grania going from him, he stood up as straight as a pillar and put on his armour and his arms, and after that he went to a door of the seven doors he had made, and he asked who was at it. "There is no enemy to you here," they said, "for there are here Oisin and Osgar and the best men of the sons of Baiscne along with us. And come out to us now, and no one will have the daring to do any harm or hurt on you." "I will not go out to you," said Diarmuid, "till I see at what door Finn himself is." He went then to another door of the seven and asked who was at it. "Caoilte, son of Ronan, and the rest of the sons of Ronan along with him; and come out to us now, and we will give ourselves for your sake." "I will not go out to you," said Diarmuid, "for I will not put you under Finn's anger for any well-doing to myself." He went on to another door then and asked who was at it. "There is Conan, son of Morna, and the rest of the sons of Morna along with him; and it is enemies to Finn we are, and you are a great deal more to us than he is, and you may come out and no one will dare lay a hand on you." "I will not indeed," said Diarmuid, "for Finn would be better pleased to see the death of every one of you than to let me escape." He went then to another door and asked who was at it. "A friend and a comrade of your own, Fionn, son of Cuadan, head of the Fianna of Munster, and his men along with him; and we are of the one country and the one soil, and we will give our bodies and our lives for your sake." "I will not go out to you," said Diarmuid, "for I would not like Finn to have a grudge against you for any good you did to me." He went then to another door and asked who was at it. "It is Fionn, son of Glor, head of the Fianna of Ulster, and his men along him; and come out now to us and there is no one will dare hurt or harm you." "I will not go out to you," said Diarmuid, "for you are a friend to me, and your father along with you, and I would not like the unfriendliness of Finn to be put on you for my sake." He went then to another door, and he asked who was at it. "There is no friend of yours here," they said, "for there is here Aodh Beag the Little from Eamhuin, and Aodh Fada the Long from Eamhuin, and Caol Crodha the Fierce, and Goineach the Wounder, and Gothan the White-fingered, and Aoife his daughter, and Cuadan the Tracker from Eamhuin; and we are unfriendly people to you, and if you come out to us we will not spare you at all, but will make an end of you." "It is a bad troop is in it," said Diarmuid; "you of the lies and of the tracking and of the one shoe, and it is not fear of your hands is upon me, but because I am your enemy I will not go out."

He went then to the last of the seven doors and asked who was at it. "No friend of yours," they said, "but it is Finn, son of Cumhal, and four hundred paid fighting men along with him; and if you will come out to us we will make opened marrow of you." "I give you my word, Finn," said Diarmuid, "that the door you are at yourself is the first door I will pass out of."

When Finn heard that, he warned his battalions on pain of lasting death not to let Diarmuid past them unknown. But when Diarmuid heard what he said, he rose on the staves of his spears and he went with a very high, light leap on far beyond Finn and his people, without their knowledge. He looked back at them then, and called out that he had gone past them, and he put his shield on his back and went straight on towards the west, and it was not long before he was out of sight of Finn and the Fianna. Then when he did not see any one coming after him, he turned back to where he saw Angus and Grania going out of the wood, and he followed on their track till he came to Ros-da-Shoileach.

He found Angus and Grania there in a sheltered, well-lighted cabin, and a great blazing fire kindled in it, and the half of a wild boar on spits. Diarmuid greeted them, and the life of Grania all to went out of her with joy before him.

Diarmuid told them his news from beginning to end, and they ate their share that night, and they went to sleep till the coming of the day and of the full light on the morrow. And Angus rose up early, and he said to Diarmuid: "I am going from you now, grandson of Duibhne; and I leave this advice with you," he said, "not to go into a tree with one trunk, and you flying before Finn, and not to be going into a cave of the earth that has but one door, and not to be going to an island of the sea that has but one harbour. And in whatever place you cook your share of food," he said, "do not eat it there; and in whatever place you eat it, do not lie down there; and in whatever place you lie down, do not rise up there on the morrow." He said farewell to them after that, and went his way.

CHAPTER III. THE GREEN CHAMPIONS

Then Diarmuid and Grania went along the right bank of the Sionnan westward till they came to Garbh-abha-na-Fiann, the rough river of the Fianna. And Diarmuid killed a salmon on the brink of the river, and put it to the fire on a spit. Then he himself and Grania went across the stream to eat it, as Angus bade them; and then they went westward to sleep.

They rose up early on the morrow, and they travelled straight westward till they came to the marsh of Finnliath.

And on the marsh they met with a young man, having a good shape and appearance, but without fitting dress or arms. Diarmuid greeted the young man, and asked news of him. "A fighting lad I am, looking for a master," he said, "and Muadhan is my name." "What would you do for me, young man?" said Diarmuid. "I would be a servant to you in the day, and watch for you in the night," he said. "I tell you to keep that young man," said Grania, "for you cannot be always without people."

Then they made an agreement with him, and bound one another, and they went on together westward till they reached the Carrthach river. And then Muadhan bade Diarmuid and Grania to go up on his back till he would carry them over the stream.

"That would be a big load for you," said Grania. But he put them upon his back and carried them over. Then they went on till they came to the Beith, and Muadhan brought them over on his back the same way. And they went into a cave at the side of Currach Cinn Adhmuid, the Woody Headland of the Bog, over Tonn Toime, and Muadhan made ready beds of soft rushes and tops of the birch for them in the far end of the cave. And he went himself into the scrub that was near, and took a straight long rod of a quicken-tree, and he put a hair and a hook on the rod, and a holly berry on the hook, and he went up the stream, and he took a salmon with the first cast. Then he put on a second berry and killed another fish, and he put on a third berry and killed the third fish. Then he put the hook and the hair under his belt, and struck the rod into the earth, and he brought the three salmon where Diarmuid and Grania were, and put them on spits. When they were done, Muadhan said: "I give the dividing of the fish to you, Diarmuid." "I would sooner you to divide it than myself," said Diarmuid. "I will give the dividing of the fish to you, so, Grania," said he. "I am better satisfied you to divide it," said Grania. "If it was you that divided the fish, Diarmuid," said Muadhan, "you would have given the best share to Grania; and if it was Grania divided it, she would have given you the best share; and as it is myself is dividing it, let you have the biggest fish, Diarmuid, and let Grania have the second biggest, and I myself will have the one is smallest."

They spent the night there, and Diarmuid and Grania slept in the far part of the cave, and Muadhan kept watch for them until the rising of the day and the full light of the morrow.

Diarmuid rose up early, and he bade Grania keep watch for Muadhan, and that he himself would go and take a walk around the country. He went out then, and he went up on a hill that was near, and he was looking about him, east and west, north and south. He was not long there till he saw a great fleet of ships coming from the west, straight to the bottom of the hill where he was. And when they were come to land, nine times nine of the chief men of the ships came on shore, and Diarmuid went down and greeted them, and asked news of them, and to what country they belonged.

"Three kings we are of the Green Champions of Muir-na-locht," said they; "and Finn, son of Cumhal, sent looking for us by cause of a thief of the woods, and an enemy of his own that has gone hiding from him; and it is to hinder him we are come. And we are twenty hundred good fighting men, and every one of us is a match for a hundred, and besides that," he said, "we have three deadly hounds with us; fire will not burn them, and water will not drown them, and arms will not redden on them, and we will lay them on his track, and it will be short till we get news of him. And tell us who you are yourself?" they said, "and have you any word of the grandson of Duibhne?" "I saw him yesterday," said Diarmuid; "and I myself," he said, "am but a fighting man, walking the world by the strength of my hand and by the hardness of my sword. And by my word," he said, "you will know Diarmuid's hand when you will meet it." "Well, we found no one up to this," said they. "What are your own names?" said Diarmuid. "Dubh-chosach, the Black-footed, Fionn-chosach, the Fair-footed, and Treun-chosach, the Strong-footed," they said.

"Is there wine in your ships?" said Diarmuid. "There is," said they. "If you have a mind to bring out a tun of wine," said Diarmuid, "I will do a trick for you." They sent men to get the tun, and when it came Diarmuid took it between his two hands and drank a drink out of it, and the others drank what was left of it. Diarmuid took up the tun after that, and brought it to the top of the hill, and he went up himself on the tun, and let it go down the steep of the hill till it was at the bottom. And then he brought the tun up the hill again, and he himself on it coming and going, and he did that trick three times before the strangers. But they said he was a man had never seen a good trick when he called that a trick; and with that a man of them went up on the tun, but Diarmuid gave a stroke of his foot at it and the young man fell from it before it began to move, and it rolled over him and crushed him, that he died. And another man went on it, and another after him again, till fifty of them were killed trying to do Diarmuid's trick, and as many of them as were not killed went back to their ships that night.

Diarmuid went back then to where he left Grania; and Muadhan put the hair and the hook on the rod till he killed three salmon; and they ate their meal that night, and he kept watch for them the same way he did before.

Diarmuid went out early the next day again to the hill, and it was not long till he saw the three strangers coming towards him, and he asked them would they like to see any more tricks. They said they would sooner get news of the grandson of Duibhne. "I saw a man that saw him yesterday," said Diarmuid. And with that he put off his arms and his clothes, all but the shirt that was next his skin, and he struck the Crann Buidhe, the spear of Manannan, into the earth with the point upwards. And then he rose with a leap and lit on the point of the spear as light as a bird, and came down off it again without a wound on him. Then a young man of the Green Champions said: "It is a man has never seen feats that would call that a feat"; and he put off his clothing and made a leap, and if he did he came down heavily on the point of the spear, and it went through his heart, and he fell to the ground. The next day Diarmuid came again, and he brought two forked poles out of the wood and put them standing upright on the hill, and he put the sword of Angus Og, the

Mor-alltach, the Big-fierce one, between the two forks on its edge. Then he raised himself lightly over it, and walked on the sword three times from the hilt to the point, and he came down and asked was there a man of them could do that feat.

"That is a foolish question," said a man of them then, "for there was never any feat done in Ireland but a man of our own would do it." And with that he rose up to walk on the sword; but it is what happened, he came down heavily on it the way he was cut in two halves.

The rest of the champions bade him take away his sword then, before any more of their people would fall by it; and they asked him had he any word of the grandson of Duibhne. "I saw a man that saw him to-day," said Diarmuid, "and I will go ask news of him to-night."

He went back then to where Grania was, and Muadhan killed three salmon for their supper, and kept a watch for them through the night. And Diarmuid rose up at the early break of day, and he put his battle clothes on him, that no weapon could go through, and he took the sword of Angus, that left no leavings after it, at his left side, and his two thick-handled spears, the Gae Buidhe and the Gae Dearg, the Yellow and the Red, that gave wounds there was no healing for. And then he wakened Grania, and he bade her to keep watch for Muadhan, and he himself would go out and take a look around.

When Grania saw him looking so brave, and dressed in his clothes of anger and of battle, great fear took hold of her, and she asked what was he going to do. "It is for fear of meeting my enemies I am like this," said he. That quieted Grania, and then Diarmuid went out to meet the Green Champions.

They came to land then, and they asked had he news of the grandson of Duibhne. "I saw him not long ago," said Diarmuid. "If that is so, let us know where is he," said they, "till we bring his head to Finn, son of Cumhal." "I would be keeping bad watch for him if I did that," said Diarmuid, "for his life and his body are under the protection of my valour, and by reason of that I will do no treachery on him." "Is that true?" said they. "It is true indeed," said Diarmuid. "Let you yourself quit this place, so," they said, "or we will bring your head to Finn since you are an enemy to him." "It is in bonds I would be," said Diarmuid, "the time I would leave my head with you." And with that he drew his sword the Mor-alltach out of its sheath, and he made a fierce blow at the head nearest him that put it in two halves. Then he made an attack on the whole host of the Green Champions, and began to destroy them, cutting through the beautiful shining armour of the men of Muir-na-locht till there was hardly a man but got shortening of life and the sorrow of death, or that could go back to give news of the fight, but only the three kings and a few of their people that made their escape back to their ships. Diarmuid turned back then without wound or hurt on him, and he went to where Crania and Muadhan were. They bade him welcome, and Grania asked him did he hear any news of Finn and the Fianna of Ireland, and he said he did not, and they ate their food and spent the night there.

He rose up again with the early light of the morrow and went back to the hill, and when he got there he struck a great blow on his shield that set the strand shaking with the sound. And Dubh-chosach heard it, and he said he himself would go fight with Diarmuid, and he went on shore there and then.

And he and Diarmuid threw the arms out of their hands and rushed on one another like wrestlers, straining their arms and their sinews, knotting their hands on one another's backs, fighting like bulls in madness, or like two daring hawks on the edge of a cliff. But at the last Diarmuid raised up Dubh-chosach on his shoulder and threw his body to the ground, and bound him fast and firm on the spot. And Fionn-chosach and Treun-chosach came one after the other to fight with him then, and he put the same binding on them; and he said he would strike the heads off them, only he thought it a worse punishment to leave them in those bonds. "For there is no one can free you," he said. And he left them there, worn out and sorrowful.

The next morning after that, Diarmuid told Grania the whole story of the strangers from beginning to end, and of all he had done to them, and how on the fifth day he had put their kings in bonds. "And they have three fierce hounds in a chain ready to hunt me," he said. "Did you take the heads off those three kings?" said Grania, "I did not," said Diarmuid, "for there is no man of the heroes of Ireland can loosen those bonds but four only, Oisin, son of Finn, and Osgar, son of Oisin, and Lugaidh's Son of the Strong Hand, and Conan, son of Morna; and I know well," he said, "none of those four will do it. But all the same, it is short till Finn will get news of them, and it is best for us to be going from this cave, or Finn and the three hounds might come on us."

After that they left the cave, and they went on till they came to the bog of

Finnliath. Grania began to fall behind them, and Muadhan put her on his back and carried her till they came to the great Slieve Luachra. Then Diarmuid sat down on the brink of the stream that was flowing through the heart of the mountain, and Grania was washing her hands, and she asked his knife from him to cut her nails with.

As to the strangers, as many of them as were alive yet, they came to the hill where their three leaders were bound, and they thought to loose them; but it is the way those bonds were, all they did by meddling with them was to draw them tighter.

And they were not long there till they saw a woman coming towards them with the quickness of a swallow or a weasel or a blast of wind over bare mountain-tops. And she asked them who was it had done that great slaughter on them. "Who are you that is asking that?" said they. "I am the Woman of the Black Mountain, the woman-messenger of Finn, son of Cumhal," she said; "and it is looking for you Finn sent me." "Indeed we do not know who it was did this slaughter," they said, "but we will tell you his appearance. A young man he was, having dark curling hair and ruddy cheeks. And it is worse again to us," they said, "our three leaders to be bound this way, and we not able to loose them." "What way did that young man go from you?" said the woman. "It was late last night he left us," they said, "and we do not know where is he gone." "I give you my word," she said, "it was Diarmuid himself that was in it; and take your hounds now and lay them on his track, and I will send Finn and the Fianna of Ireland to you."

They left a woman-Druid then attending on the three champions that were bound, and they brought their three hounds out of the ship and laid them on Diarmuid's track, and followed them till they came to the opening of the cave, and they went into the far part of it and found the beds where Diarmuid and Crania had slept. Then they went on westward till they came to the Carrthach river, and to the bog of Finnliath, and so on to the great Slieve Luachra.

But Diarmuid did not know they were after him till he got sight of them with their banners of soft silk and their three wicked hounds in the front of the troop and three strong champions holding them in chains. And when he saw them coming like that he was filled with great hatred of them.

There was one of them had a well-coloured green cloak on him, and he came out far beyond the others, and Grania gave the knife back to Diarmuid. "I think you have not much love for that young man of the green cloak, Grania," said Diarmuid. "I have not indeed," said Grania; "and it would be better if I had never given love to any man at all to this day." Diarmuid put the knife in the sheath then, and went on; and Muadhan put Grania on his back and carried her on into the mountain.

It was not long till a hound of the three hounds was loosed after Diarmuid, and Muadhan said to him to follow Grania, and he himself would check the hound. Then Muadhan turned back, and he took a whelp out of his belt, and put it on the flat of his hand. And when the whelp saw the hound rushing towards him, and its jaws open, he rose up and made a leap from Muadhan's hand into the throat of the hound, and came out of its side, bringing the heart with it, and he leaped back again to Muadhan's hand, and left the hound dead after him.

Muadhan went on then after Diarmuid and Grania, and he took up Grania again and carried her a bit of the way into the mountain. Then another hound was loosened after them, and Diarmuid said to Muadhan: "I often heard there is nothing can stand against weapons of Druid wounding, and the throat of no beast can be made safe from them. And will you stand now," he said, "till I put the Gae Dearg, the Red Spear, through that hound."

Then Muadhan and Grania stopped to see the cast. And Diarmuid made a cast at the hound, and the spear went through its body and brought out its bowels; and he took up the spear again, and they went forward.

It was not long after that the third hound was loosed. And Grania said then: "This is the one is fiercest of them, and there is great fear on me, and mind yourself now, Diarmuid."

It was not long till the hound overtook them, and the place he overtook them was Lic Dhubhain, the flag-stone of Dubhan, on Slieve Luachra. He rose with a light leap over Diarmuid, as if he had a mind to seize on Grania, but Diarmuid took him by the two hind legs, and struck a blow of his carcase against the side of the rock was nearest, till he had let out his brains through the openings of his head and of his ears. And then Diarmuid took up his arms and his battle clothes, and put his narrow-topped finger into the silken string of the Gae Dearg, and he made a good cast at the young man of the green cloak that was at the head of the troop that killed him. Then he made another cast at the second man and killed him, and the third man in the same way. And as it is not the custom to stand after leaders are fallen, the strangers when they saw what had happened took to flight.

And Diarmuid followed after them, killing and scattering, so that unless any man of them got away over the forests, or into the green earth, or under the waters, there was not a man or messenger of them left to tell the news, but only the Woman-messenger of the Black Mountain, that kept moving around about when Diarmuid was putting down the strangers.

And it was not long till Finn saw her coming towards him where he was, her legs failing, and her tongue muttering, and her eyes drooping, and he asked news of her. "It is very bad news I have to tell you," she said; "and it is what I think, that it is a person without a lord I am." Then she told Finn the whole story from beginning to end, of the destruction Diarmuid had done, and how the three deadly hounds had fallen by him. "And it is hardly I myself got away," she said. "What place did the grandson of Duibhne go to?" said Finn. "I do not know that," she said.

And when Finn heard of the Kings of the Green Champions that were bound by Diarmuid, he called his men to him, and they went by every short way and every straight path till they reached the hill, and it was torment to the heart of Finn to see the way they were. Then he said: "Oisin," he said, "loosen those three kings for me." "I will not loosen them," said Oisin, "for Diarmuid put bonds on me not to loosen any man he would bind." "Loosen them, Osgar," said Finn then. "I give my word," said Osgar, "it is more bonds I would wish to put on them sooner than to loosen them." Neither would Conan help them, or Lugaidh's Son. And any way, they were not long talking about it till the three kings died under the hardness of the bonds that were on them.

Then Finn made three wide-sodded graves for them, and a flag-stone was put over them, and another stone raised over that again, and their names were written in branching Ogham, and it is tired and heavy-hearted Finn was after that; and he and his people went back to Almhuin of Leinster.

CHAPTER IV. THE WOOD OF DUBHROS

And as to Diarmuid and Grania and Muadhan, they went on through Ui Chonaill Gabhra, and left-hand ways to Ros-da-Shoileach, and Diarmuid killed a wild deer that night, and they had their fill of meat and of pure water, and they slept till the morning of the morrow. And Muadhan rose up early, and spoke to Diarmuid, and it is what he said, that he himself was going away. "It is not right for you to do that," said Diarmuid, "for everything I promised you I fulfilled it, without any dispute."

But he could not hinder him, and Muadhan said farewell to them and left them there and then, and it is sorrowful and downhearted Diarmuid and Grania were after him.

After that they travelled on straight to the north, to Slieve Echtge, and from that to the hundred of Ui Fiachrach; and when they got there Grania was tired out, but she took courage and went on walking beside Diarmuid till they came to the wood of Dubhros.

Now, there was a wonderful quicken-tree in that wood, and the way it came to be there is this:

There rose a dispute one time between two women of the Tuatha de Danaan, Aine and Aoife, daughters of Manannan, son of Lir, for Aoife had given her love to Lugaidh's Son, and Aine had given her love to a man of her own race, and each of them said her own man was a better hurler than the other. And it came from that dispute that there was a great hurling match settled between the Men of Dea and the Fianna of Ireland, and the place it was to be played was on a beautiful plain near Loch Lein.

They all came together there, and the highest men and the most daring of the Tuatha de Danaan were there, the three Garbhs of Slieve Mis, and the three Mases of Slieve Luachra, and the three yellow-haired Murchadhs, and the three Eochaidhs of Aine, and the three Fionns of the White House, and the three Sgals of Brugh na Boinne, and the three Ronans of Ath na Riogh, and the Suirgheach Suairc, the Pleasant Wooer from Lionan, and the Man of Sweet Speech from the Boinn, and Ilbrec, the Many-Coloured, son of Manannan, and Neamhanach, son of Angus Og, and Bodb Dearg, son of the Dagda, and Manannan, son of Lir.

They themselves and the Fianna were playing the match through the length of three days and three nights, from Leamhain to the valley of the Fleisg, that is called the Crooked Valley of the Fianna, and neither of them winning a goal. And when the Tuatha de Danaan that were watching the game on each side of Leamhain saw it was so hard for their hurlers to win a goal against the Fianna, they thought it as well to go away again without playing out the game.

Now the provision the Men of Dea had brought with them from the Land of Promise was crimson nuts, and apples, and sweet-smelling rowan berries. And as they were passing through the district of Ui Fiachrach by the Muaidh, a berry of the rowan berries fell from them, and a tree grew up from it. And there was virtue in its berries, and no sickness or disease would ever come on any person that would eat them, and those that would eat them would feel the liveliness of wine and the satisfaction of mead in them, and any old person of a hundred years that would eat them would go back to be young again, and any young girl that would eat them would grow to be a flower of beauty.

And it happened one time after the tree was grown, there were messengers of the Tuatha de Danaan going through the wood of Dubhros. And they heard a great noise of birds and of bees, and they went where the noise was, and they saw the beautiful Druid tree. They went back then and told what they had seen, and all the chief men of the Tuatha de Danaan when they heard it knew the tree must have grown from a berry of the Land of the Ever-Living Living Ones. And they enquired among all their people, till they knew it was a young man of them, that was a musician, had dropped the berry.

And it is what they agreed, to send him in search of a man of Lochlann that would guard the tree by day and sleep in it by night. And the women of the Sidhe were very downhearted to see him going from them, for there was no harper could play half so sweetly on his harp as he could play on an ivy leaf.

He went on then till he came to Lochlann, and he sat down on a bank and sleep came on him. And he slept till the rising of the sun on the morrow; and when he awoke he saw a very big man coming towards him, that asked him who was he. "I am a messenger from the Men of Dea," he said; "and I am come looking for some very strong man that would be willing to guard a Druid tree that is in the wood of Dubhros. And here are some of the berries he will be eating from morning to night," he said.

And when the big man had tasted the berries, he said: "I will go and guard all the trees of the wood to get those berries."

And his name was the Searbhan Lochlannach, the Surly One of Lochlann. Very black and ugly he was, having crooked teeth, and one eye only in the middle of his forehead. And he had a thick collar of iron around his body, and it was in the prophecy that he would never die till there would be three strokes of the iron club he had, struck upon himself. And he slept in the tree by night and stopped near it in the daytime, and he made a wilderness of the whole district about him, and none of the Fianna dared go hunt there because of the dread of him that was on them.

But when Diarmuid came to the wood of Dubhros, he went into it to where the Surly One was, and he made bonds of agreement with him, and got leave from him to go hunting in the wood, so long as he would not touch the berries of the tree. And he made a cabin then for himself and for Grania in the wood.

As for Finn and his people, they were not long at Almhuin till they saw fifty armed men coming towards them, and two that were taller and handsomer than the rest in the front of them. Finn asked did any of his people know them. "We do not know them," they said, "but maybe you yourself know them, Finn." "I do not," he said; "but it seems to be they are enemies to myself." The troop of armed men came up to them then and they greeted him, and Finn asked news of them, and from what country they came. "I am Aonghus, son of Art Og of the children of Morna," one of them said, "and this is Aodh, son of Andela; and we are enemies of your own, and our fathers were at the killing of your father, and they themselves died for that deed. And it is to ask peace we are come now to you," they said. "Where were you the time my father was killed?" "In our mothers' wombs," said they; "and our mothers were two women of the Tuatha de Danaan, and it is time for us now to get our father's place among the Fianna." "I will give you that," said Finn, "but I must put a fine on you first in satisfaction for my father's death." "We have neither gold or silver or goods or cattle to give you, Finn," said they. "Do not put a fine on them, Finn," said Oisin, "beyond the death of their fathers for your father." "It is what I think," said Finn, "if any one killed myself, Oisin, it would be easy to pay the fine you would ask. And there will no one come among the Fianna," he said, "without giving what I ask in satisfaction for my father's death." "What is it you are asking of us?" said Aonghus, son of Art Og. "I am asking but the head of a champion, or the full of a fist of the berries of the quicken-tree at Dubhros." "I will give you a good advice, children of Morna," said Oisin, "to go back to the place you were reared, and not to ask peace of Finn through the length of your lives. For it is not an easy thing Finn is asking of you; and do you know whose head he is asking you to bring him?" "We do not," said they. "The head of Diarmuid, grandson of Duibhne, is the head he is asking of you. And if you were twenty hundred men in their full strength, Diarmuid would not let you take that head." "And what are the berries Finn is asking of us?" they said then. "There is nothing is harder for you to get than those berries," said Oisin.

He told them then the whole story of the tree, and of the Searbhan, the Surly One of Lochlann, that was put to mind it by the Tuatha de Danaan. But Aodh, son of Andela, spoke then, and it is what he said, that he would sooner get his death looking for those berries than to go home again to his mother's country. And he said to Oisin to care his people till he would come back again, and if anything should happen himself and his brother in their journey, to send them back again to the Land of Promise. And the two said farewell then to Oisin and to the chief men of the Fianna, and they went forward till they reached Dubhros. And they went along the wood till they found a track, and they followed it to the door of the hunting-cabin where Diarmuid and Grania were.

Diarmuid heard them coming, and he put his hand on his weapons and asked who was at the door. "We are of the children of Morna," they said, "Aodh, son of Andela, and Aonghus, son of Art Og." "What brings you to this wood?" said Diarmuid. "Finn, son of Cumhal, that put us looking for your head, if you are Diarmuid, grandson of Duibhne," said they. "I am indeed," said Diarmuid. "If that is so," they said, "Finn will take nothing from us but your head, or a fistful of the berries of the quicken-tree of Dubhros as satisfaction for the death of his father." "It is not easy for you to get either of those things," said Diarmuid, "and it is a pity for any one to be under the power of that man. And besides that," he said, "I know it was he himself made an end of your fathers, and that was enough satisfaction for him to get; and if you do bring him what he asks, it is likely he will not make peace with you in the end." "Is it not enough for you," said Aodh, "to have brought his wife away from Finn without speaking ill of him?" "It is not for the sake of speaking ill of him I said that," said Diarmuid, "but to save yourselves from the danger he has sent you into."

"What are those berries Finn is asking?" said Grania, "that they cannot be got for him?"

Diarmuid told her then the whole story of the berry the Tuatha de Danaan had lost, and of the tree that had sprung up from it, and of the man of Lochlann that was keeping the tree. "And at the time Finn sent me hiding here and became my enemy," he said, "I got leave from the Surly One to hunt, but he bade me never to meddle with the berries. And now, sons of Morna," he said, "there is your choice, to fight with me for my head, or to go asking the berries of the Surly One." "I swear by the blood of my people," said each of them, "I will fight with yourself first."

With that the two young men made ready for the fight. And it is what they chose, to fight with the strength of their hands alone. And Diarmuid put them down and bound the two of them there and then. "That is a good fight you made," said Grania. "But, by my word," she said, "although the children of Morna do not go looking for those berries, I will not lie in a bed for ever till I get a share of them; and I will not live if I do not get them," she said. "Do not make me break my peace with the Surly One," said Diarmuid, "for he will not let me take them." "Loose these tyings from us," said the two young men, "and we will go with you, and we will give ourselves for your sake." "You must not come with me," said Diarmuid; "for if you got the full of your eyes of that terrible one, you would be more likely to die than to live." "Well, do us this kindness," they said then; "loosen these bonds on us, and give us time to go by ourselves and see the fight before you strike off our heads." So Diarmuid did that for them.

Then Diarmuid went to the Surly One, and he chanced to be asleep before him, and he gave him a stroke of his foot the way he lifted his head and looked up at him, and he said: "Have you a mind to break our peace, Grandson of Duibhne?" "That is not what I want," said Diarmuid; "but it is Grania, daughter of the High King," he said, "has a desire to taste those berries, and it is to ask a handful of them I am come." "I give my word," said he, "if she is to die for it, she will never taste a berry of those berries." "I would not do treachery on you," said Diarmuid; "and so I tell you, willing or unwilling, I will take those berries from you."

When the Surly One heard that, he rose up on his feet and lifted his club and struck three great blows on Diarmuid, that gave him some little hurt in spite of his shield. But when Diarmuid saw him not minding himself, he threw down his weapons, and made a great leap and took hold of the club with his two hands. And when he had a hold of the club he struck three great blows on him that put his brains out through his head. And the two young men of the sons of Morna were looking at the whole fight; and when they saw the Surly One was killed they came out. And Diarmuid sat down, for he was spent with the dint of the fight, and he bid the young men to bury the body under the thickets of the wood, the way Grania would not see it. "And after that," he said, "let you go back to her and bring her here." So they dragged away the body and buried it, and they went then for Grania and brought her to Diarmuid.

"There are the berries you were asking, Grania," he said, "and you may take what you like of them now." "I give my word," said Grania, "I will not taste a berry of those berries but the one your own hand will pluck, Diarmuid." Diarmuid rose up then and plucked the berries for Grania, and for the children of Morna, and they ate their fill of them. And he said then to the young men: "Take all you can of these berries, and bring them with you to Finn, and tell him it was yourselves made an end of the Surly One of Lochlann." "We give you our word," said they, "we begrudge giving any of them to Finn."

But Diarmuid plucked a load of the berries for them, and they gave him great thanks for all he had done; and they went back to where Finn was with the Fianna. And Diarmuid and Grania went up into the top of the tree where the bed of the Surly One was. And the berries below were but bitter berries beside the ones above in the tree. And when the two young men came to Finn, he asked news of them. "We have killed the Surly One of Lochlann," they said; "and we have brought you berries from the quicken-tree of Dubhros, in satisfaction for your father, that we may get peace from you." They gave the berries then into Finn's hand, and he knew them, and he said to the young men: "I give you my word," he said, "it was Diarmuid himself plucked those berries, for I know the smell of his hand on them; and I know well it was he killed the Surly One, and I will go now and see is he himself alive at the quicken-tree."

After that he called for the seven battalions of the Fianna, and he set out and went forward to Dubhros. And they followed the track of Diarmuid to the foot of the quicken-tree, and they found the berries without protection, so they ate their fill of them. And the great heat of the day came on them, and Finn said they would stop where they were till the heat would be past; "for I know well," he said, "Diarmuid is up in the quicken-tree." "It is a great sign of jealousy in you, Finn," said Oisin, "to think that Diarmuid would stop there up in the quicken-tree and he knowing you are wanting to kill him."

Finn asked for a chess-board after that, and he said to Oisin: "I will play a game with you now on this." They sat down then, Oisin and Osgar and Lugaidh's Son and Diorraing on the one side of the board, and Finn on the other side.

And they were playing that game with great skill and knowledge, and Finn pressed Oisin so hard that he had no move to make but the one, and Finn said: "There is one move would win the game for you, Oisin, and I defy all that are with you to show you that move." Then Diarmuid said up in the tree where he was, and no one heard him but Grania: "It is a pity you be in straits, and without myself to show you that move." "It is worse off you are yourself," said Grania, "to be in the bed of the Surly One of Lochlann in the top of the quicken-tree, and the seven battalions of the Fianna round about it to take your life."

But Diarmuid took a berry of the tree, and aimed at the one of the chessmen that ought to be moved, and Oisin moved it and turned the game against Finn by that move. It was not long before the game was going against Oisin the second time, and when Diarmuid saw that he threw another berry at the chessman it was right to move, and Oisin moved it and turned the game against Finn in the same way. And the third time Finn was getting the game from Oisin, and Diarmuid threw the third berry on the man that would give the game to Oisin, and the Fianna gave a great shout when the game was won. Finn spoke then, and it is what he said: "It is no wonder you to win the game, Oisin, and you having the help of Osgar, and the watchfulness of Diorraing, and the skill of Lugaidh's Son, and the teaching of the grandson of Duibhne with you." "That is a great sign of jealousy in you, Finn," said Osgar, "to think Diarmuid would stop in this tree, and you so near him." "Which of us has the truth, Diarmuid, grandson of Duibhne," Finn said out then, "myself or Osgar?" "You never lost your good judgment, Finn," said Diarmuid then; "and I myself and Grania are here, in the bed of the Surly One of Lochlann." Then Diarmuid rose up and gave three kisses to Grania in the sight of Finn and the Fianna. And a scorching jealousy and a weakness came on Finn when he saw that, and he said: "It was worse to me, Diarmuid, the seven battalions of the Fianna to see what you did at Teamhair, taking away Grania the night you were yourself my guard. But for all that," he said, "you will give your head for the sake of those three kisses."

With that Finn called to the four hundred paid fighting men that were with him that they might make an end of Diarmuid; and he put their hands into one another's hands around that quicken-tree, and bade them, if they would not lose their lives, not to let Diarmuid pass out through them. And he said that to whatever man would take Diarmuid, he would give his arms and his armour, and a place among the Fianna of Ireland.

Then one of the Fianna, Garbh of Slieve Cua, said it was Diarmuid had killed his own father, and he would avenge him now, and he went up the quicken-tree to make an end of him.

Now, about that time it was made known to Angus Og, in Brugh na Boinne, the danger Diarmuid was in, and he came to his help, unknown to the Fianna. And when Garbh of Slieve Cua was coming up the tree, Diarmuid gave him a kick of his foot, and he fell down among the hired men, and they struck off his head, for Angus Og had put the appearance of Diarmuid on him. But after he was killed, his own shape came on him again, and the Fianna knew that it was Garbh was killed.

Then Garbh of Slieve Crot said it was Diarmuid had killed his father, and he went up to avenge him, and the same thing happened. And in the end all the nine Garbhs, of Slieve Guaire, and Slieve Muice, and Slieve Mor, and Slieve Lugha, and Ath Fraoch, and Slieve Mis and Drom-mor, went trying to take Diarmuid's life and lost their own lives, every one of them having the shape and appearance of Diarmuid when he died. And Finn was very sorry and discouraged when he saw that these nine men had come to their death.

Then Angus said he would bring away Grania with him. "Do so," said Diarmuid; "and if I am living at evening I will follow you." Then Angus said farewell to Diarmuid, and he put his Druid cloak about Grania and about himself, and they went away in the safety of the cloak, unknown to Finn and the Fianna, till they came to Brugh na Boinne.

Then Diarmuid, grandson of Duibhne, spoke, and it is what he said: "I will come down to you, Finn, and to the Fianna. And I will do death and destruction on you and on your people, for I am certain your mind is made up to give me no rest, but to bring me to my death in some place. And I have nowhere to go from this danger," he said, "for I have no friend or comrade under whose protection I could go in any far part of the great world, for it is often I fought against the men of the great world for love of you. For there never came battle or fight, danger or trouble on you, but I would go into it for your sake and the sake of the Fianna; and not only that, but I would fight before you and after you. And I give my word, Finn," he said, "you will pay hard for me, and you will not get me as a free gift." "It is the truth Diarmuid is speaking," said Osgar, "and give him forgiveness now, and peace." "I will not do that," said Finn, "to the end of life and time; and he will not get peace or rest for ever till I get satisfaction from him for every reproach he has put on me." "It is a great shame and a great sign of jealousy you to say that," said Osgar. "And I give the word of a true champion," he said, "that unless the skies come down upon me, or the earth opens under my feet, I will not let you or any one of the Fianna of Ireland give him cut or wound; and I take his body and his life under the protection of my valour, and I will keep him safe against all the men of Ireland." "Those are big words you have, Osgar," said Goll then, "to say you would bring a man away in spite of all the men of Ireland." "It is not you will raise them up against me, Goll," said Osgar, "for none of them would mind what you would say." "If that is what you are saying, you champion of great fights," said Goll, "let us see now what you can do." "You will have to go through with the fight you have taken on yourself," said Corrioll, son of Goll, in a loud voice. And Osgar answered him fiercely: "If I do I will shorten your bones, and your father's bones along with them. And come down now, Diarmuid," he said, "since Finn has no mind to leave you in peace, and I promise on my body and my life there will no harm be done to you to-day."

Then Diarmuid stood up on a high bough of the boughs of the tree, and he rose with a light leap by the shaft of his spear, and lit on the grass far beyond Finn and the Fianna. And he himself and Osgar went towards one another, in spite of the Fianna that went between them, and Diarmuid struck down those that were in his way; and as to Osgar, the throwing of his spears as he scattered the Fianna was like the sound of the wind going through a valley, or water falling over flag-stones. And Conan, that was always bitter, said: "Let the sons of Baiscne go on killing one another." But Finn, when he saw Diarmuid was gone from him, bade them put their weapons up, and turn back again to Almhuin.

And he sent those of his men that could be healed to places of healing, and the nine Garbhs, and the others of his men that were killed, he put into wide-sodded graves. And it is tired and downhearted and sorrowful he was after that, and he made an oath he would take no great rest till he would have avenged on Diarmuid all that he had done.

CHAPTER V. THE QUARREL

And as to Osgar and Diarmuid, they went on, and no cut or wound on them, to where Angus and Grania were at Brugh na Boinne; and there was a good welcome before them, and Diarmuid told them the whole story from beginning to end, and it is much that Grania did not die then and there, hearing all he had gone through.

And then she and Diarmuid set out again, and they went and stopped for a while in a cave that was near the sea.

And one night while they were there a great storm came on, so that they went into the far part of the cave. But bad as the night was, a man of the Fomor, Ciach, the Fierce One, his name was, came over the western ocean in a currach, with two oars, and he drew it into the cave for shelter. And Diarmuid bade him welcome, and they sat down to play chess together. And he got the best of the game, and what he asked as his winnings was Grania to be his wife, and he put his arms about her as if to bring her away. And Grania said: "I am this long time going with the third best man of the Fianna, and he never came as near as that to me."

And Diarmuid took his sword to kill Ciach, and there was anger on Grania when she saw that, and she had a knife in her hand and she struck it into Diarmuid's thigh. And Diarmuid made an end of the Fomor, and he said no word to Grania, but ran out and away through the storm.

And Grania went following after him, and calling to him, but there was great anger on him and he would not answer her. And at last at the break of day she overtook him, and after a while they heard the cry of a heron, and she asked him what was it made the heron cry out.

"Tell me that," she said, "Grandson of Duibhne, to whom I gave my love." And Diarmuid said: "O Grania, daughter of the High King, woman who never took a step aright, it is because she was frozen to the rocks she gave that cry." And Grania was asking forgiveness of him, and he was reproaching her, and it is what he said: "O Grania of the beautiful hair, though you are more beautiful than the green tree under blossom, your love passes away as quickly as the cold cloud at break of day. And you are asking a hard thing of me now," he said, "and it is a pity what you said to me, Grania, for it was you brought me away from the house of my lord, that I am banished from it to this day; and now I am troubled through the night, fretting after its delight in every place.

"I am like a wild deer, or a beast that is astray, going ever and always through the long valleys; there is great longing on me to see one of my kindred from the host.

"I left my own people that were brighter than lime or snow; their heart was full of generosity to me, like the sun that is high above us; but now they follow me angrily, to every harbour and every strand.

"I lost my people by you, and my lord, and my large bright ships on every sea; I lost my treasure and my gold; it is hunger you gave me through your love.

"I lost my country and my kindred; my men that were used to serve me; I lost quietness and affection; I lost the men of Ireland and the Fianna entirely.

"I lost delight and music; I lost my own right doing and my honour; I lost the Fianna of Ireland, my great kinsmen, for the sake of the love you gave me.

"O Grania, white as snow, it would have been a better choice for you to have given hatred to me, or gentleness to the Head of the Fianna."

And Grania said: "O Diarmuid of the face like snow, or like the down of the mountains, the sound of your voice was dearer to me than all the riches of the leader of the Fianna.

"Your blue eye is dearer to me than his strength, and his gold and his great hall; the love-spot on your forehead is better to me than honey in streams; the time I first looked on it, it was more to me than the whole host of the King of Ireland.

"My heart fell down there and then before your high beauty; when you came beside me, it was like the whole of life in one day.

"O Diarmuid of the beautiful hands, take me now the same as before; it was with me the fault was entirely; give me your promise not to leave me."

But Diarmuid said: "How can I take you again, you are a woman too fond of words; one day you give up the Head of the Fianna, and the next day myself, and no lie in it.

"It is you parted me from Finn, the way I fell under sorrow and grief; and then you left me yourself, the time I was full of affection."

And Grania said: "Do not leave me now this way, and my love for you ever growing like the fresh branches of the tree with the kind long heat of the day."

But Diarmuid would not give in to her, and he said: "You are a woman full of words, and it is you have put me under sorrow. I took you with myself, and you struck at me for the sake of the man of the Fomor."

They came then to a place where there was a cave, and water running by it, and they stopped to rest; and Grania said: "Have you a mind to eat bread and meat now, Diarmuid?"

"I would eat it indeed if I had it," said Diarmuid.

"Give me a knife, so," she said, "till I cut it." "Look for the knife in the sheath where you put it yourself," said Diarmuid.

She saw then that the knife was in his thigh where she had struck it, for he would not draw it out himself. So she drew it out then; and that was the greatest shame that ever came upon her.

They stopped then in the cave. And the next day when they went on again, Diarmuid did not leave unbroken bread like he had left every other day as a sign to Finn that he had kept his faith with him, but it was broken bread he left after him.

CHAPTER VI. THE WANDERERS

And they went on wandering after that, all through Ireland, hiding from Finn in every place, sleeping under the cromlechs, or with no shelter at all, and there was no place they would dare to stop long in. And wherever they went Finn would follow them, for he knew by his divination where they went. But one time he made out they were on a mountain, for he saw them with heather under them; and it was beside the sea they were, asleep on heather that Diarmuid had brought down from the hills for their bed; and so he went searching the hills and did not find them.

And Grania would be watching over Diarmuid while he slept, and she would make a sleepy song for him, and it is what she would be saying:

"Sleep a little, a little little, for there is nothing at all to fear, Diarmuid, grandson of Duibhne; sleep here soundly, soundly, Diarmuid, to whom I have given my love.

"It is I will keep watch for you, grandchild of shapely Duibhne; sleep a little, a blessing on you, beside the well of the strong field; my lamb from above the lake, from the banks of the strong streams.

"Let your sleep be like the sleep in the South, of Dedidach of the high poets, the time he took away old Morann's daughter, for all Conall could do against him.

"Let your sleep be like the sleep in the North, of fair comely Fionnchadh of Ess Ruadh, the time he took Slaine with bravery as we think, in spite of Failbhe of the Hard Head.

"Let your sleep be like the sleep in the West, of Aine, daughter of Gailian, the time she went on a journey in the night with Dubhthach from Doirinis, by the light of torches.

"Let your sleep be like the sleep in the East, of Deaghadh the proud, the brave fighter, the time he took Coincheann, daughter of Binn, in spite of fierce Decheall of Duibhreann. "O heart of the valour of the lands to the west of Greece, my heart will go near to breaking if I do not see you every day. The parting of us two will be the parting of two children of the one house; it will be the parting of life from the body, Diarmuid, hero of the bright lake of Carman."

And then to rouse him she would make another song, and it is what she would say: "Caoinche will be loosed on your track; it is not slow the running of Caoilte will be; do not let death reach to you, do not give yourself to sleep for ever.

"The stag to the east is not asleep, he does not cease from bellowing; though he is in the woods of the blackbirds, sleep is not in his mind; the hornless doe is not asleep, crying after her speckled fawn; she is going over the bushes, she does not sleep in her home.

"The cuckoo is not asleep, the thrush is not asleep, the tops of the trees are a noisy place; the duck is not asleep, she is made ready for good swimming; the bog lark is not asleep to-night on the high stormy bogs; the sound of her clear voice is sweet; she is not sleeping between the streams."

One time they were in a cave of Beinn Edair, and there was an old woman befriending them and helping them to keep a watch. And one day she chanced to go up to the top of Beinn Edair, and she saw an armed man coming towards her, and she did now know him to be Finn; and when he was come near she asked what was he looking for. "It is looking for a woman I am come," he said, "and for a woman's love. And will you do all I will ask you?" he said.

"I will do that," she said; for she thought it was her own love he was asking.

"Tell me then," he said, "where is Diarmuid, grandson of Duibhne?"

So she told him where he was hiding, and he bade her to keep him in the cave till such time as he would come back with his men.

The old woman went back then, and it is what she did, she dipped her cloak in the sea-water before she went into the cave; and Diarmuid asked her why was her cloak so wet. "It is," she said, "that I never saw or never heard of the like of this day for cold and for storms. There is frost on every hillside," she said, "and there is not a smooth plain in all Elga where there is not a long rushing river between every two ridges. And there is not a deer or a crow in the whole of Ireland can find a shelter in any place." And she was shaking the wet off her cloak, and she was making a complaint against the cold, and it is what she said:

"Cold, cold, cold to-night is the wide plain of Lurg; the snow is higher than the mountains, the deer cannot get at their share of food.

"Cold for ever; the storm is spread over all; every furrow on the hillside is a river, every ford is a full pool, every full loch is a great sea; every pool is a full loch; horses cannot go through the ford of Ross any more than a man on his two feet.

"The fishes of Inisfail are going astray; there is no strand or no pen against the waves; there are no dwellings in the country, there is no bell heard, no crane is calling.

"The hounds of the wood of Cuan find no rest or no sleep in their dwelling-place; the little wren cannot find shelter in her nest on the slope of Lon.

"A sharp wind and cold ice have come on the little company of birds; the blackbird cannot get a ridge to her liking or shelter for her side in the woods of Cuan.

"It is steady our great pot hangs from its hook; it is broken the cabin is on the slope of Lon; the snow has made the woods smooth, it is hard to climb to the ridge of Bennait Bo.

"The ancient bird of Glen Ride gets grief from the bitter wind; it is great is her misery and her pain, the ice will be in her mouth.

"Mind well not to rise up from coverings and from down, mind this well; there would be no good sense in it. Ice is heaped up in every ford; it is for that I am saying and ever saying 'Cold.'"

The old woman went out after that, and when she was gone, Grania took hold of the cloak she had left there and she put her tongue to it, and found the taste of salt water on it. "My grief, Diarmuid," she said then, "the old woman has betrayed us. And rise up now," she said, "and put your fighting suit upon you."

So Diarmuid did that, and he went out, and Grania along with him. And no sooner were they outside than they saw Finn and the Fianna of Ireland coming towards them. Then Diarmuid looked around him and he saw a little boat at hand in the shelter of the harbour, and he himself and Grania went into it. And there was a man before them in the boat having beautiful clothes on him, and a wide embroidered golden-yellow cloak over his shoulders behind. And they knew it was Angus was in it, that had come again to help them to escape from Finn, and they went back with him for a while to Brugh na Boinne, and Osgar came to them there.

CHAPTER VII. FIGHTING AND PEACE

And after a while Finn bade his people to make his ship ready, and to put a store of food and of drink in it. They did that, and he himself and a thousand of his men went into the ship; and they were nine days between sailing and rowing till they came to harbour in the north of Alban.

They bound the ship to the posts of the harbour then, and Finn with five of his people went to the dun of the King of Alban, and Finn struck a blow with the handwood on the door, and the door-keeper asked who was in it, and they told him it was Finn, son of Cumhal. "Let him in," said the king.

Then Finn and his people went in, and the king made them welcome, and he bade Finn to sit down in his own place, and they were given strong pleasant drinks, and the king sent for the rest of Finn's people and bade them welcome to the dun.

Then Finn told what it was brought him there, and that it was to ask help and advice against the grandson of Duibhne he was come.

"And you have a right to give me your help," he said, "for it was he that killed your father and your two brothers, and many of your best men along with them."

"That is true," said the king; "and I will give you my own two sons and a thousand men with each of them." Finn was glad when he heard that, and he and his men took leave of the king and of his household, and left wishes for life and health with them, and the king did the same by them.

And it was near Brugh na Boinne Finn and his people came to land, and Finn sent messengers to the house of Angus to give out a challenge of battle against Diarmuid, grandson of Duibhne.

"What should I do about this, Osgar?" said Diarmuid.

"We will both go out and make a stand against them, and we will not let a serving-man of them escape, but we will make an end of them all," said Osgar.

So they rose up on the morning of the morrow and they put their suits of battle on their comely bodies; and it would be a pity for those, be they many or few, that would meet those two men, and their anger on them. And they bound the rims of their shields together the way they would not be parted from one another in the right. And the sons of the King of Alban said that they themselves and their people would go first to meet them. So they came to shore, and made a rush to meet Diarmuid and Osgar. But the two fought so well that they beat them back and scattered them, and made a great slaughter, and put great terror on them, so that at the last there was not a man left to stand against them.

And after that, Finn went out again on the sea, and his people with him, and there is no word of them till they came to the Land of Promise where Finn's nurse was. And when she saw Finn coming she was very joyful before him. And Finn told her the whole story from beginning to end, and the cause of his quarrel with Diarmuid; and he said it was to ask an advice from her he was come, and that it was not possible to put him down by any strength of an army, unless enchantment would put him down. "I will go with you," said the old woman, "and I will do enchantment on him." Finn was very glad when he heard that, and he stopped there that night, and they set out for Ireland on the morrow.

And when they came to Brugh na Boinne, the nurse put a Druid mist around Finn and the Fianna, the way no one could know they were there. Now the day before that, Osgar had parted from Diarmuid, and Diarmuid was out hunting by himself. That was shown to the hag, and she took a drowned leaf having a hole in it, like the quern of a mill, and she rose with that by her enchantments on a blast of Druid wind over Diarmuid, and began to aim at him through the hole with deadly spears, till she had done him great harm, for all his arms and his clothing, and he could not make away he was so hard pressed. And every danger he was ever in was little beside that danger. And it is what he thought, that unless he could strike the old woman through the hole that was in the leaf, she would give him his death there and then. And he lay down on his back, and the Gae Dearg, the Red Spear, in his hand, and he made a great cast of the spear, that it went through the hole, and the hag fell dead on the spot. And he struck off her head and brought it back with him to Angus Og.

And the next morning early, Angus rose up, and he went where Finn was, and he asked would he make peace with Diarmuid, and Finn said he would. And then he went to the King of Ireland to ask peace for Diarmuid, and he said he would agree to it.

And then he went back to where Diarmuid and Grania were, and asked him would he make peace with the High King and with Finn. "I am willing," said Diarmuid, "if they will give the conditions I will ask." "What conditions are those?" said Angus.

"The district my father had," said Diarmuid, "that is, the district of Ui Duibhne, without right of hunting to Finn, and without rent or tribute to the King of Ireland, and with that the district of Dumhais in Leinster, for they are the best in Ireland, and the district of Ceis Corainn from the King of Ireland as a marriage portion with his daughter; and those are the conditions on which I will make peace with them." "Would you be peaceable if you got those conditions?" said Angus. "It would go easier with me to make peace if I got them," said Diarmuid.

Then Angus went with that news to where the King of Ireland was with Finn. And they gave him all those conditions, and they forgave him all he had done through the whole of the time he had been in his hiding, that was sixteen years.

And the place Diarmuid and Grania settled in was Rath Grania, in the district of Ceis Corainn, far away from Finn and from Teamhair. And Grania bore him children there, four sons and one daughter. And they lived there in peace, and the people used to be saying there was not a man living at the same time was richer as to gold and to silver, as to cattle and to sheep, than Diarmuid.

CHAPTER VIII. THE BOAR OF BEINN GULBAIN

But at last one day Grania spoke to Diarmuid, and it is what she said, that it was a shame on them, with all the people and the household they had, and all their riches, the two best men in Ireland never to have come to the house, the High King, her father, and Finn, son of Cumhal. "Why do you say that, Grania," said Diarmuid, "and they being enemies to me?"

"It is what I would wish," said Grania, "to give them a feast, the way you would get their affection." "I give leave for that," said Diarmuid.

So Grania was making ready a great feast through the length of a year, and messengers were sent for the High King of Ireland, and for Finn and the seven battalions of the Fianna; and they came, and they were using the feast from day to day through the length of a year.

And on the last night of the year, Diarmuid was in his sleep at Rath Grania; and in the night he heard the voice of hounds through his sleep, and he started up, and Grania caught him and put her two arms about him, and asked what had startled him. "The voice of a hound I heard," said he; "and it is a wonder to me to hear that in the night." "Safe keeping on you," said Grania, "for it is the Tuatha de Danaan are doing that on you, on account of Angus of Brugh na Boinn, and lie down on the bed again." But for all that no sleep came to him, and he heard the voice of the hound again, and he started up a second time to follow after it. But Grania caught hold of him the second time and bade him to lie down, and she said it was no fitting thing to go after the voice of a hound in the night. So he lay down again, and he fell asleep, but the voice of the hound awakened him the third time. And the day was come with its full light that time, and he said: "I will go after the voice of the hound now, since the day is here." "If that is so," said Grania, "bring the Mor-alltach, the Great Fierce One, the sword of Manannan, with you, and the Gae Dearg." "I will not," he said; "but I will take the Beag-alltach, the Little Fierce One, and the Gae Buidhe in the one hand, and the hound Mac an Chuill, the Son of the Hazel, in the other hand."

Then Diarmuid went out of Rath Grania, and made no delay till he came to the top of Beinn Gulbain, and he found Finn before him there, without any one at all in his company. Diarmuid gave him no greeting, but asked him was it he was making that hunt. Finn said it was not a hunt he was making, but that he and some of the Fianna had gone out after midnight; "and one of our hounds that was loose beside us, came on the track of a wild boar," he said, "and they were not able to bring him back yet. And there is no use following that boar he is after," he said, "for it is many a time the Fianna hunted him, and he went away from them every time till now, and he has killed thirty of them this morning. And he is coming up the mountain towards us," he said, "and let us leave this hill to him now."

"I will not leave the hill through fear of him," said Diarmuid. "It would be best for you, Diarmuid," said Finn, "for it is the earless Green Boar of Beinn Gulbain is in it, and it is by him you will come to your death, and Angus knew that well when he put bonds on you not to go hunting pigs." "I never knew of those bonds," said Diarmuid; "but however it is, I will not quit this through fear of him. And let you leave Bran with me now," he said, "along with Mac an Chuill." "I will not," said Finn, "for it is often he met this boar before and could do nothing against him." He went away then and left Diarmuid alone on the top of the hill. "I give my word," said Diarmuid, "you made this hunt for my death, Finn; and if it is here I am to find my death," he said, "I have no use in going aside from it now."

The boar came up the face of the mountain then, and the Fianna after him. Diarmuid loosed Mac an Chuill from his leash then, but that did not serve him, for he did not wait for the boar, but ran from him. "It is a pity not to follow the advice of a good woman," said Diarmuid, "for Grania bade me this morning to bring the Mor-alltach and the Gae Dearg with me." Then he put his finger into the silken string of the Gae Buidhe, and took a straight aim at the boar and hit him full in the face; but if he did, the spear did not so much as give him a scratch. Diarmuid was discouraged by that, but he drew the Beag-alltach, and made a full stroke at the back of the boar, but neither did that make a wound on him, but it made two halves of the sword. Then the boar made a brave charge at Diarmuid, that cut the sod from under his feet and brought him down; but Diarmuid caught hold of the boar on rising, and held on to him, having one of his legs on each side of him, and his face to his hinder parts. And the boar made away headlong down the hill, but he could not rid himself of Diarmuid; and he went on after that to Ess Ruadh, and when he came to the red stream he gave three high leaps over it, backwards and forwards, but he could not put him from his back, and he went back by the same path till he went up the height of the mountain again. And at last on the top of the mountain he freed himself, and Diarmuid fell on the ground. And then the boar made a rush at him, and ripped him open, that his bowels came out about his feet. But if he did, Diarmuid made a cast at him with the hilt of his sword that was in his hand yet, and dashed out his brains, so that he fell dead there and then. And Rath na h-Amhrann, the Rath of the Sword Hilt, is the name of that place to this day.

It was not long till Finn and the Fianna of Ireland came to the place, and the pains of death were coming on Diarmuid at that time. "It is well pleased I am to see you that way, Diarmuid," said Finn; "and it is a pity all the women of Ireland not to be looking at you now, for your great beauty is turned to ugliness, and your comely shape to uncomeliness." "For all that, you have power to heal me, Finn," said Diarmuid, "if you had a mind to do it." "What way could I heal you?" said Finn. "Easy enough," said Diarmuid, "for the time you were given the great gift of knowledge at the Boinn, you got this gift with it, that any one you would give a drink to out of the palms of your hands would be young and well again from any sickness after it." "You are not deserving of that drink from me," said Finn. "That is not true," said Diarmuid; "it is well I deserve it from you; for the time you went to the house of Dearc, son of Donnarthadh, and your chief men with you for a feast, your enemies came round the house, and gave out three great shouts against you, and threw fire and firebrands into it. And you rose up and would have gone out, but I bade you to stop there at drinking and pleasure, for that I myself would go out and put them down. And I went out, and put out the flames, and made three red rushes round the house, and I killed fifty in every rush, and I came in again without a wound. And it is glad and merry and in good courage you were that night, Finn," he said, "and if it was that night I had asked a drink of you, you would have given it; and it would be right for you to give it to me now." "That is not so," said Finn; "it is badly you have earned a drink or any good thing from me; for the night you went to Teamhair with me, you took Grania away from me in the presence of all the men of Ireland, and you being my own guard over her that night."

"Do not blame me for that, Finn," said Diarmuid, "for what did I ever do against you, east or west, but that one thing; and you know well Grania put bonds on me, and I would not fail in my bonds for the gold of the whole world. And you will know it is well I have earned a drink from you, if you bring to mind the night the feast was made in the House of the Quicken Tree, and how you and all your men were bound there till I heard of it, and came fighting and joyful, and loosed you with my own blood, and with the blood of the Three Kings of the Island of the Floods; and if I had asked a drink of you that night, Finn, you would not have refused it. And I was with you in the smiting of Lon, son of Liobhan, and you are the man that should not forsake me beyond any other man. And many is the strait has overtaken yourself and the Fianna of Ireland since I came among you, and I was ready every time to put my body and my life in danger for your sake, and you ought not to do this unkindness on me now. And besides that," he said, "there has many a good champion fallen through the things you yourself have done, and there is not an end of them yet; and there will soon come great misfortunes on the Fianna, and it is few of their seed will be left after them. And it is not for yourself I am fretting, Finn," he said, "but for Oisin and Osgar, and the rest of my dear comrades, and as for you, Oisin, you will be left lamenting after the Fianna. And it is greatly you will feel the want of me yet, Finn," he said; "and if the women of the Fianna knew I was lying in my wounds on this ridge, it is sorrowful their faces would be at this time."

And Osgar said then: "Although I am nearer in blood to you, Finn, than to Diarmuid, grandson of Duibhne, I will not let you refuse him this drink; and by my word," he said, "if any prince in the world would do the same unkindness to Diarmuid that you have done, it is only the one of us that has the strongest hand would escape alive. And give him a drink now without delay," he said.

"I do not know of any well at all on this mountain," said Finn. "That is not so," said Diarmuid, "for there is not nine footsteps from you the well that has the best fresh water that can be found in the world."

Then Finn went to the well, and he took the full of his two hands of the water. But when he was no more than half-way back, the thought of Grania came on him, and he let the water slip through his hands, and he said he was not able to bring it.

"I give my word," said Diarmuid, "it was of your own will you let it from you." Then Finn went back the second time to get the water, but coming back he let it through his hands again at the thought of Grania. And Diarmuid gave a pitiful sigh of anguish when he saw that. "I swear by my sword and by my spear," said Osgar, "that if you do not bring the water without any more delay, Finn, there will not leave this hill but yourself or myself." Finn went back the third time to the well after what Osgar said, and he brought the water to Diarmuid, but as he reached him the life went out of his body. Then the whole company of the Fianna that were there gave three great heavy shouts, keening for Diarmuid.

And Osgar looked very fiercely at Finn, and it is what he said, that it was a greater pity Diarmuid to be dead than if he himself had died. And the Fianna of Ireland had lost their yoke of battle by him, he said. "Let us leave this hill," said Finn then, "before Angus and the Tuatha de Danaan come upon us, for although we have no share in the death of Diarmuid, he would not believe the truth from us." "I give my word," said Osgar, "if I had thought it was against Diarmuid you made the hunt of Beinn Gulbain, you would never have made it"

Then Finn and the Fianna went away from the hill, and Finn leading Diarmuid's hound Mac an Chuill. But Oisin and Osgar and Caoilte and Lugaidh's Son turned back again and put their four cloaks over Diarmuid, and then they went after the rest of the Fianna.

And when they came to the Rath, Grania was out on the wall looking for news of Diarmuid; and she saw Finn and the Fianna of Ireland coming towards her. Then she said: "If Diarmuid was living, it is not led by Finn that Mac an Chuill would be coming home." And she was at that time heavy with child, and her strength went from her and she fell down from the wall. And when Oisin saw the way she was he bade Finn and the others to go on from her, but she lifted up her head and she asked Finn to leave Mac an Chuill with her. And he said he would not, and that he did not think it too much for him to inherit from Diarmuid, grandson of Duibhne.

When Oisin heard that, he snatched the hound out of Finn's hand and gave it to Grania, and then he followed after his people.

Then when Grania was certain of Diarmuid's death she gave out a long very pitiful cry that was heard through the whole place, and her women and her people came to her, and asked what ailed her to give a cry like that. And she told them how

Diarmuid had come to his death by the Boar of Beinn Gulbain in the hunt Finn had made. "And there is grief in my very heart," she said, "I not to be able to fight myself with Finn, and I would not have let him go safe out of this place."

When her people heard of the death of Diarmuid they gave three great heavy cries in the same way, that were heard in the clouds and the waste places of the sky. And then Grania bade the five hundred that she had for household to go to Beinn Gulbain for the body of Diarmuid.

And when they were bringing it back, she went out to meet them, and they put down the body of Diarmuid, and it is what she said:

"I am your wife, beautiful Diarmuid, the man I would do no hurt to; it is sorrowful I am after you to-night.

"I am looking at the hawk and the hound my secret love used to be hunting with; she that loved the three, let her be put in the grave with Diarmuid.

"Let us be glad to-night, let us make all welcome to-night, let us be openhanded to-night, since we are sitting by the body of a king.

"And O Diarmuid," she said, "it is a hard bed Finn has given you, to be lying on the stones and to be wet with the rain. Ochone!" she said, "your blue eyes to be without sight, you that were friendly and generous and pursuing. O love! O Diarmuid! it is a pity it is he sent you to your death.

"You were a champion of the men of Ireland, their prop in the middle of the fight; you were the head of every battle; your ways were glad and pleasant.

"It is sorrowful I am, without mirth, without light, but only sadness and grief and long dying; your harp used to be sweet to me, it wakened my heart to gladness. Now my courage is fallen down, I not to hear you but to be always remembering your ways. Och! my grief is going through me.

"A thousand curses on the day when Grania gave you her love, that put Finn of the princes from his wits; it is a sorrowful story your death is to-day.

"Many heroes were great and strong about me in the beautiful plain; their hands were good at wrestling and at battle; Ochone! that I did not follow them.

"You were the man was best of the Fianna, beautiful Diarmuid, that women loved. It is dark your dwelling-place is under the sod, it is mournful and cold your bed is; it is pleasant your laugh was to-day; you were my happiness, Diarmuid."

And she went back then into the Rath, and bade her people to bring the body to her there.

Now just at this time, it was showed to Angus at Brugh na Boinne that Diarmuid was dead on Beinn Gulbain, for he had kept no watch over him the night before.

And he went on the cold wind towards Beinn Gulbain, and his people with him, and on the way they met with Grania's people that were bringing the body to the Rath.

And when they saw him they held out the wrong sides of their shields as a sign of peace, and Angus knew them; and he and his people gave three great terrible cries over the body of Diarmuid.

And Angus spoke then, and it is what he said: "I was never one night since the time I brought you to Brugh na Boinne, being nine months old, without keeping watch and protection over you till last night, Diarmuid, grandson of Duibhne; and now your blood has been shed and you have been cut off sharply, and the Boar of Beinn Gulbain has put you down, Diarmuid of the bright face and the bright sword. And it is a pity Finn to have done this treachery," he said, "and you at peace with him.

"And lift up his body now," he said, "and bring it to the Brugh in the lasting rocks. And if I cannot bring him back to life," he said, "I will put life into him the way he can be talking with me every day."

Then they put his body on a golden bier, and his spears over it pointed upwards, and they went on till they came to Brugh na Boinne.

And Grania's people went to her and told her how Angus would not let them bring the body into the Rath, but brought it away himself to Brugh na Boinne. And Grania said she had no power over him.

And she sent out then for her four sons that were being reared in the district of Corca Ui Duibhne. And when they came she gave them a loving welcome, and they came into the Rath and sat down there according to their age. And Grania spoke to them with a very loud, clear voice, and it is what she said: "My dear children, your father has been killed by Finn, son of Cumhal, against his own bond and agreement of peace, and let you avenge it well upon him. And here is your share of the inheritance of your father," she said, "his arms and his armour, and his feats of valour and power; and I will share these arms among you myself," she said, "and that they may bring you victory in every battle. Here is the sword for Donnchadh," she said, "the best son Diarmuid had; and the Gae Dearg for Eochaidh; and here is the armour for Ollann, for it will keep the body it is put on in safety; and the shield for Connla. And make no delay now," she said, "but go and learn every sort of skill in fighting, till such time as you will come to your full strength to avenge your father."

So they took leave of her then, and of their household.

And some of their people said: "What must we do now, since our lords will be going into danger against Finn and the Fianna of Ireland?" And Donnchadh, son of Diarmuid, bade them stop in their own places; "for if we make peace with Finn," he said, "there need be no fear on you, and if not, you can make your choice between ourselves and him." And with that they set out on their journey.

But after a while Finn went secretly and unknown to the Fianna to the place where Grania was, and he got to see her in spite of all her high talk, and he spoke gently to her. And she would not listen to him, but bade him to get out of her sight, and whatever hard thing her tongue could say, she said it. But all the same, he went on giving her gentle talk and loving words, till in the end he brought her to his own will.

And there is no news told of them, until such time as they came to where the seven battalions of the Fianna were waiting for Finn. And when they saw him coming, and Grania with him, like any new wife with her husband, they gave a great shout of laughter and of mockery, and Grania bowed down her head with shame, "By my word, Finn," said Oisin, "you will keep a good watch on Grania from this out."

And some said the change had come on her because the mind of a woman changes like the water of a running stream; but some said it was Finn that had put enchantment on her.

And as to the sons of Diarmuid, they came back at the end of seven years, after learning all that was to be learned of valour in the far countries of the world. And when they came back to Rath Grania they were told their mother was gone away with Finn, son of Cumhal, without leaving any word for themselves or for the King of Ireland. And they said if that was so, there was nothing for them to do. But after that they said they would make an attack on Finn, and they went forward to Almhuin, and they would take no offers, but made a great slaughter of every troop that came out against them.

But at last Grania made an agreement of peace between themselves and Finn, and they got their father's place among the Fianna; and that was little good to them, for they lost their lives with the rest in the battle of Gabhra. And as to Finn and Grania, they stopped with one another to the end.

BOOK EIGHT: CNOC-AN-AIR.

CHAPTER I. TAILC, SON OF TREON

One time the Fianna were all gathered together doing feats and casting stones. And after a while the Druid of Teamhair that was with them said: "I am in dread, Finn of the Fianna, that there is some trouble near at hand; and look now at those dark clouds of blood," he said, "that are threatening us side by side overhead. And there is fear on me," he said, "that there is some destruction coming on the Fianna."

Finn looked up then, and he saw the great cloud of blood, and he called Osgar to look at it. "That need not knock a start from you," said Osgar, "with all the strength there is in your arms, and in the men that are with you." Then all the Fianna looked up at the cloud, and some of them were glad and cheerful and some were downhearted.

Then the Druid bade Finn to call all his battalions together and to divide them into two halves, that they could be watching for the coming of the enemy.

So Finn sounded the Dord Fiann, and they answered with a shout, every one hurrying to be the first. And Finn bade Osgar and Goll and Faolan to keep watch through the night, and he bade Conan the Bald to stop in the darkness of the cave of Liath Ard. "For it is you can shout loudest," he said, "to warn us if you see the enemy coming." "That I may be pierced through the middle of my body," said Conan, "if I will go watching for troubles or for armies alone, without some more of the Fianna being with me." "It is not fitting for you to refuse Finn," said Lugaidh's Son; "and it is you can shout the loudest," he said, "if the enemies come near the height." "Do not be speaking to me any more," said Conan, "for I will not go there alone, through the length of my days, for Finn and the whole of the Fianna." "Go then, Conan," said Osgar, "and Aodh Beag will go with you, and you can bring dogs with you, Bran and Sceolan and Fuaim and Fearagan; and let you go now without begrudging it," he said.

So Conan went then to Liath Ard, and Aodh Beag and Finn's hounds along with him. And as to Finn, he lay down to sleep, and it was not long till he saw through his sleep Aodh Beag his son, and he without his head. And after that he saw Goll fighting with a very strong man. And he awoke from his sleep, and called the Druid of the Fianna to him, and asked him the meaning of what he saw. "I am in dread there is some destruction coming on the Fianna," said the Druid; "but Aodh Beag will not be wounded in the fight, or Goll," he said.

And it was not long till Finn heard a great shout, and he sounded the Dord Fiann, and then he saw Conan running, and the hounds after him. And Finn sounded the Dord Fiann again before Conan came up, and when he came, Osgar asked him where was Aodh Beag. "He was at the door of the cave when I left it," said Conan, "but I did not look behind me since then," he said; "and it was not Aodh Beag was troubling me." "What was troubling you then?" said Osgar. "Nothing troubles me but myself," said Conan; "although I am well pleased at any good that comes to you," he said.

Osgar went then running hard, till he came to the cave, and there he found Aodh Beag with no fear or trouble on him at all, stopping there till he would hear the noise of the shields. And Osgar brought him back to where the Fianna were, and they saw a great army coming as if in search of them.

And a beautiful woman, having a crimson cloak, came to them over the plain, and she spoke to Finn, and her voice was as sweet as music. And Finn asked her who was she, and who did she come looking for. "I am the daughter of Garraidh, son of Dolar Dian, the Fierce," she said; "and my curse upon the King of Greece that bound me to the man that is following after me, and that I am going from, Tailc, son of Treon." "Tell me why are you shunning him, and I will protect you in spite of him," said Finn. "It is not without reason I hate him," said she, "for he has no good appearance, and his skin is of the colour of coal, and he has the head and the tail of a cat. And I have walked the world three times," she said, "and I did not leave a king or a great man without asking help from him, and I never got it yet." "I will give you protection," said Finn, "or the seven battalions of the Fianna will fall for your sake."

With that they saw the big strange man, Tailc, son of Treon, coming towards them, and he said no word at all of greeting to Finn, but he called for a battle on account of his wife.

So a thousand of the Fianna went out to meet him and his men; and if they did they all fell, and not one of them came back again. And then another thousand of the best men of the Fianna, having blue and green shields, went out under Caoilte, son of Ronan, and they were worsted by Tailc and his people. And then Osgar asked leave of Finn to go out and fight the big man. "I will give you leave," said Finn, "although I am sure you will fall by him." So Osgar went out, and he himself and Tailc, son of Treon, were fighting through the length of five days and five nights without food or drink or sleep. And at the end of that time, Osgar made an end of Tailc, and struck his head off. And when the Fianna saw that, they gave a shout of lamentation for those they had lost of the Fianna, and two shouts of joy for the death of Tailc.

And as to the young woman, when she saw all the slaughter that had been done on account of her, shame reddened her face, and she fell dead there and then. And to see her die like that, after all she had gone through, preyed more on the Fianna than any other thing.

CHAPTER II. MEARGACH'S WIFE

And while the Fianna were gathered yet on the hill where Tailc, son of Treon, had been put down, they saw a very great champion coming towards them, having an army behind him. He took no notice of any one more than another, but he asked in a very rough voice where was Finn, the Head of the Fianna. And Aodh Beag, that had a quiet heart, asked him who was he, and what was he come for. "I will tell you nothing at all, child," said the big man, "for it is short your years are, and I will tell nothing at all to any one but Finn." So Aodh Beag brought him to where Finn was, and Finn asked him his name. "Meargach of the Green Spears is my name," he said; "and arms were never reddened yet on my body, and no one ever boasted of driving me backwards. And was it you, Finn," he said, "put down Tailc, son of Treon?" "It was not by me he fell," said Finn, "but by Osgar of the strong hand." "Was it not a great shame for you, Finn," said Meargach then, "to let the queen-woman that had such a great name come to her death by the Fianna?" "It was not by myself or by any of the Fianna she got her death," said Finn; "it was seeing the army lost that brought her to her death. But if it is satisfaction for her death or the death of Tailc you want," he said, "You can get it from a man of the Fianna, or you can go quietly from this place." Then Meargach said he would fight with any man they would bring against him, to avenge Tailc, son of Treon.

And it was Osgar stood up against him, and they fought a very hard fight through the length of three days, and at one time the Fianna thought it was Osgar was worsted, and they gave a great sorrowful shout. But in the end Osgar put down Meargach and struck his head off, and at that the seven battalions of the Fianna gave a shout of victory, and the army of Meargach keened him very sorrowfully. And after that, the two sons of Meargach, Ciardan the Swift and Liagan the Nimble, came up and asked who would come against them, hand to hand, that they might get satisfaction for their father.

And it was Goll stood up against Ciardan, and it was not long till he put him down; and Conan came out against Liagan, and Liagan mocked at him and said: "It is foolishness your coming is, bald man!" But Conan made a quick blow and struck his head off before the fight was begun at all.

And Faolan said that was a shameful thing to do, not to stand his ground and make a fair fight. But Conan said: "If I could make an end of the whole army by one blow, I would do it, and I would not be ashamed, and the whole of the Fianna could not shelter them from me."

Then the two armies came towards each other, and they were making ready for the attack. And they saw a beautiful golden-haired woman coming towards them, and she crying and ever crying, and the battle was given up on both sides, waiting for her to come; and the army of Meargach knew it was their queen, Ailne of the Bright Face, and they raised a great cry of grief; and the Fianna were looking at her, and said no word.

And she asked where was her husband, and where were her two sons. "High Queen," said Finn then, "for all they were so complete and quick and strong, the three you are asking for fell in fight."

And when the queen-woman heard that, she cried out aloud, and she went to the place where her husband and her two sons were lying, and she stood over their bodies, and her golden hair hanging, and she keened them there. And her own people raised a sharp lamentation listening to her, and the Fianna themselves were under grief.

And it is what she said: "O Meargach," she said, "of the sharp green spears, it is many a fight and many a heavy battle your hard hand fought in the gathering of the armies or alone.

"I never knew any wound to be on your body after them; and it is full sure I am, it was not strength but treachery got the upper hand of you now.

"It is long your journey was from far off, from your own kind country to Inisfail, to come to Finn and the Fianna, that put my three to death through treachery.

"My grief! to have lost my husband, my head, by the treachery of the Fianna; my two sons, my two men that were rough in the fight.

"My grief! my food and my drink; my grief! my teaching everywhere; my grief! my journey from far off, and I to have lost my high heroes.

"My grief! my house thrown down; my grief! my shelter and my shield; my grief! Meargach and Ciardan; my grief! Liagan of the wide chest.

"My grief! my protection and my shelter; my grief! my strength and my power; my grief! there is darkness come from this thing; my grief to-night you to be in your weakness.

"My grief! my gladness and my pleasure; my grief! my desire in every place; my grief! my courage is gone and my strength; my grief from this night out for ever.

"My grief! my guide and my going; my grief! my desire to the day of my death; my grief! my store and my sway; my grief! my heroes that were open-handed.

"My grief! my bed and my sleep; my grief! my journey and my coming; my grief! my teacher and my share; my sorrowful grief! my three men.

"My grief! my beauty and my ornaments; my grief! my jewels and my riches; my grief! my treasures and my goods; my grief! my three Candles of Valour.

"My grief! my friends and my kindred; my grief! my people and my friends. My grief! my father and my mother; my grief and my trouble! you to be dead.

"My grief my portion and my welcome; my grief! my health at every time; my grief! my increase and my light; my sore trouble, you to be without strength.

"My grief! your spear and your sword; my grief! your gentleness and your love; my grief! your country and your home; my grief! you to be parted from my reach.

"My grief! my coasts and my harbours; my grief! my wealth and my prosperity; my grief! my greatness and my kingdom; my grief and my crying are until death.

"My grief! my luck altogether; my grief for you in time of battle; my grief! my gathering of armies; my grief! my three proud lions.

"My grief! my games and my drinking; my grief! my music and my delight; my grief! my sunny house and my women; my crying grief, you to be under defeat.

"My grief! my lands and my hunting; my grief! my three sure fighters; Och! my grief! they are my sorrow, to fall far off by the Fianna.

"I knew by the great host of the Sidhe that were fighting over the dun, giving battle to one another in the valleys of the air, that destruction would put down my three.

"I knew by the noise of the voices of the Sidhe coming into my ears, that a story of new sorrow was not far from me; it is your death it was foretelling.

"I knew at the beginning of the day when my three good men went from me, when I saw tears of blood on their cheeks, that they would not come back to me as winners.

"I knew by the voice of the battle-crow over your dun every evening, since you went from me comely and terrible, that misfortune and grief were at hand.

"It is well I remember, my three strong ones, how often I used to be telling you that if you would go to Ireland, I would not see the joy of victory on your faces.

"I knew by the voice of the raven every morning since you went from me, that your fall was sure and certain; that you would never come back to your own country.

"I knew, my three great ones, by your forgetting the thongs of your hounds, that you would not gain the day or escape from the treachery of the Fianna.

"I knew, Candles of Valour, by the stream near the dun turning to blood when you set out, that there would be treachery in Finn.

"I knew by the eagle coming every evening over the dun, that it would not be long till I would hear a story of bad news of my three.

"I knew by the withering of the tree before the dun, that you would never come back as conquerors from the treachery of Finn, son of Cumhal."

When Grania, now, heard what the woman was saying, there was anger on her, and she said: "Do not be speaking against Finn or the Fianna, Queen, for it was not by any treachery or any deceit your three men were brought to their end."

But Ailne made her no answer and gave no heed to her, but she went on with her complaint, and she crying and ever crying.

"I knew, looking after you the day you went out from the dun, by the flight of the raven before you, there was no good sign of your coming back again.

"I knew by Ciardan's hounds that were howling mournfully every evening, that it would not be long till I would have bad news of you.

"I knew by my sleep that went from me, by my tears through every lasting night, that there was no luck before you.

"I knew by the sorrowful vision that showed myself in danger, my head and my hands cut off, that it was yourselves were without sway.

"I knew by the voice of Uaithnin, the hound that is dearest to Liagan, howling early every morning, that death was certain for my three.

"I knew when I saw in a vision a lake of blood in the place of the dun, that my three were put down by the deceit that was always with Finn."

"Do not be faulting Finn," said Grania then, "however vexed your heart may be. And leave off now," she said, "speaking against the Fianna and against himself; for if your men had stopped in their own country," she said, "without coming to avenge the son of Treon, there would no harm have happened them." "I would not put any reproach on the Fianna, Grania," said Ailne, "if my three men had been put down in fair battle, but they are not living to bear witness to me," she said; "and it is likely they were put under Druid spells at the first, or they would never have given in." "If they were living, Queen," said Grania, "they would not be running down the Fianna, but they would tell you it was by bravery and the strong hand they fell." "I do not believe you or the Fianna when you say that," said Ailne; "for no one that came to meet them ever got the sway over them by the right of the sword." "If you do not believe what I am saying, beautiful Ailne," said Grania, "I tell you more of your great army will fall by the Fianna, and that not by treachery." "That is not so," said Ailne, "but I have good hopes that my own army will do destruction on the Fianna, for the sake of the men that are dead." "Well, Ailne," said Grania, "I know it is a far journey you have come. And come now and eat and drink," she said, "with myself and with the Fianna."

But Ailne would not do that, but she said it would not be fitting for her to take food from people that did such deeds, and what she wanted was satisfaction for the death of her husband and her two sons.

And first it was settled for two men of each side to go out against one another; and then Ailne said that there should be thirty men on each side, and then she said she would not be satisfied to go back to her own country till she brought the head of Finn with her, or till the last of his men had fallen. And there was a great battle fought in the end, and it is seldom the Fianna fought so hard a battle as that.

And it would be too long to tell, and it would tire the hearers, how many good men were killed on each side. But in the end Ailne of the Bright Face was worsted, and she went back with what were left of her men to their own country, and no one knew where they went. And the hill in the west those battles were fought on got the name of Cnoc-an-Air, the Hill of Slaughter.

CHAPTER III. AILNE'S REVENGE

One day Finn and his people were hunting on Slieve Fuad, and a stag stood against them for a while and fought with his great rough horns, and then he turned and ran, and the Fianna followed after him till they came to the green hill of Liadhas, and from that to rocky Cairgin. And there they lost him again for a while, till Sceolan started him again, and he went back towards Slieve Fuad, and the Fianna after him.

But Finn and Daire of the Songs, that were together, went astray and lost the rest of their people, and they did not know was it east or west they were going.

Finn sounded the Dord Fiann then, and Daire played some sorrowful music to let their people know where they were. But when the Fianna heard the music, it seemed to be a long way off; and sometimes they thought it was in the north it was, and sometimes in the east, and then it changed to the west, the way they did not know in the wide world where was it coming from.

And as to Finn and Daire, a Druid mist came about them, and they did not know what way they were going.

And after a while they met with a young woman, comely and pleasant, and they asked who was she, and what brought her there. "Glanluadh is my name," she said, "and my husband is Lobharan; and we were travelling over the plain together a while ago, and we heard the cry of hounds, and he left me and went after the hunt, and I do not know where is he, or what way did he go." "Come on then with us," said Finn, "and we will take care of you, for we ourselves do not know what way the hunt is gone, east or west." So they went on, and before long they came to a hill, and they heard sleepy music of the Sidhe beside them. And after that there came shouts and noises, and then the music began again, and heavy sleep came on Finn and Daire. And when they awoke from their sleep they saw a very large lighted house before them, and a stormy blue sea around it. Then they saw a very big grey man coming through the waves, and he took hold of Finn and of Daire, and all their strength went from them, and he brought them across the waves and into the house, and he shut the door of the house with iron hooks. "My welcome to you, Finn of the great name," he said then in a very harsh voice; "it is long we are waiting here for you."

They sat down then on the hard side of a bed, and the woman of the house came to them, and they knew her to be Ailne, wife of Meargach. "It is long I am looking for you, Finn," she said, "to get satisfaction for the treachery you did on Meargach and on my two comely young sons, and on Tailc, son of Treon, and all his people. And do you remember that, Finn?" she said. "I remember well," said Finn, "that they fell by the swords of the Fianna, not by treachery but in fighting." "It was by treachery they fell," said the Grey Man then; "and it is our witness to it, pleasant Ailne to be the way she is, and many a strong army under grief on account of her." "What is Ailne to you, man of the rough voice?" said Finn. "I am her own brother," said the man.

With that he put bonds on the three, Finn and Daire and Glanluadh, and he put them down into some deep shut place.

They were very sorrowful then, and they stopped there to the end of five days and five nights, without food, without drink, without music.

And Ailne went to see them then, and Finn said to her: "O Ailne," he said, "bring to mind the time you come to Cnoc-an-Air, and the way the Fianna treated you with generosity; and it is not fitting for you," he said, "to keep us now under shame and weakness and in danger of death." "I know well I got kind treatment from Grania," said Ailne in a sorrowful voice; "but for all that, Finn," she said, "if all the Fianna were in that prison along with you under hard bonds, it would please me well, and I would not pity their case. And what is it set you following after Finn," she said then to Glanluadh, "for that is not a fitting thing for you to do, and his own kind wife living yet."

Then Glanluadh told her the whole story, and how she was walking the plain with Lobharan her husband, and he followed the hunt, and the mist came about her that she did not know east from west, and how she met then with Finn that she never saw before that time. "If that is so," said Ailne, "it is not right for you to be under punishment without cause."

She called then to her brother the Grey Man, and bade him take the spells off Glanluadh. And when she was set free it is sorry she was to leave Daire in bonds, and Finn. And when she had bidden them farewell she went out with Ailne, and there was food brought to her, but a cloud of weakness came on her of a sudden, that it was a pity to see the way she was.

And when Ailne saw that, she brought out an enchanted cup of the Sidhe and gave her a drink from it. And no sooner did Glanluadh drink from the cup than her strength and her own appearance came back to her again; but for all that, she was fretting after Finn and Daire in their bonds. "It seems to me, Glanluadh, you are fretting after those two men," said Ailne. "I am sorry indeed," said Glanluadh, "the like of those men to be shut up without food or drink." "If it is pleasing to you to give them food you may give it," said Ailne, "for I will not make an end of them till I see can I get the rest of the Fianna into bonds along with them." The two women brought food and drink then to Finn, and to Daire; and Glanluadh gave her blessing to Finn, and she cried when she saw the way he was; but as to Ailne, she had no pity at all for the King of the Fianna.

Now as to the Grey Man, he heard them talking of the Fianna, and they were saying that Daire had a great name for the sweetness of his music. "I have a mind to hear that sweet music," said he. So he went to the place where they were, and he bade Daire to let him hear what sort of music he could make. "My music pleased the Fianna well," said Daire; "but I think it likely it would not please you." "Play it for me now, till I know if the report I heard of you is true," said the Grey Man. "Indeed, I have no mind for music," said Daire, "being weak and downhearted the way I am, through your spells that put down my courage." "I will take my spells off you for so long as you play for me," said the Grey Man. "I could never make music seeing Finn in bonds the way he is," said Daire; "for it is worse to me, he to be under trouble than myself." "I will take the power of my spells off Finn till you play for me," said the Grey Man.

He weakened the spells then, and gave them food and drink, and it pleased him greatly the way Daire played the music, and he called to Glanluadh and to Ailne to come and to listen to the sweetness of it. And they were well pleased with it, and it is glad Glanluadh was, seeing them not so discouraged as they were.

Now as to the Fianna, they were searching for Finn and for Daire in every place they had ever stopped in. And when they came to this place they could hear Daire's sweet music; and at first they were glad when they heard it, and then when they knew the way he himself and Finn were, they made an attack on Ailne's dun to release them.

But the Grey Man heard their shouts, and he put the full power of his spells again on Finn and on Daire. And the Fianna heard the music as if stammering, and then they heard a great noise like the loud roaring of waves, and when they heard that, there was not one of them but fell into a sleep and clouds of death, under those sorrowful spells.

And then the Grey Man and Ailne came out quietly from where they were, and they brought the whole of the men of the Fianna that were there into the dun. And they put hard bonds on them, and put them where Finn and Daire were. And there was great grief on Finn and Daire when they saw them, and they were all left there together for a while.

Then Glanluadh said to the Grey Man: "If Daire's music is pleasing to you, let him play it to us now." "If you have a mind for music," said the Grey Man, "Daire must play it for us, and for Finn and his army as well."

They went then to where they were, and bade Daire to play. "I could never play sweet music," said Daire, "the time the Fianna are in any trouble; for when they are in trouble, I myself am in trouble, and I could not sound any sweet string," he said, "while there is trouble on any man of them." The Grey Man weakened the spells then on them all, and Daire played first the strings of sweetness, and of the noise of shouting, and then he sang his own grief and the grief of all the Fianna. And at that the Grey Man said it would not be long before he would put the whole of the Fianna to death; and then Daire played a tune of heavy shouts of lamentation. And then at Finn's bidding he played the music of sweet strings for the Fianna.

They were kept, now, a long time in that prison, and they got very hard treatment; and sometimes Ailne's brother would come in and strike the heads off some of them, for none of them could rise up from the seats they were sitting on through his enchantments. But one time he was going to strike the bald head off Conan, and Conan made a great leap from the seat; but if he did, he left strips of his skin hanging to it, that his back was left bare. And then he came round the Grey Man with his pitiful words: "Stop your hand now," he said, "for that is enough for this time; and do not send me to my death yet awhile, and heal me of my wounds first," he said, "before you make an end of me." And the reason he said that was because he knew Ailne to have an enchanted cup in the dun, that had cured Glanluadh.

And the Grey Man took pity on his case, and he brought him out and bade Ailne to bring the cup to him and to cure his wounds. "I will not bring it," said Ailne, "for it would be best give no time at all to him or to the Fianna, but to make an end of them." "It is not to be saved from death I am asking, bright-faced Ailne," said Conan, "but only not to go to my death stripped bare the way I am." When Ailne heard that, she brought a sheepskin and she put it on Conan's back, and it fitted and grew to him, and covered his wounds. "I will not put you to death, Conan," said the Grey Man then, "but you can stop with myself to the end of your life." "You will never be without grief and danger and the fear of treachery if you keep him with you," said Ailne; "for there is treachery in his heart the same as there is in the rest of them." "There is no fear of that," said her brother, "or I will make no delay until I put the whole of the Fianna to death." And with that he brought Conan to where the enchanted cup was, and he put it in his hand. And just at that moment they heard Daire playing very sweet sorrowful music, and the Grey Man went to listen to it, very quick and proud. And Conan followed him there, and after a while the Grey Man asked him what did he do with the enchanted cup. "I left it where I found it, full of power," said Conan.

The Grey Man hurried back then to the place where the treasures of the dun were. But no sooner was he gone than Conan took out the cup that he had hidden, and he gave a drink from it to Finn and to Osgar and to the rest of the Fianna. And they that were withered and shaking, without strength, without courage, got back their own appearance and their strength again on the moment.

And when the Grey Man came back from looking for the cup, and saw what had happened, he took his sword and made a stroke at Conan. But Conan called to Osgar to defend him, and Osgar attacked the Grey Man, and it was not long till he made him acquainted with death.

And when Ailne saw that, with the grief and the dread that came on her, she fell dead then and there.

Then all the Fianna made a feast with what they found of food and of drink, and they were very joyful and merry. But when they rose up in the morning, there was no trace or tidings of the dun, but it was on the bare grass they were lying.

But as to Conan, the sheepskin never left him; and the wool used to grow on it every year, the same as it would on any other skin.

BOOK NINE: THE WEARING AWAY
OF THE FIANNA.

CHAPTER I. THE QUARREL WITH THE SONS OF MORNA

One time when the Fianna were gone here and there hunting, Black Garraidh and Caoilte were sitting beside Finn, and they were talking of the battle where Finn's father was killed. And Finn said then to Garraidh: "Tell me now, since you were there yourself, what way was it you brought my father Cumhal to his death?" "I will tell you that since you ask me," said Garraidh; "it was my own hand and the hands of the rest of the sons of Morna that made an end of him." "That is cold friendship from my followers the sons of Morna," said Finn. "If it is cold friendship," said Garraidh, "put away the liking you are letting on to have for us, and show us the hatred you have for us all the while." "If I were to lift my hand against you now, sons of Morna," said Finn, "I would be well able for you all without the help of any man." "It was by his arts Cumhal got the upper hand of us," said Garraidh; "and when he got power over us," he said, "he banished us to every far country; a share of us he sent to Alban, and a share of us to dark Lochlann, and a share of us to bright Greece, parting us from one another; and for sixteen years we were away from Ireland, and it was no small thing to us to be without seeing one another through that time. And the first day we came back to Ireland," he said, "we killed sixteen hundred men, and no lie in it, and not a man of them but would be keened by a hundred. And we took their duns after that," he said, "and we went on till we were all around one house in Munster of the red walls.

But so great was the bravery of the man in that house, that was your father, that it was easier to find him than to kill him. And we killed all that were of his race out on the hill, and then we made a quick rush at the house where Cumhal was, and every man of us made a wound on his body with his spear. And I myself was in it, and it was I gave him the first wound. And avenge it on me now, Finn, if you have a mind to," he said.

*   *   *   *   *

It was not long after that, Finn gave a feast at Almhuin for all his chief men, and there came to it two sons of the King of Alban, and sons of the kings of the great world. And when they were all sitting at the feast, the serving-men rose up and took drinking-horns worked by skilled men, and having shining stones in them, and they poured out strong drink for the champions; and it is then mirth rose up in their young men, and courage in their fighting men, and kindness and gentleness in their women, and knowledge and foreknowledge in their poets.

And then a crier rose up and shook a rough iron chain to silence the clowns and the common lads and idlers, and then he shook a chain of old silver to silence the high lords and chief men of the Fianna, and the learned men, and they all listened and were silent.

And Fergus of the True Lips rose up and sang before Finn the songs and the good poems of his forefathers; and Finn and Oisin and Lugaidh's Son rewarded him with every good thing. And then he went on to Goll, son of Morna, and told the fights and the destructions and the cattle-drivings and the courtings of his fathers; and it is well-pleased and high-minded the sons of Morna were, listening to that.

And Goll said then: "Where is my woman-messenger?" "I am here, King of the Fianna," said she. "Have you brought me my hand-tribute from the men of Lochlann?" "I have brought it surely," said she. And with that she rose up and laid on the floor of the hall before Goll a load of pure gold, the size of a good pig, and that would be a heavy load for a strong man. And Goll loosened the covering that was about it, and he gave Fergus a good reward from it as he was used to do; for there never was a wise, sharp-worded poet, or a sweet harp-player, or any learned man of Ireland or of Alban, but Goll would give him gold or silver or some good thing.

And when Finn saw that, he said: "How long is it, Goll, you have this rent on the men of Lochlann, and my own rent being on them always with it, and one of my own men, Ciaran son of Latharne, and ten hundred men of his household, guarding it and guarding my right of hunting?" And Goll saw there was anger on Finn, and he said: "It is a long time, Finn, I have that rent on the men of Lochlann, from the time your father put war and quarrels on me, and the King of Ireland joined with him, and I was made to quit Ireland by them. And I went into Britain," he said, "and I took the country and killed the king himself and did destruction on his people, but Cumhal put me out of it; and from that I went to Fionnlochlann, and the king fell by me, and his household, and Cumhal put me out of it; and I went from that to the country of the Saxons, and the king and his household fell by me, and Cumhal put me out of it. But I came back then to Ireland, and I fought a battle against your father, and he fell by me there. And it was at that time I put this rent upon the men of Lochlann. And, Finn," he said, "it is not a rent of the strong hand you have put on them, but it is a tribute for having the protection of the Fianna of Ireland, and I do not lessen that. And you need not begrudge that tribute to me," he said, "for if I had more than that again, it is to you and to the men of Ireland I would give it."

There was great anger on Finn then, and he said: "You tell me, Goll," he said, "by your own story, that you came from the city of Beirbhe to fight against my father, and that you killed him in the battle; and it is a bold thing you to tell that to me." "By your own hand," said Goll, "if you were to give me the same treatment your father gave me, I would pay you the same way as I paid him." "It would be hard for you to do that," said Finn, "for there are a hundred men in my household against every man there is in your household." "That was the same with your father," said Goll, "and I avenged my disgrace on him; and I would do the same on yourself if you earned it," he said.

Then Cairell of the White Skin, son of Finn, said: "It is many a man of Finn's household you have put down, Goll!" And Bald Conan when he heard that said: "I swear by my arms, Goll was never without having a hundred men in his household, every one of them able to get the better of yourself." "And is it to them you belong, crooked-speaking, bare-headed Conan?" said Cairell. "It is to them I belong, you black, feeble, nail-scratching, rough-skinned Cairell; and I will make you know it was Finn was in the wrong," said Conan.

With that Cairell rose up and gave a furious blow of his fist to Conan, and Conan took it with no great patience, but gave him back a blow in his teeth, and from that they went on to worse blows again. And the two sons of Goll rose up to help Conan, and Osgar went to the help of Cairell, and it was not long till many of the chief men of the Fianna were fighting on the one side or the other, on the side of Finn or on the side of the sons of Morna.

But then Fergus of the True Lips rose up, and the rest of the poets of the Fianna along with him, and they sang their songs and their poems to check and to quiet them. And they left off their fighting at the sound of the poets' songs, and they let their weapons fall on the floor, and the poets took them up, and made peace between the fighters; and they put bonds on Finn and on Goll to keep the peace for a while, till they could ask for a judgment from the High King of Ireland. And that was the end for that time of the little quarrel at Almhuin.

But it broke out again, one time there was a falling out between Finn and Goll as to the dividing of a pig of the pigs of Manannan. And at Daire Tardha, the Oak Wood of Bulls, in the province of Connacht, there was a great fight between Finn's men and the sons of Morna. And the sons of Morna were worsted, and fifteen of their men were killed; and they made their mind up that from that time they would set themselves against any friends of Finn or of his people. And it was Conan the Bald gave them that advice, for he was always bitter, and a maker of quarrels and of mischief in every place.

And they kept to their word, and spared no one. There was a yellow-haired queen that Finn loved, Berach Brec her name was, and she was wise and comely and worthy of any good man, and she had her house full of treasures, and never refused the asking of any. And any one that came to her house at Samhain time might stay till Beltaine, and have his choice then to go or to stay. And the sons of Morna had fostered her, and they went where she was and bade her to give up Finn and she need be in no dread of them. But she said she would not give up her kind lover to please them; and she was going away from them to her ship, and Art, son of Morna, made a cast of his spear that went through her body, that she died, and her people brought her up from the strand and buried her.

And as to Goll, he took a little hound that Finn thought a great deal of, Conbeg its name was, and he drowned it in the sea; and its body was brought up to shore by a wave afterwards, and it was buried under a little green hill by the Fianna. And Caoilte made a complaint over it, and he said how swift the little hound was after deer, or wild pigs, and how good at killing them, and that it was a pity it to have died, out on the cold green waves. And about that time, nine women of the Tuatha de Danaan came to meet with nine men of the Fianna, and the sons of Morna saw them coming and made an end of them.

And when Caoilte met with Goll, he made a cast of his spear at him that struck the golden helmet off his head and a piece of his flesh along with it. But Goll took it very proudly, and put on the helmet again and took up his weapons, and called out to his brothers that he was no way ashamed.

And Finn went looking for the sons of Morna in every place to do vengeance on them. They were doing robbery and destruction one time in Slieve Echtge, that got its name from Echtge, daughter of Nuada of the Silver Hand, and Finn and the Fianna were to the west, at Slieve Cairn in the district of Corcomruadh. And Finn was in doubt if the sons of Morna were gone southward into Munster or north into Connacht. So he sent Aedan and Cahal, two sons of the King of Ulster, and two hundred righting men with them, into the beautiful pleasant province of Connacht, and every day they used to go looking for the sons of Morna from place to place. But after a while the three battalions of the Fianna that were in Corcomruadh saw the track of a troop of men, and they thought it to be the track of the sons of Morna; and they closed round them at night, and made an end of them all. But when the full light came on the morrow, they knew them to be their own people, that were with the King of Ulster's sons, and they gave three great heavy cries, keening the friends they had killed in mistake.

And Caoilte and Oisin went to Rath Medba and brought a great stone and put it over the king's sons, and it was called Lia an Imracail, the Stone of the Mistake. And the place where Goll brought his men the time he parted from Finn in anger got the name of Druimscarha, the Parting Hill of Heroes.

CHAPTER II. DEATH OF GOLL

And at last it chanced that Goll and Cairell, son of Finn, met with one another, and said sharp words, and they fought in the sea near the strand, and Cairell got his death by Goll. And there was great anger and great grief on Finn, seeing his son, that was so strong and comely, lying dead and grey, like a blighted branch.

And as to Goll, he went away to a cave that was in a point stretching out into the sea; and he thought to stop there till Finn's anger would have passed.

And Osgar knew where he was, and he went to see him, that had been his comrade in so many battles. But Goll thought it was as an enemy he came, and he made a cast of his spear at him, and though Osgar got no wound by it, it struck his shield and crushed it. And Finn took notice of the way the shield was, and when he knew that Goll had made a cast at Osgar there was greater anger again on him. And he sent out his men and bade them to watch every path and every gap that led to the cave where Goll was, the way they would make an end of him.

And when Goll knew Finn to be watching for his life that way, he made no attempt to escape, but stopped where he was, without food, without drink, and he blinded with the sand that was blowing into his eyes.

And his wife came to a rock where she could speak with him, and she called to him to come to her. "Come over to me," she said; "and it is a pity you to be blinded where you are, on the rocks of the waste sea, with no drink but the salt water, a man that was first in every fight. And come now to be sleeping beside me," she said; "and in place of the hard sea-water I will nourish you from my own breast, and it is I will do your healing. And the gold of your hair is my desire for ever," she said, "and do not stop withering there like an herb in the winter-time, and my heart black with grief within me."

But Goll would not leave the spot where he was for all she could say. "It is best as it is," he said, "and I never took the advice of a woman east or west, and I never will take it. And O sweet-voiced queen," he said, "what ails you to be fretting after me; and remember now your silver and your gold, and your silks and stuffs, and remember the seven hounds I gave you at Cruadh Ceirrge, and every one of them without slackness till he has killed the deer. And do not be crying tears after me, queen with the white hands," he said; "but remember your constant lover, Aodh, the son of the best woman of the world, that came out from Spain asking for you, and that I fought at Corcar-an-Deirg; and go to him now," he said, "for it is bad when a woman is in want of a good man."

And he lay down on the rocks, and at the end of twelve days he died. And his wife keened him there, and made a great lamentation for her husband that had such a great name, and that was the second best of the Fianna of Ireland.

And when Conan heard of the death of Goll his brother, there was great anger on him, and he went to Garraidh, and asked him to go with him to Finn to ask satisfaction for Goll. "I am not willing to go," said Garraidh, "since we could get no satisfaction for the great son of Morna." "Whether you have a mind to go or not, I will go," said Conan; "and I will make an end of every man I meet with, for the sake of yellow-haired Goll; I will have the life of Oisin, Finn's great son, and of Osgar and of Caoilte and of Daire of the Songs; I will have no forgiveness for them; we must show no respect for Finn, although we may die in the fight, having no help from Goll. And let us take that work in hand, and make no delay," he said; "for if Finn is there, his strength will be there, until we put him under his flag-stone."

But it is not likely Garraidh went with him, and he after speaking such foolish words.

And what happened Conan in the end is not known. But there is a cairn of stones on a hill of Burren, near to Corcomruadh, and the people of Connacht say it is there he is buried, and that there was a stone found there one time, having on it in the old writing: "Conan the swift-footed, the bare-footed." But the Munster people say it is on their own side of Burren he is buried.

CHAPTER III. THE BATTLE OF GABHRA

Now, with one thing and another, the High King of Ireland had got to be someway bitter against Finn and the Fianna; and one time that he had a gathering of his people he spoke out to them, and he bade them to remember all the harm that had been done them through the Fianna, and all their pride, and the tribute they asked. "And as to myself," he said, "I would sooner die fighting the Fianna, if I could bring them down along with me, than live with Ireland under them the way it is now."

All his people were of the same mind, and they said they would make no delay, but would attack the Fianna and make an end of them. "And we will have good days of joy and of feasting," they said, "when once Almhuin is clear of them."

And the High King began to make plans against Finn; and he sent to all the men of Ireland to come and help him. And when all was ready, he sent and bade Osgar to come to a feast he was making at Teamhair.

And Osgar, that never was afraid before any enemy, set out for Teamhair, and three hundred of his men with him. And on the way they saw a woman of the Sidhe washing clothes at a river, and there was the colour of blood on the water where she was washing them. And Osgar said to her: "There is red on the clothes you are washing; and it is for the dead you are washing them." And the woman answered him, and it is what she said: "It is not long till the ravens will be croaking over your own head after the battle." "Is there any weakness in our eyes," said Osgar, "that a little story like that would set us crying? And do another foretelling for us now," he said, "and tell us will any man of our enemies fall by us before we ourselves are made an end of?"

"There will nine hundred fall by yourself," she said; "and the High King himself will get his death-wound from you."

Osgar and his men went on then to the king's house at Teamhair, and they got good treatment, and the feast was made ready, and they were three days at pleasure and at drinking.

And on the last day of the drinking, the High King called out with a loud voice, and he asked Osgar would he make an exchange of spears with him. "Why do you ask that exchange," said Osgar, "when I myself and my spear were often with yourself in time of battle? And you would not ask it of me," he said, "if Finn and the Fianna were with me now." "I would ask it from any fighting man among you," said the king, "and for rent and tribute along with it." "Any gold or any treasure you might ask of us, we would give it to you," said Osgar, "but it is not right for you to ask my spear." There were very high words between them then, and they threatened one another, and at the last the High King said: "I will put my spear of the seven spells out through your body." "And I give my word against that," said Osgar, "I will put my spear of the nine spells between the meeting of your hair and your beard."

With that he and his men rose up and went out of Teamhair, and they stopped to rest beside a river, and there they heard the sound of a very sorrowful tune, that was like keening, played on a harp. And there was great anger on Osgar when he heard that, and he rose up and took his arms and roused his people, and they went on again to where Finn was. And there came after them a messenger from the High King, and the message he brought was this, that he never would pay tribute to the Fianna or bear with them at all from that time.

And when Finn heard that, he sent a challenge of battle, and he gathered together all the Fianna that were left to him. But as to the sons of Morna, it was to the High King of Ireland they gathered.

And it was at the hill of Gabhra the two armies met, and there were twenty men with the King of Ireland for every man that was with Finn.

And it is a very hard battle was fought that day, and there were great deeds done on both sides; and there never was a greater battle fought in Ireland than that one.

And as to Osgar, it would be hard to tell all he killed on that day; five score of the Sons of the Gael, and five score fighting men from the Country of Snow, and seven score of the Men of Green Swords that never went a step backward, and four hundred from the Country of the Lion, and five score of the sons of kings; and the shame was for the King of Ireland.

But as to Osgar himself, that began the day so swift and so strong, at the last he was like leaves on a strong wind, or like an aspen-tree that is falling. But when he saw the High King near him, he made for him like a wave breaking on the strand; and the king saw him coming, and shook his greedy spear, and made a cast of it, and it went through his body and brought him down on his right knee, and that was the first grief of the Fianna. But Osgar himself was no way daunted, but he made a cast of his spear of the nine spells that went into the High King at the meeting of the hair and the beard, and gave him his death. And when the men nearest to the High King saw that, they put the king's helmet up on a pillar, the way his people would think he was living yet. But Osgar saw it, and he lifted a thin bit of a slab-stone that was on the ground beside him, and he made a cast of it that broke the helmet where it was; and then he himself fell like a king.

And there fell in that battle the seven sons of Caoilte, and the son of the King of Lochlann that had come to give them his help, and it would be hard to count the number of the Fianna that fell in that battle.

And when it was ended, those that were left of them went looking for their dead. And Caoilte stooped down over his seven brave sons, and every living man of the Fianna stooped over his own dear friends. And it was a lasting grief to see all that were stretched in that place, but the Fianna would not have taken it to heart the way they did, but for being as they were, a beaten race.

And as to Oisin, he went looking for Osgar, and it is the way he found him, lying stretched, and resting on his left arm and his broken shield beside him, and his sword in his hand yet, and his blood about him on every side. And he put out his hand to Oisin, and Oisin took it and gave out a very hard cry. And Osgar said: "It is glad I am to see you safe, my father." And Oisin had no answer to give him. And just then Caoilte came where they were, and he looked at Osgar. "What way are you now, my darling?" he said. "The way you would like me to be," said Osgar.

Then Caoilte searched the wound, and when he saw how the spear had torn its way through to the back, he cried out, and a cloud came over him and his strength failed him. "O Osgar," he said, "you are parted from the Fianna, and they themselves must be parted from battle from this out," he said, "and they must pay their tribute to the King of Ireland."

Then Caoilte and Oisin raised up Osgar on their shields and brought him to a smooth green hill till they would take his dress off. And there was not a handsbreadth of his white body that was without a wound.

And when the rest of the Fianna saw what way Osgar was, there was not a man of them that keened his own son or his brother, but every one of them came keening Osgar.

And after a while, at noonday, they saw Finn coming towards them, and what was left of the Sun-banner raised on a spear-shaft. All of them saluted Finn then, but he made no answer, and he came up to the hill where Osgar was. And when Osgar saw him coming he saluted him, and he said: "I have got my desire in death, Finn of the sharp arms." And Finn said: "It is worse the way you were, my son, on the day of the battle at Beinn Edair when the wild geese could swim on your breast, and it was my hand that gave you healing." "There can no healing be done for me now for ever," said Osgar, "since the King of Ireland put the spear of seven spells through my body." And Finn said: "It is a pity it was not I myself fell in sunny scarce Gabhra, and you going east and west at the head of the Fianna." "And if it was yourself fell in the battle," said Osgar, "you would not hear me keening after you; for no man ever knew any heart in me," he said, "but a heart of twisted horn, and it covered with iron. But the howling of the dogs beside me," he said, "and the keening of the old righting men, and the crying of the women one after another, those are the things that are vexing me." And Finn said: "Child of my child, calf of my calf, white and slender, it is a pity the way you are. And my heart is starting like a deer," he said, "and I am weak after you and after the Fianna of Ireland. And misfortune has followed us," he said; "and farewell now to battles and to a great name, and farewell to taking tributes; for every good thing I ever had is gone from me now," he said.

And when Osgar heard those words he stretched out his hands, and his eyelids closed. And Finn turned away from the rest, and he cried tears down; and he never shed a tear through the whole length of his lifetime but only for Osgar and for Bran.

And all that were left of the Fianna gave three gorrowful cries after Osgar, for there was not one of the Fianna beyond him, unless it might be Finn or Oisin.

And it is many of the Fianna were left dead in Gabhra, and graves were made for them. And as to Lugaidh's Son, that was so tall a man and so good a fighter, they made a very wide grave for him, as was fitting for a king. And the whole length of the rath at Gabhra, from end to end, it is that was the grave of Osgar, son of Oisin, son of Finn.

And as to Finn himself, he never had peace or pleasure again from that day.

BOOK TEN: THE END OF THE FIANNA.

CHAPTER I. DEATH OF BRAN

One day Finn was hunting, and Bran went following after a fawn. And they were coming towards Finn, and the fawn called out, and it said: "If I go into the sea below I will never come back again; and if I go up into the air above me, it will not save me from Bran." For Bran would overtake the wild geese, she was that swift.

"Go out through my legs," said Finn then. So the fawn did that, and Bran followed her; and as Bran went under him, Finn squeezed his two knees on her, that she died on the moment.

And there was great grief on him after that, and he cried tears down the same as he did when Osgar died.

And some said it was Finn's mother the fawn was, and that it was to save his mother he killed Bran. But that is not likely, for his mother was beautiful Muirne, daughter of Tadg, son of Nuada of the Tuatha de Danaan, and it was never heard that she was changed into a fawn. It is more likely it was Oisin's mother was in it.

But some say Bran and Sceolan are still seen to start at night out of the thicket on the hill of Almhuin.

CHAPTER II. THE CALL OF OISIN

One misty morning, what were left of the Fianna were gathered together to Finn, and it is sorrowful and downhearted they were after the loss of so many of their comrades.

And they went hunting near the borders of Loch Lein, where the bushes were in blossom and the birds were singing; and they were waking up the deer that were as joyful as the leaves of a tree in summer-time.

And it was not long till they saw coming towards them from the west a beautiful young woman, riding on a very fast slender white horse. A queen's crown she had on her head, and a dark cloak of silk down to the ground, having stars of red gold on it; and her eyes were blue and as clear as the dew on the grass, and a gold ring hanging down from every golden lock of her hair; and her cheeks redder than the rose, and her skin whiter than the swan upon the wave, and her lips as sweet as honey that is mixed through red wine.

And in her hand she was holding a bridle having a golden bit, and there was a saddle worked with red gold under her. And as to the horse, he had a wide smooth cloak over him, and a silver crown on the back of his head, and he was shod with shining gold.

She came to where Finn was, and she spoke with a very kind, gentle voice, and she said: "It is long my journey was, King of the Fianna." And Finn asked who was she, and what was her country and the cause of her coming. "Niamh of the Golden Head is my name," she said; "and I have a name beyond all the women of the world, for I am the daughter of the King of the Country of the Young." "What was it brought you to us from over the sea, Queen?" said Finn then. "Is it that your husband is gone from you, or what is the trouble that is on you?" "My husband is not gone from me," she said, "for I never went yet to any man. But O King of the

Fianna," she said, "I have given my love and my affection to your own son, Oisin of the strong hands." "Why did you give your love to him beyond all the troops of high princes that are under the sun?" said Finn. "It was by reason of his great name, and of the report I heard of his bravery and of his comeliness," she said. "And though there is many a king's son and high prince gave me his love, I never consented to any till I set my love on Oisin."

When Oisin heard what she was saying, there was not a limb of his body that was not in love with beautiful Niamh; and he took her hand in his hand, and he said: "A true welcome before you to this country, young queen. It is you are the shining one," he said; "it is you are the nicest and the comeliest; it is you are better to me than any other woman; it is you are my star and my choice beyond the women of the entire world." "I put on you the bonds of a true hero," said Niamh then, "you to come away with me now to the Country of the Young." And it is what she said:

"It is the country is most delightful of all that are under the sun; the trees are stooping down with fruit and with leaves and with blossom.

"Honey and wine are plentiful there, and everything the eye has ever seen; no wasting will come on you with the wasting away of time; you will never see death or lessening.

"You will get feasts, playing and drinking; you will get sweet music on the strings; you will get silver and gold and many jewels.

"You will get, and no lie in it, a hundred swords; a hundred cloaks of the dearest silk; a hundred horses, the quickest in battle; a hundred willing hounds.

"You will get the royal crown of the King of the Young that he never gave to any one under the sun. It will be a shelter to you night and day in every rough fight and in every battle.

"You will get a right suit of armour; a sword, gold-hilted, apt for striking; no one that ever saw it got away alive from it.

"A hundred coats of armour and shirts of satin; a hundred cows and a hundred calves; a hundred sheep having golden fleeces; a hundred jewels that are not of this world.

"A hundred glad young girls shining like the sun, their voices sweeter than the music of birds; a hundred armed men strong in battle, apt at feats, waiting on you, if you will come with me to the Country of the Young.

"You will get everything I have said to you, and delights beyond them, that I have no leave to tell; you will get beauty, strength and power, and I myself will be with you as a wife."

And after she had made that song, Oisin said: "O pleasant golden-haired queen, you are my choice beyond the women of the world; and I will go with you willingly," he said.

And with that he kissed Finn his father and bade him farewell, and he bade farewell to the rest of the Fianna, and he went up then on the horse with Niamh.

And the horse set out gladly, and when he came to the strand he shook himself and he neighed three times, and then he made for the sea. And when Finn and the Fianna saw Oisin facing the wide sea, they gave three great sorrowful shouts. And as to Finn, he said: "It is my grief to see you going from me; and I am without a hope," he said, "ever to see you coming back to me again."

CHAPTER III. THE LAST OF THE GREAT MEN

And indeed that was the last time Finn and Oisin and the rest of the Fianna of Ireland were gathered together, for hunting, for battle, for chessplaying, for drinking or for music; for they all wore away after that, one after another.

As to Caoilte, that was old and had lost his sons, he used to be fretting and lonesome after the old times. And one day that there was very heavy snow on the ground, he made this complaint:--

"It is cold the winter is; the wind is risen; the fierce high-couraged stag rises up; it is cold the whole mountain is to-night, yet the fierce stag is calling. The deer of Slievecarn of the gatherings does not lay his side to the ground; he no less than the stag of the top of cold Echtge hears the music of the wolves.

"I, Caoilte, and brown-haired Diarmuid and pleasant light-footed Osgar, we used to be listening to the music of the wolves through the end of the cold night. It is well the brown deer sleeps with its hide to the hollow, hidden as if in the earth, through the end of the cold night.

"To-day I am in my age, and I know but a few men; I used to shake my spear bravely in the ice-cold morning. It is often I put silence on a great army that is very cold to-night."

And after a while he went into a hill of the Sidhe to be healed of his old wounds. And whether he came back from there or not is not known; and there are some that say he used to be talking with Patrick of the Bells the same time Oisin was with him. But that is not likely, or Oisin would not have made complaints about his loneliness the way he did.

But a long time after that again, there was a king of Ireland making a journey. And he and his people missed their way, and when night-time came on, they were in a dark wood, and no path before them.

And there came to them a very tall man, that was shining like a burning flame, and he took hold of the bridle of the king's horse, and led him through the wood till they came to the right road. And the King of Ireland asked him who was he, and first he said: "I am your candlestick"; and then he said: "I was with Finn one time." And the king knew it was Caoilte, son of Ronan, was in it.

And three times nine of the rest of the Fianna came out of the west one time to Teamhair. And they took notice that now they were wanting their full strength and their great name, no one took notice of them or came to speak with them at all. And when they saw that, they lay down on the side of the hill at Teamhair, and put their lips to the earth and died.

And for three days and a month and a year from the time of the destruction of the Fianna of Ireland, Loch Dearg was under mists.

        *   *   *   *   *

And as to Finn, there are some say he died by the hand of a fisherman; but it is likely that is not true, for that would be no death for so great a man as Finn, son of Cumhal. And there are some say he never died, but is alive in some place yet.

And one time a smith made his way into a cave he saw, that had a door to it, and he made a key that opened it. And when he went in he saw a very wide place, and very big men lying on the floor. And one that was bigger than the rest was lying in the middle, and the Dord Fiann beside him; and he knew it was Finn and the Fianna were in it.

And the smith took hold of the Dord Fiann, and it is hardly he could lift it to his mouth, and he blew a very strong blast on it, and the sound it made was so great, it is much the rocks did not come down on him. And at the sound, the big men lying on the ground shook from head to foot. He gave another blast then, and they all turned on their elbows.

And great dread came on him when he saw that, and he threw down the Dord Fiann and ran from the cave and locked the door after him, and threw the key into the lake. And he heard them crying after him, "You left us worse than you found us." And the cave was not found again since that time.

But some say the day will come when the Dord Fiann will be sounded three times, and that at the sound of it the Fianna will rise up as strong and as well as ever they were. And there are some say Finn, son of Cumhal, has been on the earth now and again since the old times, in the shape of one of the heroes of Ireland.

And as to the great things he and his men did when they were together, it is well they have been kept in mind through the poets of Ireland and of Alban. And one night there were two men minding sheep in a valley, and they were saying the poems of the Fianna while they were there. And they saw two very tall shapes on the two hills on each side of the valley, and one of the tall shapes said to the other: "Do you hear that man down below? I was the second doorpost of battle at Gabhra, and that man knows all about it better than myself."

BOOK ELEVEN: OISIN AND PATRICK.

CHAPTER I. OISIN'S STORY

As to Oisin, it was a long time after he was brought away by Niamh that he came back again to Ireland. Some say it was hundreds of years he was in the Country of the Young, and some say it was thousands of years he was in it; but whatever time it was, it seemed short to him.

And whatever happened him through the time he was away, it is a withered old man he was found after coming back to Ireland, and his white horse going away from him, and he lying on the ground.

And it was S. Patrick had power at that time, and it was to him Oisin was brought; and he kept him in his house, and used to be teaching him and questioning him. And Oisin was no way pleased with the way Ireland was then, but he used to be talking of the old times, and fretting after the Fianna.

And Patrick bade him to tell what happened him the time he left Finn and the Fianna and went away with Niamh. And it is the story Oisin told:--"The time I went away with golden-haired Niamh, we turned our backs to the land, and our faces westward, and the sea was going away before us, and filling up in waves after us. And we saw wonderful things on our journey," he said, "cities and courts and duns and lime-white houses, and shining sunny-houses and palaces. And one time we saw beside us a hornless deer running hard, and an eager white red-eared hound following after it. And another time we saw a young girl on a horse and having a golden apple in her right hand, and she going over the tops of the waves; and there was following after her a young man riding a white horse, and having a crimson cloak and a gold-hilted sword in his right hand."

"Follow on with your story, pleasant Oisin," said Patrick, "for you did not tell us yet what was the country you went to."

"The Country of the Young, the Country of Victory, it was," said Oisin. "And O Patrick," he said, "there is no lie in that name; and if there are grandeurs in your Heaven the same as there are there, I would give my friendship to God.

"We turned our backs then to the dun," he said, "and the horse under us was quicker than the spring wind on the backs of the mountains. And it was not long till the sky darkened, and the wind rose in every part, and the sea was as if on fire, and there was nothing to be seen of the sun.

"But after we were looking at the clouds and the stars for a while the wind went down, and the storm, and the sun brightened. And we saw before us a very delightful country under full blossom, and smooth plains in it, and a king's dun that was very grand, and that had every colour in it, and sunny-houses beside it, and palaces of shining stones, made by skilled men. And we saw coming out to meet us three fifties of armed men, very lively and handsome. And I asked Niamh was this the Country of the Young, and she said it was. 'And indeed, Oisin,' she said, 'I told you no lie about it, and you will see all I promised you before you for ever.'

"And there came out after that a hundred beautiful young girls, having cloaks of silk worked with gold, and they gave me a welcome to their own country. And after that there came a great shining army, and with it a strong beautiful king, having a shirt of yellow silk and a golden cloak over it, and a very bright crown on his head. And there was following after him a young queen, and fifty young girls along with her.

"And when all were come to the one spot, the king took me by the hand, and he said out before them all: 'A hundred thousand welcomes before you, Oisin, son of Finn. And as to this country you are come to,' he said, 'I will tell you news of it without a lie. It is long and lasting your life will be in it, and you yourself will be young for ever. And there is no delight the heart ever thought of,' he said, 'but it is here against your coming. And you can believe my words, Oisin,' he said, 'for I myself am the King of the Country of the Young, and this is its comely queen, and it was golden-headed Niamh our daughter that went over the sea looking for you to be her husband for ever.' I gave thanks to him then, and I stooped myself down before the queen, and we went forward to the royal house, and all the high nobles came out to meet us, both men and women, and there was a great feast made there through the length of ten days and ten nights.

"And that is the way I married Niamh of the Golden Hair, and that is the way I went to the Country of the Young, although it is sorrowful to me to be telling it now, O Patrick from Rome," said Oisin.

"Follow on with your story, Oisin of the destroying arms," said Patrick, "and tell me what way did you leave the Country of the Young, for it is long to me till I hear that; and tell us now had you any children by Niamh, and was it long you were in that place."

"Two beautiful children I had by Niamh," said Oisin, "two young sons and a comely daughter. And Niamh gave the two sons the name of Finn and of Osgar, and the name I gave to the daughter was The Flower.

"And I did not feel the time passing, and it was a long time I stopped there," he said, "till the desire came on me to see Finn and my comrades again. And I asked leave of the king and of Niamh to go back to Ireland. 'You will get leave from me,' said Niamh; 'but for all that,' she said, 'it is bad news you are giving me, for I am in dread you will never come back here again through the length of your days.' But I bade her have no fear, since the white horse would bring me safe back again from Ireland. 'Bear this in mind, Oisin,' she said then, 'if you once get off the horse while you are away, or if you once put your foot to ground, you will never come back here again. And O Oisin,' she said, 'I tell it to you now for the third time, if you once get down from the horse, you will be an old man, blind and withered, without liveliness, without mirth, without running, without leaping. And it is a grief to me, Oisin,' she said, 'you ever to go back to green Ireland; and it is not now as it used to be, and you will not see Finn and his people, for there is not now in the whole of Ireland but a Father of Orders and armies of saints; and here is my kiss for you, pleasant Oisin,' she said, 'for you will never come back any more to the Country of the Young.'

"And that is my story, Patrick, and I have told you no lie in it," said Oisin. "And O Patrick," he said, "if I was the same the day I came here as I was that day, I would have made an end of all your clerks, and there would not be a head left on a neck after me."

"Go on with your story," said Patrick, "and you will get the same good treatment from me you got from Finn, for the sound of your voice is pleasing to me."

So Oisin went on with his story, and it is what he said: "I have nothing to tell of my journey till I came back into green Ireland, and I looked about me then on all sides, but there were no tidings to be got of Finn. And it was not long till I saw a great troop of riders, men and women, coming towards me from the west. And when they came near they wished me good health; and there was wonder on them all when they looked at me, seeing me so unlike themselves, and so big and so tall.

"I asked them then did they hear if Finn was still living, or any other one of the Fianna, or what had happened them. 'We often heard of Finn that lived long ago,' said they, 'and that there never was his equal for strength or bravery or a great name; and there is many a book written down,' they said, 'by the sweet poets of the Gael, about his doings and the doings of the Fianna, and it would be hard for us to tell you all of them. And we heard Finn had a son,' they said, 'that was beautiful and shining, and that there came a young girl looking for him, and he went away with her to the Country of the Young.'

"And when I knew by their talk that Finn was not living or any of the Fianna, it is downhearted I was, and tired, and very sorrowful after them. And I made no delay, but I turned my face and went on to Almhuin of Leinster. And there was great wonder on me when I came there to see no sign at all of Finn's great dun, and his great hall, and nothing in the place where it was but weeds and nettles."

And there was grief on Oisin then, and he said: "Och, Patrick! Och, ochone, my grief! It is a bad journey that was to me; and to be without tidings of Finn or the Fianna has left me under pain through my lifetime."

"Leave off fretting, Oisin," said Patrick, "and shed your tears to the God of grace. Finn and the Fianna are slack enough now, and they will get no help for ever." "It is a great pity that would be," said Oisin, "Finn to be in pain for ever; and who was it gained the victory over him, when his own hand had made an end of so many a hard fighter?"

"It is God gained the victory over Finn," said Patrick, "and not the strong hand of an enemy; and as to the Fianna, they are condemned to hell along with him, and tormented for ever."

"O Patrick," said Oisin, "show me the place where Finn and his people are, and there is not a hell or a heaven there but I will put it down. And if Osgar, my own son, is there," he said, "the hero that was bravest in heavy battles, there is not in hell or in the Heaven of God a troop so great that he could not destroy it."

"Let us leave off quarrelling on each side now," said Patrick; "and go on, Oisin, with your story. What happened you after you knew the Fianna to be at an end?"

"I will tell you that, Patrick," said Oisin. "I was turning to go away, and I saw the stone trough that the Fianna used to be putting their hands in, and it full of water. And when I saw it I had such a wish and such a feeling for it that I forgot what I was told, and I got off the horse. And in the minute all the years came on me, and I was lying on the ground, and the horse took fright and went away and left me there, an old man, weak and spent, without sight, without shape, without comeliness, without strength or understanding, without respect.

"There, Patrick, is my story for you now," said Oisin, "and no lie in it, of all that happened me going away and coming back again from the Country of the Young."

CHAPTER II. OISIN IN PATRICK'S HOUSE

And Oisin stopped on with S. Patrick, but he was not very well content with the way he was treated. And one time he said: "They say I am getting food, but God knows I am not, or drink; and I Oisin, son of Finn, under a yoke, drawing stones." "It is my opinion you are getting enough," said S. Patrick then, "and you getting a quarter of beef and a churn of butter and a griddle of bread every day." "I often saw a quarter of a blackbird bigger than your quarter of beef," said Oisin, "and a rowan berry as big as your churn of butter, and an ivy leaf as big as your griddle of bread." S, Patrick was vexed when he heard that, and he said to Oisin that he had told a lie.

There was great anger on Oisin then, and he went where there was a litter of pups, and he bade a serving-boy to nail up the hide of a freshly killed bullock to the wall, and to throw the pups against it one by one. And every one that he threw fell down from the hide till it came to the last, and he held on to it with his teeth and his nails. "Rear that one," said Oisin, "and drown all the rest."

Then he bade the boy to keep the pup in a dark place, and to care it well, and never to let it taste blood or see the daylight. And at the end of a year, Oisin was so well pleased with the pup, that he gave it the name of Bran Og, young Bran.

And one day he called to the serving-boy to come on a journey with him, and to bring the pup in a chain. And they set out and passed by Slieve-nam-ban, where the witches of the Sidhe do be spinning with their spinning-wheels; and then they turned eastward into Gleann-na-Smol. And Oisin raised a rock that was there, and he bade the lad take from under it three things, a great sounding horn of the Fianna, and a ball of iron they had for throwing, and a very sharp sword. And when Oisin saw those things, he took them in his hands, and he said: "My thousand farewells to the day when you were put here!" He bade the lad to clean them well then; and when he had done that, he bade him to sound a blast on the horn. So the boy did that, and Oisin asked him did he see anything strange. "I did not," said the boy. "Sound it again as loud as you can," said Oisin. "That is as hard as I can sound it, and I can see nothing yet," said the boy when he had done that. Then Oisin took the horn himself, and he put it to his mouth, and blew three great blasts on it. "What do you see now?" he said. "I see three great clouds coming," he said, "and they are settling down in the valley; and the first cloud is a flight of very big birds, and the second cloud is a flight of birds that are bigger again, and the third flight is of the biggest and the blackest birds the world ever saw."

"What is the dog doing?" said Oisin. "The eyes are starting from his head, and there is not a rib of hair on him but is standing up." "Let him loose now," said Oisin.

The dog rushed down to the valley then, and he made an attack on one of the birds, that was the biggest of all, and that had a shadow like a cloud. And they fought a very fierce fight, but at last Bran Og made an end of the big bird, and lapped its blood. But if he did, madness came on him, and he came rushing back towards Oisin, his jaws open and his eyes like fire. "There is dread on me, Oisin," said the boy, "for the dog is making for us, mad and raging." "Take this iron ball and make a cast at him when he comes near," said Oisin. "I am in dread to do that," said the boy. "Put it in my hand, and turn it towards him," said Oisin. The boy did that, and Oisin made a cast of the ball that went into the mouth and the throat of the dog, and choked him, and he fell down the slope, twisting and foaming.

Then they went where the great bird was left dead, and Oisin bade the lad to cut a quarter off it with the sword, and he did so. And then he bade him cut open the body, and in it he found a rowan berry, the biggest he had ever seen, and an ivy leaf that was bigger than the biggest griddle.

So Oisin turned back then, and went to where S. Patrick was, and he showed him the quarter of the bird that was bigger than any quarter of a bullock, and the rowan berry that was bigger than a churning of butter, and the leaf. "And you know now, Patrick of the Bells," he said, "that I told no lie; and it is what kept us all through our lifetime," he said, "truth that was in our hearts, and strength in our arms, and fulfilment in our tongues."

"You told no lie indeed," said Patrick.

And when Oisin had no sight left at all, he used every night to put up one of the serving-men on his shoulders, and to bring him out to see how were the cattle doing. And one night the servants had no mind to go, and they agreed together to tell him it was a very bad night.

And it is what the first of them said; "It is outside there is a heavy sound with the heavy water dropping from the tops of trees; the sound of the waves is not to be heard for the loud splashing of the rain." And then the next one said: "The trees of the wood are shivering, and the birch is turning black; the snow is killing the birds; that is the story outside." And the third said: "It is to the east they have turned their face, the white snow and the dark rain; it is what is making the plain so cold is the snow that is dripping and getting hard."

But there was a serving-girl in the house, and she said: "Rise up, Oisin, and go out to the white-headed cows, since the cold wind is plucking the trees from the hills."

Oisin went out then, and the serving-man on his shoulders; but it is what the serving-man did, he brought a vessel of water and a birch broom with him, and he was dashing water in Oisin's face, the way he would think it was rain. But when they came to the pen where the cattle were, Oisin found the night was quiet, and after that he asked no more news of the weather from the servants.

CHAPTER III. THE ARGUMENTS

And S. Patrick took in hand to convert Oisin, and to bring him to baptism; but it was no easy work he had to do, and everything he would say, Oisin would have an answer for it. And it is the way they used to be talking and arguing with one another, as it was put down afterwards by the poets of Ireland:--

PATRICK. "Oisin, it is long your sleep is. Rise up and listen to the Psalm. Your strength and your readiness are gone from you, though you used to be going into rough fights and battles."

OLSIN. "My readiness and my strength are gone from me since Finn has no armies living; I have no liking for clerks, their music is not sweet to me after his."

PATRICK. "You never heard music so good from the beginning of the world to this day; it is well you would serve an army on a hill, you that are old and silly and grey."

OLSIN. "I used to serve an army on a hill, Patrick of the closed-up mind; it is a pity you to be faulting me; there was never shame put on me till now.

"I have heard music was sweeter than your music, however much you are praising your clerks: the song of the blackbird in Leiter Laoi, and the sound of the Dord Fiann; the very sweet thrush of the Valley of the Shadow, or the sound of the boats striking the strand. The cry of the hounds was better to me than the noise of your schools, Patrick.

"Little Nut, little Nut of my heart, the little dwarf that was with Finn, when he would make tunes and songs he would put us all into deep sleep.

"The twelve hounds that belonged to Finn, the time they would be let loose facing out from the Siuir, their cry was sweeter than harps and than pipes.

"I have a little story about Finn; we were but fifteen men; we took the King of the Saxons of the feats, and we won a battle against the King of Greece.

"We fought nine battles in Spain, and nine times twenty battles in Ireland; from Lochlann and from the eastern world there was a share of gold coming to Finn.

"My grief! I to be stopping after him, and without delight in games or in music; to be withering away after my comrades; my grief it is to be living. I and the clerks of the Mass books are two that can never agree.

"If Finn and the Fianna were living, I would leave the clerks and the bells; I would follow the deer through the valleys, I would like to be close on his track.

"Ask Heaven of God, Patrick, for Finn of the Fianna and his race; make prayers for the great man; you never heard of his like."

PATRICK. "I will not ask Heaven for Finn, man of good wit that my anger is rising against, since his delight was to be living in valleys with the noise of hunts."

OISIN. "If you had been in company with the Fianna, Patrick of the joyless clerks and of the bells, you would not be attending on schools or giving heed to God."

PATRICK. "I would not part from the Son of God for all that have lived east or west; O Oisin, O shaking poet, there will harm come on you in satisfaction for the priests."

OISIN. "It was a delight to Finn the cry of his hounds on the mountains, the wild dogs leaving their harbours, the pride of his armies, those were his delights."

PATRICK. "There was many a thing Finn took delight in, and there is not much heed given to it after him; Finn and his hounds are not living now, and you yourself will not always be living, Oisin."

OISIN. "There is a greater story of Finn than of us, or of any that have lived in our time; all that are gone and all that are living, Finn was better to give out gold than themselves."

PATRICK. "All the gold you and Finn used to be giving out, it is little it does for you now; he is in Hell in bonds because he did treachery and oppression."

OISIN. "It is little I believe of your truth, man from Rome with the white books, Finn the open-handed head of the Fianna to be in the hands of devils or demons."

PATRICK. "Finn is in bonds in Hell, the pleasant man that gave out gold; in satisfaction for his disrespect to God, he is under grief in the house of pain."

OISIN. "If the sons of Morna were within it, or the strong men of the sons of Baiscne, they would take Finn out of it, or they would have the house for themselves."

PATRICK. "If the five provinces of Ireland were within it, or the strong seven battalions of the Fianna, they would not be able to bring Finn out of it, however great their strength might be."

OISIN. "If Faolan and Goll were living, and brown-haired Diarmuid and brave Osgar, Finn of the Fianna could not be held in any house that was made by God or devils."

PATRICK. "If Faolan and Goll were living, and all the Fianna that ever were, they could not bring out Finn from the house where he is in pain."

OISIN. "What did Finn do against God but to be attending on schools and on armies? Giving gold through a great part of his time, and for another while trying his hounds."

PATRICK. "In payment for thinking of his hounds and for serving the schools of the poets, and because he gave no heed to God, Finn of the Fianna is held down."

OISIN. "You say, Patrick of the Psalms, that the Fianna could not take out Finn, or the five provinces of Ireland along with them.

"I have a little story about Finn. We were but fifteen men when we took the King of Britain of the feasts by the strength of our spears and our own strength.

"We took Magnus the great, the son of the King of Lochlann of the speckled ships; we came back no way sorry or tired, we put our rent on far places.

"O Patrick, the story is pitiful, the King of the Fianna to be under locks; a heart without envy, without hatred, a heart hard in earning victory.

"It is an injustice, God to be unwilling to give food and riches; Finn never refused strong or poor, although cold Hell is now his dwelling-place.

"It is what Finn had a mind for, to be listening to the sound of Druim Dearg; to sleep at the stream of Ess Ruadh, to be hunting the deer of Gallimh of the bays.

"The cries of the blackbird of Leiter Laoi, the wave of Rudraighe beating the strand, the bellowing of the ox of Magh Maoin, the lowing of the calf of Gleann da Mhail.

"The noise of the hunt on Slieve Crot, the sound of the fawns round Slieve Cua, the scream of the sea-gulls there beyond on Iorrus, the screech of the crows over the battle.

"The waves vexing the breasts of the boats, the howling of the hounds at Druim Lis; the voice of Bran on Cnoc-an-Air, the outcry of the streams about Slieve Mis.

"The call of Osgar going to the hunt; the voice of the hounds on the road of the Fianna, to be listening to them and to the poets, that was always his desire.

"A desire of the desires of Osgar was to listen to the striking of shields; to be hacking at bones in a battle, it is what he had a mind for always.

"We went westward one time to hunt at Formaid of the Fianna, to see the first running of our hounds.

"It was Finn was holding Bran, and it is with myself Sceolan was; Diarmuid of the Women had Fearan, and Osgar had lucky Adhnuall.

"Conan the Bald had Searc; Caoilte, son of Ronan, had Daol; Lugaidh's Son and Goll were holding Fuaim and Fothran.

"That was the first day we loosed out a share of our hounds to a hunting; and Och! Patrick, of all that were in it, there is not one left living but myself.

"O Patrick, it is a pity the way I am now, a spent old man without sway, without quickness, without strength, going to Mass at the altar.

"Without the great deer of Slieve Luchra; without the hares of Slieve Cuilinn; without going into fights with Finn; without listening to the poets.

"Without battles, without taking of spoils; without playing at nimble feats; without going courting or hunting, two trades that were my delight."

PATRICK. "Leave off, old man, leave your foolishness; let what you have done be enough for you from this out. Think on the pains that are before you; the Fianna are gone, and you yourself will be going."

OISIN. "If I go, may yourself not be left after me, Patrick of the hindering heart; if Conan, the least of the Fianna, were living, your buzzing would not be left long to you."

"Or if this was the day I gave ten hundred cows to the headless woman that came to the Valley of the Two Oxen; the birds of the air brought away the ring I gave her, I never knew where she went herself from me."

PATRICK. "That is little to trouble you, Oisin; it was but for a while she was with you; it is better for you to be as you are than to be among them again."

OISIN. "O Son of Calphurn of the friendly talk, it is a pity for him that gives respect to clerks and bells; I and Caoilte my friend, we were not poor when we were together.

"The music that put Finn to his sleep was the cackling of the ducks from the lake of the Three Narrows; the scolding talk of the blackbird of Doire an Cairn, the bellowing of the ox from the Valley of the Berries.

"The whistle of the eagle from the Valley of Victories, or from the rough branches of the ridge by the stream; the grouse of the heather of Cruachan; the call of the otter of Druim-re-Coir.

"The song of the blackbird of Doire an Cairn indeed I never heard sweeter music, if I could be under its nest.

"My grief that I ever took baptism; it is little credit I got by it, being without food, without drink, doing fasting and praying."

PATRICK. "In my opinion it did not harm you, old man; you will get nine score cakes of bread, wine and meat to put a taste on it; it is bad talk you are giving."

OISIN. "This mouth that is talking with you, may it never confess to a priest, if I would not sooner have the leavings of Finn's house than a share of your own meals."

PATRICK. "He got but what he gathered from the banks, or whatever he could kill on the rough hills; he got hell at the last because of his unbelief."

OISIN. "That was not the way with us at all, but our fill of wine and of meat; justice and a right beginning at the feasts, sweet drinks and every one drinking them.

"It is fretting after Diarmuid and Goll I am, and after Fergus of the True Lips, the time you will not let me be speaking of them, O new Patrick from Rome."

PATRICK. "We would give you leave to be speaking of them, but first you should give heed to God. Since you are now at the end of your days, leave your foolishness, weak old man."

OISIN. "O Patrick, tell me as a secret, since it is you have the best knowledge, will my dog or my hound be let in with me to the court of the King of Grace?"

PATRICK. "Old man in your foolishness that I cannot put any bounds to, your dog or your hound will not be let in with you to the court of the King of Power."

OISIN. "If I had acquaintance with God, and my hound to be at hand, I would make whoever gave food to myself give a share to my hound as well.

"One strong champion that was with the Fianna of Ireland would be better than the Lord of Piety, and than you yourself, Patrick."

PATRICK. "O Oisin of the sharp blades, it is mad words you are saying. God is better for one day than the whole of the Fianna of Ireland."

OISIN. "Though I am now without sway and my life is spent to the end, do not put abuse, Patrick, on the great men of the sons of Baiscne.

"If I had Conan with me, the man that used to be running down the Fianna, it is he would break your head within among your clerks and your priests."

PATRICK. "It is a silly thing, old man, to be talking always of the Fianna; remember your end is come, and take the Son of God to help you."

OISIN. "I used to sleep out on the mountain under the grey dew; I was never used to go to bed without food, while there was a deer on the hill beyond."

PATRICK. "You are astray at the end of your life between the straight way and the crooked. Keep out from the crooked path of pains, and the angels of God will come beneath your head."

OISIN. "If myself and open-handed Fergus and Diarmuid were together now on this spot, we would go in every path we ever went in, and ask no leave of the priests."

PATRICK. "Leave off, Oisin; do not be speaking against the priests that are telling the word of God in every place. Unless you leave off your daring talk, it is great pain you will have in the end."

OISIN. "When myself and the leader of the Fianna were looking for a boar in a valley, it was worse to me not to see it than all your clerks to be without their heads."

PATRICK. "It is pitiful seeing you without sense; that is worse to you than your blindness; if you were to get sight within you, it is great your desire would be for Heaven."

OISIN. "It is little good it would be to me to be sitting in that city, without Caoilte, without Osgar, without my father being with me.

"The leap of the buck would be better to me, or the sight of badgers between two valleys, than all your mouth is promising me, and all the delights I could get in Heaven."

PATRICK. "Your thoughts are foolish, they will come to nothing; your pleasure and your mirth are gone. Unless you will take my advice to-night, you will not get leave on this side or that."

OISIN. "If myself and the Fianna were on the top of a hill to-day drawing our spear-heads, we would have our choice of being here or there in spite of books and priests and bells."

PATRICK. "You were like the smoke of a wisp, or like a stream in a valley, or like a whirling wind on the top of a hill, every tribe of you that ever lived."

OISIN. "If I was in company with the people of strong arms, the way I was at Bearna da Coill, I would sooner be looking at them than at this troop of the crooked croziers.

"If I had Scolb Sceine with me, or Osgar, that was smart in battles, I would not be without meat to-night at the sound of the bell of the seven tolls."

PATRICK. "Oisin, since your wits are gone from you be glad at what I say; it is certain to me you will leave the Fianna and that you will receive the God of the stars."

OISIN. "There is wonder on me at your hasty talk, priest that has travelled in every part, to say that I would part from the Fianna, a generous people, never niggardly."

PATRICK. "If you saw the people of God, the way they are settled at feasts, every good thing is more plentiful with them than with Finn's people, however great their name was.

"Finn and the Fianna are lying now very sorrowful on the flag-stone of pain; take the Son of God in their place; make your repentance and do not lose Heaven."

OISIN. "I do not believe your talk now. O Patrick of the crooked staves, Finn and the Fianna to be there within, unless they find pleasure being in it."

PATRICK. "Make right repentance now, before you know when your end is coming; God is better for one hour than the whole of the Fianna of Ireland."

OISIN. "That is a daring answer to make to me, Patrick of the crooked crozier; your crozier would be in little bits if I had Osgar with me now.

"If my son Osgar and God were hand to hand on the Hill of the Fianna, if I saw my son put down, I would say that God was a strong man.

"How could it be that God or his priests could be better men than Finn, the King of the Fianna, a generous man without crookedness.

"If there was a place above or below better than the Heaven of God, it is there Finn would go, and all that are with him of his people.

"You say that a generous man never goes to the hell of pain; there was not one among the Fianna that was not generous to all.

"Ask of God, Patrick, does He remember when the Fianna were alive, or has He seen east or west any man better than themselves in their fighting.

"The Fianna used not to be saying treachery; we never had the name of telling lies. By truth and the strength of our hands we came safe out of every battle.

"There never sat a priest in a church, though you think it sweet to be singing psalms, was better to his word than the Fianna, or more generous than Finn himself.

"If my comrades were living to-night, I would take no pleasure in your crooning in the church; as they are not living now, the rough voice of the bells has deafened me.

"Och! in the place of battles and heavy fights, where I used to have my place and to take my pleasure, the crozier of Patrick being carried, and his clerks at their quarrelling.

"Och! slothful, cheerless Conan, it is great abuse I used to be giving you; why do you not come to see me now? you would get leave for making fun and reviling through the whole of the niggardly clerks.

"Och! where are the strong men gone that they do not come together to help me! O Osgar of the sharp sword of victory, come and free your father from his bonds!

"Where is the strong son of Lugaidh? Och! Diarmuid of all the women! Och! Caoilte, son of Ronan, think of our love, and travel to me!"

PATRICK. "Stop your talk, you withered, witless old man; it is my King that made the Heavens, it is He that gives blossom to the trees, it is He made the moon and the sun, the fields and the grass."

OISIN. "It was not in shaping fields and grass that my king took his delight, but in overthrowing fighting men, and defending countries, and bringing his name into every part.

"In courting, in playing, in hunting, in baring his banner at the first of a fight; in playing at chess, at swimming, in looking around him at the drinking-hall.

"O Patrick, where was your God when the two came over the sea that brought away the queen of Lochlann of the Ships? Where was He when Dearg came, the son of the King of Lochlann of the golden shields? Why did not the King of Heaven protect them from the blows of the big man?

"Or when Tailc, son of Treon, came, the man that did great slaughter on the Fianna; it was not by God that champion fell, but by Osgar, in the sight of all.

"Many a battle and many a victory was gained by the Fianna of Ireland; I never heard any great deed was done by the King of Saints, or that He ever reddened His hand.

"It would be a great shame for God not to take the locks of pain off Finn; if God Himself were in bonds, my king would fight for His sake.

"Finn left no one in pain or in danger without freeing him by silver or gold, or by fighting till he got the victory.

"For the strength of your love, Patrick, do not forsake the great men; bring in the Fianna unknown to the King of Heaven.

"It is a good claim I have on your God, to be among his clerks the way I am; without food, without clothing, without music, without giving rewards to poets.

"Without the cry of the hounds or the horns, without guarding coasts, without courting generous women; for all that I have suffered by the want of food, I forgive the King of Heaven in my will."

Oisin said: "My story is sorrowful. The sound of your voice is not pleasant to me. I will cry my fill, but not for God, but because Finn and the Fianna are not living."

CHAPTER IV. OISIN'S LAMENTS

And Oisin used to be making laments, and sometimes he would be making praises of the old times and of Finn; and these are some of them that are remembered yet:--

I saw the household of Finn; it was not the household of a soft
race; I had a vision of that man yesterday.

I saw the household of the High King, he with the brown,
sweet-voiced son; I never saw a better man.

I saw the household of Finn; no one saw it as I saw it; I saw Finn
with the sword, Mac an Luin. Och! it was sorrowful to see it.

I cannot tell out every harm that is on my head; free us from our
trouble for ever; I have seen the household of Finn.

It is a week from yesterday I last saw Finn; I never saw a braver man. A king of heavy blows; my law, my adviser, my sense and my wisdom, prince and poet, braver than kings, King of the Fianna, brave in all countries; golden salmon of the sea, clean hawk of the air, rightly taught, avoiding lies; strong in his doings, a right judge, ready in courage, a high messenger in bravery and in music.

His skin lime-white, his hair golden; ready to work, gentle to women. His great green vessels full of rough sharp wine, it is rich the king was, the head of his people.

Seven sides Finn's house had, and seven score shields on every side. Fifty fighting men he had about him having woollen cloaks; ten bright drinking-cups in his hall; ten blue vessels, ten golden horns.

It is a good household Finn had, without grudging, without lust, without vain boasting, without chattering, without any slur on any one of the Fianna.

Finn never refused any man; he never put away any one that came to his house. If the brown leaves falling in the woods were gold, if the white waves were silver, Finn would have given away the whole of it.

Blackbird of Doire an Chairn, your voice is sweet; I never heard on any height of the world music was sweeter than your voice, and you at the foot of your nest.

The music is sweetest in the world, it is a pity not to be listening to it for a while, O son of Calphurn of the sweet bells, and you would overtake your nones again.

If you knew the story of the bird the way I know it, you would be crying lasting tears, and you would give no heed to your God for a while.

In the country of Lochlann of the blue streams, Finn, son of Cumhal, of the red-gold cups, found that bird you hear now; I will tell you its story truly.

Doire an Chairn, that wood there to the west, where the Fianna used to be de-laying, it is there they put the blackbird, in the beauty of the pleasant trees.

The stag of the heather of quiet Cruachan, the sorrowful croak from the ridge of the Two Lakes; the voice of the eagle of the Valley of the Shapes, the voice of the cuckoo on the Hill of Brambles.

The voice of the hounds in the pleasant valley; the scream of the eagle on the edge of the wood; the early outcry of the hounds going over the Strand of the Red Stones.

The time Finn lived and the Fianna, it was sweet to them to be listening to the whistle of the blackbird; the voice of the bells would not have been sweet to them.

There was no one of the Fianna without his fine silken shirt and his soft coat, without bright armour, without shining stones on his head, two spears in his hand, and a shield that brought victory.

If you were to search the world you would not find a harder man, best of blood, best in battle; no one got the upper hand of him. When he went out trying his white hound, which of us could be put beside Finn?

One time we went hunting on Slieve-nam-ban; the sun was beautiful overhead, the voice of the hounds went east and west, from hill to hill. Finn and Bran sat for a while on the hill, every man was jealous for the hunt. We let out three thousand hounds from their golden chains; every hound of them brought down two deer.

Patrick of the true crozier, did you ever see, east or west, a greater hunt than that hunt of Finn and the Fianna? O son of Calphurn of the bells, that day was better to me than to be listening to your lamentations in the church.

* * * * *

There is no strength in my hands to-night, there is no power within me; it is no wonder I to be sorowful, being thrown down in the sorrow of old age.

Everything is a grief to me beyond any other man on the face of the earth, to be dragging stones along to the church and the hill of the priests.

I have a little story of our people. One time Finn had a mind to make a dun on the bald hill of Cuailgne, and he put it on the Fianna of Ireland to bring stones for building it; a third on the sons of Morna, a third on myself, and a third on the sons of Baiscne.

I gave an answer to Finn, son of Cumhal; I said I would be under his sway no longer, and that I would obey him no more.

When Finn heard that, he was silent a long time, the man without a He, without fear. And he said to me then: "You yourself will be dragging stones before your death comes to you."

I rose up then with anger on me, and there followed me the fourth of the brave battalions of the Fianna. I gave my own judgments, there were many of the Fianna with me.

Now my strength is gone from me, I that was adviser to the Fianna; my whole body is tired to-night, my hands, my feet, and my head, tired, tired, tired.

It is bad the way I am after Finn of the Fianna; since he is gone away, every good is behind me.

Without great people, without mannerly ways; it is sorrowful I am after our king that is gone.

I am a shaking tree, my leaves gone from me; an empty nut, a horse without a bridle; a people without a dwelling-place, I Oisin, son of Finn.

   * * * * *

  It is long the clouds are over me to-night! it is long last night was; although this day is long, yesterday was longer again to me; every day that comes is long to me!

  That is not the way I used to be, without fighting, without battles, without learning feats, without young girls, without music, without harps, without bruising bones, without great deeds; without increase of learning, without generosity, without drinking at feasts, without courting, without hunting, the two trades I was used to; without going out to battle, Ochone! the want of them is sorrowful to me.

  No hunting of deer or stag, it is not like that I would wish to be; no leashes for our hounds, no hounds; it is long the clouds are over me to-night!

  Without rising up to do bravery as we were used, without playing as we had a mind; without swimming of our fighting men in the lake; it is long the clouds are over me to-night!

  There is no one at all in the world the way I am; it is a pity the way I am; an old man dragging stones; it is long the clouds are over me to-night!

  I am the last of the Fianna, great Oisin, son of Finn, listening to the voice of bells; it is long the clouds are over me to-night!

NOTES

I. THE APOLOGY

The Irish text of the greater number of the stories in this book has been published, and from this text I have worked, making my own translation as far as my scholarship goes, and when it fails, taking the meaning given by better scholars. In some cases the Irish text has not been printed, and I have had to work by comparing and piecing together various translations. I have had to put a connecting sentence of my own here and there, and I have fused different versions together, and condensed many passages, and I have left out many, using the choice that is a perpetual refusing, in trying to get some clear outline of the doings of the heroes.

I have found it more natural to tell the stories in the manner of the thatched houses, where I have heard so many legends of Finn and his friends, and Oisin and Patrick, and the Ever-Living Ones, and the Country of the Young, rather than in the manner of the slated houses, where I have not heard them.

Four years ago, Dr Atkinson, a Professor of Trinity College, Dublin, in his evidence before the Commission of Intermediate Education, said of the old literature of Ireland:--"It has scarcely been touched by the movements of the great literatures; it is the untrained popular feeling. Therefore it is almost intolerably low in tone--I do not mean naughty, but low; and every now and then, when the circumstance occasions it, it goes down lower than low ... If I read the books in the Greek, the Latin or the French course, in almost every one of them there is something with an ideal ring about it--something that I can read with positive pleasure--something that has what the child might take with him as a [Greek: ktema eis dei]--a perpetual treasure; but if I read the Irish books, I see nothing ideal in them, and my astonishment is that through the whole range of Irish literature that I have read (and I have read an enormous range of it), the smallness of the element of idealism is most noticeable

... And as there is very little idealism there is very little imagination ... The Irish tales as a rule are devoid of it fundamentally."

Dr Atkinson is an Englishman, but unfortunately not only fellow-professors in Trinity but undergraduates there have been influenced by his opinion, that Irish literature is a thing to be despised. I do not quote his words to draw attention to a battle that is still being fought, but to explain my own object in working, as I have worked ever since that evidence was given, to make a part of Irish literature accessible to many, especially among my young countrymen, who have not opportunity to read the translations of the chief scholars, scattered here and there in learned periodicals, or patience and time to disentangle overlapping and contradictory versions, that they may judge for themselves as to its "lowness" and "want of imagination," and the other well-known charges brought against it before the same Commission.

I believe that those who have once learned to care for the story of Cuchulain of Muirthemne, and of Finn and Lugh and Etain, and to recognise the enduring belief in an invisible world and an immortal life behind the visible and the mortal, will not be content with my redaction, but will go, first to the fuller versions of the best scholars, and then to the manuscripts themselves. I believe the forty students of old Irish lately called together by Professor Kuno Meyer will not rest satisfied until they have explored the scores and scores of uncatalogued and untranslated manuscripts in Trinity College Library, and that the enthusiasm which the Gaelic League has given birth to will lead to much fine scholarship.

A day or two ago I had a letter from one of the best Greek scholars and translators in England, who says of my "Cuchulain": "It opened up a great world of beautiful legend which, though accounting myself as an Irishman, I had never known at all. I am sending out copies to Irish friends in Australia who, I am sure, will receive the same sort of impression, almost an impression of pride in the beauty of the Irish mind, as I received myself." And President Roosevelt wrote to me a little time ago that after he had read "Cuchulain of Muirthemne," he had sent for all the other translations from the Irish he could get, to take on his journey to the Western States.

I give these appreciative words not, I think, from vanity, for they are not for me but for my material, to show the effect our old literature has on those who come fresh to it, and that they do not complain of its "want of imagination." I am, of course, very proud and glad in having had the opportunity of helping to make it known, and the task has been pleasant, although toil-some. Just now, indeed, on the 6th October, I am tired enough, and I think with sympathy of the old Highland piper, who complained that he was "withered with yelping the seven Fenian battalions."

II. THE AGE AND ORIGIN OF THE STORIES OF THE FIANNA

Mr Alfred Nutt says in ***Ossian and the Ossianic Literature,*** No. 3 of his excellent series of sixpenny pamphlets, ***Popular Studies in Mythology, Romance, and Folklore***:--

"The body of Gaelic literature connected with the name of Ossian is of very considerable extent and of respectable antiquity. The oldest texts, prose for the most part, but also in verse, are preserved in Irish MSS. of the eleventh and twelfth centuries, and go back to a period from one hundred and fifty to two hundred and fifty years older at least. The bulk of Ossianic literature is, however, of later date as far as the form under which it has come down to us is concerned. A number of important texts, prose for the most part, are preserved in MSS. of the fourteenth century, but were probably redacted in the thirteenth and twelfth centuries. But by far the largest mass consists of narrative poems, as a rule dramatic in structure. These have come down to us in MSS. written in Scotland from the end of the fifteenth to the middle of the seventeenth century, in Ireland from the sixteenth down to the middle of the nineteenth century. The Gaelic-speaking peasantry, alike in Ireland and Scotland, have preserved orally a large number of these ballads, as also a great mass of prose narratives, the heroes of which are Ossian and his comrades.

"Were all Ossianic texts preserved in MSS. older than the present century to be printed, they would fill some eight to ten thousand octavo pages. The mere bulk of the literature, even if we allow for considerable repetition of incident, arrests attention. If we further recall that for the last five hundred years this body of romance has formed the chief imaginative recreation of Gaeldom, alike in Ireland and Scotland, and that a peasantry unable to read or write has yet preserved it almost entire, its claims to consideration and study will appear manifest."

He then goes on to discuss how far the incidents in the stories can be accepted as they were accepted by Irish historical writers of the eleventh century as authentic history:--

"Fortunately there is little need for me to discuss the credibility or otherwise of the historic records concerning Finn, his family, and his band of warriors. They may be accepted or rejected according to individual bent of mind without really modifying our view of the literature. For when we turn to the romances, whether in prose or verse, we find that, although the history is professedly the same as that of the Annals, firstly, we are transported to a world entirely romantic, in which divine and semi-divine beings, ungainly monsters and giants, play a prominent part, in which men and women change shapes with animals, in which the lives of the heroes are miraculously prolonged--in short, we find ourselves in a land of Faery; secondly, we find that the historic conditions in which the heroes are represented as living do not, for the most part, answer to anything we know or can surmise of the third century. For Finn and his warriors are perpetually on the watch to guard Ireland against the attacks of over-sea raiders, styled Lochlannac by the narrators, and by them undoubtedly thought of as Norsemen. But the latter, as is well known, only came to Ireland at the close of the eighth century, and the heroic period of their invasions extended for about a century, from 825 to 925; to be followed by a period of comparative settlement during the tenth century, until at the opening of the eleventh century the battle of Clontarf, fought by Brian, the great South Irish chieftain, marked the break-up of the separate Teutonic organisations and the absorption of the Teutons into the fabric of Irish life. In these pages then we may disregard the otherwise interesting question of historic credibility in the Ossianic romances: firstly, because they have their being in a land unaffected by fact; secondly, because if they ever did reflect the history of the third century the reflection was distorted in after-times, and a pseudo-history based upon events of the ninth and tenth centuries was substituted for it. What the historian seeks for in legend is far more a picture of the society in which it took rise than a record of the events which it commemorates."

In a later part of the pamphlet Mr Nutt discusses such questions as whether we may look for examples of third-century customs in the stories, what part of the stories first found their way into writing, whether the Oisin and Patrick dialogues were written under the influence of actual Pagan feeling persisting from Pagan times, or whether "a change came over the feeling of Gaeldom during the fourteenth and fifteenth centuries," when the Oisin and Patrick dialogues in their present form began to be written. His final summing-up is that "well-nigh the same stories that were told of Finn and his warrior braves by the Gael of the eleventh century are told in well-nigh the same way by his descendant to-day." Mr Nutt does not enquire how long the stories may have been told before the first story was written down. Larminie, however, whose early death was the first great loss of our intellectual movement, pushes them backward for untold ages in the introduction to his ***West Irish Folk Tales and Romances***. He builds up a detailed and careful argument, for which I must refer readers to his book, to prove that the Scottish Highlands and Ireland have received their folk-lore both from "Aryan and Non-Aryan sources," and that in the Highlands there is more non-Aryan influence and more non-Aryan blood than in Ireland. He argues that nothing is more improbable than that all folk-tales are Aryan, as has sometimes been supposed, and sums up as follows:--

"They bear the stamp of the genius of more than one race. The pure and placid but often cold imagination of the Aryan has been at work on some. In others we trace the more picturesque fancy, the fierceness and sensuality, the greater sense of artistic elegance belonging to races whom the Aryan, in spite of his occasional faults of hardness and coarseness, has, on the whole, left behind him. But as the greatest results in the realm of the highest art have always been achieved in the case of certain blends of Aryan with other blood, I should hardly deem it extravagant if it were asserted that in the humbler regions of the folk-tale we might trace the working of the same law. The process which has gone on may in part have been as follows:--Every race which has acquired very definite characteristics must have been for a long time isolated. The Aryans during their period of isolation probably developed many of their folk-germs into their larger myths, owing to the greater constructiveness of their imagination, and thus, in a way, they used up part of their material. Afterwards, when they became blended with other races less advanced, they acquired fresh material to work on. We have in Ireland an instance to hand, of which a brief discussion may help to illustrate the whole race theory.

"The larger Irish legendary literature divides itself into three cycles--the divine, the heroic, the Fenian. Of these three the last is so well-known orally in Scotland that it has been a matter of dispute to which country it really belongs. It belongs, in fact, to both. Here, however, comes in a strange contrast with the other cycles. The first is, so far as I am aware, wholly unknown in Scotland, the second comparatively unknown. What is the explanation? Professor Zimmer not having established his late-historical view as regards Finn, and the general opinion among scholars having tended of recent years towards the mythical view, we want to know why there is so much more community in one case than in the other. Mr O'Grady long since seeing this difficulty, and then believing Finn to be historical, was induced to place the latter in point of time before Cuchulain and his compeers. But this view is of course inadmissible when Finn is seen not to be historical at all. There remains but one explanation. The various bodies of legend in question are, so far as Ireland is concerned, only earlier or later, as they came into the island with the various races to which they belonged. The wider prevalence, then, of the Finn Saga would indicate that it belonged to an early race occupying both Ireland and Scotland. Then entered the Aryan Gael, and for him henceforth, as the ruler of the island, his own gods and heroes were sung by his own bards. His legends became the subject of what I may call the court poetry, the aristocratic literature. When he conquered Scotland, he took with him his own gods and heroes; but in the latter country the bardic system never became established, and hence we find but feeble echoes of the heroic cycle among the mountains of the North. That this is the explanation is shown by what took place in Ireland. Here the heroic cycle has been handed down in remembrance almost solely by the bardic literature. The popular memory retains but few traces of it. Its essentially aristocratic character is shown by the fact that the people have all but forgotten it, if they ever knew it. But the Fenian cycle has not been forgotten. Prevailing everywhere, still cherished by the conquered peoples, it held its ground in Scotland and Ireland alike, forcing its way in the latter country even into the written literature, and so securing a twofold lease of existence ... The Fenian cycle, in a word, is non-Aryan folk-literature partially subjected to Aryan treatment."

The whole problem is extremely complex, and several other writers have written upon it. Mr Borlase, for instance, has argued in his big book on the Dolmens that the cromlechs, and presumably the Diarmuid and Crania legend, is connected with old religious rites of an erotic nature coming down from a very primitive state of society.

I have come to my own conclusion not so much because of any weight of argument, as because I found it impossible to arrange the stories in a coherent form so long as I considered them a part of history. I tried to work on the foundation of the Annalists, and fit the Fianna into a definite historical epoch, but the whole story seemed trivial and incoherent until I began to think of them as almost contemporaneous with the battle of Magh Tuireadh, which even the Annalists put back into mythical ages. In this I have only followed some of the story-tellers, who have made the mother of Lugh of the Long Hand the grandmother of Finn, and given him a shield soaked with the blood of Balor. I cannot think of any of the stories as having had a modern origin, or that the century in which each was written down gives any evidence as to its age. "How Diarmuid got his Love-Spot," for instance, which was taken down only a few years ago from some old man's recitation by Dr Hyde, may well be as old as "Finn and the Phantoms," which is in one of the earliest manuscripts. It seems to me that one cannot choose any definite period either from the vast living mass of folk-lore in the country or from the written text, and that there is as good evidence of Finn being of the blood of the gods as of his being, as some of the people tell me, "the son of an O'Shaughnessy who lived at Kiltartan Cross."

Dr Douglas Hyde, although he placed the Fenian after the Cuchulain cycle in his *History of Irish Literature*, has allowed me to print this note:--

"While believing in the real objective existence of the Fenians as a body of Janissaries who actually lived, ruled, and hunted in King Cormac's time, I think it equally certain that hundreds of stories, traits, and legends far older and more primitive than any to which they themselves could have given rise, have clustered about them. There is probably as large a bulk of primitive mythology to be found in the Finn legend as in that of the Red Branch itself. The story of the Fenians was a kind of nucleus to which a vast amount of the flotsam and jetsam of a far older period attached itself, and has thus been preserved."

As I found it impossible to give that historical date to the stories, I, while not adding in anything to support my theory, left out such names as those of Cormac and Art, and such more or less historical personages, substituting "the High King." And in the "Battle of the White Strand," I left out the name of Caelur, Tadg's wife, because I had already followed another chronicler in giving him Ethlinn for a wife. In the earlier part I have given back to Angus Og the name of "The Disturber," which had, as I believe, strayed from him to the Saint of the same name.

III. THE AUTHORITIES

The following is a list of the authorities I have been chiefly helped by in putting these stories together and in translation of the text. But I cannot make it quite accurate, for I have sometimes transferred a mere phrase, sometimes a whole passage from one story to another, where it seemed to fit better. I have sometimes, in the second part of the book, used stories preserved in the Scottish Gaelic, as will be seen by my references. I am obliged to write these notes away from libraries, and cannot verify them, but I think they are fairly correct.

PART ONE. BOOKS ONE, TWO, AND THREE
THE COMING OF THE TUATHA DE DANAAN, AND LUGH OF THE LONG HAND, AND THE COMING OF THE GAEL.--
O'Curry, *Manners and Customs of the Ancient Irish*;
MSS. Materials;
Atlantis;
De Jubainville, *Cycle Mythologique*;
Hennessy, *Chronicum Scotorum*;
Atkinson, *Book of Leinster*;
Annals of the Four Masters;
Nennius, *Hist, Brit.* (Irish Version);
Zimmer, *Glossae Hibernacae*;
Whitley Stokes, *Three Irish Glossaries*;
Revue Celtique and *Irische Texte*;
Gaedelica;
Nutt, *Voyage of Bran*;
Proceedings Ossianic Societ;
O'Beirne Crowe, *Amra Columcille*;
Dean of Lismore's Book;
Windisch, *Irische Texte*;
Hennessy and others in *Revue Celtique*;
Kilkenny Archaeological Journal;
Keatinge's *History*;

Ogyia;

Curtin's *Folk Tales*;

Proceedings Royal Irish Academy, MSS. Series;

Dr Sigerson, *Bards of Gael and Gall*;

Miscellanies, *Celtic Society*.

BOOK FOUR

THE EVER-LIVING LIVING ONES

I have used many of the above, and for separate stories, I may give these authorities:--

MIDHIR AND ETAIN.--

O'Curry, *Manners and Customs*;

Whitley Stokes, *Dinnsenchus*;

Mueller, *Revue Celtique*;

Nutt, *Voyage of Bran*;

De Jubainville, *Epopee Celtique*;

Standish Hayes O'Grady, MS. lent me by him.

MANANNAN AT PLAY.--

S. Hayes O'Grady, *Silva Gaedelica*.

HIS CALL TO BRAN.--

Professor Kuno Meyer in Nutt's *Voyage of Bran*;

S. Hayes O'Grady, *Silva Gaedelica*;

De Jubainville, *Cycle Mythologique*.

HIS THREE CALLS TO CORMAC.--

Whitley Stokes, *Irische Texte*.

CLIODNA'S WAVE.--

S. Hayes O'Grady, *Silva Gaedelica*;

Whitley Stokes, *Dinnsenchus*.

HIS CALL TO CONNLA.--

O'Beirne Crowe, *Kilkenny Arch. Journal*;

Windisch, *Irische Texte*.

TADG IN THE ISLANDS.--

S. Hayes O'Grady, *Silva Gaedelica*.

LAEGAIRE IN THE HAPPY PLAIN.--
S.H. O'Grady, *Silva Gaedelica*;
Kuno Meyer in Nutt's *Voyage of Bran*.
FATE OF THE CHILDREN OF LIR.--
O'Curry, *Atlantis*.
PART TWO. THE FIANNA
THE COMING OF FINN, AND FINN'S HOUSEHOLD.--
Proceedings Ossianic Society;
Kuno Meyer, *Four Songs of Summer and Winter*;
Revue Celtique;
S. Hayes O'Grady, *Silva Gaedelica*;
Curtin's *Folk Tales*.
BIRTH OF BRAN.--
Proc. Ossianic Society.
OISIN'S MOTHER.--
Kennedy, *Legendary Fictions Irish Celts*;
Mac Innis;
Leabhar na Feinne.
BEST MEN OF THE FIANNA.--
Dean of Lismore's Book;
Silva Gaedelica;
Leabhar na Feinne.
LAD OF THE SKINS.--
Waifs and Strays of Celtic Tradition;
Larminie's *Folk Tales*;
Curtin's *Tales*.
THE HOUND.-- *Silva Gaedelica*; Whitley Stokes, *Dinnsenchus*.
RED RIDGE.--
Silva Gaedelica.
BATTLE OF THE WHITE STRAND.--
Kuno Meyer, *Anec. Oxonienses*;
Hanmer's *Chronicle*;

Dean of Lismore;
Curtin's *Tales*;
Silva Gaedelica.
KING OF BRITAIN'S SON.--
Silva Gaedelica.
THE CAVE OF CEISCORAN.--
Silva Gaedelica.
DONN, SON OF MIDHIR.--
Silva Gaedelica.
HOSPITALITY OF CUANNA'S HOUSE.--
Proc. Ossianic Society.
CAT-HEADS AND DOG-HEADS.--
Dean of Lismore;
Leabhar na Feinne;
Campbell's *Popular Tales of the Western Highlands*.
LOMNA'S HEAD.--
O'Curry, *Orc. Treith*, O'Donovan, ed. Stokes.
ILBREC OF ESS RUADH.--
Silva Gaedelica.
CAVE OF CRUACHAN.--
Stokes, *Irische Texts.*
WEDDING AT CEANN SLIEVE.--
Proc. Ossianic Society.
THE SHADOWY ONE.--
O'Curry.
FINN'S MADNESS.--
Silva Gaedelica.
THE RED WOMAN.--
Hyde, *Sgealuidhe Gaedhealach*.
FINN AND THE PHANTOMS.--
Kuno Meyer, *Revue Celtique*.
THE PIGS OF ANGUS.--

Proc. Ossianic Society.
HUNT OF SLIEVE CUILINN.--
Proc. Ossianic Society.
OISIN'S CHILDREN.--
O'Curry;
Leabhar na Feinne;
Campbell's *Popular Tales of the Western Highlands*;
Stokes, *Irische Texte*;
Dean of Lismore;
Celtic Magazine;
Waifs and Strays of Celtic Tradition.
BIRTH OF DIARMUID.--
Pursuit of Diarmuid and Grania
(Society for Preservation of the Irish Language);
Campbell's *Popular Tales*.
HOW DIARMUID GOT HIS LOVE-SPOT.--
Hyde, *Sgealuidhe Gaedhealach*.
DAUGHTER OF KING UNDER-WAVE.--
Campbell's *Popular Tales*.
THE HARD SERVANT.--
Silva Gaedelica.
HOUSE OF THE QUICKEN TREES.--
MSS. in Royal Irish Academy, and in Dr Hyde's possession.
DIARMUID AND GRANIA.--
Text Published by S. Hayes O'Grady,
Proc. Ossianic Society,
and re-edited by N. O'Duffey for
Society for Preservation of the Irish Language;
Kuno Meyer, *Revue Celtique*, and *Four Songs*;
Leabhar na Feinne;
Campbell's *Popular Tales*;
Kilkenny Arch. Journal;

Folk Lore, vol. vii., 1896;
Dean of Lismore;
Nutt, *Waifs and Strays of Celtic Tradition*.
CNOC-AN-AIR, ETC.--
Proc. Ossianic Society.
WEARING AWAY OF THE FIANNA.--
Silva Gaedelica;
Dean of Lismore;
Leabhar na Feinne;
Campbell's *Popular Tales*;
Proc. Ossianic Society;
O'Curry;
Waifs and Strays of Celtic Tradition;
Stokes, *Irische Texte*.
THE END OF THE FIANNA.--
Hyde, *Sgealuidhe Gaedhealach*;
Proc. Ossianic Society;
Silva Gaedelica;
Miss Brooke's *Reliques*;
Annals of the Four Masters;
Celtic Magazine.
OISIN AND PATRICK, AND OISIN'S LAMENTS.--
Proc. Ossianic Society;
Dean of Lismore;
Kilkenny Arch, fournal;
Curtin's *Tales*.

I have taken Grania's sleepy song, and the description of Finn's shield and of Cumhal's treasure-bag, and the fact of Finn's descent from Ethlinn, from *Duanaire Finn*, now being edited for the Irish Texts Society by Mr John MacNeill, the proofs of which I have been kindly allowed to see. And I have used sometimes parts of stories, or comments on them gathered directly from the people, who have kept these heroes so much in mind. The story of Caoilte coming to the help of the King of Ireland in a dark wood is the only one I have given without either a literary or a folk ancestry. It was heard or read by Mr Yeats, he cannot remember where, but he had, with it in his mind, written of "Caoilte's burning hair" in one of his poems.

I and my readers owe special thanks to those good workers in the discovery of Irish literature, Professor Kuno Meyer and Mr Whitley Stokes, translators of so many manuscripts; and to my friend and kinsman Standish Hayes O'Grady, for what I have taken from that wonderful treasure-house, his **Silva Gaedelica**.

IV. THE PRONUNCIATION

This is the approximate pronunciation of some of the more difficult names:

Adhnuall	Ai-noo-al.
Ailbhe.	Alva.
Almhuin	All-oon, _or_ Alvin.
Aobh	Aev, _or_ Eev.
Aodh	Ae (rhyming to "day").
Aoibhill	Evill.
Aoife	Eefa.
Badb	Bibe.
Beltaine, or Bealtaine	Bal-tinna.
Bladhma	Bly-ma.
Bodb Dearg	Bove Darrig.
Caoilte	Cweeltia.
Cam Ruidhe	Corn Rwee.
Ciabhan	Kee-a-van.
Cliodna	Cleevna.
Coincheann	Kun-Kann.
Crann Buidhe	Cran bwee.

Credhe	Crae-a.
Cumhal	Coo-al.
Deaghadh	D'ya-a.
Dubhthach	Duffach.
Duibhreann	Dhiv-ran.
Duibhrium	Dhiv-rinn.
Dun	Doon.
Eimher	Aevir.
Emhain	Avvin.
Eochaid	Eohee.
Eoghan	Owen.
Fionnchad	Finn-ach-a.
Fodhla	Fola.
Fodla	Fola.
Gallimh	Gol-yiv.
Glas Gaibhnenn	Glos Gov-nan.
Leith Laeig	Leh Laeg.
Loch Dairbhreach	Loch Darvragh.
Lugaidh	Loo-ee, _or_ Lewy.
Lugh	Loo.
Magh an Ionganaidh	Moy-in-eean-ee.
Magh Cuillean	Moy Cullin.
Magh Feabhail	Moy Fowl.
Magh Macraimhe	Moy Mucrivva.
Magh Mell	Moy Mal.
Magh Rein	Moy Raen.
Magh Tuireadh	Moytirra.

Manannan	Mananaun.
Midhe	Mee.
Midhna	Mec-na.
Mochaomhog	Mo-cwecv-og.
Muadhan	Moo-aun.
Murchadh	Murachu.
Nemhnain	Now-nin.
Niamh	Nee-av.
Og	Og.
Rath Medba,	
or Meadhbha	Ra Maev-a.
Rudraighe	Rury.
Samhain	Sow-in.
Scathniamh	Scau-nee-av.
Sceolan	Skolaun.
Searbhan	Sharavaun.
Sidhe	Shee.
Slieve Echtge	Sleev Acht-ga.
Tadg	Teig.
Teamhair	T'yower, _or_ Tavvir.
Tuatha de Danaan	Too-a-ha dae Donnan.
Tuathmumhain	Too-moon.

I have not followed a fixed rule as to the spelling of Irish names; I have taken the spelling I give from various good authorities, but they vary so much that, complete accuracy not being easy, I sometimes look to custom and convenience. I use, for instance, "Slieve" for "Sliabh," because it comes so often, and a mispronunciation would spoil so many names. I have treated "Inbhir" (a river mouth) in the same way, spelling it "Inver," and even adopting it as an English word, because it is so useful. The forty scholars of the New School of Old Irish will do us good service if they work at the question both of spelling and of pronunciation of the old names and settle them as far as is possible.

V. THE PLACE NAMES

Accuill	Achill, Co. Mayo.
Aine Cliach	Cnoc Aine, Co. Limerick.
Almhuin	Near Kildare.
Ath Cliath	Dublin.
Athluain	Athlone.
Ath na Riogh	Athenry.
Badhamain	Cahir, Co. Tipperary.
Baile Cronin	Barony of Imokilty, Co. Cork.
Banna	The Bann.
Beare	Berehaven.
Bearna na Eadargana	Roscommon.
Bearnas Mor	Co. Donegal.
Beinn Gulbain	Benbulban, Co. Sligo.
Beire do Bhunadas	Berehaven.
Bel-atha Senaig	Ballyshannon.
Belgata	In Connemara.
Benna Boirde	Source of the Bann and Mourne Mountains.
Berramain	Near Tralee.
Bhas	River Bush.
Boinn	River Boyne.
Bri Leith	Co. Longford.
Cairbre	Carbury.
Cairgin	Three miles south of Londonderry.
Carrthach River	River Carra, near Dunkerrin Mountains.
Ceanntaile	Kinsale.

Ceiscorainn	Co. Sligo.
Cill Dolun	Killaloe, Co. Clare.
Cliodna's Wave	At Glandore, Co. Cork.
Cluantarbh	Clontarf.
Cnoc Aine	Co. Limerick.
Cnoc-an-Air	Co. Kerry.
Cnoc na righ	Co. Sligo.
Corca Duibhne	Corcaguiny, Co. Kerry.
Corrslieve	Carlow Mountains.
Crotta Cliach	Galtee Mountains.
Cruachan	Co. Roscommon.
Cruachan Aigle	Croagh Patrick.
Doire a Cairn	Derrycarn, Co. Meath.
Doire-da-Bhoth	In Slieve Echtge.
Druim Cleibh	Co. Sligo.
Druim Lis	Near Loch Gill.
Druimscarha	Near River Arighis, Co. Cork.
Dun Sobairce	Dunsevenh, Co. Antrim.
Durlas	Thurles.
Ess Dara	Near Sligo.
Ess Ruadh	Assaroe, Co. Donegal.
Fidh Gaible	Fergill, Co. Sligo.
Finntraighe	Ventry.
Fionn	The Finn.
Fionnabraic	Kilfenna, Co. Clare.
Fionntutach	Co. Limerick.
Fleisge	Co. Kerry.
Gabhra	Near Tara.
Gaibh atha na Fiann	River Leamhar, flows from Killarney.
Gairech and Ilgairech	Hills near Mullingar.

Gallimh	Galway.
Gleann na Caor	Co. Cork.
Gullach Dollairb	Barony of Rathconrath.
Hill of Bairnech	Near Killarney.
Hill of Uisnech	Co. Westmeath.
Inver Cechmaine	East coast of Ulster.
Inver Colpa	Drogheda.
Inver Slane	N.E. of Leinster.
Irrus Domnann	Erris, Co. Mayo.
Island of Toraig	Tory Island, Co. Donegal.
Laoi	River Lee.
Leith Laoi	Leitrim.
Linn Feic	Near Slaney.
Loch Bel Sead	Co. Tipperary.
Loch Ce	Co. Roscommon.
Loch Dairbhreach	Loch Derryvaragh, Co. Westmeath.
Loch Deirg Dheirc	Loch Derg on the Shannon.
Loch Eirne	Loch Erne.
Loch Feabhail	Loch Foyle.
Loch Lein	Killarney.
Loch Orbson	Loch Corrib.
Loch na-n Ean	In Co. Roscommon.
Lough Neatach	Loch Neagh.
Luimneach	Limerick.
Maev Mhagh	Plain about Loughrea.
Magh Cobha	Iveagh, Co. Down.
Magh Cuilenn	Moycullen, Co. Galway.
Magh Femen	Co. Tipperary.
Magh Larg	Co. Roscommon.

Magh Leine	King's County.
Magh Luirg	Co. Roscommon.
Magh Maini	Co. Wexford.
Magh Mucraimhe	Near Athenry.
Magh Nia	Same as Magh Tuireadh.
Magh Rein	Co. Leitrim.
Magh Tuireadh	Moytura near Sligo, scene of great battle, and Moytura, near Cong, scene of first battle.
March of Finnliath	River Lee, near Tralee.
Midhe	Meath, west of Ardagh.
Mis Geadh	In Bay of Erris.
Muaid	River Moy.
Muc-inis	Muckinish, off Connemara.
Nas	Naas.
Nem	The Nem.
Oenach Clochan	Morristown, Co. Limerick.
Osraige	Ossory.
Paps of Dana	Co. Kerry.
Portlairge	Waterford.
River Maigh	Co. Limerick.
Ros da Shioleach	Limerick.
Ruirlech	Liffey.
Samair	R. Cumhair, runs through Bruff.
Sionnan	River Shannon.
Siuir	River Suir, Co. Tipperary.
Siuir and Beoir and Berba	Suir and Nore and Barrow.

Slieve Baisne	Co. Roscommon.
Slieve Bladmai	Slieve Bloom.
Slieve Buane	Slieve Banne, Co. Roscommon.
Slieve Conaill	Border of Leitrim and Donegal.
Slieve Crot	Co. Tipperary.
Slieve Cua	Co. Waterford.
Slieve Cua and Slieve Crot	In Galtee Mountains.
Slieve Cuailgne	Co. Louth.
Slieve Echtge	Co. Galway.
Slieve Fuad	Co. Armagh.
Slieve Guaire	Co. Cavan.
Slieve Luchra	Co. Kerry.
Slieve Lugha	Co. Mayo.
Slieve Mis	Co. Kerry.
Slieve Muice	Co. Tipperary.
Slieve-nam-Ban	Co. Tipperary
Sligach	Sligo.
Srub Bruin	In West Kerry.
Sruth na Maoile	Mull of Cantire.
Tailltin	Telltown.
Teamhair	Tara, Co. Meath.
Teunhair Luchra	Near Castle Island, Co. Kerry.
The Beith	River Behy, Barony of Dunkerrin.
The Beoir	The Berba.
The Islands of Mod	In Clew Bay.
The Lemain	River Laune, Co. Kerry.
The Muaidh	River Moy, Co. Sligo.
Tonn Toime	Toines, near Killarney.
Traigh Eothaile	Near Ballisodare.
Tuathmumain	Thomond.

Ui Chonaill Gabhra	Co. Limerick.
Ui Fiachraih, Fiachraig	Co. Mayo.
Wave of Rudraighe	Bay of Dundrum.

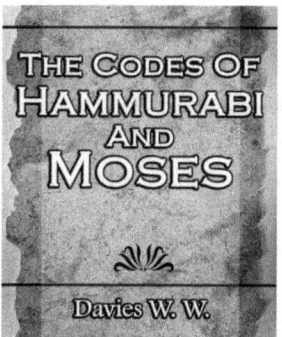

The Codes Of Hammurabi And Moses
W. W. Davies

QTY

The discovery of the Hammurabi Code is one of the greatest achievements of archaeology, and is of paramount interest, not only to the student of the Bible, but also to all those interested in ancient history...

Religion   **ISBN:** *1-59462-338-4*   **Pages:132**
MSRP $12.95

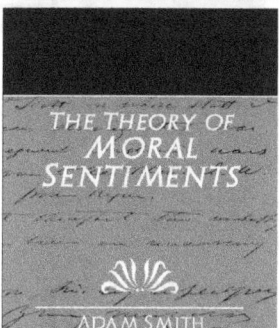

The Theory of Moral Sentiments
Adam Smith

QTY

This work from 1749. contains original theories of conscience amd moral judgment and it is the foundation for systemof morals.

Philosophy ISBN: *1-59462-777-0*   **Pages:536**
MSRP $19.95

Jessica's First Prayer
Hesba Stretton

QTY

In a screened and secluded corner of one of the many railway-bridges which span the streets of London there could be seen a few years ago, from five o'clock every morning until half past eight, a tidily set-out coffee-stall, consisting of a trestle and board, upon which stood two large tin cans, with a small fire of charcoal burning under each so as to keep the coffee boiling during the early hours of the morning when the work-people were thronging into the city on their way to their daily toil...

Childrens   ISBN: *1-59462-373-2*   **Pages:84**
MSRP $9.95

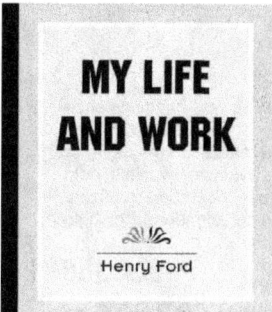

My Life and Work
Henry Ford

QTY

Henry Ford revolutionized the world with his implementation of mass production for the Model T automobile. Gain valuable business insight into his life and work with his own auto-biography... "We have only started on our development of our country we have not as yet, with all our talk of wonderful progress, done more than scratch the surface. The progress has been wonderful enough but..."

Biographies/   ISBN: *1-59462-198-5*   **Pages:300**
MSRP $21.95

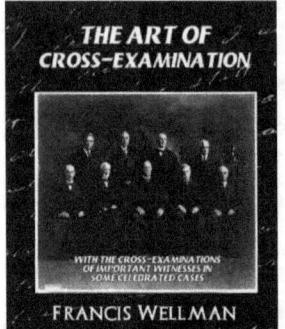

The Art of Cross-Examination
Francis Wellman

QTY

I presume it is the experience of every author, after his first book is published upon an important subject, to be almost overwhelmed with a wealth of ideas and illustrations which could readily have been included in his book, and which to his own mind, at least, seem to make a second edition inevitable. Such certainly was the case with me; and when the first edition had reached its sixth impression in five months, I rejoiced to learn that it seemed to my publishers that the book had met with a sufficiently favorable reception to justify a second and considerably enlarged edition. ..

Pages:412

Reference   ISBN: *1-59462-647-2*   *MSRP $19.95*

On the Duty of Civil Disobedience
Henry David Thoreau

QTY

Thoreau wrote his famous essay, On the Duty of Civil Disobedience, as a protest against an unjust but popular war and the immoral but popular institution of slave-owning. He did more than write—he declined to pay his taxes, and was hauled off to gaol in consequence. Who can say how much this refusal of his hastened the end of the war and of slavery ?

Law   ISBN: *1-59462-747-9*   **Pages:48**
MSRP $7.45

Dream Psychology Psychoanalysis for Beginners
Sigmund Freud

QTY

Sigmund Freud, born Sigismund Schlomo Freud (May 6, 1856 - September 23, 1939), was a Jewish-Austrian neurologist and psychiatrist who co-founded the psychoanalytic school of psychology. Freud is best known for his theories of the unconscious mind, especially involving the mechanism of repression; his redefinition of sexual desire as mobile and directed towards a wide variety of objects; and his therapeutic techniques, especially his understanding of transference in the therapeutic relationship and the presumed value of dreams as sources of insight into unconscious desires.

Pages:196

Psychology   ISBN: *1-59462-905-6*   *MSRP $15.45*

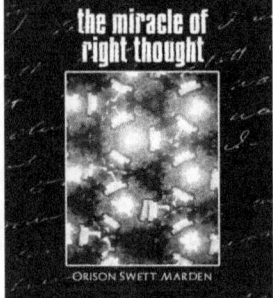

The Miracle of Right Thought
Orison Swett Marden

QTY

Believe with all of your heart that you will do what you were made to do. When the mind has once formed the habit of holding cheerful, happy, prosperous pictures, it will not be easy to form the opposite habit. It does not matter how improbable or how far away this realization may see, or how dark the prospects may be, if we visualize them as best we can, as vividly as possible, hold tenaciously to them and vigorously struggle to attain them, they will gradually become actualized, realized in the life. But a desire, a longing without endeavor, a yearning abandoned or held indifferently will vanish without realization.

Pages:360

Self Help   ISBN: *1-59462-644-8*   *MSRP $25.45*

The Rosicrucian Cosmo-Conception Mystic Christianity *by Max Heindel*   ISBN: *1-59462-188-8*   **$38.95**
The Rosicrucian Cosmo-conception is not dogmatic, neither does it appeal to any other authority than the reason of the student. It is: not controversial, but is: sent forth in the, hope that it may help to clear...   *New Age/Religion Pages 646*

Abandonment To Divine Providence *by Jean-Pierre de Caussade*   ISBN: *1-59462-228-0*   **$25.95**
"The Rev. Jean Pierre de Caussade was one of the most remarkable spiritual writers of the Society of Jesus in France in the 18th Century. His death took place at Toulouse in 1751. His works have gone through many editions and have been republished...   *Inspirational/Religion Pages 400*

Mental Chemistry *by Charles Haanel*   ISBN: *1-59462-192-6*   **$23.95**
Mental Chemistry allows the change of material conditions by combining and appropriately utilizing the power of the mind. Much like applied chemistry creates something new and unique out of careful combinations of chemicals the mastery of mental chemistry...   *New Age Pages 354*

The Letters of Robert Browning and Elizabeth Barret Barrett 1845-1846 vol II   ISBN: *1-59462-193-4*   **$35.95**
by Robert Browning and Elizabeth Barrett
                         Biographies Pages 596

Gleanings In Genesis (volume I) *by Arthur W. Pink*   ISBN: *1-59462-130-6*   **$27.45**
Appropriately has Genesis been termed "the seed plot of the Bible" for in it we have, in germ form, almost all of the great doctrines which are afterwards fully developed in the books of Scripture which follow...   *Religion/Inspirational Pages 420*

The Master Key *by L. W. de Laurence*   ISBN: *1-59462-001-6*   **$30.95**
In no branch of human knowledge has there been a more lively increase of the spirit of research during the past few years than in the study of Psychology, Concentration and Mental Discipline. The requests for authentic lessons in Thought Control, Mental Discipline and...   New Age/Business Pages 422

The Lesser Key Of Solomon Goetia *by L. W. de Laurence*   ISBN: *1-59462-092-X*   **$9.95**
This translation of the first book of the "Lernegton" which is now for the first time made accessible to students of Talismanic Magic was done, after careful collation and edition, from numerous Ancient Manuscripts in Hebrew, Latin, and French...   *New Age/Occult Pages 92*

Rubaiyat Of Omar Khayyam *by Edward Fitzgerald*   ISBN:*1-59462-332-5*   **$13.95**
Edward Fitzgerald, whom the world has already learned, in spite of his own efforts to remain within the shadow of anonymity, to look upon as one of the rarest poets of the century, was born at Bredfield, in Suffolk, on the 31st of March, 1809. He was the third son of John Purcell...   Music Pages 172

Ancient Law *by Henry Maine*   ISBN: *1-59462-128-4*   **$29.95**
The chief object of the following pages is to indicate some of the earliest ideas of mankind, as they are reflected in Ancient Law, and to point out the relation of those ideas to modern thought.   *Religiom/History Pages 452*

Far-Away Stories *by William J. Locke*   ISBN: *1-59462-129-2*   **$19.45**
"Good wine needs no bush, but a collection of mixed vintages does. And this book is just such a collection. Some of the stories I do not want to remain buried for ever in the museum files of dead magazine-numbers an author's not unpardonable vanity..."   *Fiction Pages 272*

Life of David Crockett *by David Crockett*   ISBN: *1-59462-250-7*   **$27.45**
"Colonel David Crockett was one of the most remarkable men of the times in which he lived. Born in humble life, but gifted with a strong will, an indomitable courage, and unremitting perseverance...   *Biographies/New Age Pages 424*

Lip-Reading *by Edward Nitchie*   ISBN: *1-59462-206-X*   **$25.95**
Edward B. Nitchie, founder of the New York School for the Hard of Hearing, now the Nitchie School of Lip-Reading, Inc, wrote "LIP-READING Principles and Practice". The development and perfecting of this meritorious work on lip-reading was an undertaking...   *How-to Pages 400*

A Handbook of Suggestive Therapeutics, Applied Hypnotism, Psychic Science   ISBN: *1-59462-214-0*   **$24.95**
by Henry Munro
                         Health/New Age/Health/Self-help Pages 376

A Doll's House: and Two Other Plays *by Henrik Ibsen*   ISBN: *1-59462-112-8*   **$19.95**
Henrik Ibsen created this classic when in revolutionary 1848 Rome. Introducing some striking concepts in playwriting for the realist genre, this play has been studied the world over.   *Fiction/Classics/Plays 308*

The Light of Asia *by sir Edwin Arnold*   ISBN: *1-59462-204-3*   **$13.95**
In this poetic masterpiece, Edwin Arnold describes the life and teachings of Buddha. The man who was to become known as Buddha to the world was born as Prince Gautama of India but he rejected the worldly riches and abandoned the reigns of power when...   Religion/History/Biographies Pages 170

The Complete Works of Guy de Maupassant *by Guy de Maupassant*   ISBN: *1-59462-157-8*   **$16.95**
"For days and days, nights and nights, I had dreamed of that first kiss which was to consecrate our engagement, and I knew not on what spot I should put my lips..."   *Fiction/Classics Pages 240*

The Art of Cross-Examination *by Francis L. Wellman*   ISBN: *1-59462-309-0*   **$26.95**
Written by a renowned trial lawyer, Wellman imparts his experience and uses case studies to explain how to use psychology to extract desired information through questioning.   *How-to/Science/Reference Pages 408*

Answered or Unanswered? *by Louisa Vaughan*   ISBN: *1-59462-248-5*   **$10.95**
Miracles of Faith in China
                         Religion Pages 112

The Edinburgh Lectures on Mental Science (1909) *by Thomas*   ISBN: *1-59462-008-3*   **$11.95**
This book contains the substance of a course of lectures recently given by the writer in the Queen Street Hail, Edinburgh. Its purpose is to indicate the Natural Principles governing the relation between Mental Action and Material Conditions...   *New Age Psychology Pages 148*

Ayesha *by H. Rider Haggard*   ISBN: *1-59462-301-5*   **$24.95**
Verily and indeed it is the unexpected that happens! Probably if there was one person upon the earth from whom the Editor of this, and of a certain previous history, did not expect to hear again...   *Classics Pages 380*

Ayala's Angel *by Anthony Trollope*   ISBN: *1-59462-352-X*   **$29.95**
The two girls were both pretty, but Lucy who was twenty-one who supposed to be simple and comparatively unattractive, whereas Ayala was credited, as her Bombwhat romantic name might show, with poetic charm and a taste for romance. Ayala when her father died was nineteen...   Fiction Pages 484

The American Commonwealth *by James Bryce*   ISBN: *1-59462-286-8*   **$34.45**
An interpretation of American democratic political theory. It examines political mechanics and society from the perspective of Scotsman James Bryce
                         Politics Pages 572

Stories of the Pilgrims *by Margaret P. Pumphrey*   ISBN: *1-59462-116-0*   **$17.95**
This book explores pilgrims religious oppression in England as well as their escape to Holland and eventual crossing to America on the Mayflower, and their early days in New England...   *History Pages 268*

www.bookjungle.com *email: sales@bookjungle.com fax: 630-214-0564 mail: Book Jungle PO Box 2226 Champaign, IL 61825*

QTY

The Fasting Cure *by Sinclair Upton*   **ISBN:** *1-59462-222-1*   **$13.95**
In the Cosmopolitan Magazine for May, 1910, and in the Contemporary Review (London) for April, 1910, I published an article dealing with my experi-
ences in fasting. I have written a great many magazine articles, but never one which attracted so much attention... New Age/Self Help/Health Pages 164

Hebrew Astrology *by Sepharial*   **ISBN:** *1-59462-308-2*   **$13.45**
In these days of advanced thinking it is a matter of common observation that we have left many of the old landmarks behind and that we are now pressing
forward to greater heights and to a wider horizon than that which represented the mind-content of our progenitors...   Astrology Pages 144

Thought Vibration or The Law of Attraction in the Thought World   **ISBN:** *1-59462-127-6*   **$12.95**

by William Walker Atkinson   *Psychology/Religion Pages 144*

Optimism *by Helen Keller*   **ISBN:** *1-59462-108-X*   **$15.95**
Helen Keller was blind, deaf, and mute since 19 months old, yet famously learned how to overcome these handicaps, communicate with the world, and
spread her lectures promoting optimism. An inspiring read for everyone...   Biographies/Inspirational Pages 84

Sara Crewe *by Frances Burnett*   **ISBN:** *1-59462-360-0*   **$9.45**
In the first place, Miss Minchin lived in London. Her home was a large, dull, tall one, in a large, dull square, where all the houses were alike, and all the
sparrows were alike, and where all the door-knockers made the same heavy sound...   Childrens/Classic Pages 88

The Autobiography of Benjamin Franklin *by Benjamin Franklin*   **ISBN:** *1-59462-135-7*   **$24.95**
The Autobiography of Benjamin Franklin has probably been more extensively read than any other American historical work, and no other book of its kind
has had such ups and downs of fortune. Franklin lived for many years in England, where he was agent...   Biographies/History Pages 332

Name	
Email	
Telephone	
Address	
City, State ZIP	

☐ **Credit Card**   ☐ **Check / Money Order**

Credit Card Number	
Expiration Date	
Signature	

Please Mail to: Book Jungle
PO Box 2226
Champaign, IL 61825
or Fax to: 630-214-0564

ORDERING INFORMATION

web*: www.bookjungle.com*
email*: sales@bookjungle.com*
fax*: 630-214-0564*
mail*: Book Jungle PO Box 2226 Champaign, IL 61825*
or PayPal *to sales@bookjungle.com*

Please contact us for bulk discounts